Ila's Diamonds III

Donna M. Gray-Banks

authorHOUSE®

AuthorHouse™
1663 Liberty Drive
Bloomington, IN 47403
www.authorhouse.com
Phone: 1 (800) 839-8640

Published by AuthorHouse 02/25/2019

ISBN: 978-1-5462-7879-5 (sc)
ISBN: 978-1-5462-7971-6 (e)

Library of Congress Control Number: 2010901414

Print information available on the last page.

Acknowledgments to:

Christine, Gilbert, and Jackie, Jr. (family)
My son, Gregory—you are my major accomplishment
My mother, Lorraine; my father,
Jackson W. Gray, Sr.; and
my nephew, Gary L. Hogan, who have all transitioned
My niece, Tomika—bravery unsurpassed
My GFFL—friendship. Enough said.
To Robert—it was significant.
To Ila's Poet Mike Brown – Unbelievable Talent
Dr. Seuss—thank you
To The Creator – God's Grace Is Sufficient

How is it that all my men are made of Teflon?

—Ila

The music stopped, and the door opened slowly. Eugenia was the first to leave the room. She came out in wearing a red leather pantsuit with, red stacked heels. She was, and carrying a leather purse. She stepped over Ila as if like she was a homeless person on the grate outside a subway station stop. As she got to the front door, she turned, looked at Ila, and smiled. She opened the door and left. Maurice was next. With his duffle bag on his back, he came through the door, looked down on Ila, and said, "You need to clean that shit up. I . I kept telling you, you could not turn shit into sunshine, Ila. Hunter is a faggot and a whore. Has been ever since I have known him. But now he is your faggot and whore. Don't forget to send me an invitation to the wedding." He walked briskly down the hall, opened the door, and slammed it after he left.

Ila could not believe she was coming down this yellow brick road again. Here she was with a ring on her finger, but her man's ass had a dick in it, and his dick was in another woman. There was the entire story. Maurice was fucking Hunter, and Hunter was fucking Eugenia—to "Flash Light" by Funkadelic. As Ila opened the door, all eyes turned on her. Eugenia smiled, Maurice mouthed, "I told you so," and Hunter looked like he had seen a ghost. Ila slowly closed the door to the safe house apartment and slumped to the hallway floor. She thought, *How? Why does this kind of thing keep happening to me?* Her stomach bubbled, and suddenly, she threw up all over herself. She could not move. It was as if she was having a mini nervous breakdown. The hallway went black, and for a moment, she had no idea where she was.

The music stopped, and the door opened slowly. Eugenia was the first to leave the room. She came out wearing a red leather pantsuit with red stacked heels. She was carrying a leather purse. She stepped over Ila as if she was a homeless person on the grate outside a subway station. As she got to the front door, she turned, looked at Ila, and smiled. She opened the door and left.

Maurice was next. With his duffle bag on his back, he came through the door, looked down on Ila, and said, "You need to clean that shit up. I kept telling you, you could not turn shit into sunshine, Ila. Hunter is a faggot and a whore. Has been ever since I have known him. But now he is your faggot and whore. Don't forget to send me an invitation to the wedding." He walked briskly down the hall, opened the door, and slammed it after he left.

It appeared that Hunter did not want to come out of the bedroom. Ila took off her coat and used it to clean up some of the vomit from her pants and the floor. She stood up slowly and walked to the kitchen. Sitting at the table, she cried so hard she did not hear Hunter exit the bedroom. Ila looked up. He was standing over her. "Ila, when will you understand that I'm the gift and you are just the wrapping?" She looked up from the table, gathered as much saliva as she could muster up, and spit into his eye. He grabbed her by the neck and choked her. He said, "This changes nothing. The plan is for us to get married so that we can both advance our positions. You know I can make you happy sexually. You know I know how to treat you. Maurice was just something to do. I'm no faggot. Now go wash yourself off, and let's get out of here. I'll take you home. I don't know why you came back in the first place. I could have gotten a ride to your house to get my car."

Ila could have cut his throat. She noticed that the envelope was still on the table. No one had been by to pick up the details of their undercover work. She wondered who was supposed to pick it up. She pushed the chair back and stood up. There was a knock at the door, and they heard the key in the lock. Hunter ran to the bedroom to retrieve his .38, and Ila stood there frozen. As the door opened, she heard a familiar voice. "It's friend not foe! Don't shoot!" Brock Covington entered the room. *What the hell is he doing here? This shit just gets worse and worse.* The last thing Ila remembered was hitting her head on the side of the table before she passed out.

When she came to, she could hear them shouting at each other. "Pick her up!" Hunter shouted.

"No. You get her legs. I'll put my hands under her shoulders, and we'll take her into the bedroom," Brock said.

Ila heard Hunter say, "I have a plane to catch. I don't have time for this bullshit. And why the fuck are you here? And why do you have a key?"

"We can talk about all that later. Let's just get her into the bedroom," Brock replied. They carried her down the corridor to the bedroom she occupied during their TDY (temporary duty yonder) and laid her across the bed. Ila could hear muffled voices but could not make out what they were saying. She did hear the door slam as they both left the room.

Hunter and Brock walked to the kitchen. Hunter turned to Brock with his .38 in his hand and said, "Okay, motherfucker, I'll ask you again. Why the fuck are you here? And why do you have a key?"

Brock said, "Bitch, you better put that .38 away before I make you eat it or stick it up your pussy ass. But, oh, you might like that, so I won't give you that pleasure. Uncock the gun and put it in the holster on your shoulder like a good faggot."

Hunter was fuming, but he knew there was more to this story, and he should hear Brock out. Hunter slowly sat down at the kitchen table, placing his gun on the table—aimed at Brock.

"Hunter, Ila is in great danger. She is the only person besides me who witnessed the love tryst between the chief and his protégé. The pictures, of course, are worth a thousand words, but she will have to testify in court. She needs—we need—to go back to her apartment, get as many things as possible, and bring them back to this safe house."

Hunter replied, "Where do you fit into this entire mix?"

Brock explained that he worked for the FBI and had been assigned as the chief's right-hand man. "The bureau, district, and state are ready to put the chief under arrest, but the case has to be ironclad. And it cannot be without Ila. She will have to stay out of sight until the chief goes to trial or resigns and leaves town—whatever comes first."

Hunter looked at Brock and said, "How is this my problem? I'm supposed to be on my way to my next assignment. If Ila is in a jam, I'm sorry about that, but I can't stick around to make it better or help in any way. I'll help you get her to the hospital, and then I'm on my way to National Airport."

Brock replied, "Push the envelope this way. Pick up your gun, put it in your holster, and take everything you need out of here right now, because once you walk through the door, you cannot come back."

Hunter rose slowly, placed his gun in the holster, walked backward down the hall into the bedroom, and retrieved his suitcase. He walked back down the hall, picked up his other suitcase, and headed toward the door. He stopped, turned to Brock, and said, "That woman in there is my ticket to White House detail. I need to know how to get in contact with her when this is all over. We plan to be married next year, and neither you nor your trial is going to stop that. Together, we can make it happen. She can be assigned to the first lady, and I can be assigned to the president. The blueprint has already been mapped out. So, when you get tired of playing detective, babysitter, and protector, call the Company. They can locate me. I'll come and get Ila so that we can go on with our lives. I'm sure you know the number." With that, Hunter opened the door, turned, and tossed the keys onto the table in front of Brock. Brock turned quickly and took the gun out of his holster. Hunter raised his hands and said, "Man, it's all yours for now." He then slowly walked out and closed the door.

Brock sat at the table until he heard Ila moving around in the bedroom.

All Ila could think about was leaving this condo and getting back to her apartment and back to a semi normal life. She looked around the room and decided that she might miss this kind of living, but at what cost? There was a stench in the air, and she could not figure out what it was until she looked at the coat beside her and the stains on her pants. "Shit!" she screamed. She had no more clothes at the condo and was not about to wash the clothes she'd vomited on. Ila sat up, but she got dizzy and lay back down. She could hear footsteps coming up the hallway. *Oh, here we go,* she thought. The knock at the door was slight and friendly. She knew immediately that it was not

Hunter because he would have just walked in. "Come in!" she shouted.

Brock opened the door, only to hold his nose. "Ila! My God! I forgot you vomited on yourself. Is there anything left in the apartment that you can wear?"

Ila looked at Brock and shook her head as she began to cry. This was not the condition that she wanted Brock Covington to see her in. This was not the Ila she wanted Brock to remember.

Brock stood at the door and said, "My suitcase is downstairs. Let me go retrieve it and get you something to wear." With that, he slowly closed the door. Ila stood up and took off all her clothes. Then she went to the closet and found a plastic garment bag from the cleaners. She removed the plastic from the hanger, tied the end to close the small hole, and stuffed all the vomit-covered clothes into the bag. She tightly tied the other end of the bag and placed it by the door. She would take them out to the garbage can in the parking lot when she left. It seemed that Brock was taking an awful long time. Ila decided to take a shower with what little soap was left. It seemed she had packed exactly enough toiletries to last until the day she would be leaving. She reached into the shower and turned the water to hot. All she wanted was to feel the heat on her back. She looked in the mirror and could not believe the sight. It seemed she had aged years in one day, all in the name of lust, longing, and love. Her world was once again turned upside down. She walked back to the shower and remembered she did not have a shower cap. Necessity being the mother of invention, she took a Giant Food plastic bag out of the small trash can and used it as a shower cap. Thank God, she could feel a laugh coming on. Only she would think of using a plastic bag from a grocery store for a shower cap.

When she entered the shower, the water felt like beads of hot lava sliding down her back. At one point, a long scream came out of her throat, and tears streamed down her face. Minutes went by. The water was turning cold. She seemed to have experienced a time lapse and had no idea how long she had been in the shower. As she returned to semi consciousness, she looked for a washcloth and saw one on the sink. Rather than getting out of the shower to get the washcloth, she just rubbed the bar of soap over her skin while she let the water caress her body. She closed her eyes, and there he was ... Rodney standing at her front door with coffee and bagels, smiling that Colgate smile and looking like a *Gentleman's Quarterly* model. What a vision! It was wonderful that she could call him up in her mind, even after all these years. Just thinking of him made all this palatable. Ila open her eyes, and of course, the vision was gone. She rinsed the soap off her body and exited the shower. She had forgotten to get a towel, so she had to wet the floor to get to the closet. Once there she wrapped herself in fluff. These towels were so fluffy, they didn't even absorb the water. That was the wonderful thing about being TDY. Her own towels were rough, and they cut her skin when she rubbed too hard. That made her laugh. Slowly she walked back into the bedroom. Brock had laid out clothes on the bed—a big, brown, button-down shirt; black sweatpants; and a pair of flip-flops. *Well, beggars can't be choosey*. She got dressed, crawled up on the bed, wrapped herself in the covers, and fell into a deep sleep.

Brock was sitting at the table reviewing the contents of the envelope. He was very surprised at how well the report was put together. There was so much detail. *The FBI director on this case will be very happy with this report. It leaves little to chance. The only chance is getting Ila to the trial date.* Brock believed this apartment had been compromised by Eugenia, so he and Ila would have to leave first thing in the morning. But where would they go? *Ila can't go back to her apartment. It's surely being watched, and I'm undercover, so being seen together would not be a great idea. Where would they not look for us?*

Brock decided that they would stay on or near Georgetown University. It would be the best place to hide for the three to seven months that it would take to bring the police chief up on charges of lewd and lascivious behavior along with drug distribution. Even though there were pictures and Brock and Ila were witnesses, it would not be an easy trial. Brock was still undercover, and no one knew that he would be testifying against Chief Warren Chambers. He was hoping that there was enough evidence to make him resign. But until that evidence was presented, Ila would have to be placed in protective custody. There was nothing left to do this night but secure the condo and make plans in the morning.

He was about to place a chair up under the door handle of the condo when there was a not at the door. "Who is it?" Brock called out.

"Housekeeping", the woman replied.

Brock called through the door "We'll not be leaving until tomorrow."

The housekeeper replied, "Okay," and she pushed an envelope under the door.

"Shit!" Brock said. *There is no way we can stay here tonight.* He left the envelope on the floor, retrieved the tea kettle from the kitchen area, filled it, and put it on the burner of the stove. While he waited for the water to boil, he walked over to his suitcase and got out a pair of gloves. This was so 007, but he wanted to be very careful. He pulled the gloves onto his hands, picked up the envelop, and carried it to the stove. He steamed the seal until it was loose enough to just flip open. It did not take long. Brock turned off the stove and walked over to the table. He slowly opened the envelop and pulled out a picture. There, sitting on a bench on Constitution Avenue at a bus stop, were Chief Warren and Eugenia Sumpter. Their names were written at the bottom of picture. Brock just shook his head. He knew there was something about that women. She was way too cool under fire to be just an ordinary young lady. Also in the envelope was a brief bio of Eugenia. She had been born in Warrenton, Virginia, raised in DC, and attended private schools. She attended George Mason Community College before entering the army. She became an intelligence officer in the army, did eight years, and then joined the DC police force as an undercover street officer. "Shit, shit, shit," was all Brock could say. He took one last look into the envelope. There was a hotel key. A note was attached. Someone had written "Room 394, Hyatt at Dulles Airport." *Wow, could they put us up any further out of town? But I'm sure no one will think of Dulles Airport.* Inside the envelope was also another door key and another note. "Take the stairs to the basement of this building and open the east wing door with this key. Take the stairs to the first floor and take the first exit to the right. Outside there will be a white Oldsmobile Cutlass Ciera."

He ran to the bedroom and knocked hard on the door. "Ila! Ila, wake up," Brock hollered. He did not wait for her to reply. He entered the bedroom and found her like a broken doll, curled up the fetal position.

She slowly turned over and said, "Brock, what is the matter?"

"Ila, we must leave right away.

She could see that he meant business. As she rose quickly, she could remember her father saying to her as he shot craps in the alley, "Ila, when I say run, you'd better run your ass off. Always meet me on Tioga at the Tioga Café. Never go inside. Wait in the alley, and Daddy will be right there. You understand?" *I remember just standing there and saying, "Yes, sir, I understand. But this is not my dad. It's Brock, and this is serious.* Ila got up, found the flip-flops on the floor, grabbed her plastic bag full of dirty clothes, along with her purse, and was ready to go.

Brock slowly walked Ila into the kitchen. He placed all the information back in the envelope, picked up his suitcase, and left the keys to the condo on the table. They opened the door and looked both ways down the hallway. A woman stood next to a cleaning cart at the far end of the hall away from the staircase. Ila and Brock walked in the opposite direction to the staircase. Was this a never-ending Spike Lee movie scene?

They finally reached the staircase and moved as fast as they could to the basement. Brock followed the directions, and Ila just followed and remembered her father's words, "When I say run, you run." As they finally entered the parking lot, there it sat—the Cutlass Ciera. The keys were under the mat of the front seat. Ila got in on the passenger side, tossed the dirty clothes into the backseat, and was grateful to feel the cold leather on her legs and arms. She buckled her seatbelt. Brock put his bag into the backseat, buckled his seatbelt, and remembered that he was handling precious cargo. She did not remember seeing the exit from the Watergate. She felt safe and fell into a deep sleep.

Brock cruised down Route 50 toward Dulles Airport, wondering if he should stay with Ila or go back to his own home. Lord knows he really wanted to stay at the Hyatt and take care of Ila—make her feel safe, make love to her as he was sure Hunter never could. But all of that was in the future; tonight was about safety and finding a place to stay after the condo was compromised. *That won't take long*, he thought. *Too many people, too much police presence, and too much time in one place will compromise us both.*

Brock remembered his long love affair with a coworker. She was married, and the hotel was perfect because it sat on a back road in Sterling, Virginia. The hotel was sitting there waiting for Interstate 66 West to be completed. They met there three or four times a month. The clerk finally put two and two together and began putting them in the same room each time. Brock knew better, but pussy sometimes overwhelms a person's good sense. Knowing that she would be there on those days in the same room smelling the same way, looking silky smooth, and wanting him desperately was sometimes overwhelming. Just the thought of that affair brought a rise to his pants even today.

He looked over at Ila just to make sure she hadn't seen the rise. Those types of illicit affairs never ended well, but the journey had been delicious and memorable.

One of the clerks just happened to mention to a woman friend that there was a couple who came there every week or so. He described the couple and showed her hotel camera footage. The rest was history. The clerk's friend worked for Metro, and her husband was head of the Metro system. They thought it might be a great idea to try to blackmail Mrs. Dunlap, so he wrote a letter to their home addressed to Mrs. Dunlap. Mr. Dunlap opened it by mistake. The next time Brock met Mrs. Dunlap at the hotel, Metro police were sitting in the parking lot. Brock shook his head, not wanting to relive that night.

It had started to rain slightly, and the air was cold. Patches of black ice began to form on the road. He was grateful to see the exit to Dulles Airport. He was also grateful that they did not have to check in. They could just walk through the lobby and go to the elevator. As he drove into the Hyatt's parking lot, he wanted to find a space that he could back into. And trees or brush behind the car would be good. But then he thought someone could hide in the brush. But then he might need a place to hide. So brush or trees it was. Of course, there was no parking space that backed up to any greenery. It was a wide-open space. He decided to park under one of the bright lights. Ila had gone into a full snore. It was not a very attractive look; it was very funny. He felt that a woman that beautiful in his eyes should not snore that loud or with her mouth open that wide. He sat looking at her for a few seconds. He wondered so much. *How did she get wrapped up in this business? How did she get wrapped up with Hunter? Where is she from?* So many questions. After sitting for what seemed like ten minutes, he decided to shake her gently to wake her up. She slowly opened her eyes, and she knew her mouth had been open, and maybe a bit of drool had dribbled onto her shoulder. She instantly wiped her mouth and began to laugh hard—gut-wrenching hard. Tears streamed down her face, and she began to scream.

Brock could do nothing but sit and witness a woman in a total meltdown. Her back was heaving up and down, and snot began dripping from her nose. Of course, there was nothing in the car that would help. He decided to take a piece of already-messed-up clothing from the bag in the backseat. He handed it to Ila so she could wipe her nose and face. She began to scream and cry even louder, and then she began to laugh. "Vomit and snot," she finally said. "What a pleasant picture for you!" Then there was silence. A silence that said, thank you. A silence that said, I'm so grateful that you are here. Ila's cries calmed. He could almost see her heart stop beating fast. She looked at him and said "I'm the gift. I must remember that I'm the gift." Brock had no idea what she was talking about, so he turned off the engine, removed his seatbelt, and got out of the car. He then opened the rear door and pulled out his suitcase.

Ila was still sitting in the front seat. "Ila," Brock said, "please get out of the car. Take those clothes from the backseat. We'll put them all in the nearest outside garbage can." Ila got out of the car, opened the back door, and took out those terrible-smelling clothes. She added the shirt she had wiped her face on to the bundle.

She really did not want to walk through the lobby of the hotel looking like she did, but she had no choice. Together, they walked to the front door. Before entering the building, Brock took the clothes out of Ila's hand and went to find the nearest hotel Dumpster. Fortunately, it was right around the corner from the front door. Brock slung the clothes into the Dumpster and returned to the front door. He took Ila's hand, and they entered the lobby through electronic doors. He pulled Ila close to him as if they were in love. They walked through the lobby arm in arm. It seemed that no one was paying attention to the two love birds entering the building. At the elevator, Brock continued to hold Ila close. It was not until they got into the elevator that it dawned on her that he had been shielding her face from the camera. But the cameras were everywhere.

They took the elevator to the third floor. With Ila's face still tucked into Brock's shoulder, they strolled down to room 394. Ila was having a hard time breathing under Brock's muscular arm. And he smelled a little musty, which was kind of a turn-on for her. Too funny—only she could find a little funk sexy.

Brock opened the door, and they entered a suite. There was a large kitchenette area with table and chairs; an area for sitting and relaxing with a large TV; two bedrooms; and one bathroom. The bathroom was very large with double sinks, a walk-in linen closet, a sunken tub with jets, and a wide shower that could fit two comfortably. Of course there was also a toilet area with a raised toilet with a large circumference, which was great for her. The bedrooms both had king size beds but no TVs. Very interesting. There were large, walk-in closets and sitting areas for reading.

After touring the space, Brock took his suitcase to the bedroom on the right and told Ila to take the bedroom on the left. Again, he was strategically thinking that if someone entered the suite, it would be natural for most people to go to the right first. The other interesting thing about the location of the room was that it had a balcony that was not so high it could not be used as an exit. And the room was located at the end of the hallway near the stairs. *The Company tries to think of everything for the safety of their people.*

All Ila wanted to do was take a shower. But before she could get into the shower, there was a knock on the door. Ila peeked out through the bedroom doorway.

Brock instantly pulled out his .38, and Ila took a defensive position in the bedroom with a garbage can. That was really all there was besides the telephone. Brock got down onto his stomach. Slithering like a snake, he went to the door and asked, "Who is it?"

The voice said, "Room service."

Brock hesitated and replied, "We did not order room service."

"Room service Is for the couple driving the Cutlass Ciera."

Brock slowly stood up. Holding his .38 behind his back, he opened the door. There stood a young white man—six feet tall, red hair, black pants, and black shirt. Next to him was a cart. Brock slowly let him in, never losing his grip on the 38. The young man entered the room, pushed the cart into the kitchen, handed Brock an envelope, and left.

Ila felt so stupid standing in the bedroom holding a garbage can. She knew she had to get her gun back. She didn't remember if Hunter had taken it or if she had left it at home. *Ugh. I hope I left it at my house.*

Brock kept the door open and watched the young man go down the stairwell. He came back in and closed the door. He looked at Ila, still standing in the bedroom doorway holding the garbage can. Now it was his turn to laugh until he cried. She had to laugh with him. She was curious about what was on and under the cart, but she really needed to take a shower and wash her hair.

She took off the clothes Brock had given her and walked out of the bedroom into the shared bathroom naked. Brock looked up for a second and tried to act as if he did not see her. She didn't care at that point. Soap, hot water, and shampoo were all she had on her mind. As soon as she walked into the shower and saw the new pulsating shower head, she knew she was going to be in the shower until the water ran cold. *Oh, that's right! We're in a hotel. The water does not normally run cold.* The water began to steam, and she walked into it. It felt like a rain forest. She felt as if little fingers were messaging her entire body. She didn't even bother to get the washcloth soapy; she just wanted to stand under the shower head.

Brock slowly drew his gun, not sure what he would find under the cover of the cart. He slowly pulled the cover off, and there it was—really good food. He was starving. The main course was on the first shelf, dessert on the second shelf, and ice and drinks on the third shelf. He laid the envelop down and started going through the delicious spread. First there was fruit and hot glazed salmon with new potatoes and a vegetable melody. Dessert was apple pie and chocolate pudding. The bottom shelf was stocked with water, soda, beer, a bottle of vodka, plates, condiments, and an ice bucket filled. Brock walked over to the bathroom door, opened it slightly, and shouted "Ila, how long are you going to be?"

"Five minutes."

Brock started preparing the table for the delicious meal. He turned on the radio to WHUR and made them both drinks.

Ila entered the kitchen wearing the terrycloth robe provided by the hotel. She was happy to see all the good food; she was very hungry. She kind of skipped to the table like a little girl, which sent Brock into another laughing frenzy. As he laughed, she sat at the table and downed the drink he had made for her. Then she lifted her glass for him to make another one. He laughed again. He made another drink for her and sat down to enjoy the meal.

There was not much talking; only the clanging of silverware, and in the background, the great music always played on WHUR. It took them about twenty minutes to get through the entire meal. They ate everything from the salmon to the dessert. They both sat at the table feeling so full they couldn't move for at least ten minutes. Brock finally got up to get the oversized envelope. She began clearing the table and decided to make them another drink.

Brock sat down at the table and slowly emptied the context of the envelope. First, there was a diploma stating that Ila had received a master's degree in counseling from Howard University. There was a set of keys labeled with an address to a house or apartment located near the Georgetown campus. Next was a letter of intent from Georgetown University to hire her as a diversity counselor for incoming freshman. There was also a letter stating that her rent had been paid at her current address for nine months and boxes of her belonging would be delivered to her new location on an unknown date at this time. Everything would not be brought to the new address, just pertinent items. Everything else would be provided within reason. If she needed anything, she could purchase it with the paycheck she would be receiving from Georgetown. The letter also stated that Brock should return to his assignment. The reasons he had to leave so quickly was that his favorite aunt from South Carolina had passed, and he was due back to work. Finally, there was $1,500 in fifties to be spent on necessities for Ila. They looked at each other and shook their heads. Those in charge had left no stone unturned. Of course, Brock was not surprised they had chosen Georgetown. That was exactly where he'd had in mind.

Ila finished cleaning up but wondered if there was any tea or coffee in the suite. She would love a cup of tea. She decided to look on the bottom shelf of the cart one more time, and she found tea bags, lemon, cups, saucers, and sugar. No stone left unturned. Ila began to heat up the water so she could make them each a cup of tea.

Brock took this opportunity to take a shower. She could hear his moans in the shower as the heated pulsating water hit his body. They were both drained. He returned to the kitchen in a white towel and nothing else. He thanked her for the tea, walked over to the table, placed the cup and saucer on the table, and grabbed a chair. He walked to the door and jammed the back of the chair under the doorknob. He went to the sliding doors and made sure they were locked. Then he pushed the couch against them. He turned off most of the lights, picked up his cup, and bid Ila a good night.

Ila sat at the table. She was drained, and she wondered how it all had happened so fast. What was the future going to bring? Ila began to cry again. She placed both hands over her eyes. There it was—the beautiful engagement ring she had received from Hunter. She had not even noticed it during all the commotion. What was supposed to be a symbol of dedication and love felt like a ring that had been tattooed on her finger. In the morning she would find a place to put it—a dark hiding place ... a burial ground not to be seen again. But, suddenly, she had an epiphany. *I'll have the ring made into diamond earrings! And I will never take them off.* They would be a constant reminder that Hunter had hurt her, had taken her heart and stomped on it and made her feel like shit. Every day she would look at those earrings and vow never to let her heart be the beacon for her life. The earrings would shield her heart from all men like a talisman. Perfect. As soon as she was settled at the university, she would take the ring to a local jewelry store. She would need a covering for her heart and mind to get through these next few months. She emptied her cup of tea into the sink. She clicked off the kitchen light and walked slowly to the bedroom on the left. But she decided, *No. Sleeping alone is not something I can do tonight.*

She walked slowly to the bedroom on the right and entered Brock's bedroom. He was lying with his hand behind his head wide awake. She could see his eyes and the outline of his body by the pale moonlight that entered the room. She stood at the bottom of the bed waiting to be invited in. He pulled back the covers, and she dropped her robe, climbed into the bed, and slowly wiggled down into the covers. It felt warm, cozy, and safe. She could not wait to go to sleep. Once she was in a fetal position, she felt his hand reaching for her arm. He slowly slid his hand down her arm and placed his hand in hers. She could feel her nipples getting hard and wondered if she dared to touch any part of him other than his hand. That was a fleeting thought because he took her hand and placed it on his penis. It was flaccid at first, but it grew in her hand as if it was being blown up like a balloon. She slowly moved her hand back away, thinking, *This is not what we should be doing.* He grabbed her hand again and slide it back on top of his penis. In those seconds, it had become rock hard.

Oh, Ila, resist. Tell him no. Tell him you are too fragile to have sex with anyone. Tell him you are torn, and your wounds are open. Please do not place salt into them.

Brock turned onto his side and slid closer to Ila. Her back was still facing him. He started at the nape of her neck and planted kisses all the way down her spine. As he got to her anus, his tongue began to flick. He rounded her ass and came up under her body, licking her thighs, kissing her inner thighs, and then seeking salvation in her pussy. He used his fingers to open her pussy, and he breathed into it. He did not lick it and didn't really touch it, but he breathed life into it, as if he was whispering a prayer.

With both of his hands, he began caressing her breasts while still breathing into her pussy. Ila began to cry once again. There was such relief in feeling safe from the drain of being hurt. She had developed an emotional attachment to a man who had been her protector. Suddenly, she wanted to give him everything—give him deep kisses, let him know how grateful for his presence she was. He raised up from her pussy and kissed her stomach, made love to her breasts with tiny bites and licks. Finally, he placed his lips on hers, giving her soft, slow, small intimate kisses. He took her hand once again and placed it on his dick. Ila raised her ass slowly and placed the head of his dick inside her pussy—not all the way, just the head. She played with the head of his dick for several minutes and then picked her ass up off the bed and forced his dick into her.

He began to shake at being thrown full throttle into her hot pussy. He held on to the pillows behind Ila's head, wanting desperately not to come, wanting to give her at least an hour of pleasure, but it had been some time for him. He looked down as he entered her pussy, long and hard at first, then fast, then slow, then fast … then, Ila screamed. He lost his concentration and came. His sperm came out like water from a water gun that was full. At that moment, he remembered he was fucking a woman who had been fucking a man who was bi-sexual. No condom. And no thought of a condom until now. How stupid could he be? He looked at her face. There were tears in her eyes—like crystal-clear ice from her core.

Ila began to smile. It was a smile of satisfaction and a sort of demonic pleasure. This was the beginning of her shield—feeling but not feeling, making love but feeling nothing. This was the place her mind would stay, letting nothing and no one penetrate her heart again.

Brock slowly pulled out and rolled over. He could not understand how he could have felt so much for this woman who was shielding her heart and soul, but he did, and he could not wait to make love to her again. Ila rolled over into the fetal position and went to sleep instantly. Brock slide the covers over her and lay there until he fell into a deep sleep.

As the night turned into dawn, Ila's eyes slowly opened. She had to focus because, for a moment, she had no idea where she was or who the man next to her was. It took her about a minute to rewind the events of the day before to bring her back to the present, remembering that she had made love to this man. Well, the correct term would be "had sex" with this man. Without a condom, without passion, and without purpose. Once again, a cold, salty tear rolled down her cheek.

She wanted to go home. She wanted to check on Paula and Drew. She wanted to call Dr. Zarnoff to see if she could get her old position back. She wanted to smoke weed until her head exploded. She wanted her old life back. Brock shifted positions, woke up, and sat straight up. She knew he was looking for his gun. She slowly caressed his arm, and he turned to look down at her with dark marble eyes, she saw them soften in seconds as soon as he realized he was not in danger any longer. He fell back onto the pillow hard. He turned and looked at her but said nothing. She knew the sun was rising as light began to come through the curtains. She could tell it was probably around seven o'clock. She pushed herself out of the bed and dangled her legs over the side. She needed to make sure that the blood flow had started before placing her legs on the floor. She found out the hard way that sometimes she needed to wait a minute before she started to walk from a lying down position. Only when her adrenaline was pumping was it easy to come from the lying down position to her feet. As she felt the blood start to flow, she heard another knock at the door. Damn! It was too early for room service.

She had no gun, but Brock already had his .38 in his hand and was headed to the door. Again, he waited until he was about a yard away from the door, and he got on the floor. Ila remembered her training with Hunter. From a position on the floor, it was sometimes possible to see shadows of feet under the door. That way it was easy to see how many people were on the other side of the door.

Brock crawled up to the door, looked under it, and called out, "Who is it?"

"Room service."

"We did not order room service."

The voice behind the door whispered, "It's room service from Georgetown."

Brock crawled back into the bedroom and requested that Ila get up and answer the door. She moved quickly, getting the robe from the bottom of the bed and walking to the door. Brock walked and then crawled to the door and ask her to open it slowly. She opened the door to find a different young man was standing there. She opened the door wider, and Brock stood up, holding the gun behind his back. What he forgot was that he was completely naked. As the young man entered, Ila asked that he take the cart to the second bedroom and leave it. As the man walked down the hall, Brock ran back into the bedroom and pulled on his pants. He tucked the .38 into his waist behind his back and walked back behind the door that Ila kept open. The young man came back up the hallway, with his hands out in front of him. He carried a small white envelope in one hand. He handed it to her as he walked out the door.

She closed the door quickly, and they both dropped to the floor and crawled to the kitchenette. If shots were going to be fired, they would more than likely be aimed waist high. But no shots came. They stayed on the floor for about five minutes and then got up. Ila walked slowly to the second bedroom to retrieve the cart. She was starving and was praying that the food was not tainted with something. This was a dangerous game they were playing. One wrong move made without thinking could end their lives.

Ila had not noticed until the previous evening that her hair had thinned during this operation. Her skin was not as smooth. It was not until years later that she would be diagnosed with alopecia. She wheeled the cart to the kitchen and could smell the sausage. She lifted the tablecloth off the cart. Of course, Brock still had his gun drawn. All the food was covered with cloches, but the sausage and something else smelled delicious. She removed one of the cloches to reveal link sausage, ham, and steak. Under the second warmer she found scrambled eggs, mini bagels, butter, and fried potatoes. The drinks were on the second level of the cart—coffee, juice, hot water, tea bags, milk and cream, sugar, honey, and ice water. On the last tier of the cart was a plate of mixed fruit. Ila reached onto the second tier and retrieved all the drinks and placed them on the table along with condiments, plates, cups, and saucers.

She looked at Brock as if to say, "Every man for himself." Then she grabbed a plate and filled it with a little of everything. She was not a wall flower when it came to eating. She was not much for sweets, but when it came to good food, she could eat. That was why it was so important while she'd been away at training to curtail her eating habits. She was sure that additional training was coming. Her stamina would have to be great to get through this new covert operation and the trial of the chief of police. But in the meantime, she was going to enjoy that breakfast.

Brock soon followed suit but with much more food than she could ever consume. They ate in silence but had to laugh out loud at each other after they were finished and were sitting back feeling terrible because they'd both eaten too much. They laughed hard. It felt good. Ila placed the remainder of breakfast back on the cart and went into the bedroom to take yet another shower and get ready to go. It would not take her long because all she had were Brock's clothes. Again, she jumped into the shower. Her hair was now in a semi-afro style. She had only the hotel hair dryer and the comb from her purse. It was useless. While under the shower, she braided sections of her hair. At least it would have some curl after it dried. As she left the shower, it occurred to her that they had never opened the white envelope. She toweled off, wrapped the towel around her waist, and walked toward the kitchen. Brock was sitting there very still, gun on the table, reading the contents of the white envelope. Ila walked slowly back into the bedroom and pulled on the sweatpants, brown shirt, and flip-flops Brock had given her to wear. Once dressed, she lay on the bed, knowing he would come and get her when he was ready to go. She lay there just long enough to fall asleep.

Enclosed in the envelope were plane tickets to Jacksonville, Florida. He would leave on Friday morning, attend his aunt's funeral, and return on Saturday evening. Brock would have to be at National Airport at 6:00 in the morning on Friday. His plane would land at 8:00 a.m. and he would have to report to work on Sunday morning at 6:00.

It was Tuesday, and he and Ila had only two more days together. Also in the envelope were keys and a note—an address on O Street NW and the words *safe house*. He knew he was not allowed to reach out to family members or friends to discuss funeral arrangements for his deceased Aunt Lucy, and his mother knew the routine. He had been involved in the business so long, she would just be very grateful to see him at the funeral. Brock wondered if his best friend, Morris, would be able to attend the funeral. When they were in the academy together, he often went home with Brock for a little home cooking. Morris was shocked to see scrapple. Brock remembered him coming to the kitchen to see Aunt Lucy cutting up a block of scrapple, which really looked like a block of shit. She'd asked him if he wanted one or two pieces. Morris had looked at Aunt Lucy and replied, "I'll have two pieces. Please call me when breakfast is ready. Thank you." And he'd walked out of the kitchen. Brock remembered walking by Morris in the hallway. Morris looked as if he'd seen a ghost. "Man," Brock said, "what's wrong?" Morris said, "Your aunt wants me to eat something that looks like shit!" Brock had laughed and explained that scrapple is all the stuff left over that nobody wants to use from a pig. It's thrown together, pressed into a block, and packaged. It's then sliced, seasoned, fried, and used as a breakfast meat. "Okay," Morris had said, laughing, "but I'm only eating that shit because we are at your aunt's house. The memory of the weekend slowly played like a video across Brock's mind. Those were the days.

He let the video drift off and remembered there were more important things to do than walk down memory lane. He went into the bedroom only to find Ila passed out. He turned around, walked to the bathroom, took and shower, put on the same old clothes he'd worn the day before, and went to wake up Ila. He gently shook her shoulders to wake her up. She woke up startled and looked at him as if to say, "How could you wake me up from such good sleep?"

As she swung her legs to the side of the bed and sat up, her eyes and mouth were eye level to Brock's zipper. She looked away, but Brock brought her head back to where it had been and began pulling his zipper down. Ila pushed his hand away and carefully continued unzipping his pants while rubbing his balls through his pants with her other hand. Zipper down and button undone, Ila reached into his pants. He had no underwear on! *How sexy he is!* She reached for his penis and felt it growing as she managed to get that anaconda out of his pants. It popped out and hit Ila on the nose. Brock began to laugh. Ila slowly placed his huge muscle into her mouth, sliding her tongue on the side then down the front as she slowly caressed his balls with her left hand. He grabbed his dick and began penetrating her mouth with it, all the while holding her hair. Ila could not deep throat his entire dick—that shit only happens in porno movies. Instead, she took as much as she could and sucked it until her jaws ached. He began to lean back, and Ila new any minute he was going to blow. She absolutely loved the art of giving head but hated having semen in her mouth. She backed off his dick and slowly sucked it until she got to the very end—and then she bit him. He came all over her with a growl from deep within. His legs started to tremble and he cried out, "Oh, shit!" She knew it was over, and she had to laugh. Men were so easy.

He looked down on her and gestured to the semen that was all over her and the bed. He laughed and said, "Ila, you are going to very hard to leave behind." Ila thought to herself, *He does not know it, but he will not be leaving me behind.* She smiled to herself, grabbed the towel off the bed, cleaned herself up, and wiped his dick.

Together, they gathered up the few items they had with them, and Ila made sure Brock had all the envelopes, including the original envelope they'd received when they were at the Watergate. Once again as they left, there was a cleaning woman standing at end of the hall. She wondered if it was the same lady who had been at the Watergate. She would probably go in and clean the entire suite and make sure that all finger prints were wiped down, no hairs left anywhere, and nothing personal left behind.

Ila gave that only a fleeting thought as Brock took the steps two at a time. The exit door let out to the back parking lot. Brock told Ila to stand at the door while he walked around to the front and got the Cutlass Ciera. One thing she had learned in the last three or four years was that it was best to do exactly as she had been told.

It was a warm day; spring was around the corner. The cherry blossoms would be exploding in the basin soon, and the streets would be full of tourists. There was nothing like DC in the springtime. It seemed that was when the best weed came to town, and it would be at Hains Point. Too funny—little did she know that Hunter was the dope man! Wow that seemed like a lifetime ago.

Ila wondered what was taking Brock so long. He was just going to walk to the car and come right back. He drove up slowly after about fifteen minutes, and she got into the car. He told her he had driven the car out of the parking lot, driven up the street to the store to make sure he was not being followed, and doubled back to pick her up. She buckled her seatbelt and let the sunshine fall onto her face.

She was very surprised when Brock drove back on Route 50 toward DC, but she knew asking questions would be fruitless, so she just enjoyed the tunes on WHUR and wondered what the next several months would bring. They took Route 50 onto Constitution Avenue made a left onto 19th Street. They drove to the circle and went around to P Street NW, made a left on 30th Street, and a right on O Street NW. Halfway down the block, Brock stopped in front of a red brick townhouse. Well, that is what they are called in DC; in other places they are called row houses. Ila had to laugh at that.

There was an orange cone in the space in front of the building. Brock pulled up alongside another car, got out, moved the cone, and backed into the space. Fortunately, it was in the middle of a workday and there was really no one around. By the time everyone got home, they would not remember there was a cone there in the morning and now it was gone.

Ila's first thought was, *Man, I'm going to have to move this car once a week for street cleaning.* But maybe they were exempt from that in Georgetown. She laughed again as she got out of the car and stood by the entrance to the house she thought they were going into. Brock took the envelopes from where he'd tucked them behind the visor and got out of the car. He walked over to the sidewalk, picked up the cone, and placed it into the trunk. He looked at Ila and nodded his head in the other direction.

They walked halfway down the block to the side-street entrance to a house that sat on 31st street and O. Brock used the key to open both the top and bottom lock. They entered a small hallway. Coat hooks lined the right-hand wall. On the floor, a rubber mat was ready for winter shoes and boots. They continued down the small hallway to an open area on the right that led into the kitchen. There was a small window in the kitchen that look out into the backyard. They walked through the kitchen back into the hallway. On the right was the bedroom and across the hall to the left was the bathroom. At the end of the hallway was a door that led into the backyard. Outside, next to the doorway was a flight of stairs that led to the upstairs unit. There was a single parking space in the backyard that led to an alleyway.

Ila knew that the company had picked this unit because it was strategically located on a corner so that a resident could see what was always coming, but this backyard thing had her stumped. The back door was secured by both a double lock and a dead bolt lock, just like the front door.

The apartment was furnished with only the necessary furniture, but in the bedroom, Ila noticed a pile of boxes, and she was hoping that they held some of her personal effects from her apartment. They walked back through the living room, which was furnished with a love seat, a couch, and a coffee table. There were two long pole lamps in the corners, some very large throw pillows scattered on the floor, and a square black-and-white paisley rug

under the coffee table. On the back wall by the door to
the kitchen a television sat on a stand. Just above the
television, on the wall, was a telephone, and it rang just
then, startling them.

Brock picked up the phone."Hello?"

"This is operator six-one-nine, and the phone number
to this telephone is two-zero-two-four-seven-six-nine-
nine-two-seven." The line disconnected.

Brock laughed and said, "This is really some double-
oh-seven shit. I'm afraid to leave you here." Brock walked
into the kitchen hoping to find a pencil or pen so that
he could write down the number. He found a pencil in
one of the drawers and a pad of paper. He wrote down
the number, and would give the piece of paper to Ila and
request that she memorize the number.

Ila walked into the kitchen again and opened
cupboards and the fridge, which seemed to be fully
stocked with food and all the essentials. Brock handed
her a piece of paper that had the phone number on it
and it read, memorize this. She took the piece or paper
and began walking down the hallway to the bedroom
and started to look through the boxes. The bedroom was
furnished with a queen-sized bed with no headboard, a
dresser with six drawers, and a huge mirror. Next to the
dresser was a walk-in closet of sorts. It had a pull-down
light, but was very big. She was happy to see that, even
though she had no clothes. She sat on the bed and began
to open boxes. The first box contained books; she was glad
to see them, especially the ones she'd brought but not yet
read. The next box contained her boom box and about
twenty cassette tapes. The next box contained toiletries,

including hair color. They must really want her to dye her hair honey blond, because there were eight boxes of hair color. She had never dyed her hair before. They had also packed her straightening comb; they must have seen in the kitchen on the stove. She laughed because she really needed it. She took that box into the bathroom and started emptying it out into the cabinet. The bathroom was a nice size with a full tub with a shower, basin, toilet, towel racks, and a small closet for other necessities.

It dawned on her that she had not heard a word out of Brock. She walked back down the hall, through the kitchen, and into the living room. There he was, .38 on his chest, asleep on the couch. She walked back into the bedroom and continued to unpack some of the boxes. In yet another box were purses and shoes. She didn't know who had picked what to pack, but there was a Coach bag in the box that she had not carried since Rodney died. It was a lovely black purse, but it had been a gift from Rodney, and she had placed in the darkest part of her closet in Virginia. She set the purse aside and pulled out the shoes and the three other purses. The next box contained clothes, but they were casual clothes—sweats, T-shirts, and so forth. She wondered why they hadn't packed any of her other clothes, and she figured that clothing was what the $1,500 in cash was for. She and Brock would have to go shopping before he left. First stop would be Georgetown Leather Design.

Suddenly, Ila heard a car door slam and then someone running down the steps from the upstairs apartment. She went to the back window and peeped through the small curtains. A Prince George's County patrol car was parked in the backyard. The patrolman walked through the yard and up the steps. Cracking the window, she heard the young lady who apparently lived upstairs greet him. She laughed out loud. The Company three-sixties everything. She wondered how they found out this guy was having afternoon delight, and she wondered if his patrol car would be parked out there often. Instantly, she felt a little more secure, especially because Brock was not going to be staying with her.

She decided, since Brock was asleep, to take a shower and then try to do something with her hair, since it was clear that the Company wanted her to dye it. She decided to go natural. Her hair had thinned, and this would give it time to grow strong. The color would be good protection, as people would not be looking for a woman with a honey-blonde short afro. *This is really going to alter my look. Nothing to do but to do it.* She found a pair of scissors in the bathroom. *I guess they knew that I had to do something ...* All she could do was laugh as she looked in the mirror and began to painfully cut off locks of her long, curly hair. Again she began to cry, not for the hair, but for the new beginning, knowing that for months she would be living another life. When the sink was filled with hair, she scooped it out and put it into the garbage can. Within fifteen minutes, her hair was cut very short and was ready for the color. Not knowing anything about coloring hair, she had to sit and painfully read the instructions. It did not seem like a difficult process, but she did not want her hair to be damaged. When she was ready, she stood at the sink and began the process. Two hours later, the lady in the mirror looked so different. Fortunately, the packers had included her hair grease and moisturizer from her old apartment. She applied them both, and the style began to take shape—a very curly afro, honey blonde.

As she was looking in the mirror trying to take in this new person, she felt a presence in the bathroom. When she looked up, Brock was standing in the doorway. This man was massive; he took up most of the doorway. He had taken off his shirt, and she could see that the ripples in his stomach and his arms were massive. She looked at him in the mirror and asked, "So what do you think?

He took a minute to answer. "It's not forever. It's just for right now."

A tear rolled down her face. Just then, the near future seemed like forever. He came up behind her and pressed his body against her, giving her strength. "Ila, we'll look back on this time and laugh. Blonde is just not what I expected to see when I woke up, but it doesn't matter. Come on. Let's get something to eat. We can walk to the neighborhood Chinese restaurant and get carry-out."

Ila wondered how he knew there was a neighborhood carry-out. Again, she let that go. Better just to go with it. She walked into the bedroom and pulled her favorite sweatpants from the drawer, and a Georgetown T-shirt that had arrived in the box of clothing. *Too funny*, she thought, *they remembered my Converse All Star tennis shoes.* They were brand new, and she was glad to see them. She applied a little mascara and lipstick. After she added hoop earrings, she was ready to go. Brock had gone to the Cutlass to grab his bag. He was currently in the bathroom washing up and brushing his teeth. She waited in the living room until he was ready.

There is nothing like a college town. Even though Georgetown is in the heart of DC, it feels as if it is a million miles away from the most powerful place in the world. Ila and Brock walked toward Wisconsin Avenue. By now it was early evening, and people were coming home. College students were everywhere, and the pulse of the city was evident. They walked in silence. Ila knew that Brock would be there tonight and tomorrow, and then he would be gone. There was so much to say and then nothing to say.

They turned right on Wisconsin, and there it was—a little hole-in-the-wall Chinese restaurant. People were lined up on the sidewalk to order at the walk-up window. Others were inside in the dining room. People who had ordered were hanging out front waiting for their food. When Ila and Brock walked inside, the smell of the many spices and ingredients hit her stomach. She was hungry. They waited for about five minutes to place an order because Brock had to read the entire menu. She knew what she wanted; she was such a creature of habit. They ordered and then sat at a table and watched people come and go. The food would be ready in about fifteen minutes.

They talked small talk while they waited. Brock talked about the funeral and how he could not wait to see his mother and other siblings. It had been almost a year. He also could not wait for his mother's homemade biscuits, collard greens, sweet potatoes, and other specialties. He knew all the food that would be at the repast for his aunt. She thought to herself, *If we hook up, we're going to have to go see your mother all the time because I can't cook!* She laughed to herself.

As they walked back to her new apartment, he asked Ila how she'd met Hunter and how she hadn't known he was bi-sexual. She told him the only indication I had that something was amiss was when Maurice occasionally got jealous of the time she and Hunter spent together. But she had thought little of it at the time. She had girlfriends who used to fight over who was going to sit in the front seat of her car or who got called first to go somewhere. Friendships were hard to find and hard to keep. She'd never given Maurice's attitude a second thought.

And, speaking of bi-sexual, the first time she'd seen Eugenia was in the sauna at the gym at the Watergate. For a minute, Ila thought she herself could be bi-sexual because she thought that Eugenia was so beautiful naked. So, no, she didn't give Hunter and Maurice a second thought.

Ila told Brock that what she'd seen when she walked in on Hunter, Maurice, and Eugenia would be imprinted on her mind forever. "Hopefully I'll be wiser the next time I decide to consider a relationship," she told him. "But he hid that side of himself very well."

When they arrived back at the apartment, they sat at the small dinette set, spread out all the food, and then got glasses from the cabinet and made ice water. They sat at the table and told war stories about their assignments. Brock's experience with the FBI was extensive because he'd gone to the academy. Ila, on the other hand, just seemed to always be in the right—or wrong—place and got pulled into assignments, mostly because she was an African-American female, and most people were just not thinking that an African-American female would be in an undercover position.

Ila told Brock about Dr. Zarnoff and her friends, Paula and Drew, and she told him how much she missed all of them. He was a good listener, which she found to be rare in most men. If they were talking about themselves, the conversation was great. As soon as it was the woman's turn, "Oh my, look at the time." She laughed to herself. They ate almost everything.

Ila wondered if there was a gym at the university where she might have privileges. Lord knows she'd need it after all this eating they'd been doing. They cleaned the kitchen area up and headed to the living room. Brock turned on the TV just in time for *Mod Squad*. It was a rerun, but they both enjoyed the show.

Somehow Ila felt a little awkward being in the apartment with Brock. It felt like someone's home, unlike the hotel room where perfect strangers normally would make love to each other. She decided to see if there was any alcohol in the kitchen. Maybe she would feel more comfortable if they had a drink and they both could relax. As she got up to go to the kitchen, Brock got up to secure the apartment. He placed a chair under the doorknob of each door and made sure the outside lights were on. When he went to place the chair at the back door, he saw the Prince George's County patrol car, and he began to laugh.

Ila looked in at the cabinets in the kitchen and found no alcohol. She knew that the Company usually thought of everything, so she opened the freezer, and there it was— vodka … Absolut. They always remember everything. She went to the cabinet and pulled down two tumbler glasses, figuring that, if they were going to get through this night together, they should be feeling no pain. She poured the vodka to the halfway level in the glasses and added a few cubes of ice and a splash of orange juice in each glass. Then she carried the drinks to the living room and placed them on the coffee table.

Brock had disappeared. She thought he was probably in the bathroom getting rid of his Chinese food. She was sitting on the couch watching something mindless on TV when it dawned on her that there was only one bedroom. *I do believe that the Company felt that having a Prince George's police officer visiting his girlfriend would be enough security, and Brock would feel comfortable going back to his own home.* But, as she sat there waiting for him to return to the living room, she realized that she did not want to stay in this apartment by herself.

She got up and went into the bedroom to retrieve her boom box and the few cassettes that had been packed. As she walked out of the bedroom, Brock came out of the bathroom with a towel wrapped around his waist. He was looking moist. He had said before that he liked to dry off naturally rather than use a towel. She knew they had been intimate before, but she realized that she was in such an emotional state when they were together before, that she had never really looked at him. She stared briefly and went down the hall back into the living room. Of course, all the cassettes she had in her hand were for making love. The boom box was always in her bedroom, and all she had was bedroom music. Her other music was on vinyl back at her apartment … she hoped. She had some great music that she played on her KLH turntable through KLH speakers.

But, none of that was here. She placed the boom box on the floor next to the TV and placed the Stylistics "Break Up to Make Up" cassette into the box. It was a good thing no one lived downstairs. The box had a pretty good bass coming out of it.

Brock came out of the bedroom in boxers and a T-shirt. She felt way overdressed and had to laugh to herself. She handed him his drink, which was, by now, a little diluted. He had some catching up to do. They sat and talked about getting up early and going into Georgetown to shop and then to the Waterside Mall for lunch. Ila also told him she wanted to walk around the shops on Wisconsin Avenue. She had seen a new trend—patchwork squares of suede and leather made into designer pants and matching vests. She could not wait to buy an outfit in suede. She was sure they were not ready for clothing like that at Georgetown, but she had decided that, if she had to show up with blond hair, she was going to show up dressed the part on the first day. She would tone it down on the second day.

She had always been told to give people what you've got on the first day so the rest of the days will seem mild. She was surprised that Brock liked to shop, so that would not be a problem. He told her he liked to sit and watch women model the clothes they were trying on. Boy, that was a change for her. Hunter had always just wanted her clothes off! Rodney never liked shopping, but he had wanted her to model everything when she got home after using his credit card. *Wow, got to get that vision out of my head!*

Of course, every song on the cassette was a slow song. They had both finished their drinks and were feeling no pain. The next song was "You're As Right As Rain." Brock asked her to dance. She had no idea he could dance. He held her so close she could smell his soap and cologne. The scent was unfamiliar to her. *I must ask him what he's wearing*, she thought. Once she received a paycheck, maybe she could buy him some to thank him for everything. They danced close, and she could feel the tension in his pants. He backed away from her and asked her to strip for him when the next song came on. *Strip? Here we go——another freak. She might as well have put on Funkadelic.* She smiled to herself because she was all about stripping for this man. She had never done it, but how hard could it be? She stopped the cassette and put in Teddy Pendergrass's "Turn off the Lights." He had just released the record that year, and it was being played on all the radio stations.

Brock sat down on the couch and watched with tense eyes as she prepared to take off her clothes. She walked over to the small lamp and turned it off. The only light came through the hallway from the bathroom. She started with her top and slowly let it fall to the floor. She was thinking about how sensual she could be and decided to walk over and let him help her strip. She asked him to stand up and take off her bra. She turned around, and as he started to take off her bra, she let her hands slide down his side. She slowly griped his penis in her hand then released it so she could slowly take her arms out of the bra and let it fall to the floor. She was getting nervous about the tennis shoes because how can you seductively take them off? She laughed to herself. He slowly turned her around and placed his fingertips into the top of her sweatpants and then gently pulled them and her panties to her ankles. He motioned for her to sit on the couch, and he proceeded to take her shoes, socks, pants, and panties off. While she watched, he then stripped. What a wonderful moment to see him standing there at full attention and wanting her as much as she wanted him.

He lay down on the couch next to her and gently caressed her breasts while placing his finger in her pussy, looking for her hidden clitoris. It did not take him long to find it. He started with soft round circles and slowly got rougher while sucking her breast the way a child takes milk from its mother. She could not help but moan with pleasure. She wanted to fully take control of the act but held back because this man did not truly know who she was, and she was not about to put any more cards on the table. Seeming desperate, he stood up and gestured for her to place her hand in his. They slowly walked down the hall toward the bedroom, but he made a left into the bathroom. She was confused, but thought, *Oh, yeah, he likes things very clean.* He turned on the shower and turned to kiss her deeply. When the water was warm enough, he got in and brought her in with him. He took the washcloth from the towel rack and began to lather it up. She stood like a robot waiting to take orders from this huge man who took up most of the shower. He took her breath away. He turned her slowly so that she was under the shower, and all she could think about was that she had just dyed her hair ... too funny.

He washed her from head to toe and caressed her back, relieving all the tension that was located there. She wanted to grab his penis and put it into her mouth, but she stopped herself. He turned off the shower, wrung out the washcloth, grabbed the towel from the rack, and began to dry her off—not all the way, just slightly until she was still damp. He got out of the shower first and grabbed her hand to help her out of the shower. She was sorry to see that his hardness had dissolved, but he seemed to be enjoying himself, so she was happy. They walked into the bedroom, and he asked her to lie sideways on the bed. He walked back into the bathroom, took the lotion from the cabinet, and brought it back into the bedroom. At this point, the only sound they could hear was from the springs of the bed in the bedroom upstairs where the police officer and his girlfriend were heavily in to sexual intercourse, or perhaps bondage, she thought. Again, too funny.

Brock slowly anointed her body with lotion, making slow circular motions on her back, arms and legs. He then turned her over and did the same to her breasts, arms, thighs, and feet. She was filled with pleasure. He had magic hands. When he finished her feet, he spread her legs and slowly placed his finger in her vagina, slowly opening the walls. He stuck his tongue full in like a dog licking his pan of water. She came instantly, and he went to the bathroom for a towel. He cleaned her off and started again. She could not stop screaming with emotion. She'd had some awesome cunnilingus before, but this man had a tongue that was as good as a dick. She had begun to sweat, and after about twenty minutes, she could hear herself scream as her feet turned up like the dead wicked witch's feet in the *Wizard of Oz*. Once again, he cleaned her vagina. He got up, turned off the bathroom light, walked back into the bedroom, and asked her to get under the covers and roll over to the left-hand side of the bed. She did as she was told. He walked into the living room, retrieved his .38, and placed it on the floor next to the bed. He was left handed, so he could reach it easily if he needed it. He kissed her on the forehead and said good night. She lay their misty eyed. She did not believe this had ever happened to her before. It was a feeling of satisfaction and no satisfaction at the same time. A very mixed bag. She lay there wondering what she should think about what just happened. There was a snore from the other side of the bed that shook the walls. She decided that whatever that had all been about, she was glad to not be alone and grateful to be with someone who was so giving.

After what had seemed like hours of sleeping, they heard steps coming down the stairs from the apartment above them. Then they heard the car door slam and the car drive off. They looked at each other and laughed and went back to sleep. As the dust of morning light came through the window, she had to get up and go to the bathroom. As she rolled out of bed trying not to disturb Brock, she could see him reaching for his gun. She gently stroked his arm and told him she was going to the bathroom. His body had tensed up just that quickly. After he had heard her voice, it seemed as if someone had let the air out of a balloon. She could see his body relax. She went into the bathroom, sat on the toilet, and peed for what seemed like ten minutes. It reminded her of the night she had gone to a Georgetown game with Rodney. As they were about to leave, he decided he had to pee. He found a dark corner of the parking lot, but he seemed to pee for a very long time—so long that she began to laugh hysterically, and then people started to notice. She told him if he did not stop, they were going to be arrested for being lewd and lascivious. After going down that yellow brick road again, it dawned on her that she had been on the toilet for some time. She heard Brock rustling as he got out of bed, and before she knew it he was standing at the bathroom door. He came in. He asked her to spread her legs, and he peed right between them. He took a piece of toilet paper, tapped the end of his penis, threw the toilet paper into the toilet, washed his hands in the basin, and left the bathroom. She sat there a little longer thinking, *What the fuck just happened?* And she laughed again, hard. Once she had recuperated, she washed her hands and headed toward the living room only to see Brock in his boxers eating cereal and watching *Underdog. Wow ... you just never know.*

She turned around and went into the kitchen to make coffee and to see if she could find something other than cereal to eat. Yup, everything was there—bagels, eggs, and sausage. So she went to work and fixed breakfast for two just in case his cereal was not enough. As she turned the last sausage, there was a knock on the front door. She could hear Brock get up quickly, run into the bedroom, put on his jeans, get his .38, and head out the back door. She decided just to stand at the living room door and yell out, "Who is it?"

The person behind the door said, "I have a package for this address." Then she heard him talking to someone, and she knew Brock had come around the house and come upon this young man from the sidewalk. She could hear a change in the young man's voice, and then there was a second knock at the door.

"Who is it?" she said again.

"It's me, Brock." She slowly went to the door but peeked out the window just to make sure it was him. She opened the door, and Brock came in carrying an envelope, which he threw onto the coffee table after making sure the back door was locked. That was something she had not even thought of. *Oh, shit … what am I going to do when I'm alone?*

She placed breakfast food on plates and carried them into the living room. Brock looked up from cartoons and was glad to see more food. They consumed coffee and breakfast and again laughed about him peeing between her legs. He thought that was hilarious, and said he wished he'd had had a camera so he could show her the look on her face when he did it. He got up, picked up both their plates and cups, and proceeded to the kitchen. She could hear him running water and washing the dishes, and she was truly glad to see that happen. He got many brownie points for that.

He came back out of the living room and said, "Okay, let's get ready to go exercise. I'm a runner," he said loudly, "but I know you don't run, so we'll walk to the university, walk around the track, and walk back. She looked at him as if he had two heads, but she knew it was something she should do, so she got her ass up and went into the bedroom to get dressed. She picked up the sweatpants from the floor which she had tossed there after her strip tease. She got her Converse tennis shoes out of a box, found a bra in another box. Brock had thrown a T-shirt at her. She threw some water and grease in her hair, put on some lipstick, and was ready to go.

She was not sure where Brock was going to put his .38, but she saw that he had decided to holster it since they were walking not running. He had put on an oversized T-shirt and Adidas tennis shoes, a brand she was unfamiliar with. He was ready and looking fine and masculine. They did not talk about last night. It seemed he felt it was very natural. She thought it was very different and wondered if he preferred to masturbate over having sex with a woman. It would not be out of the question. Men who work for the government and are away on assignments to places they can barely pronounce are told to be very careful where they stick their wicks because they just might bring something through customs they cannot get rid of. Condoms were available but not comfortable to get. A guy would get in the checkout line to buy lambskin Trojans and, of course, the clerk would have to call for a price check over the loud speaker. Unbelievable, but it had happened to her more than once. Then she decided that maybe she should just go to the health department to get condoms, so off she'd gone one day. After signing in and sitting for an hour, someone handed her a brown paper bag with two condoms in it. She laughed all the way to her car because the man she was dating at that time could use those condoms only as water balloons. Funny how quickly you can remember things that happen so long ago, but can't remember yesterday.

Brock and Ila headed to the door and had to look for the keys. Brock found them next to the envelope that had contained the money and tickets. They left the apartment. Ila left from the front door after removing the chair from under the doorknob. She locked the door after her. Brock left from the back door. Always security conscience. Ila stood on the sidewalk waiting for Brock. He jogged around the corner, stopped in front of the apartment, and kissed her softly. He started doing jumping jacks and touching his toes, looking at her sideways because she was standing there watching him. He nodded his head for her to join him. She did as he requested, and within five minutes, she had a full sweat going, and he looked the same way he did when he'd jogged around the corner. Ten minutes later, they started to walk. She realized that warming up was important but … come on.

They walked briskly up O Street toward the university. The street was lined with townhomes that had been turned into apartments for students—one in the basement and two each on the first, second, and third floors. It was a beautiful day, and people were everywhere. Students were sitting in the local park reading or listening to music. Jewish families walked together to temple, and members of the university track team were running on both sides of the street. The activity made for a wonderful walking experience. They were in full stride and she was really enjoying every moment. Ila looked over at Brock, who finally was in a full sweat.

After they entered the gates of the university, they walked around the back of Healy Hall. This was the building she would be working in on Monday morning. It was named after Patrick F. Healy, who was president of the university from 1873 to 1882 and was the first African American to head a major, predominately white university. She was extremely proud to be able to work in a building with that kind of history, and to be a part of a university experience.

As they headed toward the track, they noticed that the track team members had come full circle back to the stadium and were working out. Brock decided that, since they couldn't walk the track, they would exercise on the steps of the stadium. Now, that was where Ila drew the line. She sat in the bleachers and looked at him. He nodded and continued his quest. He began running the steps. *Oh my God.* She looked down at the field. The team was leaving; practice was over. So she wouldn't look like a real slug, she got up, walked down the stairs to the track, and started a brisk walk. She understood from her training in Virginia that four laps around the field would equal about one mile, so the quest for the day was to do eight laps. She hoped to be able to do it at least three times a week. With Brock leaving soon, it would be hard to be motivated, but she was willing to give it a try.

She zoned out for a moment and started to think about what had happened in the last six months. A tear rolled down her face. It was hard to believe that she would probably never see Drew and Paula again, and that Dr. Zarnoff had a new assistant, and her time with the Company would be terminated after the court case.

She was sure they would transfer her to another agency, but she had really enjoyed her service and was a little perturbed that she would be requested to leave because she had been on a difficult assignment because they had achieved the outcome they wanted, but they had also received too much publicity. More tears came, not for the job, but because she had not seen or heard from any of her family members in sometime. She had not had a chance to sit on the stoop of her own apartment, play cards with the police officers, or smoke a joint with Paula and Drew. And Drew was sick, which made her even sadder that she hadn't been able to contact them. She wondered if Brock could find a way for her to visit just once before he left on Sunday. Halfway through her first mile, Brock joined her, looked her in the eyes, and said, "I'm here for you. Please don't be sad."

She stopped and kissed him hard. He was her life jacket at that point. As they made their way around for the second mile, Brock said, "Ila, when we get near the door of the gym, walk straight to the door and see if it's open." She looked up at him and did not say a word. He picked up the pace, and they sprinted for the door of the gym. There was a guard at the door. As Ila and Brock approached the door, the guard was about to say something, but Brock flashed his badge. They walked right in went to the left toward the restrooms. In the gym, the track team members were lifting weights and working out. Brock told her to go into the ladies' room and wait. *Damn*, she thought to herself, *how could they have found us in that short period of time?* She went into the ladies' room and sat on the toilet. Her tears became a river. She heaved for all the things that had happened and screamed out loud, and almost instantly felt better.

Brock headed back to the front door and asked the guard if he recognized the people with binoculars who were on the top deck of the stairs. The security guard looked and shook his head. He headed out the door and requested that Brock stay at the door until he returned. The guys in the gym had no idea what was going on they were so focused on their workout and listening to Guns and Roses "Into the Fire." The music was very loud, and they were pumped up. The security guard returned and said the people were from the Audubon Society, and they were looking at a nest that a pair of eagles had built on top of the score board. It was a very rare occurrence, and they wanted to keep close contact with it. They even wanted the university to make the area secure, but unfortunately there was a huge track meet scheduled over the next several days, and the stadium would be filled with people. So, all they can do was track the days and wait for the eggs to hatch and video what they could about the experience of the bald eagle nest at the stadium.

The guard said he had forgotten about the nest. It had gotten a lot of attention about a month ago when it first appeared, but people seemed to have forgotten about it. Brock asked the guard if the people had shown the guard any ID. The guard said they'd shown Audubon IDs. Brock shook his hand and walked back to the ladies' room. He cracked the door and called for Ila to come out.

She got up off the toilet and walked slowly to the door. *What a life.* As she slowly opened the door, Brock placed her head in a friendly hand lock. She knew then that the coast was clear. They thanked the security guard and left the building. She turned right to go back to the apartment, but of course, Brock turned left, and they took the very long way back—all the way down 37th Street and back up O Street. She was exhausted when they arrived back to the apartment. She went through the front door, and Brock walked back to the back door. As he rounded the corner to the alley, the Prince George's County patrol car was just pulling up into the ally way. The officer spied Brock and slowly pulled the car into the spot. He put the car in park and watched as Brock headed for the short flight of steps that led to the back door of the downstairs apartment. The officer got out of his car and closed the door. When Brock got to the door, he turned around and sat down on the steps. The police officer pinched the strap on his gun and walked slowly toward Brock. He said, "Do you have business at this apartment?"

Brock replied, "Yes, this apartment, not that apartment." He pointed upstairs.

The officer replied, "Do you have any ID?"

"Yes." There was a thirty second silence between them. Brock finally replied, "We are brothers in blue."

The officer said, "Sit on the steps and put your hands behind your head." Brock did as he was told. The officer came up the first two steps and said "If we are brothers, you have a badge. Where is it?"

"It's in my pants pocket." The officer took his gun from its holster and ordered Brock to produce the badge in two movements. With his left hand, Brock reached into his pocket and pulled out his badge. The officer walked up the last step, pointed his Glock between Brocks legs, and took the badge. He inspected it and told Brock to turn slowly. He handed the badge back to Brock, placed his gun back in the holster, and helped Brock get up. All the while Ila and the woman who lived upstairs were standing inside their respective doors looking at the action outside. Ila was trying not to scream out.

As Brock walked up the remaining step, Ila open the door slowly while the door to the upstairs apartment also slowly opened. Ila walked out and looked up to get a glimpse of the lady and received a shock. It was Eugenia. They stared at each other and then closed their doors. "Shit," Ila said aloud to herself. "This shit cannot get any worse. What the hell is she doing here?"

She looked at Brock and said, "Do you know who that was?"

"No. I didn't get a good look at the lady. Considering the fact that the officer had his gun in between my legs, looking to the left was not on my mind."

"It was Eugenia," she replied. Brock looked at her and told her to sit down. She sat in the chair in the kitchen and waited for the story. Brock explained that Eugenia was playing both sides of the fence. "She's working undercover for the chief and for the Company," he explained. "She's a duel agent, and her current assignment is to keep an eye on you for two reasons—so you will not be killed by one of Chief Warren's people, and also to make sure you show up for the trail because I have to leave in a couple of days."

This was all extremely complicated, and Ila needed an Absolut absolutely. She went straight to the refrigerator and got the vodka out of the freezer. She reached into the cabinet for a glass and poured a very large drink. She looked up, and Brock was standing in the doorway. She took another glass from the cabinet and poured him a drink just as strong. She added a splash of orange juice to each glass. She handed Brock his glass, and he took a big gulp. She decided she needed to be sitting down to hear the rest of the story.

She walked to the living room and sat on the couch. Brock followed slowly and sat on the couch beside her. He said nothing for some time. All she could hear were the sounds of cars going back and forth and the footsteps of people passing by. Brock finally broke the silence. "Ila," he said, "you must understand that the fewer people involved in your protection the better. Eugenia is a great agent who has worked her way up. She's an excellent marksman. She'll be working as an assistant to the director of athletics. His real assistant was promoted to executive liaison for this investigation. She, of course, does not know that, but the school officials and the director are aware of the situation. That's already too many people. People run their mouths, and one slip could put you in real danger."

Ila had nothing to say. All she wanted was her life back, and it seemed that was never going to happen. She finished her drink, got up, walked to the kitchen, and decided to cook a meal. Brock sat on the couch and finally got up and turned on the TV. He sat and watched something mindless while the smells from the kitchen invaded the apartment.

Ila had to laugh. She was not much of a cook, so she must have been drunk to come into the kitchen and act as if she knew how to prepare a meal. But, after sipping on that drink, she felt as if she could do anything. She found salmon fillets in the freezer. She turned the oven on to about three hundred and let it heat up while she rinsed two of the fillets and placed them on a baking pan. She looked in the cabinets and found some olive oil and lemon juice, which she used to season the fish. She placed the salmon into the oven. She gathered salad ingredients she found in the refrigerator. She figured the salmon would take about thirty minutes because it was frozen. Hopefully that would work. She prepared the salad with spinach, lettuce, goat cheese, and almonds from a can. She placed the salad in the refrigerator so it would remain cold while the salmon finished cooking. There was only wheat bread in the cabinets, so she took out four pieces, spread them with butter, and sprinkled on some garlic powder. *Garlic bread ... too funny.* Ila remembered her mother making garlic bread that way, but with Wonder white bread. She drifted back in time thinking about how she used to go to a store called Loblaws with one dollar and get a loaf of bread, a pound of chipped ham, a gallon of milk, and four cans of tomato soup. And she'd go home with some change!

In the short time she'd drifted off into the past, she began to smell the salmon. She opened the oven. It was perfect, thank goodness. She placed the garlic bread on the oven rack to toast. She checked to make sure the salmon was cooked all the way through. Then she sat and finished her drink. She thought, *Another one of those and I won't be able to sit at the table because I'll be under the table!* She prepared two plates and placed them on the table. She called for Brock, but he didn't answer. *He probably fell asleep.* She walked to the living room to find him again on the couch with his Glock on his chest. She decided not to startle him by touching him, so she called his name several times quietly, and he woke up. Slowly, he placed his hand on his gun, put the safety back on, and put the gun on the table. Ila wondered if he ever got a good night's sleep.

Brock got up slowly and followed Ila into the kitchen. He was hungry and could not wait to eat. He knew it would not be a gourmet meal, but it would be filling. He was surprised at how good the food looked; he couldn't wait to eat. They both sat and talked about the garlic bread. They walked down memory lane, as they had both grown up in large families and had plenty of stories to tell. After dinner, Brock got up and cleared the table and washed the dishes.

Ila knew she could get very use to a man who was grateful to anyone who cooked for him and showed it by taking the time to clean up. She spent time in the living room while he cleaned the kitchen. Suddenly there was a knock on the back door. Brock's gun was on the table in the living room, and he was in the kitchen. Ila picked up the gun, crawled to the kitchen, and handed the gun to Brock. He called out "Who is it?"

"Eugenia."

With caution, Brock walked against the wall to the front door. Before he ran out the door, he motioned to Ila to close and lock the door, which she did quickly. Minutes later, she could hear voices at the back door, and then there was a knock. Brock yelled, "Ila, open the door." She ran to the back door and opened it. Eugenia walked in first, and Brock followed her, his gun nowhere in sight.

Eugenia walked to the living room and sat on the couch. Brock went into the kitchen to get a chair, and Ila stood in the hallway not knowing what to do. Brock pushed her slightly, urging her to go into the living room. He sat his chair between the hallway and the living room. Ila sat next to Eugenia. Damn, she was beautiful—and deadly. Ila wanted to go comb her hair and put on some lipstick. Eugenia had let her hair grow slightly, and she was wearing a Nike navy-blue warm-up suit and those new Adidas tennis shoes. Her skin was flawless—just a touch of mascara and no lipstick. Ila remembered seeing her in the sauna at the Watergate and thinking how beautiful she was. Little did she know that she would play such an important part in her life.

There was a dead silence in the room. Eugenia decided to speak first. "Ila, let me apologize to you for the last time we saw each other. I was in a compromising position, and so were you. It was not my intention for you to see what you saw, but I'm certainly glad you did. Hunter is bi-sexual and has been for many years. It was the end of his assignment and not the first time we had been together. We've known it each other for many years. Hunter and I were in the bedroom, and Maurice got jealous and came in to join us. I got caught up in the moment. It was actually very exciting and sexually satisfying in a sick kind of way."

Ila's stomach was turning over, but she would not give this woman the satisfaction of seeing her throw up again.

Brock interrupted the apology by stating, "All of that is in the past. We must move on to the present. Eugenia, what is the game plan?"

Eugenia stated that her office would be right across the hall from Ila's and that she would keep an eye on Ila's office door at all times. She told Ila that they would have to become friends and have lunch together. "After the first week, we'll appear get to know each other and then start spending a lot of time together. As far as getting back and forth to work, the Company would prefer if you walk some days and drive some days. They do not want your schedule to be regular. Some mornings you will go in at eight o'clock, and some days you'll go in at ten. And you won't leave by the front door every day. You must mix it up—go out the front door, look as if you've changed your mind, go back into the house, and go out the back door. Someone will also be around while you walk or ride to work. I'll be your friend only at the job. I have another apartment closer to the school that I'll be going to daily, and at night, I'll come to the apartment in this building. We are hoping to have all the evidence we need in about a month, and then Chief Warren will be arrested. In the meantime, you are the only witness to his sexual experience with a male we think is underage but cannot prove it at this time." She looked at Brock and said, "When are you reporting for your next assignment?"

Brock said, "I have to go to a funeral, and then I have to report to headquarters."

"I'll be at headquarters on Sunday," Eugenia said

"This Sunday?" Brock replied.

"Yes." Eugenia looked at Ila and asked her if she had any questions. Ila said she didn't, and she got up and walked into the bedroom. Eugenia and Brock stayed in the living room discussing the assignment and how Eugenia was going to keep track of Ila and the protective measures that were going to be taken. Eugenia stayed for about thirty additional minutes, and then she left by the back door.

Ila could hear a car door close as Eugenia left, and she wondered what the real story was between her and the Prince George's County police officer. *I'm sure that was another assignment, but she never mentioned it.*

Ila heard Brock check the doors, place the chair at the back door, and walk to the kitchen. As she lay in the bed in a fetal position, she thought, *What the fuck? Last year at this time, I was living a normal life. Yes, I had lost the love of my life two years before that, but I had gotten back to a sense of normal. Wow, how fleeting a sense of normal really is. I should have taken the time to enjoy it! I should have enjoyed people, and I should have realized how important friendships really are. I should have … I could have … I would have if I had known my life's axis would turn ever so slightly and place me into a nexus—a black hole!* Then she started to laugh, she watched too much *Star Trek*.

Brock went into the kitchen and fixed a bowl of cereal so that he could eat it while he watched his favorite TV show, *Gun Smoke*. He was all set to watch the show when Ila walked in looking as if she had seen a ghost. All he could do was pat the cushion beside him and beckon her to sit down.

She walked slowly to the couch and sat down. She laid her head on his lap, and fell into a deep sleep. Brock sat uncomfortably and tried to eat his cereal and watch TV at the same time. There were back to back episodes on, so it was a great night of TV for him. Ila began to snore halfway through the second episode, so he woke her up and told her to go to bed. She woke up slowly, sat up for a minute, and then slowly walked to the bedroom.

Ila was not looking forward to Saturday morning; she and Brock had only one more day together. She slowly stripped and walked into the bathroom to take a shower. She could hear Brock still crunching on cereal; he must have gone back to get a refill. The water took some time to get hot, so she took the time to spend on the toilet to get rid of her day. And, like clockwork, as soon as she was finished, in walked Brock who had to pee. He told her to open her legs, and again he peed between her legs. Ila just looked at him. He began to laugh hysterically. He thought that was the funniest thing. Ila decided she would get him when it was his turn to shower. He walked out the bathroom laughing, and as he left, Ila slammed the door. She could hear him laughing as he went down the hall.

The water was finally hot, so she stepped into the shower and felt the stream of hot droplets on her back and on the top of her head. Since she had gone natural and blond, there was no need not to get her hair wet. She washed up slowly as she went over the events of the day. Then she thought about tomorrow and wondered what shops they would hit—Georgetown Leather Design, Charlotte's Boutique, Simple's Shoe Store, and that great Chinese restaurant.

As she was going through her tomorrow, she heard the door open, and she knew Brock was about to enter the shower. She rinsed off quickly and turned the water to cold. "Hey, Brock, I'm done. Come on in." Ila left the shower. She knew that Brock would hop in thinking that the water was hot. But it was ice cold. Ila grabbed her towel. Now it was her turn to laugh as she ran down the hall.

Brock screamed like a girl when he entered the shower, and that made Ila laugh more. She walked back into the bedroom and found an old T-shirt in one of the boxes. She would have plenty of time to unpack those boxes when Brock was gone. She walked down the hall to the kitchen to make drinks for both—strong drinks. It had been a day to remember.

She could hear the water turn off in the bathroom. She walked slowly to the living room and placed the drinks on the table. As fate would have it, as she sat down, *I Spy* was coming on. She could hear Brock in the bedroom looking for his pajama bottoms. She figured he wouldn't want to miss a moment of the show. He kind of skipped down the hall and landed on the couch hard, ready to watch one of his favorite shows. She was sure he had not forgotten the cold water; she would just have to wait for his revenge. They watched the show very intently; it was great to see a black man on a national TV show. *I Spy* with Bill Cosby had been one of her favorites. When the show was over, Brock got up, turned off the TV, checked the doors as usual, and gave her his hand to help her off the couch. She was tired but had wanted to watch the show with him, so taking his hand was not a problem because she was ready to go to bed.

Brock turned off the lights as they walked down the hallway together. He was holding her hand, and she felt safe and secure. As they entered the bedroom, she walked to the right, and he walked to the left. He left the bedroom door open but placed one of the boxes in the open doorway. The house was dark without lights on. He looked around the room, took his gun off the night stand, took off the safety, and placed the weapon behind the light. Ila had curled up into a fetal position. She did not remember anything more until the morning light beamed through the window at seven thirty.

Ila heard water running in the bathroom, and she turned slightly to see that Brock had already risen. She got up and placed her legs over the side of the bed so the blood could flow to her toes. She heard him call out as he walked up the hall, "Ila, put on your sweatpants, tennis shoes, and a top. We are walking to breakfast."

Really, she thought. *I'll be in the best shape of my life if we stay together.* She got up went into the bathroom, washed her face, brushed her teeth, applied a bit of foundation and some deodorant, and put some grease in her hair, which she proceeded to pick out. When she was finally ready, she walked back to the bedroom and pulled on her sweatpants and T-shirt—no bra—socks, tennis shoes, and earrings. She grabbed her lip gloss and ID. These she would give to Brock to put in his pocket.

She walked down the hall to find him sitting on the couch watching the morning news. He looked at her and said, "You might need a jacket." She walked back to the bedroom and retrieved a Georgetown nylon jacket from one of the boxes of clothing. Brock was standing by the door when she walked back down the hallway. He said, "This time you go out the back door, and I'll go out the front." She turned around, walked to the back door, removed the chair from the handle. He walked behind her. She opened the door and walked out to the steps. He locked the door behind her. As she walked down the steps, she could hear laughter behind her. She turned slightly to see the police officer leaving Eugenia's apartment. When Ila got to the bottom of the step, she turned left down the alleyway. Brock must have jogged to the end of the alleyway, as she could see him standing there waiting for her. Walking toward him, she could feel his energy. *Could this really be the man for me? Could this be the man that I've been waiting for? Look at him standing there looking so good and chocolate with his legs spread so wide you could drive a bicycle through them!* She snapped out of it when he hollered, "Ila, come on!" Okay, so he is not Prince Charming. She laughed out loud. He looked at her and said, "What are you laughing at?"

She said, "I saw the policeman leaving Eugenia's apartment, and I just thought how funny that was."

They walked in silence, watching the city wake up on a work day. The city was bustling already. Chocolate City—Washington DC—never slept. The Metro and the bus services ran most of the night. People working the night shift had to have a way to get home also. It was about nine blocks to the I Hop. And, of course it was crowded, so they had a fifteen-minute wait. they sat on the bench outside of the restaurant making small talk. It was nine o'clock before they got to eat breakfast.

Brock seemed to order everything on the menu, and so did Ila. They ate in silence, afterwards both wondering why they had eaten so much. They sat for a while and drank water to make all the food move. They decided to give up the booth they were sitting in before the waitress suggested they should pay rent.

Ila could not wait to go back to the apartment, change, and go shopping. As they left the restaurant, Brock took her hand, and they headed toward the Metro. Ila did not ask him why. His grip was very tight, as if to say, "No questions, Ila." They walked about five blocks to the Metro and took the long escalator down to the platform. The train came in about ten minutes. Still holding hands, they went all the way to the very back of the last car. Brock had gotten spooked in the I Hop, and Ila had no idea what he had seen or felt. They stayed on the train for five stops and immediately got off and got a transfer toward Virginia. They got on the yellow line and headed toward the Pentagon. They sat in silence. As they crossed the water into Virginia, memories of times with Rodney came to Ila and then swiftly went. They were in danger, and she could not let herself drift off into memory land.

They stayed on the train until they got to Crystal City, which kind of reminded her of Oz. They got off the train and came from underground to all the hustle and bustle of the workday in Virginia. They swiftly walked to the Crystal City Marriott, walked through the lobby, and out the side door to the AMC theater where they bought tickets to a movie she had never heard of. They headed toward theater number five to the see the movie *Cornbread, Earl and Me*. Brock took the steps two at a time to the top of the theater. Ila knew he wanted to be able to see both exits clearly. They sat in silence watching previews. He finally said, "I'm pretty sure we were being followed, but I'm hopeful that we lost whoever it was. I made sure I checked the windows as we walked toward the Marriott and once we got in the Marriott. This movie is about two hours long I think, so it will be mid-afternoon by the time we leave, and we'll leave out of the back-exit door."

The theater started to fill up, which was surprising to Ila since it was a work day, but ten minutes before the movie started, half of the theater was full. She could feel Brock becoming more tense as each person walked in. He had taken his gun out of the holster; it was now lying in his lap with the safety off. The movie began, and she was intrigued. It was an extremely good movie. But she was sure Brock had seen only half of the movie because every time someone moved, he had tensed up. The ending was heartbreaking and left her not wanting to love anyone for any reason. Because each person brings so much baggage and garbage into a relationship, having to peel back all of that was work—work that she was unwilling to do at that time.

They, of course, waited until the theater was empty. Brock told Ila to walk down the other side of the stairs and to go out the opposite door. He would meet her in the lobby of the Marriott hotel. She almost ran down the steps. As she turned the corner to leave, she almost bumped into the young man who had come into the theater to clean it. She apologized and kept moving fast. She went out the side door, walked around to the front, and continued to walk to the Marriott. She decided to walk through the front door and take a seat in the lobby. It seemed like a lifetime before she saw Brock coming in a side door. He took a seat at the other end of the lobby. They sat there looking at all the people coming and going for about half an hour. Brock got up and went to the men's room. She did not move. When he returned from the men's room, he walked over to the ladies' room and stood outside of the door. She got up, walked over to the ladies' room, and was very happy that he understood that she was about to pee all over herself at this point. She walked past him as if he was a stranger and ran into a stall. She almost could not hold it any longer. She was doing the pee-pee dance as she tried to get her sweat pants down. Then … the relief. It came out fast and went everywhere—all over the seat—but she was very glad to empty her bladder. After she cleaned up the seat and herself, she walked out of the stall to wash her hands. She was surprised to see Brock standing inside the door. She washed fast, grabbed a paper towel, and walked fast to the door. He grabbed her hand once again, and they headed for the street. Brock walked into Crystal Plaza One building, went to the elevator, and headed down toward the underground. They walked to the end of the underground, took the escalator up, and caught the yellow line back to DC.

Ila was worn out, and her hand hurt from Brock holding it so tight. They rode the line in silence, transferred, and headed to Georgetown. She was very happy to get off the train and glad to be walking back to the apartment. As they got closer to the apartment, Brock handed her the key and he took off running. She knew that he was going to go to the back door.

So much for the shopping trip. Brock was leaving on Saturday morning, and there would be no time tomorrow. He would have to pack his few things here, go back to his own apartment, pack what he needed, and be on an early-morning flight on Saturday. Once again, she felt like throwing up, and then it dawned on her—had she had a period? *Oh, shit! Do not tell me I'm pregnant again.* As she walked to the bedroom, she heard Brock coming in from the back door. *I'll not mention it to him. I'll just take care of it while he's gone. Dang! Shades of years ago. I'll have to do better. How many abortions can you have before your uterus gives up?*

Ila took her clothes off and tossed them into a box that had become a laundry basket. She was running out of everything. Maybe tomorrow they would do something romantic and go to the Laundromat. She had seen one just down the street. She lay across the bed, just exhausted from the day—and hungry. She heard Brock in the kitchen, and she really hoped he was cooking something, because breakfast was gone. He came into the room about ten minutes later with a Dagwood lunchmeat sandwich cut in half with dill pickles on the side and two glasses of vodka on the rocks. She laughed because he knew she was hungry, and he knew she needed a drink. He placed a towel on the bed and put the sandwich plate on the towel. He handed her a drink, and he placed his glass on the night stand. He stood up and took off all his clothes. He was a good-looking man, no doubt about it. But he was strange as hell. He picked up his clothes and placed them in the cardboard laundry box she'd been using. She hadn't noticed that that he'd been putting his dirty clothes also. She figured she'd be washing laundry for both of them tomorrow. *And I did not mind ... hmmm, that is a switch.* He sat on the bed in a crossed legged position and picked up his half of the sandwich. She took all the pillows and placed them against the backboard. Then she sat against them and began to eat her half of the sandwich. It was so good. He had toasted the wheat bread, put yellow mustard on one slice of the bread and mayonnaise on the other. He'd added a large helping of chipped ham between the slices of bread along with American cheese, lettuce, and sliced sweet pickles. *Okay. Now I'm thinking Brock has all the symptoms of being pregnant, bringing this sandwich in the bedroom.* All she could do was laugh.

He had put so much mayo on the sandwich that, when she bit into it, a big blob fell out and landed on her stomach. He took that opportunity to bend over and lick it off. That gave her a sensation down her legs that made them tremble. She laughed, and they continued to eat the sandwich and talk about the crazy day. She asked him what he had seen in I Hop, and he said that it didn't matter. He was sure the threat was taken care of. They finished the sandwich and talked about the movie and how Laurence Fishburne was going to be a star in Hollywood.

When they finished eating, he took the plate back into the kitchen. Ila could hear him running the water.

She would have left the plate in the sink, but Brock was not about to leave dirty dishes in the sink.

He walked back to the bedroom to find that she had assumed her position. He crawled up behind me and began running his tongue between her butt cheeks. *Ugh ... after all the running we did, it must smell back there.* But he continued. He lifted her butt up with one hand and placed his other hand in her pussy, finding her clitoris with little effort and slowly making circles around it until she could feel herself coming slightly at first. As he felt her pussy swell and become super wet, he mounted her and placed his penis in her pussy at an angle from behind. She wanted to scream with pleasure, but he said in a very soft voice, "No words. No moans. I just want to hear my dick coming in and out of your pussy. I want you to concentrate squeezing your vaginal muscles as I come in and out." She, of course, did exactly that and could not believe how many times she came just holding her muscles tight. He had her ass so far up in the air at one point that she thought they were going to be making love standing up. He cupped her breasts and made circular motions with both hands. She had lost her ability to hold the muscles when he whispered, "Concentrate!" So, she concentrated on holding the muscle. When she came, she felt as if she had to pee. Then she felt his penis grow as if it was going to explode, and it did. She could feel the air leave his body. He gently laid her back down on the bed, slowly pulled his penis out of her vagina, and patted the bed to find the towel. He told her to turn over so that he could wipe her pussy. After she turned over, he got up and went into the bathroom. He came back, and the towel was wet and warm. He cleaned the lips of her vagina and then parted the lips and cleaned inside. He then wiped his penis off with the towel. He tossed the towel into the laundry box, fell down face forward, and said, "Good night." In what seemed like seconds he was a sleep. And there she was looking at the ceiling thinking, *What just happened? It was good and strange at the same time.* It was not long before her eyes closed and she fell into a deep sleep.

Once again, Ila woke up to the sound of Brock doing something in the kitchen. She looked at the clock. Seven thirty. She sat up and thought about last night and smiled. She could hear him coming up the hall. He stood in the doorway and said, "I have to do laundry. Would you like to come and do yours with me?"

"At seven thirty in the morning?"

"Yes! For sure no one will be there this time of morning."

She looked at him and said, "Do I have time to take a shower?"

"No. Just brush your teeth, wash your face, and comb your hair. We'll be getting sweaty walking to the Laundromat."

"Why don't we take the car?"

"Because this will be our exercise for the day." She looked at him and crossed her eyes. He shouted as he walked back down the hall, "The early bird gets the clean washing machine!" She laughed, got up out of the bed, and walked slowly to the bathroom. On the mirror, there was a promise written in lipstick.

I promise to take care of you.

I promise to complete your happiness.

I promise to be your partner, friend, and lover.

I promise to protect you.

I promise to give you unconditional love.

I promise to be a dedicated husband and father to our children.

Lastly, I promise to keep your heart from hurt, harm, or danger.

Ila began to cry. She sat on the toilet and thanked God for another chance at happiness—for another chance at love, for keeping her from hurt, and for allowing her to once again open her heart to the possibility of believing in love one more time. She also prayed that she would not take for granted this gift that had been bestowed upon her once again.

She wiped her eyes, brushed her teeth, washed her face, combed her hair, and removed the promise off the mirror. He was leaving in the morning, and that promise could mean nothing in a week. *I'll keep in my heart and not speak about it until he returns.* She slowly walked back into the bedroom, rooted through the boxes for yet another pair of sweatpants, found a pair of black ones and a black-and-gold top. She had to root even further for additional underwear and a bra. She would really have to organize this after Brock left. There was a dresser in the bedroom and closet space. She had her work cut out for her considering she had no idea how long she was going to be there.

She wanted to get back to Arlington so that she could see Paula and Drew. She had heard some time ago that he was not doing well, and she really wanted to see them both. *After Brock leaves, I'll take a ride to Virginia to see if I can get in touch.* The last time she had tried the phone number, it had been changed.

She got dressed and went back to the bathroom to put on foundation, lip gloss, and mascara. Finally, he walked into the front room. He had already gathered up their clothes and had placed them in pillow cases. She didn't know why she was so surprised. *The combination of Company training on top of military training can't be beat!* she thought. *There is a way to do everything.* She laughed to herself. "I'm ready," she said.

He looked up at her as if he wanted to say something about time, but no words were uttered. She knew he was waiting for her to say something about the promise, but her lips would not part to even speak about the words he had written on the mirror. She picked up the keys and walked to the door. To her surprise, he walked toward the front door also. She did not question his judgment, but as she placed her hand on the handle to turn it, she remembered she had forgotten her purse. She did not know how long they would be gone, so she wanted to at least have her lip gloss. *So vain.* She stopped at the door and turned around. Brock said, "What's wrong?"

"I forgot something."

He laughed hard. "What? Your lip gloss?" She did not think it was funny. And, then, there was a knock at the door, Brock hit the floor, and she walked fast to the back door. She lay against the wall next to the door and moved the curtain a bit to see if anyone was in the parking lot or standing in the alleyway. But there was nothing there but the police car.

Brock called out, "Who is it?" No answer. He waited about a minute and crawled to the back door, unlocked it, and sprinted to the alley so he could run around to the front door. By the time he got there, the person had gone, having left a manila envelope at the front door. Brock stood looking up and down the street for about five minutes, and then he decided to walk over and retrieve the envelope. He squeezed the envelope and decided the contents felt like keys and possibly money. Instead of taking the envelope into the house, Brock walked swiftly to the alley and turned the envelope upside down so the contents fell onto the grass. Just as he had suspected, there was a set of keys. There was also a name plate and a letter addressed to Ila and about two hundred dollars in cash. He felt that the Company should find a better way to communicate, but he could not think of a better way. He picked up the items and began placing them back in the envelope only to find another envelope addressed to him. The letter requested that he report to the Pentagon when he returned on Sunday. He was to see a four-star general, Jefferson Owens. He had no idea what that was about, and he would not know until Sunday.

Brock ran back to the back door of the apartment. Ila was still standing against the wall straight as a board. He laughed and told her she could stop standing at attention. They both laughed. Brock took the envelope into the kitchen and put it down next to the sink. They could discuss the contents when they got back. He went to the front door and picked up the laundry and headed toward the back door. Ila had the keys, so they walked out the back door together. As they were walking out, the Prince George's police officer was leaving the upstairs apartment. Only niceties were exchanged—no words. He got in his car and left, and Brock and Ila walked toward the alley. The officer got into his car and pulled off slowly, and they kept walking. Brock carried the two pillow cases, one in each hand. They were no longer the real early birds after all the interruptions, but it was still early, and hopefully the Laundromat would not be completely full. They walked in silence, knowing that this was Brock's last day and knowing that they had to talk about the promise.

The streets were full of students and people headed to the metro. They entered the Laundromat and inhaled the aroma of Clorox and Gain detergent, the products that were sold in the vending machine. Brock walked over to an elderly black lady. He handed her the laundry and gave her money. She took the money and began sorting the clothes into laundry baskets. Ila stood there not sure what to do, but very happy that they were not doing laundry. Brock walked back to the door where she was standing and said, "Let's go." She did not say a word. She was happy not to do laundry and would try to get the information out of him on the hook-up before he left—and how much it costs. She laughed to herself. *If there is a second chance at life I want to come back as a good looking, intelligent black man with a big penis.*

They walked onto O Street again and made a right onto Potomac. She started getting girlie jitters because, if they were going to Garfinkle's, that would be fabulous. He held her hand tightly as they walked. Ten minutes into our walk he said, "Did you read the promise?"

She looked at him, and her eyes filled with tears. He did not mention it again on this day. They got to Garfinkle's, and it felt like Oz. She was singing in her head "You're out of the woods, you're out of the woods." Entering Garfinkle's from M Street, they saw a small deli. Ila was starving. They had not eaten anything that morning, and she was a breakfast lady. She could skip all other meals, but breakfast was something she had to have. They walked into the deli and inhaled the smell of the fresh bread, bagels, lox, and cinnamon. She walked over to the bagel case and saw the huge bagels and thought to herself that each one alone was about three hundred calories, but she would be walking them off right away. They patiently waited their turn. Ila ordered a cinnamon bagel with lox, cream cheese, and sliced tomatoes on the side. She also ordered a large deep-roasted coffee with cream and sugar. Brock ordered a multi grain bagel, lox, cream cheese, onion, and tomato. His drinks of choice were orange juice and water. Ila also requested water. They walked to the cash register, paid for their breakfast, found a cozy table, and waited on the server to bring their food.

They talked about the morning, and she asked him, "How did you know there would be someone there to do the laundry?"

"The Company has arranged everything. You just have to be safe to testify. When you are ready to do laundry again, just take it to Mrs. Early, and she will take care of it. I have paid her for it in advance plus a little more."

"Does she work for the Company?" He did not reply. *Okay. I get it—need-to-know basis.* Their breakfast finally arrived, and they stopped talking and ate. The lox was cut perfectly thin, and the cream cheese tasted homemade. The waitress also bought them a new item on the menu— the restaurant was trying out a spread called hummus. Ila was willing to give it a try, but Brock looked at it and said it looked like porridge. She saved a quarter of her bagel for the hummus and found that it was delicious. They talked more about how the process was going to go for the trial. They both hoped that all the evidence would be gathered within the next couple of months. During the week the trail started, Ila would have to go deep undercover to a hotel. She would have to testify only once, but it was going to be grueling.

Brock said, "They are going to try to trick you on the stand—say you did not see what you saw. I'm sure they told their lawyers about the .38 incident and me eating your pussy, but make sure they understand that you were in a compromising position and just wanted to get out of that room alive." They sat in silence for a while and started to people watch. Brock finally got up, cleaned up the table, and took everything to the trash can. He came back to the table and said, "Okay. I'm going to lift your spirits. We are going to the Fox Trapp tonight, so I want you to buy something sexy to wear, including a great pair of shoes. We'll celebrate my going and my coming back on the same night."

Ila jumped up. She was all for shopping—and going and coming. She laughed to herself. They headed into the clothing area of Garfinkel's. In the store, Brock asked to see the manager. He spoke to her over in a corner, and then came back to where Ila was standing at the dress rack. He said, "You're all set. Shop away." He looked at her, winked, and left the store. She had no idea where he was going. He shouted back over his shoulder, "I'll be back in an hour." She heard his beeper go off as he walked away

Ila felt as if she was on the good ship *Lollipop*. She almost ran from rack to rack, but then she decided she had to control herself. She pulled several things to try on. One was a red form-fitting dress with a v-cut in the back. She also grabbed some black shoes and some red ones. She pulled down a tan pants suit that had a single-button jacket. She found a mustard shirt that would go with it. At the shirt rack she decided on a basic black fitted shirt and a French-cut white shirt. She grabbed some black-and-white heels. She was looking for heels for the tan suit when the manager approached her and said, "I've got the perfect pair of boots for that pant suit." They walked over to where the boots were displayed, and the manager showed her a pair of tan, black, and brown patchwork boots. Ila was in heaven. She went into the dressing room and tried on everything. Perfect fit. She hadn't looked at the prices of these items until she was about the leave the fitting room. She shook her head. *There is no way I'll be able to get everything.*

Brock walked back to the front of the Garfinkle's and stood on the side of the front door. His beeper had gone off—911. He decided to walk across the street so that he could see who was coming and going. Once across the street he stood against a light pole and waited. In about twenty minutes, a black town car pulled up, but there were no places to park, so the driver of the car put on the emergency blinkers and pulled as close to the curb as he could get. The door opened, and Hunter got out of the car, looked around, and spotted Brock across the street. He ran swiftly across the street. Brock slowly placed his hand inside his shirt just to let Hunter know he was packing. And Hunter did the same. Hunter walked over to the left of Brock so that they could talk. Hunter asked, "Where is Ila? How can I get in touch with her?"

Brock replied, "You of all people should know that Ila is in deep cover. No one knows where she is. Why are you asking me?"

Hunter said, "I'm asking you because you are the last motherfucker I saw her with, and I know you are playing both sides of the fence. So, if anyone would know, you would."

Brock replied, "Is there something else I can help you with? If not, this conversation is over."

Hunter looked at Brock and said, "She has to come up for air sooner or later, and I'll find her. If you happen to see her in your travels, tell her to start planning our wedding day." Hunter ran back across the street, got into his town car, and drove off.

In the meantime, Ila had purchased her clothing. She had to take a deep breath when the lady told her to give Brock the receipt, which came to a thousand dollars and some change. Ila took the receipt and was tempted to return everything, but Brock had planned for her to spend the money so ... what's a lady to do? She laughed to herself and walked out the store with only four bags for all that money. She looked around for Brock and decided to use protocol and find a place to sit or stand and wait for him to come looking for her.

She went back into the store and told the manager that, if Brock came back looking for her, the manager could say that Ila would be standing out front. Ila left the store again and walked toward the front door. As she walked through the double doors, she looked across the street and saw Hunter and Brock. She turned around quickly and went back into Garfinkel's. She sat on a bench and waited. How the fuck had she left the apartment without her beeper? Oh, she had her lip gloss, but no beeper. Stupid, stupid, stupid. She sat for what seemed to be thirty minutes and finally decided to just go out another door and walk back to the apartment. She walked back to a side door and ended up on Wisconsin Avenue. She made a left back to M Street and headed toward O Street. This was the longer route but probably the safest route because Hunter would be trying to follow Brock. She walked briskly toward O Street and made a left back to the apartment. Eugenia was standing in front of the apartment and started walking back toward the alley. Ila followed her as she walked down the alley to the back of the apartment. As they turned into the small parking lot, they saw Brock and the Prince George's officer sitting in the car. Ila was so relieved to see Brock. She walked past the car and went up the steps to the apartment. Eugenia had gone ahead of her and opened the door. Ila entered the apartment and went straight to the bathroom. She had to throw up. What a day. The most wonderful thing about the entire day was that, when she was in the bathroom, she discovered that she'd started her period. She started to cry … yet again.

She heard Brock enter the apartment and lock the back door. He came to the bathroom door, picked up the bags, and closed the door. She sat there until her butt started to hurt. She retrieved a sanitary napkin from the cabinet under the sink and placed it in her panties. Then she pulled off her sweats off, took an ibuprofen, walked out of the bathroom to the bedroom, fell across the bed, and immediately fell asleep.

When Ila woke up, she could hear *The Quiet Storm* on the radio. She knew it had to be around eight o'clock in the evening. Melvin Lindsey's voice on the radio always signaled that time of day—time to whine down. She looked down and had a mess going on. Fortunately, nothing had gotten on the bed. She jumped up grabbed another pair of panties out of the box and went to the bathroom to clean up. There was not a sound coming from the living room. She wondered if Brock was even in the house.

After cleaning up, she walked to the living room and found him sitting on the couch with a glass of vodka on the rocks listening to the radio. He saw her enter the room and patted the cushion next to him—an invitation for her to sit down. They sat in silence for what seemed to be an hour. He finally said, "I saw you come out of the building today. Fortunately, Hunter was running his mouth so much he didn't see you. I know you're afraid, but he has no idea where you are. He got my beeper number from the Company using his influence. He was just on a fishing expedition. Eugenia will take great care of you. And I know you can take care of yourself. I'm leaving you my .38 because that's what you were trained on. There's plenty of ammunition in the box. I'll clean the weapon tonight, so be careful—the trigger will be very fast. I know you carry a purse with all your female things in it, but I want you to carry the gun in there too. You should have a dedicated bag that you carry everywhere.

There was no going to the Fox Trapp that evening. Ila felt like shit; she was bleeding as if someone had stuck her. She lay across Brock's lap, and he rubbed her hair as she cried big tears because she knew this was his last night. He rubbed her back and began talking about his aunt and his cousins and how he could not wait to see his best friend and roommate from the academy, Morris. It had been a long time. His friend would be flying in from California.

After she fell asleep, Brock whispered in her ear to wake up so that they could go to bed. She woke up slowly, walked to the bathroom before going to the bedroom, changed her sanitary napkin, looked for a black towel for the bed, found one, brushed her teeth, washed her face, and walked to the bedroom. She pulled back the covers, put the towel on her side of the bed, and tucked it in slightly. She had to walk back to the bathroom because the cramps were starting to make her teeth hurt. She took three ibuprofen, went back to the bedroom, and crawled into bed. Brock was catching the seven o'clock flight, so he would have to get up at four thirty to get to National Airport. She heard him preparing the apartment for the night, checking locks and moving chairs. That was the last thing she heard until four the next morning.

Ila could feel Brock stirring. She knew it was time for him to get up so he could catch the plane. She reached for him, and he reached for her. He whispered, "Don't forget my promise."

She looked up. "I have to go to the bathroom, but don't move until I get back." She walked to the bathroom cleaned herself up, and placed a new napkin in her panties. As she walked back into the bedroom, he sat straight up, and so did his dick.

Not wanting to take for granted that he did not care if she was menstruating, she got back under the covers and acted as if she had not seen his erection. She wrapped her arms around his chest and lay her head on his chest to hear his heart beat. It was rapid and steady. He pulled her on top of him and told her to straddle him and stand up. She did. He slowly pulled down her panties. He held one of her hands as she pulled her left leg free. Then he held her other hand as she pulled her right leg out of the panty. She then sat on his dick. He raised his ass at an angle, and she rode that penis like a stallion. After about fifteen minutes of steady thrust, she could feel her cum coming down along with all the blood. He cupped her ass with his hands to make sure that every inch of his penis was penetrating her body, and once again his penis swelled, and a moan of enjoyment came from his lips. His thrust became slower, and he lowered his ass to the bed. She had to carefully roll off his penis onto the bed so the mess from her cycle would not be everywhere. As she rolled over, he took the towel and cupped her vagina with it to stem the flow of blood. He got up quickly to take a shower. She laughed. *I guess he enjoyed it, but not enough to let blood and cum dry on his penis*. When he returned from the bathroom, she jumped up to also take a shower. She knew she would not have time to fix him breakfast, but she thought it would be nice to see him off. After her quick shower, she dressed and came back to the bedroom. He was in the kitchen. When she walked into the kitchen, he was writing a list of things she had to do:

(1) Return to the laundry and pick up our things
(2) Read the letter the company sent
(3) Make sure you wear your beeper
(4) Always carry the gun
(5) Ask Eugenia for anything that you might need
(6) Remember the promise

She took his note and held it close. He walked out of the kitchen to get his bag. As he walked back to the bedroom, his beeper went off, and two seconds later, there was a knock at the door. Brock walked back to the kitchen, kissed Ila, walked slowly to the door, and then turned to go out the back door once again. As he walked to the back door, he whispered, "Come lock the door." She followed behind him, and an empty feeling developed in the pit of her stomach. *Will I ever see him again?* He opened the door, kissed her, reminded her again to lock the door, and left. Ila stood in the silence for what seemed like thirty minutes in a statue stance not knowing what to do. It was Saturday, early morning. She was bleeding, and her head was hurting. What to do next? *Go to bed and wake up in a few hours. Then decide what the day is going to be like.* She took two more ibuprofen and went back to bed.

Ila woke up suddenly to a noise that sounded like a buzzer, only to discover it was her beeper. She looked down at the number but did not recognize it. She got up quickly. She felt lightheaded, so she sat back down for a few seconds, forgetting that she was on her cycle, which seemed worse than ever. After sitting for a few minutes, she went to use the house phone and remembered that might not be a good idea. She would get dressed, walk up to the college, and use a pay phone on campus to return the call. But first, more ibuprofen and some coffee. She walked to the kitchen, put coffee in the maker, poured water into the reservoir, and waited for the aroma to fill the house. She walked back to the living room and put a tape in by the Average White Band just to get herself moving. She danced around the room while the coffee was brewing. It had been a long time since she had really danced, and it felt great. *Maybe I could go out to the Fox*

Trapp tonight by myself just to see what kind of trouble I could get myself into. That was a fleeting thought. *Dang ... what am I going to do without Brock?*

She walked back into the kitchen, poured a cup of steaming coffee, added half and half and three teaspoons of sugar, and sat down at the kitchen table. She began to cry. *What a mess I'm in. All because I wanted to advance my career.* She had been having a great time working for Dr. Zarnoff, but there had not been any room for advancement there.

Ila took a little time to just feel sorry for herself, but then she remembered the call on the beeper. She pulled herself together, picked up her coffee, walked to the refrigerator, and wondered what quick item she could eat before walking to the college. The message had not included the code 911, so she had some time. Ila opened and closed the refrigerator. She looked around the kitchen and spied the bagels and peanut butter. Perfect. She slowly opened the wheat bagel bag, placed a sliced bagel into the toaster, poured a second cup of coffee, and waited for the bagel to pop up. She liked to spread the peanut butter onto the bagel quickly so it would melt and run down the sides ... heaven. As soon as the bagel slices popped out of the toaster, she grabbed them and spread a generous amount of peanut butter on each one. She was going to savor this tasty treat. She placed the bagel on a plate and sat at the table. It felt very strange sitting there all by herself. She would really have to think of things to do while Brock was gone. Maybe she would buy a puzzle today and set it out on the coffee table. She could work on it at night. Maybe she could purchase a few books to read.

She was immersed in thought when she heard her beeper go off again. She decided it was time to get her ass in gear and return that call. She finished off the bagel and did not bother to clean up since Brock was not there. She ran into the bedroom to find yet another pair of sweatpants and a sweatshirt because a chill was in the air. Fall was on its way. Quickly she changed her pad, brushed her teeth, picked her blonde afro, put on deodorant, lip gloss, and mascara. She was ready to go. She put on her Converse All Stars with tube socks, and she was ready to go. Being paranoid, she decided to go out the back door and walk around and then head toward the college. *Shit! Backtrack. Forgot my beeper.* She went back to the bedroom to pick up the beeper, and then she went out the back door. Just like clockwork, the police car slowly pulled up, and the officer watched her as she walked down the steps and through the alley. She thought she saw him pick up his radio as she passed the car, but she wasn't sure. That had nothing to do with her. She walked swiftly to the college to make the call.

When she found a telephone, she got the operator to place a collect call to the number on the beeper. The phone rang about four times before she heard a voice on the other end. The operator said, "Collect call from Ila Montgomery."

The person on the other end accepted the charges. "Hi, Ila!" Brock said.

"Hey, Brock. How is it going?"

"Missing you", he replied. After a small pause, he said, "Are you all right?"

"Yes, good," she said.

After another small pause, he said, "My roommate arrived. We were just having a couple of beers. The service is at one this afternoon and will probably go on most of the day. County funerals are all-day affairs."

She laughed and said, "I'm sure you'll have some fun in the middle of your sadness. Don't give me a second thought, do what you have to do and then come back." He reminded her that he had to report to headquarters on Sunday and was unsure when he was going to return.

"I know," she said.

"But, as soon as they release me, I'll run to the apartment to see you all the way from headquarters." They both laughed and said good-bye. She hung up the phone and turned to walk back to the apartment. But then she decided to go into the building where she would be working in on Monday. It was a beautiful building filled with Old World charm.

Patrick F. Healy, S. J., had been president of this Georgetown from 1873 to 1882. He was the first African American to head a major, predominantly white university. Healy Hall where her office was located, had been added to the National Register of Historic Places and had also been recognized as a National Historic Landmark. This was going to be a major move on Ila's part. She could only imagine what the first day was going to be like. She would have to do some research on her job title and description on Sunday so that she would have some idea of what to do. She walked the massive hall. The doors on either side were so large and heavy she felt that maybe she should start lifting weights so she'd be able to open them. Her position was diversity counselor. She wasn't sure how many minority students were enrolled; she would have to find out more in her research.

She strolled through the halls until she found her office—G19. The desk was massive. There were lots of file cabinets, and an Apple computer sat on the desk. *Sweet! This should be fun.* She was just turning to walk out of the building when she noticed a person in the hallway. The black man was dressed in a janitorial uniform. She walked over to him to ask if he could tell her how many black students attended the school. She tapped him on his shoulder to get his attention. It startled him. He turned around and made the American Sign Language—ASL— sign for "hi." She returned the sign and told him that she was going to be working there on Monday and that it was nice to meet him. He just nodded and pulled out a booklet from his shirt pocket. He wrote, "I'll see you on Monday. Everyone is very nice here." She thanked him and walked away saying good-bye in sign language. It would be months later when she would realize that the door to her office should not have been open at that time.

She had forgotten that Gallaudet University was a federally chartered private university for the education of the deaf and hard of hearing, and it was in Washington DC. This university probably employed several people from Gallaudet. This was going to be a wonderful position. Too bad it was just temporary. She walked slowly out of the building and strolled back to the apartment not wanting to really spend a lot of time in it alone.

Back at the apartment, she decided to get the keys to the Cutlass and drive to Arlington to see Drew and Paula. There might not be another time for that to happen. She would be very careful to make sure she wasn't followed, and she would park in the Giant Food parking lot and walk to the apartments just to make sure there were no detectives in unmarked cars watching the apartment building. She rounded the alleyway and made her way up the steps. As she unlocked the door, right on cue, the police officer was leaving the upstairs apartment. She hoped Eugenia was not having sex with him every day. *Her pussy probably looks like that of a rhesus monkey in heat.* She laughed hard at that visual.

Inside, she locked the door, went to the bedroom, got the .38, and placed it into her purse with the safety on. She checked her beeper and went into the kitchen to get some of the money Brock had left in the refrigerator in an empty ice cream carton. She took out $25, as she thought she would go to the car wash and give that old Cutlass a bath before heading to DC. Plan in place, she left the apartment by the front door, locking it before she walked to the Cutlass.

It was a busy Saturday, and she knew once she moved the car she would lose the parking space, but she needed to get away, smoke a joint, and see old friends. This house arrest stuff was horse shit. The Cutlass has a great engine. It turned right over, and the gas gauge red full She pulled out into traffic and decided to wait until she got to Virginia to get the car washed. There was a car wash on Arlington Boulevard that did an excellent job.

It was a beautiful day. She inserted a cassette into the player and listened to the Ohio Players. It took a minute to navigate the traffic in DC to cross the 14th Street Bridge. As she got onto the bridge, her feet went cold. This was the bridge on which Rodney had died when Air Florida Flight 90 crashed into it. Tears rolled down her face as she crossed the bridge. She could not wait to get to the other side. She would not be traveling back that way. To many memories … waiting for him at her apartment only to find out he was not behind her and he never would be.

She got across the bridge and wiped the tears away. She drove another five blocks to the Crystal Clean car wash. It was only five dollars, and there were about six different settings. The Cutlass would drive better clean. She laughed out loud thinking about the Cutlass smiling as it went through the car wash. Since it was such a nice day, there were several cars ahead of her, but she didn't mind because she had placed the Ohio Players on repeat, and the music was loud. The attendant finally indicated it was her turn. "Straighten the wheels, put the transmission in neutral, and we are not responsible for any damage."

"Check," she told the attendant. The belt pulled the car—all windows up music playing. She marveled at the technology it took to get the car washed, waxed, and blown dry. As the car entered the last step—the blow-dry step—she noticed two men standing at the end of the car wash. *Wow, they've added towel dryers. That's a great amenity for five dollars.* As the car came to the end of the car wash and the light turned green to go, she slowed down so the guys could wipe the car off.

Suddenly, one of the men jumped into the front seat of her car, and the other jumped into the backseat. She had forgotten to make sure all the doors were locked. She had not given it a second thought to lock the car doors. She pulled slowly into a parking space trying to get the attention of the people who were having their car detailed on the other side of the car wash.

The man sitting in the passenger side had a .22 aimed at her knee, and the man in the backseat had a .22 aimed at her neck. Anyone familiar with a .22-caliber pistol knows it can be very deadly. Because of the size of the bullet, after it enters the body, it boomerangs all through the body.

Ila placed the car in park and waited for instructions. The man in the passenger seat said in a slow low voice, "You should have stayed your ass wherever you were. Did you have no idea that there was a cop with a copy of your picture stationed at every major bridge leading out of DC hoping you would show up in Virginia? And here you are."

She could hear Hunter's voice in her head: "Think smart if you cannot get to your gun." As the man in the front seat continued to talk, a car pulled up beside them. There were two guys in it. Immediately, Ila turned up the radio and whipped her top off with one quick movement. Then she took off her bra. By that time she had the attention of the men in the other car. She could hear the click of the .22 as it was put into safe mode. The guys came over to the car and asked if they could join the party. The gunman in the front of her car got out first, and the gunman in the back screamed, "Testify and you are dead!" They walked away from the car laughing telling the other hopeful partiers that she was crazy and they shouldn't waste their time at that party.

Ila put the car in gear and peeled out of the parking lot. She did not head back to Virginia; instead, she pulled into the Giant Food parking lot. After replacing her clothes, she sat in the parking lot for three hours until she felt she had lost the men who had been looking for her. She took route 50 back to DC, crying the entire time. She drove the car to the Georgetown school parking lot and prayed it would not be towed before Monday. As she was getting out of the car, from out of nowhere came the maintenance man who was hearing impaired. He read her lips as she told him what she needed. He pulled out his pad and wrote: "I'll take care of it. Don't worry." She hugged him and walked slowly back to the apartment.

As she turned into the alleyway, she saw that the police car was not there. *Dang, there's some comfort having it parked there all the time.* As she turned the bend toward the apartment, she saw Eugenia sitting on the steps holding her .38 across her lap. Ila walked up the steps and sat down beside her. Eugenia said, "Do not leave this apartment again without telling me. I beeped you on several occasions, and you did not return the call. I was about to call out the troops to try to find you. You are really being very naive about your situation, and that naiveté is going to get you killed."

Ila looked at her and said, "Understood." She got up, pulled the keys from her purse, and unlocked the door. As she turned to close the door, the police car was pulling up into the alleyway.

Shit, shit, shit! Brock is going to be pissed when he finds out about my escapade. I've got to face the fact that I'm confined to the apartment and to the school until the trial is over. She began to cry again. She had not spoken to her mother and father in months, and she knew that her family members worried about her all the time. She tucked kitchen chairs under the knobs of both the back and front doors. Then she turned off all the lights, walked to the bedroom, stripped, and got into the bed. The next thing she heard was Sunday morning traffic.

Ila could not believe what had happened the day before. She decided to write the incident down, just in case she did not make it to trial. And, yes, she was going to be very careful about how she spent her time until Brock came back. She got up, went into the bathroom, and turned on the shower. While she waited for the water to get hot, she walked to the kitchen, put coffee and water in the coffee maker, and turned it on.

The temperature of the water in the shower was just right, and she stood under it until the water went cold. She enjoyed the water running down her back and over her head. Her period had gotten lighter and would probably be done that day. Hopefully it would be all clear before Brock returned. She got out of the shower, dried off, and looked in the mirror. Her roots were turning black. She would have to touch up the die job very soon.

Brock would be headed to his meeting and should be back in town soon, but there was no telling when she would see him again. It was time to get something in her stomach. She slowly walked to the kitchen, looked in the refrigerator, and saw nothing appetizing. The coffee was ready. She washed out yesterday's cup and set it on the counter while she went to the refrigerator only to find out that there was no cream.

She walked into the living room and turned on the TV. The only thing worth looking at was *CBS News Sunday Morning* with Charles Kuralt. She was still very hungry and wondered if she should get dressed and walk to the bakery for a bagel with lox and cream cheese and a double roasted coffee with vanilla creamer. Charles Kuralt was taking viewers on a trip through Amish country in Pennsylvania, and she was so surprised to see that the Amish people were still stuck in time and didn't want to get into the new age of television, telephones, and other technology. She watched as the show took viewers back in time and showed how the Amish were so self-sufficient, raising dairy cows along with chickens, ducks, and turkeys. They even made all their clothes.

Ila somehow got so engrossed in the show that she did not notice the shadow that flashed across the front window, which was something Brock would have never missed. Suddenly, there was a knock at the door, and an envelope was pushed under the door. Ila, now alert, immediately lay on the floor and crawled toward the door. She could see that the shadow from under the door was gone. She crawled over to where the enveloped had landed and decided to lie on the floor for another five minutes before getting up.

Finally, she opened the envelope while she was still on the floor. It was a simple hand-written note that read: "Your groceries are at the back door. Agent Brock Covington has been delayed and will not be returning to this assignment until the end of next week."

Ila could not believe it. She now thought the apartment was bugged. How else would they know she was almost out of food? *They have this shit down to a science. That is what they pay all those very intelligent people for.* She started laughing and then began to cry. Brock would not be back for a week. She had really thought he would walk in the door sometime that evening after his meeting with the general, even if it was to just say hello and good-bye.

Ila peeled herself off the floor and walked back to the back door to get the groceries. She stood next to the door and opened the curtain a tiny bit to make sure there was no one standing there. No one was there, but the Prince George's cop was sitting in his car looking at the door. As she slowly opened the door, he rolled down his windowed and said, "I wish I could get that kind of delivery." That was the first time he had said anything to her. She just waved at him and took the first two bags off the step, placing them inside the door. Then she retrieved the other two bags. As she turned around with the bags, she saw Eugenia coming out of the apartment. She walked down the stairs, stood next to Ila, and waved to ask the police officer to get out of the car. She was wearing red leather hot pants, leather knee-high black boots, a black see-through top with no bra, and a black vest with fringe. She also wore a black short-cut wig and large hoop earrings.

Ila could not take her eyes off Eugenia. She was truly beautiful—and deadly. Like a black widow spider. Coming back to earth, Ila said, "Hey, Eugenia, how are you?"

Eugenia said, "Would you like to join us after you put your groceries away?"

I replied, "No I'm just going to make a little meal and get ready to go to work tomorrow." She could hear the police officer securing his car and walking up the alleyway.

Eugenia said, "Ila, I need you to join us in thirty minutes. I promised the police officer that you would join us tonight."

Ila looked at her long and hard and said, "Give me hour." Eugenia nodded her head. Ila went into the apartment, closed the door, and locked it. *God damn! What is this going to be about?* She took two bags to the kitchen and then went back for the other bags. As she was turning back into the kitchen, there was a knock at the back door. *Here we go again.* She crawled to the door and said, "Who is it?"

"Eugenia."

Ila stood up, positioned herself at the side of the door, and open the door slowly. Eugenia handed a black sleeveless dress through the narrow opening. "Please wear this. No stocking. No panties. No shoes. Page me nine-one-one when you are ready." Eugenia nodded her head at Ila and left.

Ila slowly closed the door. She was going to have to have a drink to get through the night. She decided to put away the groceries and then get dressed. She did not remember if she and Brock had finished the vodka. *What is this shit going to be about?* She emptied the bags and, of course, everything she needed was there along with some extra things—things for Brock like razors, shaving cream, and deodorant. She unpacked humus, bagels, milk, coffee, creamer, eggs, sausage, turkey bacon, and chicken wings that had to be cooked. Someone had made a mistake. She began to laugh. Lettuce, tomatoes, orange juice, cranberry juice … excellent. The last bag had the essentials—vodka, Hennessy cognac, Coke, toothpaste. She laughed out loud.

After she'd put all the groceries away, she decided a large drink was in order. Before opening the new vodka, she checked the freezer. She believed there was still vodka in the bottle she'd shared with Brock. And, sure enough, there was enough left for a solid drink. She placed the old bottle on the table and the new bottle in the freezer. She had a suspicion that she would need a drink after her escapade upstairs. She poured the cold vodka into a tall glass, added cranberry juice and orange juice from the refrigerator, and stirred it with a spoon. She looked in the kitchen drawer because it was clear she needed a straw. Finding one, she sat at the table began sipping the drink. She could feel the warmth of the alcohol going down her throat into her stomach.

After a few sips, her nerves began to calm, and she felt able to get dressed. She had showered earlier, so she decided just to wash up. She put lotion, put on hoop earrings, picked out her blond afro, and put on ruby-red lipstick, eye liner, and mascara. She went to the bed and pulled the black dress over her head. She had been given explicit instructions not to wear underwear, stockings, or shoes. So there it was … it was about to go down.

She placed her essentials into a small bag along with Brock's .38. She also placed a pair if panties and a pad just in care her period had not completely ended. Then she picked up her beeper and keys and beeped Eugenia 9-1-1. After only what seemed like two seconds, Eugenia was knocking on the back door. Ila turned off the lights in the bedroom and walked down the hall, but she stopped in her tracks. She walked to the door sideways and peeked through the curtains. Eugenia and the officer stood there with drinks in hand, and Eugenia was holding a pink bag.

Ila slowly opened the door, and they both walked in. Eugenia said, "Ila, this is Officer Franklin Waters." Ila put her purse in her left hand and shook his hand. Eugenia said, "I know you have a tape player. Where do you keep it?"

"In the living room." Eugenia walked to the living room, unplugged the tape player, and walked back down the hallway to the bedroom.

Officer Waters and Ila were still standing in the hallway. Ila left him there and walked into the bedroom and said, "What the fuck is going on?"

"I need you to just be cool and follow directions. Go invite the officer into the kitchen and make him a drink while I prepare the bedroom. And put your .38 in the closet. I've got your back."

Ila walked to the closet and placed her purse on a shelf. Then she walked back into the hallway. The officer was standing at attention waiting for orders. She walked up to him and asked if she could top off his drink. He nodded his head and followed her down the hallway. She could feel his green eyes on her ass. He was not a bad looking man. She was not sure if he was a white/black or black/Hispanic, or something in the middle, but he was built very well and had large feet. *So, now I know why Eugenia was spending so much time.* She had to smile to herself.

As she turned into the kitchen, she realized that she did not hear his footsteps. She turned around to see him crawling on the floor behind her into the kitchen. In the kitchen, he stood up and sat in the chair. Ila went to the refrigerator to get the vodka. As she turned around, he was standing in front of her. She didn't know exactly what to say, so she said, "Will vodka be okay?" He nodded. "Do you want cranberry juice or orange juice or both?

He said, "Both." Then he walked to the sink and washed his hands.

Ila pulled out the juice. She was adding ice to his glass when he walked over to her, grabbed her arm, and said, "I want you to go to the end of the table and lie over it."

She looked at him and thought to herself, *Oh this man is crazy.* But, since he still had all his police regalia on, including his Glock, she did exactly what he'd ordered her to do. She wondered where the hell Eugenia was.

Ila walked to the end of the table and leaned over. He walked down to the end of the table, pulled her dress up over her ass, and began running his fingers down the crack of her ass and into her pussy. She dared not move or make a sound because she did not know what was about to come next. But she heard Eugenia coming down the hall. Ila's heart stood still. *This is her man and here I was stretched across the table with his hand up my pussy!*

Eugenia ran into the kitchen, and Ila heard a crack. The officer jumped away from her, and Ila decided to stand up slowly. Eugenia was saying, "You asshole! You couldn't wait! I should beat you till you bleed." Eugenia began to whip the officer with a spanking whip, and he looked like he had tears in his eyes. She said, "Go into the bedroom and take off all of your clothes. I'll be right in." He once again got down on all fours and crawled to the bedroom.

Ila looked at Eugenia and said again, "What the fuck is going on?"

Eugenia said, "Finish making his drink and get a strong one for yourself. It's going to be a long night." Then she turned and walked back down the hallway.

Ila stood there for what seemed like forever thinking, *This is crazy.* She finished making his drink and topped off her own. After putting everything back into the refrigerator, she walked slowly down the hall, dreading what was going to happen next. As she turned into the bedroom, she saw the officer lying across the bed. Eugenia was whipping his behind, and he was holding the bedspread, obviously trying not to scream. Ila walked over and put the drinks down on a crate that had been left in the room. The apartment had minimal furniture. Then she walked to the kitchen, got a chair, and brought it back into the bedroom so that she could watch the show. When she returned, Officer Waters began to scream, and then Ila saw why. Eugenia was placing ice from her glass on his ass on the places where she had just whipped him. He screamed and then hopped up and grabbed her and started to cry.

Eugenia signaled Ila to get up. Ila set her drink on the floor and walked up behind the naked police officer and began to rub his back. He turned around and asked her to lie on the bed. Eugenia nodded, so Ila followed his instructions. He then got up, pulled her dress up once again, and requested that she bend her knees. He bent over and placed his entire head between her legs. The man's tongue was long and wide like a dick. She could not believe the sensation he was giving her. She tried her best to keep one eye on Eugenia, but she could feel herself coming. She closed her eyes and enjoyed the sensation of the warm fluid leaving her body. He began to moan and lick her pussy as if he was licking ice cream from a bowl.

Then she heard the sharp crack of the whip. Eugenia began whipping Officer Franklin Waters on the ass and calling him names. The more lashes he got, the more he ate pussy. She whipped harder, and he screamed. He got up and turned to Eugenia. Ila moved swiftly off the bed and slowly went to the closet to be closer to her .38. Franklin stood in front of Eugenia and began calling her names, "You cunt! You whore! I Hate you!" Eugenia walked around him and waved Ila back to the bed.

Ila walked slowly and stood at the head of the bed waiting for instruction. Eugenia lay down on the bed and motioned for Franklin to come to the bed. He was still calling her names. He walked to the bed. As he began taking her boots off, he began to cry. He placed the boots on the floor, and he looked at Eugenia. "You did not take pictures," he said.

Eugenia motioned to Ila to pick up the pink bag. Inside she found an Instamatic camera. She took it back to the head of the bed. Eugenia said, "I want you to take pictures. Use up all the shots." Franklin continued undressing Eugenia, first her panties, then her sheer black covering. He was very meticulous. As he took the clothing off, he folded each piece and placed it on the floor. Her bra opened in the front, and he released it with ease. He did not remove the bra; instead, he dove onto her breasts and licked them with such passion that Ila began to come just watching. She almost forget to take pictures. Franklin looked up at Ila with a glare in his eye, and she raised the camera and continued to take pictures.

Ila took about four shots of him licking her breasts and thought she should save some film for whatever was coming next. Eugenia raised her ass so high up in the air he was almost thrown off the bed. He regained his composure and stood up. Ila had not really seen his penis, but when she did, she saw that it was short and wide. It looked almost three to four inches wide! She could not imagine taking that dick in her pussy. She took a picture of him standing straight up, and Eugenia then turned over and got up on her knees. Officer Waters held his penis and ran it up and down the crack of Eugenia's ass while she screamed, "Stick it in! Stick it in!" He stroked her ass a few more times and then slowly stuck his dick into Eugenia's pussy. She screamed with pleasure, and he came. The last picture Ila took was him slowly pulling his dick out of Eugenia's pussy. She had come around to the side of the bed to get a better angle.

Franklin stood there while Eugenia got up and began putting on her clothes. When she was dressed, she helped him put his police regalia back on. Ila stood by the closet door not sure what was going to happen next. It took a few minutes for each of them to get dressed. At that point, they all stood there in silence. After Eugenia finished placing items back into her pink bag, she asked Ila for the camera. Then she said, "Walk us to the door."

As they were walking to the door, Eugenia turned around and returned to the bedroom. She came out with the two glasses they'd brought with them. Officer Waters went to his car, and Eugenia went down the steps behind him to see him off.

Ila slowly closed the door, locked it, retrieved the chair from the bedroom, and wedged it under the doorknob. Then she went into the bathroom to take a shower. It was getting late, and she knew she had to report to Georgetown in the morning. She would have to walk since she'd left the car at the university. She looked at her hair and remembered that she needed to lighten her roots. She found her bleach and developer and gloves. It took her only about twenty minutes to apply the bleach to her hair and wrap her head in a plastic cap. She would have to wait for another twenty minutes before washing her hair.

While she decided what to do while she waited, she tried to rewind the last two hours in her head. She knew that it all was part of something larger, but she could not connect the dots. She knew it would all come together at some point. Finally, she decided that a drink would sure taste good. She forgot she'd left her glass in the bedroom. When she went to retrieve it, she immediately saw the camera in the middle of the bed. Eugenia had made her give her the camera and then when she came back for the glasses she left the camera. *Holy shit! This just got taken to another level!* She looked at the camera and wondered what she was supposed to do with it. She decided to put it in her purse. She'd be taking that purse to the university tomorrow. Knowing her colleague, she was sure Eugenia (or someone) would be looking for that camera tomorrow. And leaving it in the apartment would not be a good thing.

She took her glass to the kitchen, filled it halfway with vodka and a splash of cranberry juice, and returned to the bathroom to rinse out her hair before it turned orange. It always took some time for the water to get hot. She stood under the showerhead letting the hot water caress her body. Soon the fragrance of her shampoo filled the bathroom. Rodney used to love to wash her hair. It seemed he had come for a brief visit to let her know that he was around to give her spiritual protection. And just as quickly as the smell had filled the bathroom, it was gone. A tear rolled down her face. His love would be everlasting in her heart. She finished washing her hair, washed her body, towel dried her hair, and air dried her body. She carried her glass to the bedroom, lay across the bed, and then it was morning.

Ila's natural body clock woke her up at six thirty in the morning. It looked like a beautiful fall morning. The sun was shining, and the day was filled with promise. She had not set an alarm and had not thought about what she was going to wear on her first day. She jumped up and looked through the boxes. She really had to organize this mess. She was going to wear something new, but decided against showing off her first day. She found black slacks and a black-and-white boxy blouse. She had not seen an iron or an ironing board in the apartment, as she had been living her life in sweats and t-shirts. She decided to look around; surely there was an iron and ironing board here somewhere. She looked everywhere, but time was running out. Her last thought was to look under the bed. And sure, enough she found an iron and an ironing board.

My goodness, they thought of everything. I must think like an operative. The iron could also be used as a weapon if necessary. She could not stop laughing. The people at the Company were all crazy, but that sort of people were necessary for keeping our country safe. She set up the ironing board near the plug at the bedroom window. She had to go to the kitchen to get water to put in the iron. *I'm sure it would not work with vodka and cranberry juice.* She really wanted to sip that drink before she left for the university. The drink had sat there all night. She could add a few ice cubes and take a couple of sips just to get the butterflies out of her stomach.

Ila filled the iron with water and began to press the pants and the blouse. When she was finished, she remembered that she needed to find her credentials and a pair of shoes. Looking through boxes, she found a pair of Nine West black pumps. She would carry them in her purse and wear her tennis shoes for the walk to the university. In the living room, she found the envelope that contained the credentials sitting on the coffee table. She carried it back to the bedroom and put it into her purse. The purse was going to be heavy. Okay, time for coffee. She looked at the clock. Seven fifteen. She had to get going. She opted for no coffee and was praying that there would be coffee at the university. She pressed on. In the bathroom, she applied foundation, mascara, blush, eye liner, and red lipstick. She put all those items in a makeup bag and added it to the things in her purse, which was already quite full. In the bedroom, she looked for panties and a bra. *I'll not let another day go by without putting these items away*, she thought. *But where?* She would conquer that question this evening. She got dressed and realized she needed a belt. So, she looked though the boxes again and found a jewel box that she had totally forgotten about. It would be nice to have a different pair of earrings to wear. She placed the box on the bed and continued to look for a belt. Of course, it was at the bottom of one box. She threaded her beeper onto the belt before putting it on. *Okay—beeper, .38, shoes, camera, credentials, makeup. I'm ready to leave. Oh, earrings!* She opened the jewel box. Inside she found a folded piece of paper, but no jewelry. She unfolded the paper. It was a love message that Rodney had written to her so many years ago.

New Life

From your ever-flowing stream of sweetness, I celebrate you. Your new life has begun. You and life are now bound as one, so lift your spirit to the sky. Pledge an oath to life that you will live and love and enjoy the rest of your beautiful existence. Fashion strength as your shield, and let your heart be your sword.

Spring will come again for you after you smile though a thousand tears. After you laugh a crying melody, the dawn of a new day is yours for the choosing. A far more beautiful place awaits you. Listen sweetly and you will hear life calling you like a lover's caress. Feel me, touch me with your hands so soft.

Whisper to life your words of desire and it will honor your glorious being. As a flower, your petals fell to the ground, but seeds also fell and sprouted to give you a new beginning and a new strength. You are a soldier of the sun, and your smile and your hopes will dance across the sky. Every moment in your life will be peaceful and lovely. Sorrow cried as it walked away from you because it saw no place any more in your life, but joy smiled knowing it had a place in your life. Your freedom will be a house of refuge. Your intelligence will be your thunder, and life will demand fate to be kind. Love will command tribulations to flee, and you will feel the cool misty droplets of happiness shine on your face.

Endurance, preparation, opportunity, strength, determination, and intelligence are your arrows. Shoot them well and life and comfort are yours. You are my love, and I celebrate your new life with this poem.

These were his words of encouragement. When he wrote them, he knew he was being sent to California, and Ila had no idea where her next assignment would be. She paused for a moment, not having time to really reflect on what the poem said. She folded the piece of paper and placed it back in the jewelry box. Then she ran to the bathroom and put on the hoop earrings.

At the front door, she had to remove the "security chair." She felt as if she was living in a fortress. *Where are my keys?* She ran back to the bedroom and found the keys in the closet. She had put them there next to the .38. She ran back to the front door and was finally on her way.

The sun was bright, and she had left her sunglasses in the Cutlass, which was parked on the campus. She could hear Brock's voice: "Don't leave the apartment the same way every day, and never come home the same way. Park the car in different locations and sometimes walk." *So, okay. Today I walk.* The streets were busy with cars and people on bikes.

The sidewalks were busy with pedestrians—lots of them students— and people standing outside the coffee shop. Ila crossed the street three times looking in windows to make sure she was not being followed. She stopped at a news stand and pretended to look at the local paper. She brought the paper and continued her walk. She entered the campus, and the atmosphere changed. It was quiet and regal. She could hear the encouraging screams from coaches as the track-and-field students practiced and the sounds of maintenance men taking care of the grounds.

As she entered Healy Hall, the hearing-impaired maintenance man approached her out of nowhere. She signed hello. He signed hello and waved for her to follow him. She did not think he knew that she already knew where she was going, but she followed him nevertheless. He walked slowly and showed her to her office. The door was unlocked, so they walked right in.

She sat her purse on the desk chair and took out her heels so that she would be dressed appropriately when people started arriving to introduce themselves. As she was taking her shoes out of her purse, the maintenance man surprised her by speaking. He said, "Do you have the camera?"

She almost lost her footing. "What camera?" He looked at her and told her to put the camera in the pocket of his jean jacket. At that moment, the office door opened and Eugenia walked in. She was wearing a dark-blue suit with a ruffled blouse and three-inch heels.

The maintenance man said to Eugenia, "She does not have the camera."

Eugenia looked at Ila and said, "Did you bring the camera?" Ila turned to get the camera from her purse, but Eugenia instantly took her .38 from inside her jacket and aimed it at her.

Ila placed her hands in the air and said, "It's in my purse."

Eugenia did not put her .38 away. She stood very still as Ila slowly pulled the camera out of the purse. The maintenance man came around the desk, and Ila placed the camera in his hand. He walked swiftly out the door. Eugenia holstered her .38 and began to apologize for pulling a gun on Ila.

Ila said, "The next time you draw your pistol on me, be prepared to shoot me because I'll shoot you, and that is a promise.

Eugenia said, "I'll be back to formally introduce myself. People should be filing into their offices in about fifteen minutes. Things don't really get started here as far as faculty and staff is concerned until nine o'clock." Eugenia turned, and as she was leaving, a lady was attempting to come into the office. They spoke to each other, and Eugenia left to go to her office. "Hi", Ila said to the lady.

"Hello," she replied. "My name is Carole Russell, and I work in personnel. I have some paperwork I need you to complete. If you have time, I would love to review and complete it with you now."

It took Ila a minute to compose herself. Carole lifted Ila's purse off the chair and sat down. She seemed very efficient. Ila had a feeling she was working with the Company, but they did not discuss that nature of Carole's position. Ila had to sign a W9 and other paperwork to become a paid employee of Georgetown University. Carole went through all the material in about an hour. At the end of session, she asked if Ila had any questions. Ila said, "I'll surely have a question the minute you leave my office, but for right now, I'm okay."

Carole nodded her head and gathered up her paperwork. She handed Ila her business card and said, "You should have everything you need to conduct business in your office already, but if you need anything, just pick up the phone and dial two-five-five-seven for my assistant, Cheryl. She'll be able to help you. With that she headed for the door. But she paused, turned, and said, "A complete description of your position is in the top right-hand drawer. You will not be seeing students today, as we would like you to become acquainted with the campus. Walk around, introduce yourself, have lunch in the dining hall, and tomorrow we'll start to send you minority students who may be having a hard time adjusting to campus life." With that she left the office.

Ila's office was approximate twenty by twenty, and the ceilings looked to be about fifteen feet high. The desk and side table were made of cherrywood. The chair was covered in hard, black leather. There was an apple computer and a tall filing cabinet with a combination lock. A black phone and a phone book sat on the desk. All the necessities were in the drawers. Ila retrieved her job description and began to review her assignment. Inside the drawer where she found the job description, she also found a piece of paper that contained the combination to the filing cabinet along with her direct phone number. She also found a box of business cards. It was a lovely office, but there was only one exit. There was a huge window that rolled up and locked at the top. The window gave her a beautiful view of the front of the building. She could see some of Bishop John Carroll's statue, which sat in front of the building leading up to the massive entrance. Bishop John Carroll was the founding father of Georgetown University. When people walked up to the entrance, they often felt as if his eyes were following them as they passed.

Ila decided to see if the window would open. Then she decided against it. She would ask the maintenance man when she saw him. She could feel air circulating from somewhere, so she decided, as long as it was comfortable in the office, she would mind her own business. But that single exit bothered her a lot. Even if she could throw the chair through the window, the chair would not penetrate those windows encased in stone.

Ila took the combination out of the desk and unlocked the filing cabinet/safe lock. It had been some time since she'd had to lock and unlock a safe, but it came very naturally back to her. She grabbed her purse up and put it in the safe, but not before she removed her .38 and put it in one of the desk drawers. She was still wearing her tennis shoes, and she thought it would be a good time to take a stroll. She looked for the keys to the door, but could not find them. Then she remembered reading that all keys are kept in the combination safe. She quickly found the key. Fortunately, the combination was easy to remember because it was the day she had entered the Company. Before she left the office, she tore the piece of paper into tiny pieces and tossed it into the trashcan.

She took the keys out of the safe, closed the safe, and turned the combination lock three times. It would be a good time to walk the campus and talk to people or just get some sunshine on this beautiful cool crisp fall day.

The door was enormous and very heavy. She grabbed the handle, opened the door slowly, and locked it. She decided to make a right and head toward the front of the building. Things were moving now. There were students everywhere. Everyone was greeting everyone else. Students were saying hello to her, but she heard one of them saying as he walked away, "Who is that? I never saw her before."

Ila walked up to a group of African American students and introduced herself as the new diversity counselor. She told them she hoped to get to know each of them during the semester. "Please do not hesitate to come see me in Healy Hall, room G19," she told them. They all nodded and said they would come to visit. She continued walking around the campus introducing herself to students and enjoying the day.

After a while, she looked up and was in front of the faculty lounge. She did not have identification and wondered why she had not received an ID card from the personnel department. There was a gentleman standing at the front door greeting faculty members and letting them know what was for breakfast and what would be for lunch. He also told them what coffees had just been refreshed and which ones they might want to wait on. Ila walked in, and he greeted her also. He did not request ID and gave her his spiel about where everything was. Ila didn't know if this gentleman would be there all the time, or if things had changed since last semester. Then she saw the sign: Welcome to the newly renovated faulty lounge. *Okay, that explains it.*

Ila headed for the coffee and made herself a concoction of more sugar and cream than coffee. After putting a lid on it, she headed to the cashier. But, on her way, she saw bagels and cream cheese, so she immediately made an about face. The bagels looked fresh and plump. She picked up a piece of waxed paper, picked up the bagel and looked for the cream cheese. There it was. She placed two packages onto a paper plate along with the bagel and then looked for plastic cutlery. She noticed it was at the checkout along with metal cutlery.

As she walked to the cashier, she could see the maintenance man out of the corner of her eye. He pretended that he was mopping a spot on the floor. She looked at him and signed "hello." He, in turn, did the same. The cashier told Ila her bill came to $5.00. Ila was glad she had decided to get food; she was going to enjoy this bagel. The maintenance man slowly made his way over to her and took out a pad and a pencil. He wrote, "Check your beeper at 5:00 p.m. And the camera is in good hands. Place this piece of paper into your coffee cup when you are almost done." He then turned and walked away with his cart. Ila paid for her breakfast and walked over to a table close to a window and sat down.

She was surrounded by Company people. She did not need her .38; they were everywhere. She smiled and was about to give the bagel her full attention when she heard the click of high heels. *Shit that could only be Eugenia.* Ila looked up, and there she stood. "May I sit down?" Eugenia said.

"Do I have a choice?" Ila replied, so Eugenia sat down. Ila looked at her as if to say. "What?"

Eugenia looked around the lounge and then said, "Have you seen the maintenance man?"

"Yes. He strolled through about ten minutes ago."

Eugenia stood up and walked away. Ila said to herself, *That bitch is crazy, but I guess you must be crazy to do the work we do. But, that would make me a crazy bitch too!* She laughed out loud. The man at the front door looked at her and smiled. She finally finished her bagel and drank most of her coffee. She picked up the piece of paper, which she had placed under the plate—good thing since Eugenia had showed up—removed the top from her paper cup, and put the paper into the cup, which still contained a bit of coffee. She stirred the paper and coffee with the knife, placed the top back, stood up and took the cup to the trashcan along with the rest of her trash. She went out of the front door and said good-bye to the gentleman who was stationed there. He stopped her and said, "My name is Jefferson. I have not seen you here before, so I'll take it for granted you are a new faculty member." She reached into her coat pocket and handed him a card. He nodded his head and said, "Ms. Montgomery, have a great day." She wished him the same and left.

It was a beautiful day. She strolled along giving her cards to students and requesting that they stop and say hello to the new faculty member on the block. They all laughed when she said that. She decided to go to the practice field and sit in the sunlight for a few minutes before returning to her office. There was no sunlight in the Healy Building. She climbed onto the bleachers not really thinking that she could be a sitting duck for anyone to take a shot at her. Rather, she was thinking about how nice it was to be a part of the campus and how, when this was all over, she could go back to school and complete her education and maybe even get a PhD.

She sat just reflecting upon the last several months and wondered if it would ever be over. Would she ever get back to her so-called normal life? She stood up slowly and walked down the steps toward the breezeway that connected the stadium to the college. There was a man standing at the end of the breezeway, and she decided not to complete her plan. Rather, she turned around and walked back toward the bleachers. As she turned the corner, members of the track team were running up the steps toward the breezeway. She waited until five or six of the team members walked toward the breezeway and decided to take the opportunity to introduce herself and walk along with them. The man she had seen was no longer there.

Man, was she seeing a ghost now? She just shook her head as she entered the campus along with the athletes, who went one way running as she walked toward her office.

There were three students standing outside the office door when she arrived. Personnel had said not to see any students until tomorrow, but since the students were there she decided to see them anyway. She introduced herself and invited them in. Each had a myriad of items to discuss. Before she knew it, it was 4:45 p.m. The last student left at 4:50, and she knew she would be waiting for a message on her beeper. She gathered her things and changed her shoes. There was no reason to try to drive back to the apartment, but it was going to be getting dark at around quarter to six. *I'll have to hustle back.* Her beeper started going off. There was no call back number, just a bunch of numbers: 4, 15, 14, 15, 20, 23,15 18,18, 25,1, 2,15, 21 20, 20, 8, 5, 20, 18, 9, 1, 12.

It took Ila a minute to understand what was going on. She quickly reached in to the top drawer of the desk, took out a pad and a pen. She knew this was an alpha code. After decoding, the message read, "Do not worry about the trial." Tears rolled down her face. She had no idea who the page had come from, but she really hoped that the message was true. She sat a moment, erased the numbers off the beeper, and collected herself for the walk home.

The sun was setting fast, so Ila had to pick up her steps. She walked back to the apartment on the opposite side of the street from the apartment. She stood across the street from the apartment for about five minutes just watching people come and go. She decided to take the alley and enter the apartment from back. As she walked down the alleyway, she saw the police car parked in its usual spot. It looked as if there were two people sitting in the car. She took it for granted that the second person was Eugenia. But she thought she had seen Eugenia still in her office when she left. Maybe Officer Waters had picked her up.

Ila waved to the officer and smiled about last night. What a freak. As she looked for her keys, she heard the police car door open. She looked over her shoulder and saw someone running toward her up the steps. As she fumbled for her keys, she found her .38. The damn safety was on, and by the time she got the gun in her hand, a massive body stood behind her with a gun at her back. She dropped the .38 back into her bag.

A voice said in her ear, "Open the door slowly." She had managed to get hold of the keys, so she opened the door. The man pushed her inside. She fell to the floor, dropping her purse, but she knew she had to get to her gun or whoever this was going to kill her.

The man picked up her purse and slowly walked back to the door where he waved to the officer. When he closed the door, the hallway was dim, so she still did not know if she knew the intruder. He walked to the kitchen entrance and turned on the light. She was still on the floor but had gathered herself up to sit against the wall. She looked up. "Hunter!" she said.

"Surprise!" he said. "I know you thought Brock would be coming back for you, but we made sure his assignment would not require him to come back here." She looked at him with sheer disgust, and then she remembered that Hunter was the biggest narcissist in the world. It was always about him.

She got up from the floor and walked to the bedroom as he continued to speak, all the while thinking that his conversation just sounded like white noise. She took off her clothes, walked to the bathroom, turned on the shower, looked in the mirror and mouthed to herself, *You know this motherfucker. There are things that you do and things that you don't do. Do this motherfucker so he can move on.* She knew he would come into the shower with her because he could not help himself.

She had been in the shower for nearly five minutes before she heard his footsteps. He took off his clothes and got into the shower. Because she knew this man, she took control of the situation. He always felt it was her place to satisfy him, and if she got satisfied in the process that was a bonus for her. She looked at him and knew that the only way to get out of this jam was to fuck his lights out and hope that he would leave.

"You missed me, right?" he said. She did not reply. She just began to soap his body up. She didn't look into his eyes because tears were running down her face along with the water from the shower. She rubbed his balls, and instantly his penis got hard. She quickly dropped to her knees, but then she remembered that he did not come from being given head. She could be there all night and all day, and he would not come. She messaged his balls and placed his dick in her mouth—what she could handle of it. She had forgotten that his dick was long and wide. She sucked it until the water began to get tepid.

She stood up, and he turned her around. "Hands on the wall," he said. She knew then that he was going to enter her pussy from behind. She was hoping that he would not try to put his big dick in her ass. She turned around and bent over instead, letting him know that her ass was off limits. He slowly lifted her ass while holding her around the waist and forced his dick into her pussy. It was a very uncomfortable position for her, but if she remembered correctly, it would not last long. But she was wrong. She did not know this Hunter. He took his time, and she tried not to be aroused, but as he brought his dick in and out of her pussy while the flowing water kissed her ass, she could not help but come and come again. She could feel the head of his dick get wider and his body tense up. He held her almost straight up as he came with a roar.

He softly put her down. He had taken her off her feet. He looked at her, picked up the washcloth, cleaned his dick, and left the shower.

By this time, the water had turned cold. She washed up quickly and got out of the shower. The apartment had gotten cold. She thought she would wrap herself up in a towel and run out the back door, but that was a fleeting thought. What would she do then? Run to Eugenia's? She was probably the one who had set this shit up. Instead, she wrapped herself in a towel, went to the bedroom, found her flip-flops, and headed to the kitchen. Hunter was cooking breakfast for supper. She smelled bacon and sausage. Well that was something that he had not forgotten. Breakfast was her favorite meal.

She unwrapped the towel, laid it across the kitchen chair, sat down, and watched as he prepared the meal. He was skillful in the kitchen. He talked the entire time about how he had been assigned to Brussels for six months, but as soon as he came back, they could start preparations for their wedding. Ultimately, they were going to be assigned to the White House and live happily ever after.

Ila had gone into survival mode. She knew the best thing to do was to let him talk. He prepared, eggs, bacon, toast, and fresh fruit. He gave her a tall glass of water with lots of ice. She was very hungry. It had been a long time since the bagel at the university. He placed the food in front of her. She had just begun to eat when he said, "We should say grace." She almost choked on the food. She stopped eating while he said a grace. *Who is this man? This Hunter is different from the one I left at the safe house with Maurice's dick in his ass and his penis in Eugenia.*

She was silent and ate everything on her plate. Then he started in on her: "Same old Ila. Always needed to lose ten pounds. Well, that's not going to be a problem because, when I get back, we are going to go into strict training. You don't want to be a fat bride walking down the aisle!"

She wanted to say, "Motherfucker, I'm not fat." But she sat quietly knowing the night was going to be long enough. She looked around for her purse, but it was nowhere in sight. He picked up her plate and began cleaning the kitchen. He was meticulous and talked about how she would have to learn how to cook and clean better once they were married. After cleaning up the kitchen, he took out tumblers to make drinks. He got the vodka from the freezer, poured almost have a tumbler of vodka into each glass. The only thing she could think about was that she had to go to work in the morning. He added iced and a splash of cranberry juice to the vodka. He picked up both glasses and walked toward the bedroom. He placed both glasses on the floor and came back into the kitchen for additional ice in a bowl.

She was still sitting at the table waiting for instruction. As he got the bowl of ice, he said, "It's time. Come to bed." She got up, picked up the towel, and walked behind him into the bedroom. He turned the lights out in the bedroom and left the light on in the bathroom. He then went through the house, and she could hear him securing all the doors and windows. When he came back to the bedroom, she was sitting on the edge of the bed waiting for further instruction.

He placed his .44 Magnum under the pillow on the left side of the bed. He walked back to the other side of the bed, laid the other pillow on the floor, and handed Ila her drink. He knelt on the pillow, picked up his drink, and began to talk again. She sipped her drink slowly, as she did not want to get drunk. He drank his quickly and set the glass back on the floor. He took her glass out of her hand and pushed her gently toward the bed. She lay on her back, and he pulled her ass toward the edge of the bed, spread her legs, and began to eat her pussy.

He reached for ice and placed a piece between the lips of her pussy and sucked on the ice. She knew she should not enjoy it, but, my goodness, this man was a professional at eating pussy. She could not help but come and come again, screaming and holding onto the covers of the bed so tightly her knuckles were turning white. He had found her clitoris and was licking it like a dog licks water. She could not help but scream. She felt as if he had been eating pussy for an hour, but she was sure it had been only about twenty minutes. She was exhausted from coming. He could see she had gone completely limp.

He stood up and reached out for her hand. She grabbed his hand, and he pulled her up from the bed. He stood her up, turned her around, and told her to kneel on the bed and bend over. He grabbed her ass and jammed his dick into her pussy. He slowly pushed her to the bed, closed her legs so that he could barely get his dick in and out of her pussy, and he came—with another roar.

He was very still. She dared not to move. He finally rose up and once again assisted her up from the bed. He said, "I have to get some rest. I have a plane to catch at six in the morning." She did not say a word. She walked to the opposite side of the bed, got under the covers, curled up in a fetal position, and remained very still. He got into bed and draped his massive leg across her body so that he would know whenever she moved. She had to go to the bathroom, but she would rather pee in the bed than try to make a move. He was not in the bed ten minutes before he was snoring. She thought that she would never fall asleep, but soon she was asleep herself. She figured a person could not come that many times and not be exhausted.

Ila woke up at around four in the morning, unable to hold her urine any longer. She moved, and Hunter woke up instantly. As he moved, his beeper went off. He jumped up, looked at his beeper, and then started putting on his clothes. She jumped up and went to the bathroom; her bladder was about the burst.

Hunter came into the bathroom, turned on the water in the sink, wet a washcloth, and wiped his face. He was completely dressed. He carried his Magnum in his shoulder holster. He left the bathroom, came back wearing a light jacket, and said, "Get off the toilet and secure the apartment. I'll see you in six months."

She rose quickly, wanting him out of the apartment. He walked to the back door removed the chair unlocked the security lock, and turned around. "See you soon. I'll tell Brock you said hello when we meet in Brussels." With that he left.

She closed the door, pulled back the curtain, and watched him leap down the steps and get into the police car. She secured the lock, placed the chair back under the knob, and walked slowly to the bedroom. She almost stepped into the bowl of water, which had once been ice cubes. She crawled back into bed thinking about Brock and how she might never see him again. She fell back into a deep sleep.

The next thing she heard was traffic on the main street. Light was shining through the window. Fortunately, it was only 6:45 a.m., so she had plenty of time. She slowly got up and tried to think about how it had all happened. She tried to connect the dots. She walked slowly to the kitchen to make coffee and decided to make tea instead. She sat and waited for the water to boil wondering what this day would bring. As she poured the hot water onto the tea bag, she heard her beeper go off. She placed the kettle back on the stove and ran down the hall toward the living room where Hunter had put her purse. More numbers.

She pulled a small scratch pad out of the purse and began writing down the numbers: 2, 1, 20, 23,15,18,11,1, 20,14, 9,14, 5. "B at work at nine." So, she had to get moving. Still there was no return number on the beeper. Ila went back to the kitchen, picked up the cup of tea, and headed to the bathroom. She was still full from the meal Hunter had made; she was hoping to dump it in the bathroom to get it out of her stomach. Fortunately, she was able to SSS (shit, shave, and shower). Her mind was reeling as she had to once again go through boxes, iron clothes, and complete so many other tasks in preparation for going to work. Hopefully things would settle down and she would settle into some kind of routine. Fall was slowly turning into winter, and she had not seen any winter clothing in those boxes. Her clothes, she guessed were still at her apartment. But the company motto was "Never have anything or anyone you cannot leave in fifteen minutes." What a life.

When she was finally dressed, she looked for her tennis shoes as she would be walking to the university once again. She put her heels into her purse, found her keys, and was finally ready to go out the back door. No, she would go out the front door today; she'd gone out the back door yesterday. She turned around and headed toward the front door.

Her beeper went off again. She dropped everything and looked for a scratch pad in her purse because she knew there would be more numbers. She looked at beeper: 9, 12, 15, 22, 5, 21, 2, 18, 15, 3, 11. Her knees got weak. "I love U, Brock." She really hoped Hunter had been lying about seeing Brock in Brussels. She removed the chair from the front door, unlocked the security lock, and opened the door to the bright sunshine. This was truly a God-filled day, and she was going to try her best to enjoy just being alive.

Ila locked the front door and turned left instead of right. She walked down the street a block, crossed the street, walked back up O Street, and headed toward the university. She must remember to get her sunglasses out of the Cutlass; this sun was intense. The walk cleared her head, but her stomach was in a knot. She saw one of the students she had spoken to the day before. He hollered, "I'll be back to see you soon." She felt good about that. Basically, she was just a sounding board for them. She really had no authority. She just took notes and passed the notes onto the dean of students, who would see if their concerns could be addressed. There were some items that she would keep to herself, as they were confidential, and the students did not want that information passed on.

She walked past the huge statue; she could see the maintenance man out of the corner of her eye. He nodded. She nodded and kept walking. As she arrived at her office, she saw that there were two students standing outside her door. Great! This was going to be a busy day, and that is what she needed. The last thing she needed was time to think about Hunter, Brock, and Eugenia. She wanted to forget for a little while about that triangle. She opened the office door and walked to her desk. The students followed in behind her. She would have to give them appointments because her office did not have an additional partition for privacy. As she began to make their appointments, she looked at the clock: 8:55 a.m. The message had ordered her to be at work by 9:00. She made the first appointment for 10:00 and the next for 11:00. The students left, and she was finally able to sit for a minute at her desk, change her shoes, unlock the safe, and place her purse inside.

She wanted to walk to the faculty cafeteria for coffee. She never had finished the cup of tea she'd made at home. And of course there were the bagels at the cafeteria. She opened the center drawer to get pens and paper out so she could start the day. Lying on top of the pens and note pads was a copy of the *Washington Post*. The headline read: "Police Chief Shot by Alleged Lover." She could not believe it. The article went on to say that Police Chief Warren Chambers was in critical condition, and the shooter was in custody. The shooter, Henry Dubois, had allegedly been romantically involved with the chief. There was a statement by the chief's wife stating that Mr. Dubois was just a perpetrator who had an ax to grind with the chief, and his allegations of homosexual behavior with her husband were totally unfounded. She also stated that Mr. Dubois should plan on finding himself in a new kind of hell in the penal system. There was a picture of Dubois in the paper. It was the same gentleman who had been in the room that night with the chief so long ago. He looked devastated and confused in the picture. She could see that a defense of being totally crazy could get him off the hook.

She folded the paper and put it back into the drawer. She could feel a wave of relief come over her, and her stomach became very queasy. She looked for the trashcan. It was located behind her; the maintenance man or cleaning people must have moved it. She grabbed the can and threw up repeatedly into the plastic liner. It was at that moment she decided to leave the Company. It was time for her to try to have a life, if that was even possible. She looked around for napkins or something to wipe her mouth with and found tissues in one of the desk drawers.

Of course, the trashcan smelled to high heaven. She wrapped up the bag and found clean bags on the bottom of the can. She gathered up the bag and walked to the door to find a place to discard it. As she opened the door, she found Eugenia standing outside. As Eugenia walked toward Ila, the click of her high heels made Ila's stomach turn again. She almost threw up all over her Nine West shoes.

Eugenia came very close to Ila and whispered, "Have you heard the news?" Ila nodded. "You may be off the hook." Ila nodded again. Eugenia whispered in Ila's ear, "The police officer really enjoyed himself. We'll have to do it again real soon." She laughed and walked away.

There was a large trash receptacle close to Ila's office, so she did not have to go far to discard the bag. She walked back into the office and retrieved the keys so she could lock the door. She needed to make her way to the cafeteria for coffee and a bagel. Maybe that would quiet her stomach before the first student arrived. She walked swiftly to the faculty lounge. The gentleman was there again greeting everyone, letting them know what roasted coffee was available and what had been freshly brewed. She greeted him and quickly grabbed coffee and a bagel. This time there was strawberry cream cheese, and that sounded just right. She gathered up her breakfast, paid the five dollars, and exited the lounge.

It was approximately 9:50. She had a few minutes to eat the bagel before the first student would arrive. She unlocked her office, sat down at her desk, and managed to eat half the bagel before the door opened and the first student of the day arrived. She put the other half aside and got to work.

The day moved along swiftly. It looked as if she was going to see all kinds of students. But she guessed that is what was meant by *diversity*. She had thought she would be dealing mainly with minority students, but it seemed that everyone needed a shoulder to cry on and solutions to situations. She looked at the clock at two o'clock. She looked up again, and it was five o'clock. Time to go home. She walked the last student out of the office and locked it as he left.

She just wanted to take a minute to exhale. As she walked back to her desk, the weight of last night's events crashed down upon her. She wanted to just sit in the chair and go to sleep, but she decided to go through the ritual—shoes, safe, and so forth. She walked back to the apartment. She had no idea where the Cutlass was, and she had no idea where the maintenance man was hiding out. She decided to make sure she got the keys from him tomorrow.

The days and nights were endless without Brock. She saw Eugenia only at work, and Eugenia never brought the Officer Waters back to her apartment. The work at the university was the only thing keeping her sane. Police Chief Warren was still fighting for his life, and she would have to start giving her deposition in a few days. The lawyers had decided to come to the university for her deposition. Each day at lunchtime, the Company investigator came to her office to ask questions, and she would answer them to the best of her recollection. The event had happened almost six months ago, and her memory had faded, but she had written a full report right after the incident, so all the facts did not have to be exact. She gave them her deposition in real time with the report. She believed this deposition was to make sure everything she said the first time could be repeated. It was going to be difficult on the stand. The chief's lawyers would be twisting and turning the evidence and the circumstances.

The nights were long. After being used to having sex almost nightly, it was difficult for her to not think about it. Masturbation was her nightly ritual, but even that was starting to wear on her. Plus, she had not seen a period this month, and her nipples were rock hard. She knew she was pregnant. *Here we go again. Damn it! That Hunter has powerful sperm.* The last thing she wanted to do was to have another abortion. If her period did not come in the next several weeks, she would have to contact the Company and decide whether to keep the baby or abort.

She had decided to leave the Cutlass at the university and not drive to work at all. Every day she walked and took a different route. The maintenance man wrote her a note and told her that he had been driving the car on his lunch hour. She did not ask any questions.

As her pants got tighter by the week, she knew she had to face the music. The baby felt good in her stomach, and she felt that she wanted to have this child even through it belonged to a demon seed. She was not getting any younger, and having children was something she wanted to do and needed for herself.

The winter was on its way, and winters in DC could be brutal. The wind was most telling. Ila's eyes watered all the way to work and all the way home from work. She finally requested that the maintenance man retrieve her sunglasses from the Cutlass. He brought them to her office. She thanked him and could not wait to try them on the way home so that the howling wind would not grab her eyes and remove the cornea.

As she walked home that day, her stomach began to cramp. She thought it was because she had not had a bowel movement in several days, but the pain kept getting worse as she got closer to the apartment. It felt as if she had to go the bathroom immediately. It would be a relief to get rid of the waste that had been lingering in her body. She walked faster and went in through the front door.

The pain was worse than any pain she had felt before. As she ran to the bathroom, a trail of blood followed. What was this a period or ... *Oh, my God, a miscarriage!* She did not know whether to throw up or sit on the toilet. She decided to sit on the toilet and to see what would happen. A cramp came through her stomach and through her throat. She threw up all over the floor, and then a cramp came that felt as if her insides were turned inside out. She heard something hit the water in the toilet. Her child was a huge glob of blood and material that was indescribable. The blood was still coming fast. She got up and went to the cabinet to get a sanitary napkin. She placed a towel between her legs and took her pants off. Still bleeding, she walked to the bedroom and retrieved another pair of panties.

The pains in her abdomen were still coming fast and furious. She had dropped her purse at the door. She walked slowly to the door and picked it up. Her equilibrium was off, and she held on to the door knob and began to cry. The pain was intense. She grabbed her beeper, looked for Eugenia's number, and beeped her 911. She walked over to the couch and sat down bent over from the pain.

Suddenly, as quickly as the pain had come, it stopped. It took only about five minutes for the pad to be completely saturated. As she walked back to the bathroom to retrieve another pad, she heard Eugenia at the back door. She was using her key, but the chair was preventing the door from opening. Ila walked to the back door and removed the chair. Eugenia busted into the apartment with gun in hand. She took one look at Ila and the trail of blood on the floor and shouted, "Go lie down on the bed. I'll get help right away."

Ila walked slowly to the bedroom room. She tried to change the pad, but felt lightheaded. She lay across the bed and passed out for a few minutes. The next thing she knew, the medics from the Walter Reed Hospital were there asking her to sit up. When she did, they asked if she could walk. She could. She walked over to the gurney and lay down.

The next time she woke up she was in a private room at Walter Reed with tubes in one arm and a saline drip in the other arm. And, she was alone. The nurses came in and out of the room—blood pressure checks, bathroom checks, bag replacement checks and food. She did try to eat some of the food, but it was horrible, and she just did not have an appetite. She wondered why each time someone came through the door there was a hesitation. And then she saw the Secret Service agent at the door. Every now and then he would peek into the room. She knew the case was big, but not big enough for her to be guarded by the Secret Service.

Ila slipped in and out of consciousness most of the day. She really did not know what day it was, but it seemed she had been in the hospital for some time. The sun went down and came back up, it had to be maybe the third day. She wondered how they had covered for her at the university. And what about the apartment? Once again, the faucet of tears streamed down her face.

She heard a man with a very official voice enter the room. She turned her head to wipe the tears away. He stood by the bed and said, "Hello, Ila. I'm Dr. Shepard.

I want to discuss the procedure that was done and what you will need to do during your recovery."

Ila decided to be as attentive as possible as he explained. He went on to say. "After we gave you a sedative to help you relax, we performed a dilation and curettage—or D&C for short. You are now receiving antibiotics intravenously to prevent infection. We did a vacuum aspiration to make sure that all the tissue was extracted from your uterus. We sent the tissue that was captured to pathology for testing. The tissue came back inconclusive; it showed no signs of disease or cancer. These things just happen sometimes. We find that most women who are in stressful situations or have high blood pressure or diabetes have a high risk of miscarriage, and since you do not have high blood pressure or diabetes, we can only deduce that it might have been stress. We'll be releasing you in a couple of hours, and we understand that you will have a caregiver for a day or two to make sure you have no complications. Do you have any questions?"

Ila shook her head. He then said, "We'll be sending you home with pain medication and something to calm you nerves during your healing process. It should take only five days for the bleeding to stop. Then the pain will subside. If that does not happen, be sure to come back to the hospital. Please do not go to any other hospital or physician."

Ila nodded, and the doctor left the room. At his point, Ila had not a tear left. She looked out the window at the cold day and thought, *I'm done with this life. I'm ready for a position in an office pushing paper, or maybe an assignment to a satellite office where only domestic work is done—no intelligence, no undercover.* It was time. She had been in the game for enough years. With that thought, she fell asleep again. The next time she woke up, Eugenia was there, and the nurse was there with discharge papers. Ila was given prescriptions. Eugenia had brought a pair of sweatpants, a T-shirt, a jacket, and flip-flops. Ila guessed Eugenia had not thought about what time of year it was. But she was grateful Eugenia was there.

The nursed wheeled Ila out of the back door of the hospital. Ila was surprised to see the Cutlass with the maintenance man in the driver's seat. She had to laugh inside. The Company she worked for was incredible; they looked at all angles. Eugenia and the nurse helped her into the front seat and closed the door. Eugenia got into the backseat, and the maintenance man drove them off.

There was no talking during the twenty-minute ride back to Georgetown. Ila was grateful that he pulled up to the front door as she did not want to have to climb steps. There was a black Riviera parked in front of the apartment that pulled off as they drove up. Eugenia jumped out of the backseat and opened the front door of the apartment. The maintenance man pulled his gun from under the driver's seat and laid it on the seat beside them. Eugenia left the door wide open and came back to get Ila from the car. She was very calm and very gentle. This was a Eugenia Ila had not seen before. Eugenia asked Ila to place both feet out of the car before trying to stand up so that all her weight would be on both feet. She did as she was told. Eugenia placed one arm under Ila's arm and the other arm on the car for balance. Ila stood up, and they began to walk toward the front door.

Once inside, Ila walked to the bedroom and was very happy to see that the apartment had been cleaned up. She removed her flip-flops and fell across the bed into a deep sleep.

Eugenia went back out to the car and gave the maintenance man his instructions. When she came back into the apartment, she locked the door and secured it with a chair. It had been an exhausting two days for her. The police officer had been blowing up her beeper, Hunter had been blowing up her beeper, and the Company had told her that she would be reassigned soon. What Ila did not know while she was in the hospital was that Chief Warren had died, and his funeral was going to be tomorrow. The protégé had pleaded guilty to second-degree murder, and there would not be a trial because his attorney had said that he was not mentally stable enough to withstand a trial at the time. He would have to be examined by an independent group of physicians at the Walter Reed Naval Hospital. All Eugenia could do was laugh out loud. They were going to find him crazy as hell and lock his stupid ass up in the west wing of the hospital until he was old and gray.

Eugenia went to the bedroom to check on Ila. She covered the sleeping woman with a blanket from the closet and decided that eating would be a great thing to do. It seemed that it had been some time since she had eaten. She went into the kitchen and opened the refrigerator. There was a note on the top shelf. "Have Ila beep me when she is feeling better, fondly Hunter." *Goddamn! how did he get someone to come in here from the Company and leave that note? I thought he was out of the country. He must have long-reaching tentacles.* Eugenia was afraid for Ila. Hunter was crazy and madly in love with Ila. That was a most dangerous combination. She took the note and tore it up into tiny little pieces.

Eugenia began making a salad. She put some eggs on to boil. Then she chopped up onions, tomatoes, Swiss cheese, kale, and spinach. If was very quiet in the apartment. She wanted to turn on the TV but thought it would awaken Ila. She prepared the salad with care, but had to wait for the eggs to cook. She had made a huge salad just in case Ila woke up hungry. She knew Ila thought she was the enemy, but truth be told, Ila would never know that Eugenia worked for the Company and the FBI as a duel agent and could flip flop at any time. It was a life she had chosen to live, and she had no regrets. There would never be children in her future, never a husband or a white picket fence. Her life was dedicated to her country and that was that.

When the eggs were done, she dunked them in ice water to cool them. Then she peeled and sliced them and added them to the salad along with some crumbled bacon and avocado slices. In the refrigerator she found ranch and thousand island dressings. She mixed a little of each in a bowl. What a beautiful combination. She poured the dressing over the salad and took a big bite, savoring the flavors. Before she could take a second bite, she heard footsteps and reached for her gun. But then she relaxed. it could only be Ila. Eugenia jumped up and stood beside the kitchen entrance just in case.

Ila slowly walked into the kitchen. She saw Eugenia exhale and sit back down at the table. Ila slowly went the refrigerator and got some water. When she saw the salad, her stomach started doing flip-flops. She felt as if she had not eaten in days. She got a bowl from the cabinet, filled it, looked at the combination of salad dressings on the counter, looked at Eugenia, and started to laugh. She poured some of Eugenia's concoction onto her salad and sat at the table with Eugenia. She began eating slowly at first, and then faster. She was very hungry. They sat in silence. Eugenia finally broke the silence and said, "I'm sorry."

Ila looked at her and said, "So am I." They sat in silence the rest of the time. Eventually, they cleaned up the kitchen. When they were finished, Ila turned left to the bedroom, and Eugenia turned right to the living room.

The morning light was clear, and it had gotten cold in the apartment. Ila got up slowly, not wanting to rush into anything. She could still feel some blood flow, but it did not seem to be intense. There were no stains on the sheets, and she was feeling eighty percent better. She walked to the bathroom, looked into the mirror, and almost screamed. Her black roots were full and in control, the bags under her eyes were heavy, and her color was chalky. There was paperwork on the sink from the doctor, along with the prescriptions. Her instructions were no tampons, no baths, no heavy lifting or strenuous exercise. She had decided not to take the pain medication as she had an addictive personality, and she knew it would be easy to get hooked on those types of prescriptions. She would ask

Eugenia to go to the store and get more hair color. She turned on the shower and waited for it to get hot. She climbed into the shower and let the water run down her head onto her body. She could still see the marks on her arms from all the tubes and bandages. She began to cry just to relieve the pressure of it all. *Was it a boy or a girl? What kind of life could I have given a child? Why was I not blessed to keep it?* Then she began to laugh because it had originated from a demon seed. She was blessed not to have had Hunter's child. The thought of spending the rest of her life with Hunter was truly frightening.

She washed her hair, and while she was rinsing, she began to smell coffee and bacon. Eugenia must be cooking. She was glad about that. She finished her shower, got another pad, dried off, and walked to the bedroom to find another pair of panties. She would have to go to the laundry soon. The laundry had been brought in from the laundry mat previously. She had not been since Brock left. That would be another trip she guessed she would have to make with Eugenia. When she was dressed, she found her flip-flops and strolled down the hallway toward the kitchen.

Eugenia must have gone upstairs and showered as she had on fresh pajamas, slippers, and no makeup. Eugenia was a mystery to Ila and would probably always be. Eugenia smiled as Ila entered the kitchen and said, "I bet you thought I didn't know how to cook."

Ila smiled and replied, "The thought had entered my mind, but from the smell of things it seems you know your way around a stove." She had made eggs, bacon, and French toast, something Ila had not had in a long time.

She could not wait to have a slice. Eugenia fixed two plates and poured coffee. They sat down to devour another meal together in silence.

Ila finally asked what Eugenia had told the university staff about her absence. She said, "I told them you got the flu that was going around campus and that you would probably be out for a week." Ila nodded her head. That was great. She wouldn't have to tell anyone about the horrific experience she had just gone through.

As Ila popped the last piece of French toast into her mouth and savoring the flavor, Eugenia said, "Chief Warren is dead, and his protégé has taken the insanity plea for killing him."

Ila replied, "Say that again?" Eugenia repeated her statement. Once again, Ila was speechless. She rose from the chair, gathered up both plates and her cup, and took them to the sink. She returned to the table, and they sat in silence.

After fifteen minutes, Eugenia's beeper went off. She got up, handed Ila her cup, thanked her for breakfast—because she'd used the food in Ila's apartment and not hers—and left out the back door. She hollered from door, "Come put the lock on the door."

After locking the door, Ila noticed the Prince George's police car. Officer Waters was still sitting in the driver's seat. Ila went back to the kitchen to wash the dishes. She was so excited to think that her deep cover days were about to come to an end and that she would be headed back to a semi-normal life. She could not wait for the day to come. Since the chief was dead, there would be no reason for her to testify unless the protégé actually did go to trial, but that would probably be years in the future since he had filed a plea of temporary insanity.

After Ila cleaned the kitchen, she made sure the apartment was secure. Then she took a quick shower and fell across the bed. Next thing, it was morning once again.

Ila felt as if the weight of the world had been lifted. Her life could go back to normal—Brock would come home, and they would get married and have children. The future, in her mind, was looking incredibly bright. She sat on the side of the bed and made plans to have breakfast and to go to the Laundromat. She rose and placed her dirty clothes in two pillow cases. She looked at her bed linen and comforter and thought to herself, *That bed has been through a lot. Those items really need to be washed.* She was unsure how she was going to get all that stuff to the Laundromat. She found another pillow case and stuffed the sheets into it. The comforter would have to wait. Ila decided to only have a cup of coffee and to go to the bagel shop and get a bagel after dropping off the clothes at the Laundromat. She had taken a shower the night before, so she decided to just wash particular parts, brush her teeth, put on mascara, lip gloss, and blush and call it a day.

As she looked in the mirror, she noticed once again that the dark roots had come back strong. She had gotten used to being blonde. She made a mental note to pick up hair color at the local drug store. She went back into the bedroom and looked for sweats, tennis shoes, and a sweatshirt. It had gotten cold outside. The fall had turned into full winter in a matter of days it seemed.

There was a box she had not opened. She hoped it contained winter clothing, and she was rewarded with coats, hats, sweatshirts, double-knit pants, and sweaters. She looked at the closet and decided that, if she had to stay there, she should make it as comfortable as possible, and that would begin with getting some hangers. She found everything she needed in the box—a little wrinkled, but it did not matter because she was in a college town. Everyone was a little wrinkled. She laughed out loud. She found her favorite hooded sweatshirt with the Georgetown emblem on it. She was true college basketball fan and loved Georgetown basketball. She had never dreamed that she would be working there.

Ila quickly got dressed. She picked up her purse and made sure it contained her .38 and her ID. When she was ready to leave, she decided to go out the front door because she could see the sun shining through the small opening between the curtains. She hauled the three pillow cases to the door and was about to open it when someone knocked on it. She hit the floor and grabbed her purse to get the gun. Damn it! This was supposed to be an uneventful day. The person knocked again. Ila got up, went to the back door, moved the chair, placed her .38 in the pocket of her sweatpants, and ran down the steps to the alley. She continued up the alleyway to the street.

She ran across the street so that she could see who was at the front door. The first thing she saw was the Cutlass parked in front of the house. The man had his back turned to her now and was still knocking at the door. He finally turned around to walk toward the Cutlass when he noticed her across the street. He waited until she walked across the street. He stood by the side of his car. She told him she would be right back. She ran back down the alleyway to the back door and, of course, who was sitting there? The Prince George's police car. Did this dude ever work? She ran up the steps, opened the door, re-secured it with the chair, ran to the front door, gathered up her things, and remembered that she did not have the beeper. She went back to the bedroom to get the beeper, ran back to the front door, and opened it.

The maintenance man was still standing by the car. She pulled all the dirty clothes out of the apartment onto the sidewalk, retrieved her keys, and locked the door. The maintenance picked up the dirty clothes and headed toward the car. She said, "I was on my way to the Laundromat."

He said, "I'll take you there. Please sit in the backseat of the car." She opened the back door and slid into the backseat. He then piled the clothes onto the front seat. He closed the door and ran to the driver's side. When he turned the key in the ignition, the engine turned over like a hot rod engine. He must have done some work on it. She could only laugh to herself. He pulled off, and she said, "The Laundromat—"

He waved his hand and laughed and said, "I know where it is." He drove to the Laundromat in silence and parked in the alley. He got out of the car and knocked on the back door. The same lady that Brock had given the clothes to when they were there before came to the back door. He handed her the three pillow cases.

She said. "They will be ready tomorrow same time, and I'll put them in a basket." They both laughed. The maintenance man got back into the car and began to drive off.

Ila said, "I was going to breakfast after I dropped the clothes off. I'm very hungry."

He said, "We got a message from your neighbor, Paula, that her boyfriend, Drew, is very sick and only has days to live. If you like, I can drive you to to Alexandria Hospital so that you can see Drew. Maybe we can get something to eat afterwards. In the meantime, we'll run down to the coffee shop get a cup of coffee and a bagel. We'll have to keep moving."

She just nodded her head. They knew her routine anyway. She didn't know why she was surprised at what he had said. That was exactly what she'd been planning to do anyway.

When they got to the coffee shop, he said, "Please stay in the car." She decided not to even tell him what she wanted on her bagel; she was sure he had been told exactly what she liked. He'd had to park about a half a block away as most people got there very early, parked, fed the meters, and strolled around Georgetown for the rest of the day. He walked swiftly down the street and went into the shop. The town was in full hustle—people shopping, students going to and from the university. The smell—a combination of car fumes and food—would make the non-city person's stomach quiver. Ila enjoyed the city and was convinced that, once this assignment was over, she was going to move to DC and leave the Virginia suburbs. She daydreamed about the move and where she would go. DC was a bit expensive, but she also really loved Hyattsville, Maryland.

She was deep in thought when the maintenance man walked up to the door and asked her to roll down the window. He handed her a cup of hot coffee and a small brown bag. He had another cup of coffee and another small brown bag. As he walked around the car to the driver's side and slid into the car, she put her coffee in the seat next to her and opened the brown bad. Inside was a bagel. It looked like cinnamon swirl. It was toasted and had peanut butter on it. She looked at the bagel and she looked at the maintenance man. He said. "I can feel your eyes on the back of my head, but don't you know you are watched every morning you go to the cafeteria? Everyone knows you like peanut butter on your bagels."

She did not respond because she was so hungry. She broke off a small piece of the bagel, and peanut butter oozed out of the sides. Ila was too hungry to argue. She plopped the piece of bagel into her mouth. They sat silently eating for about ten minutes. He turned over the engine, and they were on their way to Alexandria. The traffic crossing the 14th Street Bridge was horrible. Ila had to hold her breath as they crossed the bridge, which she avoided all the time. As they crossed, she could see in her mind the snow falling and the ice on the road from that fateful night, cars inching along trying to get across the bridge in rush-hour traffic in the worst ice snow storm DC had seen in a long time. She herself crossing the bridge and looking in the rearview mirror for Rodney ... and the news broadcast as she walked into my apartment: "Flight 90 leaving the National Airport has just struck the 14th Street Bridge." Rodney never arrived that night. Tears rolled down her face as they crossed the bridge.

The maintenance man looked into his rearview mirror and wondered why she was crying. *She must really have a strong friendship with the people we are about to see*, he thought.

They got across the bridge and headed toward the hospital. She was eager to see Paula and very sad that Drew was about to transition, but there was no cure for Hepatitis C, and he had lived a long time with the disease.

When they pulled up to the hospital she realized it was much larger than she had remembered. *They must have added some wings because it seems massive to me.* The maintenance man parked the car and said, "I have an errand to run. Beep my number when you are ready, and I'll meet you back here."

She nodded and said, "Thank you very much for breakfast. It was delicious."

As she got out of the car and he began to pull off, she panicked. He must have seen her stop and look around because he turned the car around and came back to the entrance. He parked and jumped out of the car. "What is the matter?" he said.

She replied, "You are coming back, right?"

He laughed and said, "Ila, I'll be back." He got in the car and drove off. She stood in front of the hospital for what seemed an hour but was only minutes. She walked through the electronic door and asked the volunteers at the visitor's desk for Drew Henderson's room number. It was room 290. She thanked them and proceeded to the elevator. She had to pass the chapel to get to the elevator, so she took a moment and sat in the chair closest to the door and said a prayer for herself, for Drew, for Paula, and for her family members, whom she had not seen in such a long time. She walked toward the elevator and pushed the button.

Feeling a presence behind her, Ila turned around to see Paula standing behind her with tears streaming down her face. It was clear she had been outside smoking a joint. Ila could smell the perfume and weed. She took Paula's hand, brought it up to her lips, and kissed it. There were no words to say, only memories of a man who had lived his life fearlessly with love, compassion, and weed.

Drew loved to get high. He worked for the Department of Sanitation and was able to beat the pee test. Or, as she suspected, it was so hard finding workers who did not smoked weed that they overlooked it and concentrated on the hard stuff—heroine, opiates, crack, and meth.

The two women entered the elevator together holding hands like young school girls about to enter a spooky movie. After exiting the elevator, they walked down to room 290, and as they entered, Ila almost screamed. This was not what she had been expecting. There he was—a shell of the man she remembered. He was lying there with tubes and monitors everywhere. He saw Ila as she came in, and he began to smile. "'Bout time you brought your ass to see me," he said.

"I tried on at least two occasions, but I was stopped by very crazy circumstances."

"I bet," he said. "I remember those crazy motherfuckers you work for." They both laughed. "You know I'm not going to get better, so please check in on my lady when you can. She is really going to miss me."

"Even if you are not here in body, you are too mean to leave this earthly planet!" she said. "I'm not even worried about Paula because I know you'll be haunting every motherfucker who tries to get near her." They all laughed, but this time when he laughed, he began to cough, and all the bells and buzzers started going off. The nurses ran in and put an oxygen mask on his face.

Ila began to cry, for so many reasons. He had been her protector for so many years when she lived right next door to him. He would find her keys in her door because she'd been so drunk and high she'd forgotten she left them there. He always knew when she needed a shot of Hennessy and a joint before she could close her eyes after a full day of covert work. He was Paula's man, but he was also her friend—like a brother to her.

After Drew breathed the oxygen for a bit, he closed his eyes and fell into a deep sleep. He was also in love with the musical group Blue Magic, and so was Ila. There was not an evening when she got home or a Saturday when she woke up when she had not heard their music coming through the walls—"Loneliest House on the Block," "Thirteen Blue Magic Lane." She began to cry deeply and could not believe that this was going to be the last time she would see this gentle soul.

Paula came over to the chair and gave her a handful of paper towels. "You sure are ugly when you're snooting and crying." They both broke out into uncontrollable laughter. They sat together for about an hour. Paula finally said, 'Ila, go home or wherever it is you live now. Once Drew leaves us, I'll be sending the body back to Philadelphia. His parents have family plots in a cemetery in the town he grew up in. I'll not be having a service here for him. Say good-bye now. He loves you, and that is all that matters."

Ila reached for Paula's hand once again and kissed it. Paula was being so strong. Ila got up, walked over to the bed, and kissed Drew on the forehead. She hugged Paula and told her to beep her if she needed anything. She gave Paula her beeper number and hoped that it would be the same in the next couple of months. Paula said, "Thank you. This way I won't have to call headquarters to get a message to you. Ila took what cash she had out of her purse and handed it to her friend. "Buy some more weed. You're going to need it to get through all of this." Paula nodded and thanked her. Ila hugged her tightly, turned, and left the room.

The walk to the elevator seemed so long. She took the elevator down and was walking out the visitor door when she remembered she had not beeped the maintenance man. She walked down the driveway to sit on the bench so that she could beep him, but just then she heard a car horn. He was sitting in the car waiting for her. She jumped up and walked to where the car was parked. She collapsed onto the backseat without even closing the door. He got out of the car, came around to the back door, closed it and returned to the driver's seat. The last thing she remembered was the maintenance man pulling the car out of the parking lot. She was exhausted from sorrow. When she woke up, he was pulling into a parking space a few yards away from the apartment. He got out of the car and told her to get out on the street side as there were so many cars driving by. She straightened up, grabbed her purse, and slid out of the car. "Are you hungry?" he said.

"Yes. Let's walk to the Chinese restaurant. Oh, and by the way, I gave all my money to my friend Paula."

"No problem." They walked in silence the five blocks to the Chinese restaurant. It was crowded as usual. There was some seating outside, but the day had turned chilly, so everyone had chosen to huddle inside the small restaurant. They walked in and reviewed the menu. She ordered Hunan chicken, and he ordered moo goo gai pan. they walked over to an empty spot on the wall to wait for their order. It took about fifteen minutes, but the people watching was entertaining. Most of the students were eating and reading. Most of the residents were waiting anxiously, and still others decided that eating all the fortune cookies while waiting was an acceptable behavior. Their order was soon ready. The maintenance man went to the counter and paid. It had gotten even chiller while they got their food, so they walked quickly back to the apartment. Ila was glad she had gotten into a habit of putting her apartment keys in her pocket and not her purse. She would have been digging for minutes trying to find them in her purse.

As they approached the door, Ila said, "Would you like to come in and eat your dinner?"

"No. I have an early day tomorrow. Remember I'm the maintenance man. I have to be at work at seven. Would you like me to leave the car here?"

"No, thanks. I'll walk to work tomorrow. Thank you for everything." She placed the key in the lock. He waited until he heard the dead bolt lock click, and she watched him proceed to the car. Ila could not wait to eat the food. It had been a long time since she eaten that bagel. She placed the food on the kitchen table, turned on the TV for noise, took her purse to the bedroom, and returned to the kitchen. The restaurant had provided a plate, fork, and napkins. She immediately ripped open the bag, opened the containers, and plowed into the meal. After eating a complete plateful, Ila got up to get cold water from the refrigerator. She returned to the table and devoured another plateful. She drank the full glass of water, put the remnants of the Chinese food into the refrigerator, tossed the trash, and left the kitchen. She walked back to the bedroom, removed all her clothes, crawled into the bed, and prayed she would wake up. The last thing she heard was the theme music to *Miami Vice*.

Ila woke up to traffic sounds and street sweeper sounds. It was wonderful not to have to get up and move the Cutlass because of the street cleaning. She sat on the side of the bed and reflected on the last seventy-two hours. She remembered that she had lost a child and was about to lose a friend in that short period of time. It is amazing what the mind and body can absorb and still stand firm. For the next two days, Ila got up, ate and went back to bed. She could feel herself healing. On the third day, she dressed in sweatpants, and old sweatshirt that belonged to Brock, tennis shoes, and a scarf she found in the bottom of a box. She decided that life was for the living. What had happened had happened, and it was time to move on. She threw water on her face, brushed her teeth, and looked for a skull cap. She thought there should be one in one of the boxes. Digging deep, she found her Georgetown skull cap, which she'd had for many years. Beeper, keys, .38 in her purse. She headed for the door.

As she opened the door, the chill came into the room. It seems the temperature had really dropped in the last few days. She closed the door, placed her purse on the couch, and went to look for gloves. Digging again in the boxes, she found her leather gloves. *Dang! Gloves, hat, sweats. Okay, I'm ready.* Ila walked back through the living room, picked up her purse, and headed out the door.

The sun was shining, but the air was cold. She decided to walk to the school and walk around the track and come back. She walked slowly, crossing the street several times making sure she was not being followed. When she reached the school, she jogged slowly to the track. She was glad to find that the track field was empty. She was about the run down the steps when she saw the maintenance man. He walked up to her and just looked at her. She said. "I needed to get out of the house, and I wanted to get some exercise." He was silent, as she was sure everyone there thought he could not talk. He held out his hand, and, she said, "What do you want?" He pointed to her purse. She said, "My gun is in my purse." He nodded his head and pointed to the four corners of the stadium. There was already protection. They were disguised as maintenance men. At that point, she wondered how many operatives were really working at Georgetown University. Was it because of her, or was it because of the kids who went to school there who were members of dignitary families from all over the world? She decided it was the latter. It was a very prestigious school and very well secured. She had nodded to about four security guards. By now she was sure they knew who she was or they would have stopped her. She handed the maintenance man her purse, and he took a seat on a bench. Ila continued down the steps to the track and around the track three times, sometimes running and sometimes walking. She could feel her lungs starting to burn. But she was not going to let another pound jump onto her body. Brock would be very disappointed that she had not kept up her exercise routine. Telling him about Hunter and the baby episode was going to be difficult. On the other hand, maybe it would be her secret. Well, the Company's secret.

As she finished her laps and climbed slowly up the stairs, the maintenance man rose up, handed her the purse, and walked away. He laughed out loud. She had no idea what he was laughing at, but it was probably because she looked as if someone had stomped her. She had to laugh herself.

This became her routine for the next week—up early, walk to the school, run the track, and walk home. The next week, she knew, she would have to return to work. She had beeped Paula to see how she was doing. She had left the apartment number, but since there was no answering machine, she had no idea whether Paula had tried to call or not.

It was Monday morning. The sun was shining, and the noise from the traffic was an automatic alarm clock. Ila looked around the bedroom and heard noise coming from the living room, only to remember that she had left the TV on. She jumped up and walked to the living room to turn the TV off, only to see a special bulletin— Chief Chambers' protégé had killed himself in his jail cell. There was no reason to think there was foul play because an empty bottle of Drano was found next to his bed. However, how he obtained the drain cleaner was still under investigation. There would be more details during the eleven-o'clock news broadcast. Ila stood in front of the television and felt a shudder of relief that came over her. She sat on the couch and wondered if she should go to work after this dreadful news. But she felt that going to work would keep her mind off everything. She was sure there were students waiting to see her with a myriad of problems to solve, and she could not wait to sink her teeth into doing something helpful.

This spy business could get the best of you. She walked slowly to the bathroom to take a shower. Again she noticed her hair was truly blacker than blonde at this point. But since the danger seemed to be over, going back to her natural hair color seemed like a good idea. She turned on the water for the shower and new it would take a while to get hot, so she began to brush her teeth and looked at the little hairs that had begun to grow under her chin. She looked for a razor and finally found some under the sink. The razors were Brock's, and the blades looked like they could cut a person's throat. She gently rubbed a little soap under her chin and then clipped off the hairs with the razor. By the time she was finished, she could see the steam coming from the shower. She hopped in and let the hot water roll down from the top of her head to her feet. The great thing about having short hair was that she could dry it with a towel, work in some gel, and she could be out the door. She would probably never have long hair again. She turned the knob so that the water would be tepid and finished washing her body. *Dang, I forgot that the pants I had found in the box need to be ironed.*

She finished up quickly so that there would be enough hot water left to steam her pants. She hated ironing. She finished and got out of the shower, towel dried her body, but not completely. She found she did like her body to air dry. She moisturized her face, towel dried her hair, and worked curling gel in it so that it would set. She did her makeup—foundation, eye liner, mascara, blush, and red lipstick. She picked up the red lipstick so that she wouldn't forget to put it in her purse along with a compact. She was not very good about remembering to take her makeup with her. For her job, she was always moving and working undercover, so making sure how she looked was never the top priority. She laughed to herself. It was going to be a great new start.

She walked to the bedroom, pulled the pants out of the box, creased them, and hung them on a hanger, one of the last ones in the closet. She remembered she was supposed to pick up more. She took the pants into the bathroom and hung them on the shower curtain rod. She turned the water to hot, turned off the light, and partially closed the door so that the steam would stay in the bathroom. After five or six minutes, most of the wrinkles should be gone, and she'd be able to put them on, even though they would feel a little wet. She looked around the bedroom to fine her heels, tennis shoes, socks, and a sweater. Then she remembered that most of her clothes were still at the laundry. *Damn it!*

Suddenly there was a knock at the back door, but quickly she decided that anyone wanting to kill her would not come to the back door knowing that the Prince George's police car was parked there most of the time. She walked sideways up the hall and yelled out, "Who is it?" It was the maintenance man. She moved the chair out of the way and opened the door. There he stood with all her laundry, some in a pillow case and the rest in a laundry basket. She smiled and laughed and asked him if he wanted to come in for coffee. He said, "No, I'll be waiting for you in the alley. You can have coffee at work. It's getting late. The laundry didn't open until seven thirty this morning. That's why I'm just getting here."

"Okay," she said. "Give me ten minutes. I'll be right out." She took the pillow case from him, and he placed the basket in the hallway and left. She closed and locked the door and was very happy to see clean underwear. She thought, *I was going to have to wear the ones I had on yesterday.* She was not above doing that, but she just did not want to do it her first day back at the university. She laughed to herself. *Like anyone would know.* She finished getting dressed and grabbed the pants out of the shower. The steam had worked perfectly. She grabbed a sweater from the box and checked her purse—gun, beeper, makeup, shoes. Her keys were in her pocket. She was ready to walk out the door. As she walked to the door, a feeling came over her. She felt that she was forgetting something. She stopped in her tracks but could not remember. She opened the door, closed it tightly, and was headed down the steps when the Prince George's patrol car pulled up. She continued down the steps and acknowledged him as she turned left to walk up the alley.

The Cutlass was parked next to the building. She got into the backseat and locked the door. The maintenance man put the car into reverse. He was going to back out into the street, which was probably going to be a little difficult considering the traffic. He inched his way out into the street; he was an excellent driver. He had to turn in the opposite direction of the school. She thought he was going to the light and turn around, but he went through the light. She said, "Where are we going?"

He said, "To your favorite coffee shop for a bagel. We have time. You know—to get you that bagel and peanut butter that you love so well."

She laughed. He was right; those bagels were very good. It was a beautiful fall day. The sun was shining, and the steam from the subway was coming up through the grates into the streets. Near the bagel shop, the maintenance man pulled all the way to the corner, but there was no place to park. As the car came to a stop, a man with a beard and a skull cap jumped into the car on the passenger side. *Oh, shit! Now what?* The man told the maintenance man to drive him to the subway and to take Ila to the Crystal City Marriott.

The man turned around. His smile could light up a city. He looked at her, and she knew it was Brock. She almost peed herself. She looked at him and said, "What took you so long?"

"I hit a lot of traffic coming from Europe." They all laughed out loud. The maintenance man dropped Brock at the subway and then continued to Virginia.

Ila asked him not to take the 14th Street Bridge. "If you could please take Route Fifty that would be perfect."

He did not ask any questions, he made a right onto Constitution Avenue, which would take them to Route 50. He took the Jefferson Davis Highway straight into Crystal City. He let Ila out in front of the Crystal City Marriott. Through the open driver's window, he handed her a room key to room 376. She smiled from ear to ear, and he laughed and said, "I'll be back to get you at around five this evening."

"What about work?"

"You're still on sick leave. You don't have to return until Wednesday." Ila almost jumped out of her skin. She leaned into the car, grabbed his neck, and kissed him on the cheek. He blushed and pulled off.

She walked—skipped—into the Marriott and walked fast to the elevator. She remembered that she had to be cautious, so she took the stairs up one flight and then took the elevator. Room 376 which was at the end of the hallway, of course, by the stairwell. *Nothing changes.* She did not think Brock had made it to the hotel before she did, but they had experienced some traffic. When she opened the door, she heard the shower. Her heart started beating fast.

The suite consisted of a sitting room in colors of burnt orange and sand and a bedroom with a huge king-size bed. The colors in the bedroom were reversed; sand was the dominate color, and splashes of burnt orange served as accents. Ila felt like a bag lady. She would not have brought all the stuff if she had known she was going to spend the day in a hotel. She could not wait to have Brock in her arms, mouth, her pussy, her … everywhere.

She decided to take off her shoes and just lie across the bed until he came out of the shower. She listened as he made noises in the shower as if someone was throwing cold water on him. She jumped up to secure all the locks on the door and then walked back into the bedroom as he was coming out of the shower.

He flinched, looking for his gun, but then realized it had been Ila securing the door. At the same time, he knew that if it had been another circumstance, he would be dead. Just the split second of not knowing where his gun was would be all it took. Letting his edge slip was dangerous—even deadly. After that scenario went through his head like a mini movie, he began to smile and wondered what he would have to do to make this woman his wife. It would take some maneuvering with the Company, but he believed he had accumulated enough political favors that he could arrange whatever personnel changes had to be done for them to be together.

He'd had to use a lot of his clout to get Hunter sent to Libya on a fact-finding mission. They were in the room together when they received their assignments. Hunter thought that Brock was going to Libya and he was going to be reassigned to the Pentagon. Wrong. Hunter did not have the political connections to have Brock sent to Libya, but Brock had the connections to have Hunter sent. As they both opened their assignment folders, Hunter hadn't said a word except to ask the four-star if there was anything else; he had to leave to prepare for his new assignment. The four-star dismissed him. Brock stood there reading his assignment, which sent him back to the Pentagon to complete the paperwork and close the case on the police chief and to make sure all the paperwork related to the case was secured top secret and all the rest of the paper trail was shredded, including pictures. Brock gratefully accepted the assignment and requested to be dismissed. Permission was granted, and he'd left the room.

He'd almost skipped down the hall but saw that Hunter was waiting for him at the elevator. Hunter let the elevator come and go. Brock decided to take the stairs because, if this motherfucker had anything to say to him, he did not want to have a conversation on the elevator. When Brock turned left toward the stairs, he could hear Hunter's footsteps coming up fast behind him. He stopped quickly as he got to the door of the stairs, opened the door, and let Hunter walk through it. Brock came through the door, and they both stood on the landing for a few seconds. Hunter said, "So now that you've got my ass sent to fucking Libya, let me tell you something. I visited Ila while you were gone, and she and I have made plans to get married as soon as I get back from this assignment. So, enjoy your time in DC, but keep your black ass away from Ila. I have told you more than once that she is part of my career plan, and that plan does not include you! Oh, and by the way, she is delicious!"

Brock started to laugh. He said "Man, by the time you get back, Ila and I will be married, and we'll even have children. Enjoy your time in the sand. We'll send you a wedding invitation." Brock took the steps down to the first floor two at a time while Hunter was screaming some bullshit down the steps. All Brock could do was laugh. And he yelled up over his shoulder, "Bye, bitch! See you in a year!" And he laughed louder.

Ila stood there looking at a man who looked like Adonis. Brock had a six pack, arms that were chiseled, and thighs that could bend steel. She did not want to take her clothes off because she had not done intense exercise, just on the track a couple of times and walking back and forth to work. He walked over and engulfed her in a bear hug. She started to cry. He said "Ila, stop I'm back." She could not help it, she had missed his touch, and how she felt safe in the cradle of his arms. He held her close until her tears subsided. He walked her over to the bed and told her to relax for a moment.

He went back into the bathroom and turned on the water in the tub until it was hot. He ran the water in the tub until it was half full and then turned the water to cold so that it would be just the right temperature. He lit the candles he had purchased. He turned down the lights, turned the water off, and went back to get Ila. She was sitting on the bed like a withered plant that needed to be watered. And he was going to do just that. He walked over to her told her to stand up. He unzipped her pants and pulled them to her ankles and asked her to step out of them. He laid them across the chair. He took off her panties and put those across the chair. He took her sweater off along with her bra and laid them on the chair. He took her hand and guided her into the bathroom. She stepped into the tub, and he went to get a chair from the sitting room. He sat while Ila washed up. He talked about his aunt's funeral and how he had gained ten pounds over the weekend. He told her that he and his roommate had had a chance to go to the local VFW and hang out, drink, and play cards after the funeral. His aunt had been a veteran, so the repast was held at the local VFW. Drinks flowed, and the food was excellent. It seemed that everyone in the little town of Gastonia had brought a dish. There was enough food there for an army. They played darts and there was a jut box that still took quarters and played forty-fives. It had been great to see family members and friends.

Brock's roommate remembered a lot of the people from all the time Brock had spent there with him during training camp and visits over the years. His roommate, Morris, showed him pictures of his family, and he was a bit envious that he had gotten an assignment on a major base and was able to start a life there and a family. The children were beautiful, and his wife was lovely. Brock told Ila all about the old men playing horseshoes and telling lies, and how they all smoked weed. They both laughed. He said that the funeral had been elegant and country at the same time. People sang off key and dressed in their Sunday best. His mother had stayed busy with arrangements, food, greeting people, and really did not have time to really think about her sister being dead. Sunday, when he was about to leave, she had broken down. It was going to be hard for her. She and her sister had been so close. Brock told Ila that, after the wedding, they would go back to Gastonia and spend some time with his mother.

Ila looked at him and said, "After the wedding?"

"Yes," he replied. "You will marry me, won't you?"

Ila looked at her body, her toes, her knees to make sure she was not dreaming. She replied, "Spending the rest of my life with you would be my joy, my pleasure, and my appointment in life. Yes, of course." He reached out for her to help her out of the tub. She stood up, and he grabbed her hand to help her out onto the mat. He patted her down with the towel and then walked her into the bedroom. He laid her on the bed slowly. He began to kiss her ankles. He kissed her knees, her thighs, and made his way up to her navel. He blew kisses into her navel and then reached down to feel her pussy throbbing. He was so excited he had to take small breaths so that he would not come all over her leg. He slowly opened her pussy with his fingers and darted his tongue inside.

She had lain back by this time and was enjoying in the sensation. Her legs started to quiver, and her body began to shake. This man was everything she had ever dreamed of. She was in her world, safe, secure. He turned her over and asked her to get on her knees. He ate her pussy from behind. At this point, it felt as if she was peeing on him, but he kept wiping her pussy dry with the towel and starting again. At one point, Ila thought she had passed out. He turned her over and rubbed every part of her body. His penis was rock hard. When she went to grab it, he said no, he was not done with her. He went back into the bathroom and returned with baby oil. He poured it between her breasts and slowly rotated his hands all over her body, down to her toes. It felt incredible. As he came up, he slid her buttocks to the end of the bed and entered her with just the head, in and out, then more, then a little more. She felt his body tighten up and knew that the end was coming soon, but she was completely satisfied. She lifted her ass high so that he could get his entire penis into her canal. He called out her name, and she came in a way that she had never come before. He could not hold it any longer. She could feel the hot semen penetrate her vagina and was happy that he was completely satisfied.

He stood still for a minute, opened his eyes, and started to laugh. "Oh, my God. I have been waiting for that for a long time!" She laughed with him. He pulled out and picked up the towel. He cleaned her first and then cleaned himself. He pushed her over so that he could fall on the bed. All she could do was laugh. He lay with his head on the pillow. He did not speak, but she could feel his heartbeat through his back. She wrapped herself around him as he fell asleep.

They both woke up when their beepers went off. He looked at his, and she looked at hers. It was the maintenance man. It was 3:30 p.m. They had been sleeping for hours. She number texted the maintenance man "ten minutes." Ila got up and walked into the bathroom to take a shower. She turned on the water and looked for the towels and washcloths. Plush white cloths and towels were hanging on the side of the vanity. The shower was steaming. She got in and let the water roll down her back. She remembered what had happened earlier and prayed that she could have this man forever. She had her eyes closed when Brock entered that shower. He held her close and just let the water run. Then they got out of the shower. They got dressed in silence. As they were walking out of the door he said, "Can you start planning our special day? I would like to keep it simple, but I'm up for whatever you want to do. Beep me the date you come up with," he said, "and I'll make sure you get the money you need for deposits—photographer, caterer, venue, whatever. Just please keep me out of it, tell me what color to wear, where it's going to be, what hotels people can stay in, and I'll take care of the honeymoon."

Ila smiled and said nothing. She was good at taking orders. She just laughed to herself. What exactly had she just signed up for? Whatever it was, she was more than willing to take the ride and stay on until the ride stopped. He opened the door to leave, but then closed it. He took her in his arms and hugged her so hard her ribs hurt. "See you soon, and remember the promise. I love you." He opened the door and ran toward the stairs.

Ila stood at the door looking both ways and remembered that she had left the keys to the room on the vanity. She walked back to the bathroom, picked up the room key, and placed it in her purse. She opened the door and almost shit her pants. The maintenance man was standing there looking at his watch. "Ten minutes," he said. She looked at him and laughed. They walked down the hall in silence. He had been parked in front of the hotel, and hotel staff were not happy about him being parked there so long. As they walked out of the hotel, he handed the valet a twenty-dollar bill. She jumped in the car, and he ran around to the driver's side. As they sped off, she said, "Please do not take the Fourteenth Street Bridge.

He replied, "I remember." They drove without talking as they listened to WHUR radio.

She said to the maintenance man, "Brock and I are going to get married."

"Really?"

"Yes, maybe on New Year's Eve."

"Don't forget to send me an invitation. Brock and I have been colleagues for many years. It would be great to see him married and content."

"What about happy?"

"I don't believe Brock will ever be completely happy, but you are making him smile, so that is all right by me."

Somehow, Ila did not want to know why the maintenance man felt Brock could never be happy. There were some things that just needed to be left unsaid.

When they arrived at the apartment; Ila thanked the maintenance man for everything and got out of the car. He carefully opened his door, got out, and ran around the car so he could walk her to the door. She had found her keys, and she held them in her hand. As she put the key in the lock, he said "What name are you going to put on my invitation?"

She said, "Maintenance Man, of course." And they both laughed.

"My name is Stephen Stevens, but as far as you are concerned, on campus and off campus, I'm the maintenance man."

"Understood. Thank you, Mr. Stevens, for all you have done and will do."

"Do you want me to leave the car?"

"No. I'll repack my bag and get ready for work tomorrow." She thanked him again and went into the apartment.

She entered, locked the dead bolt, placed a chair under the knob. What a wonderful afternoon. She felt better than she had in weeks. She was very surprised that she had not bled during sex with Brock considering it had only been two weeks since her miscarriage. She could have played it off and told him she was on her period, but she was glad she hadn't had to go through the period thing with towels and all the mess. It had been a wonderful afternoon.

She walked back to the bedroom, took off all her clothes, and laid them on the bed. She slipped into a T-shirt from the basket of clean clothes and walked back to the kitchen to eat. It was very quiet, so she walked to the living room to turn on the radio to WHUR. When the phone rang, it scared her. She could not remember the last time she'd heard it ring. She let it ring three times before picking it up. "Hello?" she said.

"Hey, Ila. It's Paula."

"Lady, I was just thinking about you, how are you? Has Drew transitioned or is still holding on? I'm sure he is not ready to go."

"Yes, he transitioned. He went peacefully in the night. I had just gone home and was about to get into bed when the phone rang. I got dressed again and drove back to the hospital. I said good-bye for the last time. When he was gone, I signed all the paperwork and waited for the transport people to take his body to the funeral home. I decided to have him cremated because of the cost for transport of his body. After he's cremated, I'll put his ashes into two urns. I'll keep one and send the other to his mother. His family can't afford to come to DC, and I can't afford to send his body home, so that was the compromise." Then she began to cry. "Oh, Ila," she said after a moment, "I miss him so much. I'm going to move out of the apartment to another apartment across town. I don't want to really, but I just can't bear every day to come home to the apartment building where we spent our time together. Especially since you're no longer there, it is just not the same."

Ila did not say a word; rather, she let Paula continue to talk. "I found a place not far from here. I'll miss being able to walk to everything. This place is a diamond in the rough. Drew had a great insurance policy at work, so I'll be all right for a while." She paused and said, "I've quit smoking weed. I realized that I just smoked it because he smoked it. I guess I only enjoyed it because he enjoyed it so much."

There was a pause in the conversation. Ila said, "I have good news. Brock and I are going to get married."

Paula screamed, "No shit! When?"

"I think in March, right after the winter breaks."

"Why are you going to wait that long? Girl, life is short. You'd better grab that man and love him for the time you can. Believe me, moments missed are precious, and time marches on with or without you. You might as well spend as much time as his wife as possible. You no spring chicken anyway." They both laughed.

"Okay," Ila said, "how about New Year's Eve? He doesn't want a big wedding. Actually, he told me just to tell him what to wear and where to be and let him know if I needed money." They laughed again because that was so Brock.

Paula said, "Oh, this is exactly what I need to keep my brain busy. When can we get started looking for a place?"

"Well, it's the middle of November, so we don't have much time."

Paula said, "I really won't have to start working right away, so let me look at some places. When I have three for you to look at, we can meet and go see each place."

Ila replied, "That sounds wonderful. I can use all the help I can get." Then there was silence. Ila said, "There will be life and love for you after Drew, Paula. It will just take time—and an open heart and open mind from you."

"I know, Ila, but it is going to be hard. I didn't have to work. He was my life, and that's my fault. I let him consume the core of my being, but I felt so secure in his arms that sometimes time stood still."

Ila laughed. "You know, Paula, that's how I feel about Brock. Maybe it's my turn to feel what you've felt all these years. I'm looking forward to it."

Paula said, "There is nothing like it. There are times when I felt his breath on my neck and I wanted to consume his soul. If I find anything close to that again, I'll grab onto it and never let go."

Ila replied, "Pray for me because you know I can take a yacht and turn it into the *Titanic*." They laughed and said good night.

After hanging up the phone, Ila secured the apartment and walked to the bedroom. This place was so empty without Brock. He could take the air out of a room and make a person glad to be choking. Ila laughed and began to take her clothes off. It had been a wonderful day, and she hoped she would have many days of happiness with Brock. But she also understood that happiness is like a sparkling jewel that we all reach for but most of us never get. She was completely naked and decided just to lie across the bed for a few minutes. She would then get up and take a shower, decide about what to wear to work, and then go to bed. She lay across the bed and fell into a deep sleep.

Once again, she woke up to the sound of cars outside and the trash men picking up the trash in the alley. She snapped up and looked around the room to get her bearings. It took her a minute to remember the day before and how wonderful it had been. She let the blood flow down to the bottom of her feet because they had been hanging over the bed most of the night. She reflected that one day soon her name would be Ila Montgomery-Covington. She could not wait! She got up from the bed and went to the boxes. Because it was so cold out now, she needed something warm to wear. She found a pair of lined navy-blue pants and a light blue cowl-neck sweater. Perfect. She hung the pants up on a hanger and placed them in the bathroom to let the steam work on the wrinkles. It would take a minute, of course, for the water to get hot, so she went to the kitchen and put the kettle on the stove on low. She was going to have a hot cup of tea this winter morning. As she turned back around the corner, she could see the steam coming from the bathroom. She rushed down the hall and hopped into the shower, letting the water run down her back for what seemed like minutes. It was great to feel almost whole again. *I'll remember the promise until he returns.*

Ila got out of the shower and heard the tea kettle whistling. She quickly dried herself off and ran down the hall to the kitchen. There was nothing like a hot cup of tea and toast with so much grape jam on it that poured out of the corners of her mouth. She put two large pieces of wheat bread into the toaster, pulled out the jam from the refrigerator, and waited patiently for the toast to pop up. She had to make sure that the jam was spread on the toast while it was hot. The toast popped up, and she immediately put a glob of jam on each piece. She poured hot water into a cup to warm it, emptied out the water, put a tea bag in the cup, and poured steaming water over it. She had begun drinking her tea without sugar. It just was not as good, but sugar was something she was trying desperately to take out of her daily routine. She placed the towel on the chair and sat down, ready to devour this quick delicacy. And, just as she had imagined she had placed so much jam on the toast that it quickly dripped off both sides of the toast. She had to use her tongue to catch the dripping jam. She laughed out loud because only a child would do what she had just done. But it was that kind of morning—cool, crisp, and childlike. It was a new day dawning, and she was breathing in fresh air. After she finished her delicacy, she cleaned up the kitchen and walked back to the bedroom to get dressed. As she walked down the hall, she saw a shadow come across the back door. She immediately got on the floor. She set the cup down softly and crawled slowly down the hall on her elbows, hoping that whoever was at the door was friend not foe, and that she could get to her gun before she knew which one it was.

The shadowed figure knocked on the door. She knew that Eugenia had a key, so she had no idea who might be at the back door. She found her gun, checked the chamber, and crawled back to the door. She knocked on the door with her gun and shouted, "Who is it?"

A man's voice replied, "The maintenance man."

Ila crawled back to the bedroom and wrapped a towel around her. She walked back to the door with her back against the wall. When she got close to the door, she shouted, "What is your real name?"

"Stephen."

Ila moved the curtain back slowly, and there he was—Stephen Stevens. *What in the world does he want?* She slowly opened the door and said, "Morning. Is there something wrong?"

"There is a mandatory staff meeting at eight thirty this morning. I was unaware of it until I got to work this morning at seven. So, could you please get the lead out and get ready? I have the car in the alley."

Ila replied, "Do you want to wait inside?"

"No. Please just get dressed and come to the alley." He turned and walked down the steps.

Ila ran down the hallway, went into the bathroom to retrieve her pants, and then ran back to the bedroom to finish getting dressed. She quickly put on her pants, sweater, and pumps. She put tennis shoes in the bag just in case she had to walk back to the apartment at the end of the day. She walked back to the bathroom, ran some gel through her hair, put on foundation, lipstick, and mascara, and she was ready to walk out the door. She ran back to the bedroom, put her gun and her makeup into her purse, and grabbed her leather coat.

When she got to the back door, she heard a noise coming from outside. She walked slowly to the door and saw Eugenia and the maintenance man having an intense conversation. Ila walked back into the kitchen and turned off the light. Whatever they were discussing, she just hoped it had nothing to do with her moving again. She wanted to stay put until Brock was able to be with her and they could plan the wedding together. She walked back to the back door and opened it. It seemed as if the conversation had ended; Stephen had gone back to the car, and Eugenia was nowhere to be seen. Ila slowly went down the stairs, looking around carefully. Suddenly, a chill ran down her back to her feet. She stood still for a minute waiting to see if something was going to happen after the chill, but her insides became calm again. She walked slowly to the car. Stephen had the engine running. He looked a bit disturbed that it had taken her a little while to finish getting ready.

They rode to the university in silence. As they entered the gate, he made a left instead of heading to her office in Healy Hall. She sat silently waiting for an explanation that never came. He pulled up in front of Copley Hall. He said, "Please get out of the car. I have something to show you."

They walked into the Copley Hall and made a right to the entrance of St. William Chapel. The maintenance man opened the huge doors. The space looked like something from Oz. The aisle to the front of the chapel was twenty feet long. And there was a beautiful stained-glass window at the end of the chapel that looked like something out of the Vatican. The dark-wood pews were polished and shone in the dark like diamonds. Stephen turned on the hanging lights, which looked like crosses shining brightly all the way to the altar. She looked at Stephen, and he said, "Walk down the aisle and see how it feels. This is the only chapel on campus that allows marriages of any denomination. And, since I know people, I was told that it would be available on New Year's Eve, if you could arrange the proper security for the wedding." He laughed. "I wanted to tell the university president that there'll be so many guns at this wedding he wouldn't have to worry about that. But what I did tell him was that you would hire campus security for the event and pay them time and a half for coming out on New Year's Eve. The president even said that, if you wanted to do a small reception in the hallway for about an hour after the wedding, that would be fine as long as everything was over by midnight. He also said that it would be great if you would invite the fifty or so students who usually are on campus because their homes are far away. So, what do you think?"

Ila walked down the aisle and got misty eyed. She had known there was a chapel on campus in which any denomination could be married, but she hadn't thought there was any way she would be able to get married in any chapel on New Year's Eve. When she got near the altar, she sat on the first pew and cried. Stephen walked down and sat beside her. He said, "Brock is a good friend of mine. I knew it would be hard with his schedule to plan a wedding or make it too complicated. This would be perfect for both of you, I think. It seats a hundred twenty-five people. I know fifty kids are a lot, but all fifty won't come, and I have no idea how many people you and Brock would invite. The president also said that the side gate would be left open for your guests to enter and exit. And there are dressing rooms you and Brock can use if you want to. I had no idea how many people you were going to have involved, so I didn't take that off the table just in case it would work for you." He continued, "But, there is a catch—there's a fee of a thousand dollars for using the chapel, and you will have to use the catering company that does food for the university, which will probably cost you another two thousand. The catering company will take care of all the arrangements for the reception. There will be seating for fifty people, but mostly there will be table tops since the reception is only going to last for an hour."

As he was talking, Ila was adding up the total in her head. They could probably do the entire wedding for $6,000, including her dress, his tuxedo, a tuxedo for his best man, dresses for Paula and Eugenia, flowers, food, and so forth. It might go to $7,000, but Ila was going to try to keep it to $6,000. She looked up at Stephen and said, "I'm overwhelmed with your generosity and your kindness. This would be perfect for Brock and me! I cannot tell you what a relief it is to have all this tied up in a bow without having to seek out places, caterers, arrangements for parking ... so many details! My cup runneth over. Thank you so much." She paused and then thought of something else. "Did they say when we had to pay for these accommodations?"

Stephen said, "The catering company will need a deposit, and the school would appreciate payment for the chapel and security thirty days before the wedding." All Ila could do at this point was to hug Stephen as hard as she could. This had made it possible for her to marry the man she loved without any hassle. She released her bear hug, wiped her eyes, and prayed that her mascara had stayed in place. Stephen said, "The students will be here for chapel soon, so we'd better go."

They took the long walk back to the front door. Outside, they turned right to go back to the car. As they were exiting the building, Ila told Stephen that she wanted to stop by the cafeteria for coffee and a bagel. He laughed and turned into his other persona as they existed the building—he no longer spoke. Rather, he was a man who was deaf and could read lips. He walked to the car while Ila made a left turn toward the cafeteria. She was so excited she felt like jumping up and down, but since that was so much out of her character, she felt it was not wise. She didn't want anyone calling the people in the white van to pick her up. She laughed out loud.

As Ila turned the corner to the cafeteria, she saw Eugenia entering the cafeteria. She picked up her pace so that she could tell Eugenia the good news. She went through the door, spoke to the security guard, and made her way over to the coffee station where Eugenia was standing. Ila tapped her on the shoulder. Eugenia turned quickly and said, "Hey! How are you?"

"Fine! And I have great news."

"What news would that be? That you and Brock are getting married on New Year's Eve?"

Ila stood there with her mouth hung open. "How did you know?"

"The maintenance man and I went together to the president to work out the accommodations. Are you happy with what the president agreed to?"

"Yes, yes, yes!" said Ila. "And I want you to be in my wedding along with my girlfriend, Paula."

There was silence from Eugenia. She turned around and continued to make her coffee. Ila thought, *Does she have tears in her eyes? I must be seeing things.* Eugenia turned back around after she regained her composure and said, "I would be honored. I have never been asked to be in a wedding before. Let me know the details—you know, color, shoes, and so forth, soon so that I can fit that kind of girly stuff into my calendar."

They both laughed, and Eugenia walked off. Ila got her bagel and coffee. She knew she should not be having anything else until lunch, but who can stay away from roasted coffee accompanied by a homemade Jewish bagel, toasted with peanut butter? Nobody. She gathered up her second breakfast and began walking to her office.

When she arrived, there were three students sitting outside on the bench waiting to see her. It was going to be a long day, but she enjoyed listening to the students about their problems, especially their love lives, and making them understand that, no matter what, it would all work out. They just had to get the details straightened out and they could solve whatever problem they were having. She greeted the students and asked them to wait just a minute until she opened her office and prepared for the day. She turned on the lights, secured her purse, turned on her computer, and was ready for the day. She looked at her telephone and saw the light blinking, notifying her that there were messages. She decided to listen to the messages before her day got started just in case there was something she needed to respond to right away. The first message was about a mandatory fire drill for the building on Friday at two o'clock: "Be prepared to evacuate the building and secure your safe and office before leaving the building." The second message was about the debate team having their annual debate workshop in December. The professor wanted to know if Ila would moderate the debate. The third message was from Hunter: "Hello, Ila. Just wanted to let you know that the clock is ticking. I need to know that you are going to be available to me when I return to the country. Hope you have a wonderful day." Ila held the phone for a second and remembered how her feet had gone cold earlier in the morning. She wondered if he was back in the country already. She believed he could talk his way out of any assignment, but Brock had taken care of Hunter, so she was not going to give him anymore space in her brain. All she wanted to do was get the wedding preparations finished so that, in six weeks or so, she would be Mrs. Ila Montgomery-Covington.

Ila hung up the phone and opened her office door so that she could begin seeing students. The line had grown to about eight in that short period of time. She saw each student one by one, and each had unique circumstances to discuss with her. One needed a secure phone card so that she could reach her parents who were working for the State Department in the Netherlands. Another had a situation with a professor about a report that was turned in on time but received points off for being late according to the professor. Others were checking up on how they could change roommates for one reason or another. And yet others just wanted to talk. The day went by swiftly. Before Ila knew it, it was three o'clock—just another two hours before it would be time to go home. She knew the cafeteria was closed while the staff prepared dinner for the students, but all she needed was a cup of tea. She secured her desk and walked to the door. Just as she was about to leave, the door opened. It was the maintenance man.

He walked in pushing his cleaning cart. With his head, he beckoned her to go back to her desk. As she sat down, she wondered what in the world he could want. After the great news he had given her that morning, it must not be good news by the look on his face. He turned and locked the door. Stephen walked back to Ila's desk and said "Hunter has a ten o'clock flight tonight at Dulles airport. He's on his way to Cameroon then on to Libya, and he wants to see you to talk about your future."

Ila could not reply. *How in the world had Hunter reached the maintenance man? His tentacles were long and wide.*

Stephen continued, "I'm supposed to drive you to the airport. We are supposed to meet him at the international baggage carrousel of United Airlines."

She finally caught her breath. "Okay," she said, "I need to put an end to the madness. We'll leave at five. It will take us an hour and half to get there through the traffic. We should get there at around six thirty. We can meet him at seven and be out of there well before eight."

Stephen stood there for a minute, and then he replied, "I will not let you out of my sight. I don't think you really know Hunter."

"I know Hunter very, very, well. I just need to play my cards right with him—keep him off guard."

"I'll be back in an hour to pick you up," said Stephen. He turned and slowly walked out the door. Ila could not remember why she had been leaving her office. The news about Hunter had left her uneasy. Hunter could be mean and forceful. All Ila wanted to do was keep him at bay until she was Mrs. Ila Montgomery-Covington. She decided she didn't have to leave her office after all, so she decided to finish up some paperwork. The maintenance man would be back in an hour. Unfortunately, however, she could not focus on her paperwork because her mind kept going over why Hunter would want to see her. Was he still trying to make trouble for Brock? It was incredible to her how all the men were connected when, in fact, in the beginning, she'd had no idea. Then her mind drifted off to the wedding. What color dress? Silver. What color tux? Maybe silver jacket with tails and black pants? Eugenia and Paula would wear silver or black. She started to write it all down so she would not forget. There was so much going on.

Just as she finished, there was a knock at the door, and the maintenance man came in. "Are you ready?"

"Yes." She took just a minute to straighten up her desk, turn the dial on the combination lock, grab her purse and keys. When she was ready, she walked toward the door with her keys in her hand.

Stephen said, "I got it. Remember—I'm the maintenance man." They both laughed. She went through the door and so did he, and he locked it. They walked down the hallway to the back of the building where Stephen had parked the car. She was glad that the Company did all of the maintenance on the vehicle so she would not have to. She trusted that Stephen knew that he could not drive a car that was not in great condition. He had to be prepared for any situation he might find himself in. He opened the back door, and Ila slid onto the backseat. She really could get used to being driven around. As they pulled off Stephen asked, "Do you have your weapon?"

"I try very hard not to leave home without it," she replied, and they both laughed. They were in traffic for some time before they were able to reach Interstate 66. Stephen had WHUR on the radio. That station always played great music, so the ride was comfortable and relaxing. It became not so comfortable when Ila saw the signs that said Dulles Airport 15 miles. She could feel her blood pressure start to rise. She quickly calmed herself down. One hour, and she'd be out. Stephen would be there waiting for her.

Stephen pulled into the short-term parking lot and found a space quickly. He backed into the space, as that was the rule—never put yourself in a situation where you must back out. He smiled. Never forget your training, he thought to himself. He got out of the car to open the door for her when a young man on a golf cart pulled up alongside the car. Stephen quickly closed Ila's door and felt to make sure his gun was holstered. He walked back to the front of the car. He asked the young man, "Is there something I can do for you?"

The young man said, "I'm here to take your passenger to her destination."

"Credentials, please," Stephen replied.

The young man pulled up his left shirt sleeve. On his arm there was a tattoo of a compass.

Stephen looked to make sure that, under the compass, were the Pentagon latitude and longitude. He asked the young man, "Where are you taking my passenger?"

"To the security office on the lower level of baggage claim. We have only two hours before takeoff, so your passenger will be back within the hour."

"What is your name, soldier?"

"Spencer," the soldier replied.

Stephen reached for his gun, but Spencer immediately said loud, "Sir, I have given you all the credentials I can give you at this point. You must know that I'll bring Ms. Montgomery back within one hour. If she is not back within one hour, you know the drill. You should return to your post and forget you were here."

Stephen nodded and walked back to the car to open the door for Ila. He explained the situation. Ila had not been able to hear the conversation, but she had looked at the tattoo on the young man's arm. It was the same tattoo that Hunter, Brock, and Eugenia had. Rodney had had it too. When Ila got out of the car, Stephen explained that he would not be going with her, but this young soldier would be taking her to her destination and bringing her back within one hour.

Ila looked at Stephen and said, "Is there anything else I should know? Should I be afraid?"

"I'll be here waiting for you. One hour. Leave your purse and your gun if you have it with you."

"Leave my gun and my purse?"

"Yes."

Ila took her purse from her shoulder and handed it to Stephen. "You will be here when I get back?"

"I'll be right here."

Ila walked to the golf cart and got in. She did not engage in conversation with the young soldier. Her stomach suddenly was on fire, and she felt as if she might throw up. The young soldier reached to the side of the cart and handed her a can of soda. She looked at him as if to say, "How the hell did you know I was about the throw up?"

He looked at her and smiled and said, "You will be back within the hour." The road to the end of the arrival area went around the back to a checkpoint. At the checkpoint, the soldier showed his airport badge and the guard let him through. The golf cart rounded the corner, and the soldier parked at a door that was labeled Security. He got out of the cart and assisted Ila to get out also. He swiped his badge on a security pad, and the door opened to a small hallway. He pushed the door open. "Go to the end of the hallway," he told Ila, "and enter the office marked Security."

She looked at the young soldier and said, "You are not accompanying me to the office?"

"I'll be on the other side of this door. It's now nineteen hundred hours. Please make your way back by twenty hundred.

"What if he doesn't let me come back?"

"You know the drill. I'll leave this area and act as if I had never been here. You know if he decides to put you on the plane with him, there is nothing I can do."

"I'll be back in an hour. Please wait for me." He nodded his head and closed the door.

Ila walked slowly down the hallway. When she got to the security office, the door slowly opened. She should have known there were cameras in the hallway, and he would know the minute she was outside the door. She smiled at Hunter, who by the way, looked good as hell in an all-black suit and black-and-white shoes. He smiled and asked her to have a seat. He got right to the point. He offered her a glass of wine or water. Ila chose the wine since she found herself to be a little nervous. She looked around the room wondering how he had got security to leave their base for an hour. She just smiled to herself. She knew his reach was far and wide.

He poured her a glass of wine and started in on his fairytale story about their lives. "Well," he said, "you know Brock tried to get me shipped away for two years, but he doesn't understand that the tables will turn on him soon, and he'll be the one going away for two years. I thought you should know that so that we can now plan our wedding. I'd like to get married at Mt. Zion Methodist Church on Sixteenth Street—a formal evening wedding with a candlelight service. We'll have a formal reception immediately following at the Intercontinental Hotel on Pennsylvania Avenue. Here is the checkbook to the account I have set up for you to take care of the financial responsibilities. Oh, yes, we want an open bar one hour before the reception with finger foods—your choice. And the bar should be open for two hours during dinner. After that, the guests will have to pay cash for their drinks. The dinner will include a soup or salad, fish, beef, or chicken, vegetable medley, mashed or baked potato, champagne on every table. No wedding cake, but three different types of cake—red velvet, lemon cake, and chocolate cake with chocolate icing. And, please do not forget the chocolate fountain, where people can dip apples, bananas, strawberries, and other treats."

Ila sat quietly, nodding her head. She took the checkbook out of his hand. He said, "Please make the date sometime in February or March. By that time I'll be back in the States and will be able to help you arrange things. But for now, you have your marching orders."

Ila sat quiet waiting for more orders. She sat and sipped her wine as she tried not to look at the clock in the office. She had only thirty more minutes to be in the same room with this narcissistic asshole. He finally sat down and poured himself a glass of wine. He looked at Ila for a few minutes, and then he began to rub his dick as he looked at Ila with lust. He said, "Please take off your pants and panties and come over here and sit on this big black dick that you love so much." Ila did not move. He said, "Put down your wine, take off your pants and panties, leave your heels on, walk over here, and sit on my dick."

Ila knew that his next move would be to yank her up out of the chair and force her to sit on his dick. Since time was ticking away, she slowly removed her pants and panties, laid them over the chair, and walked over to his chair with her heels on. She stood in front of him and reminded him that she had no protection and was not taking the pill. He stood up, pulled a condom out of his pocket, dropped his pants, and asked Ila to suck his dick and then place the condom on it. She got on her knees and placed his dick in her mouth, slowly sucking the head and then taking his entire dick into her mouth slowly. Now she knew this was the time to just bite it, but the truth was, she was afraid of Hunter. She took his balls into her hand and messaged them slowly and placed her middle finger into his asshole, knowing that's what he liked. He moaned with pleasure, and before Ila knew what he was doing, he had turned around and bent over the chair so that she could put more than one finger up his ass. The entrance to his asshole had gotten moist, and two fingers slid right in. He then said, "Use your thumb." Ila took her two fingers out of his ass and replaced them with her thumb. He bent over more. Ila thought he was going to touch his toes. She forced her thumb in and out of his asshole, slowly at first and then with more force. He had grabbed his own dick at this point and was rocking it slowly back and forth with his hand. The rocking became faster and faster as Ila forced her thumb deeper and deeper into his ass. Suddenly his butt cheeks got tight. Ila thought her thumb would fall off. He moaned, and there it was all over the chair. She was grateful that he had come so that she would not have to have intercourse with him. Ila stood to her feet and walked backwards to her chair to place her panties and pants back on. Hunter stood over the chair still releasing a huge stream of semen all over the chair. She thought, *Whoever sits in that chair might get pregnant.* She laughed to herself. He finally turned around, pulled up his underwear and pants, and walked to the bathroom. Ila heard the water running, and he returned with a handful of soapy paper towels. He began washing down the chair. Ila quickly finished putting on her clothes and sat back in the chair to finish her wine. She placed the checkbook in her bra and sat quietly.

After he had sufficiently washed down the chair, he returned to the bathroom to discard the towels. It was 7:55 p.m. *Great. Five more minutes.* He returned from the bathroom, walked over to her chair, and told her to stand up. He held her close and whispered in her ear, "If you fuck up my career, you will live to regret it."

Ila, for once in her life, said nothing. There was a knock at the door. Hunter called out, "Come in." The young lady at the door announced that Ila had to leave now so he could get through security and to get on the plane for first-class boarding. He replied, "Close the door. I'll be right out, and you can escort me to the appropriate gate to board." The door closed slowly. Hunter turned slowly to Ila and kissed her on the cheek. He picked up his duffle bag and walked toward the door. He turned and said, "Your ride will be at the back door waiting for you at the end of the hallway. I'll be in touch." With that, he walked out the door.

Ila could hear voices coming toward the door, and just like that the door opened and two women came in. They began to clean up the office, corking the wine, taking the glasses to the bathroom to wash them, and placing the wine in the small refrigerator. Ila stood still like a statue for what seem like minutes but was really seconds. She headed for the door, and the ladies said good-bye.

Ila made a left out the of the door and walked down the same hallway that had brought her to the security office. When she got to the back door, it slowly opened and there was Spencer waiting for her. She slowly got into the golf cart. He said nothing and did not ask any questions. They rode in silence back to the short-term parking lot. As they got closer to the car, Stephen got out of the car and waited for them to arrive. Stephen greeted Spencer and asked Ila if she was all right. Ila nodded as she got out of the cart. She thanked Spencer for bringing her back safely. Then she slowly walked toward the car. Stephen thanked the young man, and Spencer turned the golf cart around and headed back in the direction he'd come from. Stephen skipped to get to the back door to open it for Ila. She waited and got in after he opened the door. When she was in, he closed the door and walked fast to the driver's side to begin the drive back to Georgetown.

They rode in silence. As they were crossing into DC, he said, "Did everything go well?"

"Hunter is Hunter."

He nodded and left that conversation alone. Back at the apartment, he parked in the alleyway and told Ila to get her keys out of her purse. She did as he asked. He said, "I'm going to watch you climb the steps and go inside. Once you're inside, please go through the apartment and then flicker the lights for an all clear signal."

Ila nodded and got out of the car. She walked ten feet to the steps and climbed them slowly. She opened the back door and went inside. She turned on the lights in the hallway and walked all through the apartment, even checking the closets and the bathroom. When she was done, she flicked the back light on and off so Stephen could go home. He had to be at the school early, and then he had to come back and get Ila. Not that he had to, but that is what he had been doing. She could hear him drive out the back of the alley because the driveway turned to gravel at the back end of the alleyway.

Ila was exhausted. She went to the bedroom, took off her clothes, threw the checkbook into one of the boxes of clothes, and got into bed. She got right back up, however, as going to bed with makeup on was a taboo. Ila could hear her grandmother in her head: "Ila, makeup left on overnight means blackheads in the future." She walked slowly to the bathroom and thought about the very strange evening. Her stomach reminded her that she had not eaten. After washing her face and smoothing on a light moisturizer, she walked to the kitchen. She looked at the clock and could not believe it was only 10:00 p.m. She felt as if it was after midnight.

She filled the tea kettle and put it on the stove to boil. Ila knew that there was very little in the refrigerator, and she'd probably had to settle for a peanut butter and jelly sandwich. She opened the refrigerator, and holy shit! It was filled! She had forgotten how well the Company took care of her and Brock. What would she do when she had to go grocery shopping for herself? So, instead of peanut butter and jelly, she could have a cinnamon raisin bagel toasted with peanut butter. She laughed out loud as the tea kettle started to sing. Ila made the tea, pulled the bagel out of the toaster, and lathered it with fresh peanut butter—just enough to squeeze out the sides. What a big kid she was. She ate the bagel drank the tea in silence. It was different being there alone—no TV on, no radio playing. Brock likes noise. She thought it distracted him from all the thinking he did in his head. She remembered the promise he had written:

I promise to take care of you.

I promise to complete your happiness.

I promise to be your partner, friend and lover.

I promise to protect you.

I promise to give you unconditional love.

I promise to be a dedicated husband and father to our children.

Lastly, I promise to keep your heart from hurt, harm or danger.

Ila walked to the bedroom, rolled into the covers, thanked the Creator, and fell asleep.

Brock could not believe all the things he'd found out about the police chief. He wanted to wrap up all the details and get back to Ila and that cozy apartment in Georgetown. He was working in a small office in the lower level of the Pentagon. There weren't many people around, but it was a nice and quiet workplace, so he would soon be finished with the report he was putting together, and he could put an end to this part of his life and go on to a new assignment. The office was equipped with a TV, a computer, and a refrigerator. The bathroom was just down the hall. Brock was not a computer man. He had turned it on a few times to connect to the intranet to get information, but other than that, he preferred to do all his background work by typing it on the typewriter or writing it out in long hand. He was sure that, when he was done, whatever young assistant who had to type everything up would not be happy. He knew that Hunter was pissed and that he would have to use all his connections to keep him in Libya until after he and Ila were married.

Brock went back to his work and tried to stop thinking about the what-ifs in his life. He had been at it for about three hours when there was a knock on the door. In walked the four-star general, Jefferson Owens. *Shit. What could this be about?* Brock stood at attention, and the general said, "At ease."

Brock took his seat and the four-star continued to stand. Brock said, "Would you like to have a seat, sir?"

"No. I have a special request from the US representative to the North Atlantic Treaty Organization (NATO). He is going to NATO headquarters in Brussels on special assignment for a month, and he needs a body guard. As you are one of a handful of people who have a NATO clearance, we wondered if you would be willing to accept this assignment."

Brock replied, "Are you asking me or telling me?"

"I'm giving you a chance to say yes before I tell you that it's mandatory for you to take this assignment."

"No disrespect, sir, but I'm planning on getting married in a couple of months, and I wanted to be in the United States to assist with the planning." Of course, that was a lie, but if it worked.

General Owens replied, "This is November. When are you planning on getting married?"

"The date hasn't been set because I'm on assignment. I didn't want to set a date until I knew my time would be free and clear."

"Well, you'd better drill down and get the wedding scheduled. The US representative to NATO wants to begin his special assignment in Brussels in January—around the fifteenth of the month."

Brock replied, "It will be done, and I would be honored to accept this assignment."

"I don't have to tell you that this type of assignment doesn't come along every day. The Company will take care of you when you return as long as you return the representative back to the States safely. I believe that you are the right man for this assignment, and I have full confidence that you will be able to guard him with your life. You'll receive orders in the next couple of days with dates, flight times, and so forth. You're a good man, Covington. Your career is about to soar." And, with that he turned around and walked out the door. Hunter looked around the room for his beeper. He began to type: 9, 14, 5, 5, 4, 20, 8, 5, 4, 1, 20, 5 ("I need the date"). He thought that Ila should be up by now and moving around. Ten seconds later his beeper went off: 453, 31 "(December 31"). He replied: 7,18, 5, 1, 20 ("Great")

Ila jumped up! She was excited that Brock was interested in the date she'd suggested for their wedding. He'd sounded so uninterested before; it seemed he'd just wanted to get it done. She was happy he had finally come around. Maybe he'd even want to get more involved with the wedding planning. She sent him another number text: "I love you."

She walked down to the kitchen to put the kettle on for tea. It seemed lately that she preferred tea in the mornings. Probably because it was cold outside, and tea was very soothing. She went through her routine—clothes in the bathroom to let the steam get the wrinkles out, shower on, pee, shit, and jump into the shower before the water went cold. She knew that Brock was not far away, but he might as well be in China since she was unable to see him. The apartment was so quiet. She thought, *Today I'm going to listen to WHUR while I'm getting dressed.* She walked down the hall to the living room and saw an envelope that had been left on the couch. Whoever had left this envelope had no idea that it might be days before she walked into the living room. She picked up the envelope, which must have been left when an operative came to replenish the supplies in her refrigerator. Brock's name was on the front of the envelope. She wondered if she should open it but decided to take it back to the bedroom and put in the closet until Brock returned.

Brock felt better that the wedding was going to be on December 31, but he had no idea how he was going to tell Ila that he would be leaving two weeks after their wedding on TDY. He would make it up to her on the honeymoon. But he had to tell her that the honeymoon could not be more than a week. He would plan to meet her in Crystal City again, and he would tell her next week. He got back to the business at hand, and that was wrapping up the paperwork on the death of Chief Warren Chambers.

For some reason Ila just could not get it into gear. Before she knew it, Stephen was knocking at the back door. He knocked three times and left. She ran to put on her shoes. She tossed her gun into her purse, and she found her ID, which she'd left in another jacket pocket. She put on her blue pea coat and grabbed her keys. Money. She had no money. She would have to ask the cafeteria lady to put breakfast on her tab until she went to the bank. She had everything—purse, gun, shoes, and tennis shoes—in a bag just in case Stephen could not bring her home. She checked the stove and went out the front door to walk around to the alleyway. *Never leave a building the same way each day.* But that was hard considering there were only two doors. Ila did sometimes remember the rule, but it had slipped her mind. It seemed to have slipped Stephen's mind also.

She secured the double lock on the door and looked down to the corner. Stephen had driven out of the alleyway and parked at the end of the street. All of this had happened without communication. Ila crossed the street and walked in the other direction. Stephen made a U-turn in the street, and caught up with Ila about a block away. She was grateful because she was wearing her heels. He pulled up along the curb, and Ila got into the backseat. "Good morning," she said.

Stephen replied, "Brock would like to see you sometime this week. Good morning. I'll let you know a day in advance of when and where."

Ila nodded. They drove the rest of the way in silence. He pulled up to Healy Hall, and Ila got out of the car. Stephen got out of the driver's side and said, "You might want to start getting some exercise." He laughed and got back into the car. *What was he saying?* Well, it was clear that she had not been doing any exercise. So, he was right. During her lunch break, she would put on her tennis shoes and walk once around the track. That was probably all she could do at that point. She laughed out loud as she climbed the stairs to enter Healy. She walked to her office, unlocked the door, and placed her purse in the desk. She did not unlock her safe because she needed to go get coffee and a bagel. She walked back out of her office door and locked it. The doors at Healy Hall were huge and weighed a ton. Ila thought, *If I stand in front of my office and open the door back and forth for about a hundred times a day, it would build up the muscles in my arms so they would look really good by December thirty-first.* She could not believe that her wedding was less than thirty days away. How exciting. She walked quickly to the cafeteria, spoke to the security guard, and walked over to the cashier. She knew her name was Ms. Miller, but they'd never really had a conversation except for a cordial good morning. There was a line of customers ahead of Ila, so Ila decided to get her coffee and her toasted bagel with peanut butter. Then she would have a conversation with Ms. Miller. She stood in line and waited her turn. When she reached the front of the line, she explained her situation about having no money. Ms. Miller said, "Here is a form. Complete it and bring it back tomorrow. We can take your cafeteria bill out of your paycheck so that you don't have to worry about money, Ms. Ila."

Ila smiled because she didn't know the woman knew her name. "Thank you so much," Ila replied. She wondered why no one had told her about that policy. She shook her head and decided that it was not that important. She walked out of the cafeteria and told the security guard to have a nice day. She wanted to sit down and eat her bagel, but she thought it was getting late. She would have enough time to eat it at her desk. She walked down the hall quickly. She always forgot what a balancing act it was to get her keys in the door while holding the coffee and bagel at the same time. As she got close to the door, Stephen was leaving the maintenance closet. He walked over to the door and opened it. He laughed, held the door open, and let Ila walk through.

The day went by with no unusual events. Ila was grateful for a day that had no surprises. As she was packing up her desk the phone rang. She answered it: "Ila Montgomery."

"Hey, lady! This is Paula. How you doing?"

"Hi," Ila said. "What you up to?"

"I thought we'd better go shopping and look for our dresses," Paula replied.

All of sudden there was a smile on Ila's face so wide, anyone looking at her would be able to see her tonsils. She replied, "Yes! Yes! Let's go. Where shall I meet you?"

"Meet me in Alexandria in Old Town at Rita's Italian Restaurant."

"Great. I'll meet you there at five thirty. What time does the store close?"

"Don't worry. It will be open for us."

"Okay! See you there." Ila hung up the phone and finished packing up her desk. She might have to walk to the Metro if Stephen was still working. But that was not a problem. She had her tennis shoes in her bag. But it was cold. She was hoping to find Stephen so that he could drive her to Alexandria. Just as she finished clearing her desk and was walking to the safe to lock it, the door opened.

Stephen waited until the door closed and said, "You ready to go?" Stephen said.

She jumped. "Are you done with work for the day? Because Paula and I are going to shop for wedding dresses."

"Yes, done for the day. Where are you going?" Ila told Stephen that she was meeting Paula at Rita's in Old Town. He nodded and asked Ila if she was ready. She locked the safe, picked up her purse, bag, and keys and was ready to go. Stephen opened the door and used his keys to lock it behind them.

As they turned the corner, headed toward the back parking lot, they ran into Eugenia. "Hey, there," Ila said. "Paula and I are going to Old Town to look for wedding dresses. Do you want to come?"

Eugenia said "I wear a size nine dress and nine shoes. No, I do not want to go shopping, but I really want to be in the wedding, so help a sister out and get all that I need. I'll pay you for it."

"Come on," Ila said. "It'll be fun."

Eugenia looked at Ila as if to say, "You know I don't shop."

"Okay. Okay. I'll let you know if we find anything," said Ila. Eugenia looked at her and smiled. Yes, that is exactly what she wanted to hear. Ila and Stephen walked toward the car while Eugenia headed back toward the building. Stephen looked back at Eugenia with a puzzled look on his face. Ila did not respond one way or the other. All she wanted to do was get a dress.

Traffic in DC is always terrible, but Stephen knew all the right bridges to cross and the back roads to get to Alexandria, Virginia, from Georgetown. It still took about forty minutes to get to their destination in rush-hour traffic. Ila was sure Paula would wait for her. They slowly rolled down King Street until they arrived at Rita's. There was no sign of Paula. Stephen said, "There is nowhere to park here. Shall I go around the corner to see if there's additional parking?"

Ila replied, No. I'll jump right here. Can you meet me back here later, or is your evening tied up?"

Stephen replied, "I have to go back to the university for about an hour and finish something up. What time do you think you will be finished?"

"About nine? I'm sure the store doesn't stay open past then on weekdays." Ila replied.

Stephen nodded his head and said, "I'll be in front of Rita's at nine. Ila jumped out of the car and headed toward Rita's. She could feel Stephen looking at her in his rearview mirror as he drove slowly away. When he saw Paula coming out of the restaurant, he sped off.

Ila hugged Paula hard when she saw her. They had been through so much together; this was a special occasion for them to be together celebrating. They stood there for a minute exchanging the usual conversation. Paula took Ila's hand, and they began walking down King Street. Ila did not ask any questions. She trusted that Paula knew exactly what she needed because they had known each other for so long. They got to a small side street that had residential houses on it. Again, Ila did not ask any questions.

Paula had been born and raised in Virginia. She knew her way around the area and probably knew quaint places where the perfect dresses could be found. They walked and talked and came upon a little house that looked like a fairytale gingerbread house. The sign outside said Ms. Virginia's Sewing Shop.

They walked up to the front door, and Paula rang the bell. They were buzzed in. Ila looked around as they entered and noticed that there were security cameras all around the little house and at the front door. As they entered, they were greeted by a woman who looked to be in her sixties. She was dressed in a lime-green tailored pant suit with a mint-colored scoop-necked blouse. She called Paula's name out loud and walked quickly forward to greet her. "Hi, Aunt Virginia", Paula said

The lady replied, "It's so nice to see you! How is your mother?"

"She's well."

"How are you doing?" asked the lady. "I heard you lost your boyfriend. I'm so sorry. You were together for a very long time."

"Yes. It's been difficult. Not sure if I'm going to move or stay in the apartment we were sharing."

"Remember that I have that small apartment complex in Southeast DC. It is not the best, but you know your uncle takes really good care of it, and there's security and free parking. I believe we'll have an opening right after the first of the year, and you are more than welcome to live there."

Paula's eyes welled up, and she hugged the lady. "Oh, where are my manners?" Paula turned to Ila. "Aunt Virginia, this is my really good friend, Ila. She is the one getting married."

Aunt Virginia gave Ila a bear hug. For a moment, Ila's eyes welled up. It had been a long time since she had felt a motherly hug. She had been away from her mother and father for so long, the hug really felt good. "It is so nice to meet you," said Aunt Virginia. "And I have something very special to show you. Paula has told me all about you, and I came up with a design for your wedding dress that I think you'll really like. She also has a concept for her own dress and for the other lady. I'll need to know her size before you leave today, and she'll have to come by and be fitted."

Aunt Virginia began to walk into a back room, so Ila and Paula followed her. They entered a room that Ila never thought could be in that gingerbread house. It was full of manikins wearing beautiful wedding dresses—some beaded, some lacey. Some had full trains. There were other dresses in a variety of colors. It was like being in a Paris boutique. Ila walked around with her mouth hanging open. She loved the lace and fine wear, but she was hoping that Aunt Virginia knew that was not what she was looking for. While she was walking around, Paula and Aunt Virginia disappeared. Ila sat in a chair until they returned, each carrying a black clothing bag. Ila remained in the chair.

Aunt Virginia removed a beautiful silver dress out of the bag she was carrying. It was not yet completed, but it was ready for Ila to try on. Ila said to Aunt Virginia, "I'm a size twelve—possibly fourteen." Aunt Virginia said, "I know." Ila smiled. The dress was a simple silver knit. It was off the shoulder, long sleeved, and had a belted waist. The hem would come to the top of her shoes. Also in the bag was a silver beaded shawl to wrap around her shoulders since it was probably going to be cold. Finally, Aunt Virginia produced a beaded comb that would hold a short silver veil. The veil would fall to her shoulders. Ila was thrilled. This was *all* just what she wanted, and the guys could wear silver tuxedo jackets with black pants, shoes, and shirts. And they could wear silver bow ties. It was going to be wonderful.

Paula opened her bag. Her dress and Eugenia's were also very simple—black knit, off the shoulder, long sleeve, hem at the top of their shoes. Their dresses had beaded silver belts. Also in the dress bag were very large combs that were beaded to match the belt that she and Eugenia could wear in their hair.

Aunt Virginia said, "Come on, Ila. Come to the dressing room so I can pin you up. Let me just say that, from this day, you must watch what you eat because this is not the kind of dress that can be let out once it is completed. It will be fitted so you will be able to sit and dance in comfort, but there will be no room for weight gain."

Ila nodded her head and thought she would eat lettuce every day to make sure she got into this dress on New Year's Eve. It was already late November. The wedding was almost only thirty days away. Back in the fitting room, Aunt Virginia pinned the dress to her body. With the dress pinned, she tried on the scarf and the veil. The image in the mirror brought tears to Ila's eyes. She turned from the mirror and big tear drops came down her face.

Virginia ran to the tissue box and said, "No crying on this dress! The material will spot! Stop it!"

Ila took the tissue from her hand and wiped her eyes. She said, "Aunt Virginia, I could not ask for anything more. I'm so grateful to you and Paula for making my dream come true.

At that moment, Paula came of out of the dressing room with her dress on. That was the moment Ila knew that this was really going to happen. Paula looked stunning. She carried a picture of Drew in her hand and said. "Ila, he would want to be with us." Ila lost it at that point, and Aunt Virginia worked to get the dress off her as fast as she could.

Paula began to cry too, and Aunt Virginia said, "Girl, go get out of the dress before you ruin it." Paula began to laugh and ran back into the dressing room to remove her dress. Aunt Virginia unpinned Ila and took the dress to her workroom. Ila got dressed and went back out to the open area with all the beautiful dresses. She sat down to wait for Paula. Then it dawned on her—how much was this going to cost? She was doing the numbers in her head when Aunt Virginia and Paula came into the big room, and it was as if Paula had been reading her mind.

Aunt Virginia handed a shoebox to Ila, saying, "To top it off, Cinderella, here are your silver slippers." Ila opened the box. There, nestled in tissue, was a pair of Nine West silver boots decorated with rhinestones, size nine. Paula showed Ila their boots, which were black with silver rhinestones. Aunt Virginia said, "Since you are my niece's best friend, even though I'm an exclusive tailor for most of the dignitaries in DC, I'll not charge you for Paula's dress. For everything else, the cost will be a thousand dollars. I must ask that it be paid in full before I'll release your dresses and shoes."

Ila began to cry again. The cost was within her budget, and the dresses were exquisite. "Paula," Aunt Virginia said, "come get this water bug out of my shop before she wets up everything."

Ila began to laugh. Paula came out of the dressing room laughing. Her dress had already been tailored, and she was taking it home along with her shoes. Aunt Virginia had disappeared and came back with glasses of white wine on a tray. She placed the tray on the table and gave each woman a glass. She held her own up for a toast. Ila and Paula followed her lead. "Believe in love," Aunt Virginia began, "believe in truth, and remember we are all wonderfully made in God's eyes. Congratulations, Ila. Your journey has just begun."

Ila began to cry again. "Oh, God!" Aunt Virginia said. "Get her out of here!" They all stood quietly drinking the wine. Ila was speechless. "I'll call you when I've completed the alternations," Aunt Virginia said. "Please have the other young lady call me and make an appointment for a fitting. I'd like to have the dress completed in two weeks, so if she could come for her fitting next week, that would be wonderful." At that point she handed Ila her card. They finished the wine, and Aunt Virginia ushered them out of the front door. "See you soon!" she said to Ila. Ila turned around and gave her the kind of hug that Aunt Virginia had given Ila when she came through the door. Paula hugged her aunt and thanked her very much.

As they walked out the door, the Cutlass drove up. Okay, so Stephen had followed them to that location and then had gone back to the university. She laughed out loud. Paula said, "Ila what is wrong?"

"Our driver is waiting for us." They both laughed. Stephen got out of the car and opened the passenger door for Ila and the backseat door for Paula. Paula smiled. "You sure do know how to live, Ila." But little did she know that time spent with her friend could be dangerous.

Stephen had timed it perfectly. It was about 8:45 p.m., and it had been a long day for everyone. He did not have to ask Paula where she lived because he knew that it was the same apartment building where Ila lived. He made his way to Arlington, Virginia, to her apartment. There was very little conversation, but he finally did ask, "Well, Ila, do you have a dress?"

Ila replied, "Yes." And yet another tear came down her cheek.

Stephen did not trust Eugenia. He wondered why she was going back to the university after the workday was over. He went around the block and watched, driving slowly behind Paula and Ila to the side street. He watched them go into the house. He knew that Ila knew she was being followed. She saw the Cutlass in one of the windows along the street they had turned onto. No problem, then. She knew that Stephen knew where they were in case he needed to get back in a hurry, or if she sent him a 911 on her beeper. He saw them enter the dress shop and continued down the street to return to the university.

Once there, he decided not to park in his regular spot. He had slipped up and talked while Paula was in the car. He hoped that would not be something that would come back up. He hoped Paula would not talk about the man she'd met with Ila. But she had known Ila long enough to know that talking about Ila or anyone she was associated with could be dangerous.

Stephen also took down the license number of another car that seemed to be following them. It may have been nothing, but he sent the license plate to Brock so that he could trace it. He was at the Pentagon, so a quick trace shouldn't be hard to do. He decided to park around the back where all the maintenance trucks were. He slowly pulled in between two other trucks so the Cutlass could not be seen. He saw Eugenia's car still in the parking lot. Why would she still be on campus at 7:00 p.m.?

As Stephen walked slowly through the parking lot, he spotted Maurice and Eugenia. What the hell could they be meeting about? He hung back and watched them deep in conversation for about ten minutes. Maurice finally walked to his car, which was parked in the same parking lot, and Eugenia turned to walk back into the building.

But she stopped for a minute as if her Spidey sense had been awakened. She turned around and placed her hand on her gun. She looked very intently into the parking lot, but her senses finally seemed to stand down and she seemed to relax. She walked to the door, unlocked it, and went into the building. Stephen waited for about thirty minutes to make sure she was gone before he left the parking lot. He slowly drove with his lights out to the front parking lot and saw that her car was gone. He put his lights on and went through the front gate.

Eugenia had moved her car. She watched as Stephen drove off.

When Stephen dropped Paula off, Paula told Ila that they would talk the next day. Ila was a little worried about Paula being in the apartment by herself, especially as Ila's apartment next door was still empty. She was sure there were some lonely nights ahead for her friend.

As they drove off, Ila asked Stephen, "Do you know how long they're going to pay for my apartment to be empty?"

"When the case of the police chief is closed, they may let you return to your apartment, but more than likely they will move you to a new location. It's hard to say right now. Once Brock takes care of the final paperwork, things for you should be smoother, and the transition will be swift and secure." Stephen drove the car across the 14th Street Bridge once again forgetting that it was the bridge where Rodney had died. Ila did not remind him this time. She had hoped that not using the bridge would soften the memory, but it did not.

Stephen pulled in behind the apartment down the gravel driveway, stopped the car, and let Ila out. It was getting late, and Ila could not wait to relax in the apartment and go to bed. It had been a long but marvelous night. The dresses were perfect, and all the plans were coming together. She would meet with Eugenia tomorrow and let her know she had to go for a fitting at the dress shop. She would probably be mad that she had to go, but how else would the dress fit? She'd have to go down on a Saturday morning and just get it done. The wedding was less than thirty days away.

Stephen got out of the car and opened the back door to let Ila out. He was such a gentleman. Ila wished she knew more about him, but one thing she had learned in her job—the less you know the less you can tell. She got out of the car, hugged him, and thanked him. As she began walking to the stairs, the patrol car came creeping up behind the Cutlass. Stephen jumped into the car and moved it slowly toward the driveway that exited out to the main street. But he wanted to make sure Ila got inside before he left. Ila waved to Stephen and to the police officer as she entered the apartment.

She ran to the bedroom, took off all her clothes, and fell across the bed. She knew she was hungry, but she couldn't get herself up to go get something to eat. She instantly fell into a deep sleep. She woke up at around 11:30 p.m. to a rapping on the back door. *Who the hell would be at the door this time of night?* She reached for her purse and got her gun. She crawled on the floor to the hallway and shouted, "Who is it?"

"Eugenia."

Ila shouted, "What is my last name?"

"Montgomery."

Ila stood up and went to one of the boxes to find a T-shirt. She kept her gun in her hand and walked along the left-hand side of the wall to the door. At the door, she pulled back the curtain to see Eugenia and Officer Waters. She slowly opened the door. Eugenia walked in, and Officer Waters also walked in—slowly. "What in the world do you guys want?" Ila said.

Eugenia replied, "I told Officer Waters that you were getting married in thirty days, and he said it would be a shame not to have one more threesome before you got married. He goes on the day shift next week and won't be able to spend as much time here because there are more oversight officers on duty during the day."

While Ila and Eugenia were talking, Officer Waters had walked into the bedroom, removed his uniform, folded it up, and set his gun on the chair. He was now on his way to the shower. He looked down the hallway and said, "You two need to join me in the shower, and, Eugenia, bring the toy you have in your bag."

Eugenia and Ila looked at each other. Ila said, "Come on … it's late, and I'm tired."

Eugenia replied, "This is the last time. Let's just get it over with."

Ila replied, "When this is all over, you'll have to tell me what this situation is all about."

Eugenia said, "It's all about you." Ila just shook her head. Eugenia walked slowly to the bedroom, removed her clothes, and put her gun under the pillow. Ila walked to the bed and picked up her clothes, folded them, and laid them back into one of the boxes that she had been living out of for months. They could hear the water running, and Ila knew by now it was good and hot. Ila took off her T-shirt and walked with Eugenia into the bathroom. Officer Waters was standing in the shower just waiting for them to join him.

Eugenia had the toy, and Ila wondered to herself, I hope it's waterproof.

Eugenia laughed and said, "Yes, it's water proof." They both laughed, and Ila thought, H*ow did she know what I was thinking?* Eugenia stopped outside of the shower and gave Ila the toy. "Just turn the bottom. There are three settings."

Ila said, "What shall I do with it?"

Eugenia said, "Stick it up his ass."

"What are you going to be doing?"

"Sucking his dick", said Eugenia.

Shit, Ila thought, *this should be very interesting.* Eugenia got into the shower first and immediately got on her knees. The shower was not that big. Ila got in and stood behind Officer Waters with the toy in her hand. He handed her a washcloth, which he had lathered up. He bent over. Eugenia sat all the way at the end of the shower and began to suck his dick. Ila began to slowly wash his ass with the soapy cloth. She made sure his asshole was good and soapy. With her thumb, she slowly entered his asshole, thinking that it would take some time for it to open.

But her thumb slid right in. He was ready. She dropped the cloth onto the floor of the shower and turned on the toy. She slowly pushed the toy into the hole and began slowly pulling it in and out. He moaned with pleasure. Ila decided to get more aggressive and began pushing it in and out with force. He began to scream with pleasure. Ila didn't know how Eugenia was keeping his dick in her mouth. What an expert.

Ila began to laugh. She turned the bottom of the handle on the toy and it was motorized. She started out at level one, while Eugenia left his dick and went to his balls. Slowly in and out. This guy was going crazy. Eugenia left his balls and went back to his dick and Ila went to level two and the toy began to vibrate faster. He turned and shouted "faster." Eugenia looked up at Ila and nodded. Ila turned the dial to level three and jammed it into his asshole as hard as she could. He screamed and came all over Eugenia, screaming, "Bitch, drink this shit!" Eugenia put her mouth back on his dick and drank his semen. He held his dick in his hand and began pumping out the last bit of semen. Ila still had the toy in his ass. She slowly took it out and stood there waiting to see what the next move would be. The toy was vibrating in her hand.

Eugenia stood up, walked around the officer, and took the toy from Ila's hand. She whispered, "You can leave now." Ila stepped out of the shower. She grabbed her towel and went to the small towel cabinet to get towels for Eugenia and Waters. Ila wrapped her towel around herself and walked out of the bathroom. She closed the door and walked slowly down the hall hoping that she would not be called back in. She went to the kitchen. No better time to have a cup of tea. She put the kettle on and waited for it to boil.

Eugenia turned Officer Waters around and told him to touch his toes. He did, and she jammed the toy up his ass again. He placed his long arms up against the back of wall of the shower.

Ila heard Eugenia say, "Who's the bitch now?" Officer Waters did not reply, or Ila did not hear his reply. The kettle was screaming. Ila took it off the burner and made a cup of tea. She decided, since she was wide awake and hungry, why not have a bagel? She laughed out loud as she went to the bread box, got a bagel, and placed it in the toaster. She went to the refrigerator and got grape jam. As she waited for the toaster to pop, she heard the water being turned off and Eugenia and Officer Waters talking as if they had just had dinner. Ila continued her task and sat at the table to enjoy her bagel and tea. She listened as her "guests" chatted as if nothing had just happened. Ten minutes later, Eugenia came to the kitchen and said, "Come lock the door. I'll see you tomorrow at work."

Ila got up, towel still wrapped around her, and walked Eugenia to the door. Officer Waters was already standing at the door waiting. He said to Ila, "Congratulations. It has been a pleasure." He opened the door and walked out. Eugenia turned and looked at Ila and smiled. She then walked out the door, walked down the stairs, and walked up the stairs to her apartment. The officer walked to his car, got in, and drove off. Ila locked the door, turned off the outside light, went to the kitchen, put her bagel in the refrigerator, poured her tea down the drain, walked down the hall to the bedroom, crawled into bed, and fell fast asleep. What a day. What a night.

Brock was falling asleep at his desk. He could not wait for this assignment to be over. He was almost there. Chief Chamberlin was dead, most if not all the evidence had been tagged and recorded. Some evidence was even stamped Secret. There were certain things the public just did not need to know. Brock had decided to stay the course, finish the project, and be done by Christmas. He would then get ready for the wedding and be ready to take off for the honeymoon. He had not decided where it was going to be yet. Ila would love Aruba or Bora Bora—places where they could just be alone for two weeks, drink, make love, and make babies. Brock could not wait to start a family. If he had a family, they would give him a permanent assignment, hopefully in Washington DC, Richmond, or North Carolina. Any one of those places would do. But, with his luck, they would probably have to go to Utah for two years. He did not care, and Ila would not either if they were together. He would call Ila at work tomorrow and tell her that he was going to stay until the assignment was over and then they could be together. He needed to know the colors for the wedding so that he could call his roommate, Morris, and let him know. He would have to fly in the day before. Morris would probably stay with his family members in DC, but he would surely get him a hotel room if he needed it. They could get their tuxedoes from the Men's Wearhouse, which was a new franchise, but they had a large inventory of high-quality clothing. Morris might have to bring his family, but that would be okay too. Brock would call him tomorrow after talking to Ila about the arrangements.

Ila woke up and felt as if she had been drinking the night before. Outside, the day was in full gear—cars, children's voices, students walking by. The sun was shining, but it was cold outside. She wondered if Stephen was coming to pick her up when her beeper when off: 2, 20,8,5,18,5 120, 597820. ("B There At Eight"). Ila said to herself, *I'll really be glad when this cellular phone thing happens.* After decoding, she ran to the kitchen and got a glass of water. She felt super dehydrated that morning. She drank two glasses of water quickly. She would wait and have coffee and a bagel at work. It was already seven o'clock, and Stephen would be there soon. Once again, she was running out of clothes. She did not have to take a shower; heaven knew she had been in water for a long time last night. But she decided a shower would wake her up. She laughed out loud. She walked to the bathroom and turned on the water. It would be about five minutes before it would be hot. She walked into the bedroom and looked into the closet and the boxes. Slim pickings. She would have to do laundry this week. She grabbed a pair of wool gray lined pants from the closet and a long-sleeved turtle-neck sweater from the box. She hung them on hangers so that they could be steamed while she was in the shower. By the time she did all that, the steam was coming from the bathroom. She rushed in, hung everything up, and jumped into the shower. She looked at her body. She would have to do some exercising to tone up a bit before the wedding. She didn't have many days left. She washed up quickly and, remembering the scene in the bathroom last night, she began to laugh uncontrollably. *How the hell? What the hell had happened?* She was so glad she did not have to have sex with anyone; she had just been a participant in a sexual crime. She laughed again.

She exited the shower. She had to get another towel because the one she'd used last night had gone to bed with her. She would have to go get it and hang it up. She washed her face, brushed her teeth, and started her facial regimen—moisturizes toner, foundation, eyeliner, mascara, and lipstick. She looked in the mirror and decided that she would have Paula do her makeup for the wedding. She was very good at it. Getting Eugenia to get her makeup done will be problematic, but she was so beautiful it wouldn't matter. After her regimen, she looked at the clothes and prayed that the wrinkles would had come out. Her hair was growing fast. She would have it cut short for the wedding so that the veil would fit properly. Ila took down the clothes and walked to the bedroom to get dressed. She dug into the box for panties and bra.

She put her tennis shoes and socks and some workout clothes in a bag just in case she got motivated to go to the school gym or to walk the track. She put on her clothes, knee-highs, and pumps. She put her gun, makeup, beeper, and ID into her bag and went to find her belt. Finally, she was ready to go.

Her beeper went off right at 8:00 a.m.: 15,22,20,19,9,4,5 ("Out Side"). She pulled on her leather jacket, grabbed a scarf and gloves, picked up her bag and her purse, and headed for the front door. And there it was—another manila envelope. She picked it up and decided to wait and read it at work. She unlatched the sliding lock and the dead bolt lock and exited the apartment. She had forgotten to put her keys in her hand.

She re-entered the apartment, but eventually found the keys in the bottom of her purse. She exited the apartment again with her keys in her hand. As she turned to lock the door, she could feel someone walking up behind her. She locked the door quickly and headed toward the school walking.

Ila walked fast and felt the person on her heels. She wanted to get to a storefront so that she could see who it was that was following her. She had got about two blocks down the road when Stephen pulled over to the curb, put the car in park, and jumped out. He motioned her to get into the car, which she did quickly. He stood by the car while the gentleman who was following her crossed the street. The man looked back at them with distain. "Oh Shit!" Ila said.

Stephen got back into the car and looked back at Ila. "Who was that?"

"Maurice." They rode the rest of the way in silence.

Ila was spooked. Why would Maurice be in Georgetown? She had thought he was off on assignment like Hunter. She jumped out of the car and walked slowly to her office. Stephen was planning to take the car around to the maintenance parking area. As she placed her key in the lock, Eugenia came out of her office. "Hey there," she said. When Ila turned to look at her, Eugenia said, "What in the world is wrong?"

Ila replied, "I just saw Maurice."

"Hunter's Maurice?"

"Yes," Ila said. She pushed open the office door and turned on the lights. She had her gun out of the holster as she entered the office. Ila turned and locked the door from the inside just in case. The office was clear.

Eugenia sat in the chair and said, "Okay, what shit is about to go down? I thought Maurice was on assignment."

"So, did I," Ila said.

Eugenia knew full well why Maurice was in town. He, of course, had heard about the wedding because there are no secrets in the intelligence community family. He wanted to confront Ila to remind her that Hunter was bi-sexual and that marrying Brock would be best for everyone. Eugenia, of course, had told Maurice to go back to his assignment wherever it was, and to let things happen the way they were supposed to happen.

Hunter would still be overseas when Ila and Brock got married. Maurice and Hunter would be able to live happily ever after. Eugenia told Maurice not to bother Ila. She was not his problem. Hunter was his problem. Any fight he had should be with Hunter, not Ila. She remembered that he had calmed down a bit after their conversation, but to be out stocking Ila—that was another story. Eugenia made a mental note to call the Company and make sure Maurice was back on assignment. He shouldn't be showing his face in a place where there was still an active investigation going on, and Ila was still undercover.

Ila looked at Eugenia and said, "What could he possibly want?"

"Well, he wants you and Hunter to be done with each other so that he can have Hunter all to himself. That's the only thing I can think of."

Ila said, "He can have Hunter; does he not know that by now?"

Eugenia got up and walked toward the door. "Ila, keep your gun close. I'm going to try to find out what the fuck is going on." With that she opened the door and left the office.

Ila sat for a moment to regroup. There was no way she was going to let Maurice and Hunter ruin her day. Even if she had to elope. She placed her purse in the desk, took out her gun, and slid it into the top drawer. She opened the safe so that she could start her day. Just then the phone rang. She ran over to catch it. "Hello?"

"Hi there, Mrs. Covington," Brock said. Ila instantly had a smile on her face. "Stop smiling so hard," Brock said and laughed.

"Hi, Honey. I really love the sound of that name. I can't wait until it is official."

Brock was silent for a moment. "Ila, I'm not going to try to see you before Christmas. I want to stay here and finish this assignment so I don't have to come back until after we are married and have been on our honeymoon."

It was Ila's turn to be silent. She had been looking forward to seeing Brock. A tear trickled down her face.

"Don't cry," Brock said.

"I'm not crying … just a little sad. It's very lonely in the apartment without you, and you said you would be back."

"Ila, it only makes sense. It is just two more weeks, and then the assignment will be over and I'll be all yours until after the honeymoon. By the way, where would you like to go?

"I want to spend two weeks in a five-star secluded place—just the two of us. Throw a dart at the globe, and wherever it lands, that is where we'll go. As long as we're together, it doesn't matter where we are." Then she laughed and added, "As long as it's hot." They both laughed.

"Ila, I'll see you in two weeks. The time will go by really fast." Tears were streaming down her face. She wanted to tell him she was afraid, tell him about Hunter, tell him about Maurice, tell him about the police officer and how she needed his protection. But all she could say was, "Okay, honey. See you in two weeks."

Brock said, "I love you, Ila. Remember my promise. See you really soon." With that he hung up.

Ila stood there with the phone in her hand, hot tears flowing fast and furious down her face, messing up the little bit of makeup she had applied that morning. *Damn it!* was all she could say in her head. She hung up the phone and reached into the bottom drawer of her desk to find tissues. She patted her face, reached into her purse for her makeup bag, replaced her lipstick, patted her face with a makeup sponge, and called it a day. As she was replacing all the makeup items, there was a knock on the door, and a student came in. "Hi, Ms. Montgomery. Do you have a minute?" And thus started the day.

Eugenia was going to call headquarters on the private line to see what the hell Maurice was up to. As she walked slowly to her office, she was glad to see the students waiting in the hallway to see Ila. She turned around and headed to the cafeteria. What a way to start your day, being stocked by a man who wants a man you are supposed to be sleeping with. What a drag. She walked quickly through the cafeteria and picked up coffee and bagel. She knew Ila liked her bagels toasted, but Eugenia had work to do, so she got an untoasted bagel and packets of peanut butter along with the coffee. It would have to do. The lady at the cafeteria register gave her a look because she knew Eugenia would not eat a bagel and certainly not peanut butter in the morning. That made Eugenia laugh. Was she that rigid in her thinking that having a bagel with peanut butter was out of the question?

Eugenia walked swiftly out of the cafeteria, acknowledged the security guard, and walked to Ila's office. There was still a line of students sitting waiting for her. As Eugenia got close to the door, one of the students stood up and opened Ila's door for her.

Ila was in the middle of a conversation with a student when she looked up and saw the coffee, bagel, and peanut butter. Her mouth began to water. Eugenia slowly placed the items on her desk and began to laugh softly. She knew Ila could not wait to get to that food. She probably had not eaten in ten hours. Eugenia quietly walked out of the office and walked across the hallway to her office. She knew that Ila would come out and tell the students she was taking a ten-minute break. If they wanted to wait, okay, but if they wanted to come back, that would be okay also. Most would stay because they had arranged the time in their schedules to be there.

Ila finished up and walked the student to the door. She opened the door and announced that she needed ten minutes. After she gave them options, everyone said in unison that they would wait. She smiled and walked fast back to her desk. Of course, Eugenia had not brought utensils. Ila had to use her finger to spread the peanut butter across the bagel. She didn't care; she was starving. The bad part about being that hungry is that you don't take the time to savor the taste. The food just all goes down very fast.

The day went by swiftly. There were so many students to see. Many had situations she would have to try to resolve, and some just needed a listening ear. Most of the students from overseas had no support and wanted just to know that there was a lifeline out there if they needed it. Ila reassured them that the university's priority was to make sure that each student was safe, secure, fed, housed, and emotionally cared for. There were some that slipped through the cracks, but for the most part the university did an excellent job of providing safety nets for all their students including their overseas students.

The last student left her office at 4:30 p.m. She realized that she had not eaten anything since the bagel Eugenia had brought for her. She had drunk a lot of water, something she was trying desperately to do more of. She began the process of shutting down her office, logging in all the students she had seen, keeping notes about their concerns and what actions steps would be taken to resolve their issues. By the time she logged in all the students and made recommendations for follow-up or resolutions, it was 5:15 p.m.

She could hear her door open slowly. She was almost afraid to look up after the morning she'd had with Maurice. She finally looked up after making sure her gun was within reach. It was the maintenance man, Stephen. He said, "You ready to go?"

"Yes, but I'm starving. Can you take me somewhere to get a bite to eat?"

He nodded. Ila gathered her things, locked the safe, and looked around to make sure there were no papers left on her desk. Some of the material the students discussed was confidential, and she did not want the cleaning people to have access to her paperwork. After one last look, she walked toward the door. Stephen was standing on the outside of the door waiting for her. They walked in silence. She really liked Stephen. He was a man of few words, not because he was pretending not to be able to speak, but because he was crystal clear with the words he did speak, and he was always on time. She never had to worry about where she stood with him. In a few words, he would let her know.

Ila climbed into the back of the car, and Stephen jumped into the front. She finally said, "Stephen, I need to start exercising to make sure I'm able to still fit into my wedding dress on my wedding day. What can we do together?"

He looked in the rearview mirror. "Ila, the university gym is open to the faculty. You can use it anytime. Your ID is the pass key to get in. Just let me know what days you want to go and I'll wait for you. You shouldn't walk home, even in Georgetown, late at night."

"Okay," Ila said. "Next week, I'll start on Monday. I'll do Monday, Wednesday, and Thursday.

"That will be fine,"= Stephen replied.

As they drove past the apartment, she wondered where he was taking her to eat, but he quickly made a right into the back alley of the apartment. He parked in front of the steps.

Ila said, "I thought you were taking me to get something to eat."

"Well, you should start your eating program today. You know there's food in the apartment. Take the time to make yourself something healthy. See you in the morning."

Ila gave him a dirty look and got out of the car. She started up the steps, stopped to get her keys, and again turned around to give Stephen a glare. She continued up the steps and then looked back again. Stephen was laughing. She glared at him again, put the key in the lock, walked into the apartment, and closed the door hard. She froze for a moment because the TV was on. She knew that anyone in the apartment would know she was there because she had just slammed the door. She stood very still, laid all her paraphernalia on the floor, and pulled her gun out of her purse. She removed the safety and held it behind her back.

Brock had gone into the bathroom to take a shower. He wanted to surprise Ila. She was not expecting to see him for several weeks, but he was very horny and had decided to come hold his baby and have quiet, calm, sexy sex. He exited the shower when he heard the door slam. Damn, he'd left his gun in the bedroom. He grabbed a towel, wrapped it around his waist, and hollered, "Ila, its Brock!"

Ila hollered back, "Show yourself!" Brock slowly opened the bathroom door, and Ila slowly brought her gun from behind her back. Brock walked into the hallway slowly, and Ila slowly lowered the gun and put the safety on. She placed the gun on the floor and ran to Brock. She held him close for at least ten minutes. His towel fell to the floor, and his dick was standing at attention. Ila had been at work all day and wanted to take a shower, but Brock gently took her hand and led her to the bedroom. "Please sit here a moment," he said.

Brock walked nude to the front room and checked the front door. Then walked to the back door and placed the dead bolt and picked Ila's gun up off the floor. Back in the bedroom, he placed her gun on the night stand and stood in front of Ila, and she started to cry. Tears streamed down her face. She was so glad to see him she could not talk. He lifted her legs and removed her heels, lifted her up and unbuttoned her pants, removed her sweater. He turned her around to unbutton her bra. Her folded all her clothing and placed them on the floor. He slowly removed her panties, folded them up, and placed them on the floor. Brock took her hand and headed for the bed. Ila wanted to say, "Please let me shower." But she decided not to ruin the moment. He turned the covers back and asked Ila to get in the bed. She did. He in turn got into the bed. He asked her to turn around and place her ass into his dick. She turned around and scooted her ass close to his dick. He slowly entered her pussy from behind. Very slowly, in and out. They could hear the suction of his dick entering her pussy and slowly coming out. Ila's tears became a full cry. He kissed her neck and cupped her breasts. His thrusts became faster but sensitive nonetheless. Ila had bent over completely, and he was almost on top of her, stroking her breast and kissing her neck. She could feel her pussy swell and increase so that his dick could penetrate her entire canal. She screamed, and he shivered and groaned and came. The love making was intense. She so wanted to grab his dick and place it as far down her throat as she could. But instead, she straightened up, and he placed his dick between her legs. He pulled her close and fell asleep. She cried for a few minutes more and then fell into a deep sleep—the kind of sleep she had not had in weeks. And she forgot she was hungry.

The sun peeked through the window, and Brock began to stir. He jumped up, walked into the bathroom, and took a quick shower. He picked up his clothes, which he had left on the floor the night before. He got dressed in the bathroom so that he would not wake Ila up. He'd left his shoes in the living room. He walked quietly into the living room, put on his shoes, picked up his gun, his Pentagon pass, and his briefcase, and he left through the front door. He made sure the door was secured, and he walked swiftly to the Metro station. As he was walking, he could feel someone behind him. He moved swiftly down the escalator so that he could get into a secure position to see who was following him. He heard a car horn blowing as he bounded down the escalator. He had forgotten his beeper at the office.

Stephen had slept in the car that night, knowing that some bad shit might go down with Maurice lurking in the area. As the sun rose, he woke and kept his eye on the front door. He did not know why he thought Brock would leave out of the front door, but that is exactly what he did. As Brock walked swiftly down O Street toward the metro, Stephen saw Maurice get out of a dark-blue sedan. Stephen slowly pulled out of the parking space and drove slowly behind Maurice.

Maurice could feel the tail as he walked, but he was determined to have a conversation with Brock. He picked up the pace. He could see the Cutlass out of the corner of his eye, and knew that Stephen was following him. As Brock got close to the Metro and was about the make his way down the escalator, Stephen started blowing the car horn. Maurice was furious. That would surely spook Brock, and he would be nowhere to be found after Maurice got into the underground Metro. Maurice turned and headed back to his car. Stephen stopped the car and rolled down the window on the passenger side and shouted. "Maurice, make this the last time I see you in this area. We would hate to make one of us a fatal statistic, but we will."

Brock stood behind a pole so that he could see who might come down the escalator or stairs. He let two trains go by. After not seeing anyone that might be of interest, he got on the third train and headed toward the Pentagon.

Ila woke up and found Brock gone. She cried again. How could she not have awakened to see him off? She did not know how exhausted she had been. He had folded up her clothes and placed them on the floor with gentle care. She picked them up and placed them in the dirty clothes basket. It was completely full. She would have to get Stephen to take her to the Laundromat. As she walked slowly to the kitchen to put water in the kettle for tea, her stomach reminded her that she was hungry. She filled the kettle and put it on the stove. She quickly turned to the refrigerator, opened it, and found they had again replenished it with food. She did not know what she was going to do when she returned to her normal life. She would have to go to the grocery store. She laughed out loud. She saw fresh cherries, bananas, oranges. She decided to peel a banana and peel an orange and sit down to enjoy their flavors. The kettle began to whistle. She quickly made her cup of tea. She sat at the table and enjoyed the fruit. She also decided that she would give up bagels every morning, which she thought really did not help her weight-loss efforts. She finished her breakfast and then placed an apple, cherries, another banana, and another orange into a freezer bag. She would take these items to the university and just get a cup of coffee and munch on the fruit during the day.

She looked at the clock on the wall and got up running. Stephen would be here in twenty minutes. She picked up her tea and hurried down the hall. She looked into the closet and again into the box. Options were getting very limited. She decided to wear a pair of black slacks, a red pullover sweater, and a black-and-red scarf. The scarf could use an ironing, so she folded it and placed it in between the mattress and box spring. Her pumps were at the end of the bed, and she had never unpacked her bag yesterday.

Ila ran into the bathroom and turned the shower. She looked in the mirror and had to take a minute to pluck her eye brows as they had grown in quite a bit. Her hair was almost completely black again, and she was not going to lighten it any more. She also had to shave the little hairs that were growing out of her chin. *When had that started to happen?* She laughed and thought about her mother who would have said, "Ila, it is all part of the process."

The shower was steamy hot, and she had to turn the handle back a bit before she got into the shower. She jumped in quickly and hit all the important spots. She got out quickly, dried off, brushed her teeth, and began the face regimen. She was out of the bathroom in record time. As she crossed the hall, she saw a shadow at the back door. *Damn!*

"Ila, hurry up. I'll be outside," Stephen said. Ila laughed. This man was like an alarm clock. She rushed into the bedroom, found panties, put on the same bra Brock had left on the floor. She had not removed her earrings, so no need to look for some. She wore very little jewelry, she was ready to go. She grabbed her bag and her leather jacket, made sure her gun was in her purse, and hurried toward the door. She forgot about the scarf she had placed under the mattress.

Stephen was sitting in the car wondering if he should tell Ila about Maurice stalking Brock. On one hand, he felt she should know, on the other hand, he felt she had been spooked enough. He decided to keep the sighting of Maurice to himself. He would call Brock at the Pentagon that afternoon to let him know Maurice was in the area. And to let him know that Eugenia and Maurice had been having conversations. Ila was a lady he could spend time with. Unfortunately, he had met her at the wrong time. His assignment with the university would be over when she left. He was scheduled to go to Brussels for the next two years on special assignment. The Company tried to keep married people at home, but in this job, it was very hard to get to know anyone, especially as there were things you could not talk about, and you might have to travel for months at a time without letting anyone know where you were. The only connection family members had was with the Company. Stephen had been in South Africa when he found out his mother had passed, and he had been unable to get home in time for the funeral. When he finally arrived home, all he could do was go to the cemetery and lay flowers. That was a very sad and pivotal segment in his life.

After that time, he became completely dedicated to the Company, spending time all over the world making sure he made no commitments for love or family. But Ila could have changed all that if the timing had been right. His feelings for her, he felt, were obvious, but Ila, he was sure, had no idea how he felt about her. He looked at his watch and looked at the back door. Where was she? Ah, there she was—flawless—coming down the steps. It had gotten cold and a snow storm was on the way. She was wearing only a short leather jacket. She must be very sure he would pick her up from the university, and she was right. She walked swiftly to the car and got in to the backseat on the passenger side.

Ila placed all her paraphernalia on the seat and looked at Stephen. She saw a look that she had never seen before. What was that look? She smiled; Stephen had a crush on her. How sweet. She quickly began a conversation before something came out of his mouth that was too difficult to talk about. "Hi there. Sorry it took me so long, but you gave me a great surprise last night. Thank you so very much."

Stephen responded, "My pleasure." They rode to the university in silence. It was Friday, and she had to convince Eugenia to go to the dressmaker for a fitting on Saturday. Ila got out of the car, thanked Stephen, and told him she had to convince Eugenia to go to Alexandria on Saturday to try on her dress. Stephen said, "Make sure you mention wine and lunch. I'm sure she'll be more than willing to go." They laughed. He drove off, and Ila entered the building.

It was still early, and she was going to stick to her guns—she'd go to the cafeteria, get a cup of coffee, and eat her fruit. She unlocked her office and turned on the light. She smelled something different in her office. It smelled like a men's cologne. It was probably from a member of the cleaning crew. Ila went to her desk and placed all her belonging in the large drawer. She put her gun in the top drawer. She left her office, locking her door behind her. She walked slowly to the cafeteria, greeting students and faculty alike. She entered the cafeteria, greeted the security officer, and looked around at the tables. Eugenia was sitting down eating breakfast. Normally that was not a problem, but in all the months Ila had been working there, she had never seen Eugenia sit and eat.

Ila walked over to her and sat down. Eugenia gave her the usual look, as if to say, "Did anyone ask you to sit down?" Eugenia was a strange bird. Ila laughed to herself. Ila said, "Eugenia, you need to go to the dress maker in Alexandria tomorrow to be fitted and to try on your shoes."

Eugenia looked up from her coffee and said, "Did you give her my measurements and my shoe size?" Ila nodded. "Then it will be fine."

Ila said, "Eugenia this is a one-of-a-kind dress, and I want you to look your absolute best in the wedding. You come in first—you start the procession. I need you to be striking."

Eugenia looked up again and said, "What time tomorrow? Are you buying lunch? And is Stephen driving us? Because I do not want to take the Metro."

Ila nodded and said, "We'll leave at ten and we'll be back before four."

Eugenia grabbed her coffee, got up, and said. "See you in the alley at ten."

Ila thought she would call Paula to see if she could meet them at her aunt's place the next day. And she would have to talk to Stephen to see if he could drive them to Alexandria. She had no idea what he did with his weekends. Ila got up and walked toward the coffee, but to get to the coffee, she had to walk past the wheat, plain, and cinnamon raisin bagels. The guard saw her hesitation and began to laugh. Ila had to laugh also because, in the split second that she decided not to get the bagel, there was a cinnamon raisin one on her plate. She popped the bagel into the toaster and cranked the dial to medium brown. As soon as the bagel popped up, she placed it back on the plate and grabbed two containers of peanut butter. After she spread the melting peanut butter on the bagel, she began to smile. She cleaned up the area, picked up the bagel, and headed toward the coffee. She could not wait to eat the bagel. She made her coffee and decided she still had time to sit and enjoy her breakfast. She slid into a back table so that she could see everyone who walked into the cafeteria while she ate.

After a while, she looked up and saw Stephen walking toward her with a pad and pencil in his hand. *Sometimes I forget he pretends to be unable to talk.* But that was his cover, and he did it very well. He came and sat at the table. He wrote on the pad that he had spoken to Eugenia and that he would meet them in the alley at ten o'clock the following morning. She nodded, and he got up and walked off. Ila sat and savored the last bite of her bagel and the last sip of her coffee. It was most satisfying. She would have to eat the fruit for lunch. She smiled, cleaned up her area, threw her trash away, and walked out of the cafeteria. As she past the security guard she gently punched him in the arm, and he laughed again.

As Ila walked swiftly down the hallway, she could see students sitting on the bench outside of her office. As she got nearer, they began to tell Ila the order in which they had arrived. She decided she should post a signup sheet outside her office. As she got to the door, one of the students gave her a list. She looked at the list and asked Mr. Avery to follow her into the office. She walked to her desk, sat in her chair, and let Mr. Avery sign in. He had multiple issues, so Ila told him everything could not be accomplished today, but they would address everything by the end of the week. For the moment, she would call financial aid to find out why his book allowance had not been posted at the book store. And, so the day began.

Ila looked up. It was two o'clock in the afternoon. At that moment, she had seen all the students. She was able to begin her daily notes and spend the remaining two hours finishing them and making recommendations for the students.

Maurice sat in the dark apartment. He was letting this illness get the best of him. He had lost weight and had taken leave under the Family Emergency Medical Leave Act (FEMLA). Everyone thought that he had gone AWOL from his post, but he had to leave the Company for now.

There was a new drug being released to help him with his HIV, but his t-cell count was so low, it probably would not help him. He knew Hunter was not going to miss the wedding. He had not returned any of his phone calls. Hunter knew Maurice had the virus but was unwilling to talk to him about it. He thought Hunter had given it to him, when in fact Maurice had probably given it to

Hunter. All Maurice wanted to do was stop the madness. He hoped that Hunter had not had sex with Ila. He did not think they had seen each other for some time, so Ila was safe, but she should know. All he wanted to do was to let her know in case Hunter came sniffing around her before the wedding trying to get her to reconsider.

Maurice began to cry. It was so difficult being gay in this line of work. There was no coming out unless you got caught red handed as he and Hunter had been years ago. Everyone was shocked when Ila walked into the room and they were having a threesome. Maurice had already spoken to Eugenia. She had been very angry. But as Maurice told her, he probably did not have the disease back then. But Eugenia had told Maurice that there was a ten-year incubation period for some people. He didn't know when the fuck he'd got it. Eugenia had begun to cry. Maurice had walked away and so had Eugenia.

Stephen knocked on the door and came into the office. It was around 4:30 in the afternoon, and Ila had just wrapped up her notes. She looked up and saw that Stephen looked particularly tired this evening. "Hi, there. You okay?" Ila said.

Stephen nodded and said, "Ila, if you don't mind, I'm very tired. Could you wrap up so I can drop you off?"

"Certainly. I'm done. Let me close-up, and we can be on our way. And, if you don't feel like driving into Alexandria tomorrow, just let me know. If you dial your number on my beeper in the morning, I'll know that you're just not up to it.

Stephen walked back to the door and waited outside for Ila. She quickly got herself together, locked the safe, and hurried to turn off the lights. When she opened the door, Stephen was sitting on the bench where the students usually sat. He got up when he saw her and began walking toward the back of the building. He had not brought the Cutlass around to the front. That was very strange.

Ila hurried to catch up with him. "Something wrong?" Ila said. They were not out of the building yet, so Stephen did not respond. Ila had forgotten. She walked in silence. He had parked the car some distance away. She wondered why he had not told her. She would have changed into her tennis shoes. But they forged on. Once in the back parking lot, Stephen opened the back passenger-side door for her. She got in with all her baggage, and he laughed. She knew he was laughing at her. He ran around to the driver's side, got in, and started the car.

Ila said again, "Something wrong?"

"I got some unsettling news today, but everything will be all right."

"Can I help you in some way?"

"No, but thanks." He had nothing else to say. They rode the rest of the way in silence. He drove around the back to the alley and stopped. Ila got out of the car, said good-bye, and headed toward the steps. Stephen hollered out the window, "See you tomorrow morning at ten." Ila turned around and smiled and waved good-bye again.

Stephen drove slowly to his apartment behind the university. There was nothing worse than unrequited love. He wanted to tell her, but what was the point knowing she was going to marry Brock in just a few short weeks? This was not a fairy tale. She was not going to run away with him after he told her how much he loved her. This would be a love that he would place in the back of his heart, and he would hope that someday he would meet another lady who made his heart beat fast with just the sound of her voice.

Ila walked slowly up the steps, got her key out of her purse, and opened the back door. Stephen had not even waited for her to get into the apartment. That was very strange. Ila double locked the door and went straight to the bedroom. She could feel herself fading, and it was only 5:00 p.m. She made herself hang up her clothes. She walked slowly to the bathroom, turned on the water, and washed her face. She wanted to get something to eat, but she was too tired. She walked straight to the bedroom instead and crawled into the bed. She had a long and undisturbed sleep.

When she woke up, it was seven in the morning, and she was starving. She slowly moved around in the bed and decided she would not masturbate anymore until after the wedding. She was not sure she could hold that promise, but she was going to give it her best shot. She was hoping her dress would be ready after the last fitting and she could bring it back to the apartment.

She could not wait to get to a place she could call home. She would probably move in with Brock. This was something they had not talked about. His apartment was very nice—small but nice. If the Company allowed them to stay there until they found another place, that would be wonderful. Brock's apartment could be subleased or just given up. That was one thing about living in the Metro area—if you gave up your rental house or apartment, you could be assured that it will be re-rented within twenty-four hours. Ila's apartment in Alexandria, on the other hand, was larger and in a great location. She had a feeling that she would never be able to go back there. The Company would just pack up the rest of her things and move her and Brock wherever they decided to relocate her. But because she and Brock were getting married, the destination would probably be any place they decide to send Brock since he out ranked Ila in government status. It did not matter. She would move to Utah … well, maybe not Utah. She laughed.

It felt colder in the apartment than usual; it was probably colder outside. Ila decided to look out the back window, and indeed, she saw a dusting of snow. The weather in the Metro area could be very hard to predict. She was slowly walking to the kitchen to begin preparing breakfast when she heard loud voices coming from the front of the apartment. She ran to the front room and looked out the window. It was Maurice and Stephen. Maurice was screaming "I have something to tell her! It won't take long."

Stephen replied, "You know she is undercover. Why are you hanging around here? What if someone recognizes you?"

"You don't understand. It's very important!"

"I've called the Company. Field personnel are on the way here to get you if you don't leave."

"You asshole! You did not call the Company."

"Yes, I did. Stay here five more minutes and see. Now get to stepping before they get here and, man, please don't come around here again. The next time there might be a real problem."

Maurice turned and walked away, looking very defeated. Ila closed the curtain. What in the world could Maurice have to tell her? And what was Stephen doing in the area so early? She was too exhausted to think about it. Suddenly Ila's stomach was in a knot. She sat down on the couch. She was so close to having everything she ever wanted. Maurice looked horrible and seemed disoriented. She wanted to talk to him. If he was sick or needed anything, she wanted to help him. Okay, so she had seen him in a threesome with Eugenia and Hunter. But they had all been high, and it was "a moment." *Who among us has not had a moment?* She thought about the moments with Eugenia and the police officer and laughed again. *Yeah, who among us has not had a moment?* She sat for a about another ten minutes wondering why her stomach was not feeling well. She thought about what she had eaten. Oh, right—nothing. She laughed again, got up, and walked slowly to the kitchen to have tea.

Just as she had picked up the kettle, there was a knock at the back door. *Shit! What kind of morning is this?* Ila called out, "Who is it?"

"It's Eugenia. I have breakfast."

Ila walked quickly to the back door and covertly looked out the window. Ila almost danced. Ila opened the door and Eugenia walked toward the kitchen. Ila re-bolted the door. There she was with a platter of food. Eugenia walked in with bacon, sausage, melon, croissants, and small jars of jam. Eugenia was wearing her gun holster under her pajamas. *Dang, what a life we lead.*

Eugenia placed the platter on the table, got plates from the cabinet, and then went to the refrigerator to get cranberry juice. Ila was looking at her thinking, *Who is this person and what have they done with Eugenia?* Ila walked over to the stove and picked up the kettle again. Ila looked at Eugenia and said, "You never eat this way. What's the celebration?"

"It's Fat Saturday, girl. Come on and eat. I eat like this only on Saturday mornings."

Ila laughed, sat down, and made a plate. The kettle began to sing. Ila asked Eugenia if she wanted tea or coffee. She declined both. Ila made a cup of tea quickly so that she could get back to the breakfast. They ate in silence. It was wonderful to eat this way. It made Ila feel so much better to know that Eugenia really was not a robot. Ila finally broke the silence. "Did you hear the argument this morning between Stephen and Maurice?

Eugenia looked up. Her eyes got big. "Maurice is still in town?"

"Yes."

There was a long pause. "No, I didn't hear an argument this morning. I'll have to have a conversation with Stephen about why Maurice is in town without the Company knowing. I wonder where he's staying."

"I have no idea, but he kept saying that he needed to talk to me. Do you have any idea what that could be about?"

Eugenia shook her head and said, "I have no idea."

Eugenia almost cried. She was going to be HIV tested at Walter Reed Hospital next Thursday. She wanted desperately to tell Ila, but if Ila was HIV positive, they would have found that out after her miscarriage. People who went into the hospital for anything these days were tested for HIV.

Ila and Eugenia cleaned the platter, and they both laughed. Ila then became concerned that she would not be able to fit into her dress. Eugenia said, "Now you want to think about that?" They both laughed. After they cleaned up the kitchen, Eugenia picked up the platter and said, "See you at ten." Ila walked her to the back door, and she left.

Ila bolted the door and was tempted to get back in the bed. But it was already nearly nine, and they had to meet Stephen at ten. Ila went the phone to call Paula to see if she wanted to meet them at the dress shop. Paula picked up on the second ring. "Hello?"

"Hi! It's Ila. How you doing?"

"Good," Paula replied.

"Eugenia and I are going to the dress shop today for Eugenia's fitting. Do you want to meet us there?"

"No. Drew's brother is in town, and we're going to lunch. Would you like to join us?"

"No, we'll probably have lunch in Alexandria. Thanks for the invite, though."

"Okay. Ila, your wedding is only three weeks away. We need to finalize the menu and think about the music, and a few other details."

Ila said, "I don't care if they play 'Tiptoe through the Tulips' as long as I walk down the aisle and marry Brock." They both laughed.

Paula said, "No, we will not be playing 'Tiptoe through the Tulips'! Girl, you are crazy."

"We'll get together next week and put the menu and music together," Ila said.

"Great. Just let me know your schedule." They both laughed "Oh, by the way, some man moved into your apartment. Seems nice. Doesn't talk much."

"Really," Ila said. "That seems unusual. The Company didn't let me know that someone was living there. But it's their money. It's probably someone here for a temporary assignment. No worries. You're safe. They wouldn't let anyone live there who hadn't been background checked. But I'm curious. See if you can find out more about him."

Paula said, "Yes, I will."

They both hung up. Ila wondered why the Company had not told her that someone was living in her apartment.

This motherfucker going to make me kill him! Stephen said to himself. Maurice had just left the area quickly in the dark-blue sedan. Stephen had noted the license number of the sedan and would give it to the Company so they could find out what address it was linked to. Stephen had wanted to follow Maurice, but he had business to take care of before picking up Ila and Eugenia at ten.

Stephen drove slowly to Walter Reed Hospital. He had an appointment at 8:30 a.m. to be HIV tested. They told him it would take seven to ten days to get the results. He had had sex with Eugenia only twice. Both times, they were drunk and in her apartment. *Shit! How did I let this happen?* Well a hard dick has no conscience. That's how it happened. He could only smile and pray that the results would be negative. He had used a condom the first time but not the second time. *Stupid!*

Ila walked to the bathroom, turned on the shower, and waited for the water to heat up. After looking in the mirror, she decided her eyebrows needed to be plucked and her mustache needed to be shaved. It was amazing— the older she got the more hair grew on her upper lip. Time had been kind to her, but age lines from her trials and tribulations were starting to show. She had to hurry and marry Brock before the lines began to resemble the San Andreas Fault. She laughed.

When the water was hot enough, she jumped into the shower and washed quickly. She remembered that she had nothing to wear. She had to go to the laundry and to the cleaners. She quickly did her make-up routine and walked to the bedroom to see what she could grab to put on. She knew she needed a scarf, her leather jacket, and gloves. It was cold outside. She looked in the bottom of one of the boxes and found a red sweatshirt and red sweatpants. She pulled them out and tried to get the wrinkles out. She did not want to pull out the ironing board. She decided not to worry about it since she was just trying on her dress and probably going to lunch at a very inexpensive place. She found what she thought was clean underwear and bra. She started to laugh again. *Who lives like this?*

Just as she was putting her tennis shoes on, there was a knock at the back door. "Come on, Ila!" she heard Eugenia shout. "We're waiting for you."

Ila looked at the clock. *Shit! It's ten o'clock! Where did the time go?* She yelled, "Coming right now!" She grabbed her leather coat, scarf, and gloves and ran to the back door. It had started to snow. She descended the steps carefully. It didn't snow a lot in the metropolitan area, but when it started, it usually snowed every day—just enough to make the morning commute miserable.

Eugenia and Stephen were in the car. When Ila got into the backseat where she normally sat, she had a feeling that they had just had a heated discussion. She decided not to enter that world. She greeted them both. Eugenia was in the front passenger side, looking as if she wanted to cry. They rode slowly and silently through the streets; it would take about an hour to get to Alexandria. On a normal day it would take about half that time.

Stephen drove up to Ms. Virginia's Sewing Shop, parked, and got out to open their doors. He was such a gentleman. Eugenia got out and said that she would talk to him later. He opened Ila's door and said, "What time shall I return?"

"Knowing Eugenia, I don't think we'll be here long. If you could just hang around Alexandria, I'll send my phone number to your beeper when we're ready." He nodded.

Eugenia and Ila headed to the front door, and Stephen got back into the car. Ila was listening for the car engine to turn over. She turned around to see that Stephen had put the seat back, locked the doors, and was going to take a snooze. That was probably the best idea. After Ila rang the doorbell, she could hear the clicking of Virginia's heels as the woman walked to the door. Virginia opened the door with a wide smile. 'Hi, ladies," she said. "You must be Eugenia."

"Yes. Very nice to meet you. Ila has spoken about you and your talent. I can't wait to try on my dress."

Ila looked at Eugenia. *This woman never ceases to amaze me.* They walked to the display room where all the puffy dresses were lined up. Eugenia turned around and looked at Ila when she saw the dresses. Ila shook her head and laughed. "No, Eugenia, we'll not be wearing anything like this."

Ms. Virginia went into the back room and came out with a black garment bag. She motioned to Eugenia to come into the back room so that she could try on the dress. Eugenia followed her to the dressing room.

Ila sat in the chair looking at bridal magazines and wondered if marrying Brock was the right thing to do at this time. So much was up in the air. As she looked at the magazine page by page, she wondered what was taking Eugenia so long. She heard the click of heels. Ila looked up to see Eugenia standing there in the very simple, black knit, off-the-shoulder, long-sleeved dress. The hem touched the tops of her shoes, and the beaded silver belt sparkled. Eugenia was even wearing the black beaded boots and the fancy comb. She walked slowly to the three-sided mirror. Eugenia looked stunning, and Ila began to cry. Eugenia got misty eyed and said, "We wanted to surprise you. I've already been here for the fitting, and this is the result. Are you happy? I hope so, because I have never looked so beautiful," Eugenia said.

"Happy?" Ila said. "I'm delirious. You look stunning. I could not ask for more."

"Great!" Eugenia said. "Now can I get out of this shit before I really start to believe that this could happen for me one day?"

Ila nodded. "Yes, Eugenia, please do, but know how grateful I am to you for being a part of my special day."

As Eugenia patted her eyes and walked back to the dressing room, Ila could hear Ms. Virginia coming down the hall. She appeared carrying a tray with glasses of wine on it. "Ila, we are going to toast to your happiness when Eugenia comes out of the dressing room." They sat and made small talk. Ila asked her if she wanted to come to the wedding. Ms. Virginia said Ila was the first person ever to invite her to a wedding for which she'd made the dresses. She accepted the invitation. Shortly afterwards, Eugenia came into the room with her black garment bag, which contained everything. She placed it gently on the couch. Ms. Virginia gave each of them a glass and lifted her glass high. She said, "Good friends are like diamonds. They are hard to find." They all toasted to that. Then Ms. Virginia said, "I have a surprise for you. Your dress is ready!"

Ila screamed, "May I try it on now, Ms. Virginia?"

"Go ahead. It's hanging up in the dressing room." Both Virginia and Eugenia started to laugh. Ila fast-walked to the dressing room, and there it hung—the most beautiful sight ever. Ila ripped her clothes off and removed the dress from the hanger. She stepped into the dress and pulled it up. She could tell it was going to fit perfectly. She looked in the mirror, and her eyes welled up. Eugenia and Virginia walked back and saw Ila and gasped. She looked so beautiful. Virginia said, "Let's try on everything!" She got the veil and the shoes and helped Ila put them on. Ila could hear Virginia's clicking heels as she ran back to her office and ran back with a camera in her hand. She took three pictures. She placed one on her beautiful display board and gave each of the women a copy. Ila began to cry, and Virginia reminded her firmly, "Take the gown off before you leave tear stains on it."

Ila walked over to the table to get some tissues. She dried her eyes and walked back to the mirror for one last look. This was a day she had thought would never happen for her. Most of the women who worked for the Company made their jobs their lives and never got married, never had children. She was glad to be one of the ones to break the mold. She removed her dress carefully, placed it on the satin hanger, and put it into the garment bag. She put her boots in the clear bag Virginia provided, and carefully put the veil and belt in the box Virginia provided. She put her own clothes back on and walked over to Virginia. Giving her the biggest hug, Ila said, "I can never repay you for what you have done, but I can pay you for what you have done. Please let me pay you today."

Ms. Virginia replied, "That bill has already been paid."

"By whom?"

Ms. Virginia said, "The gentleman said he was a friend, so I didn't ask any questions. I just took his money."

"Did he tell you his name?"

"Yes, he said his name was Drew." As I said, he paid cash. I gave him a receipt, and he left. I thought you would be happy."

Ila replied, "Drew is dead." They all looked at each other.

Ms. Virginia said, "Well, he had earthly money." They all laughed.

Ms. Virginia walked them to the door. She told them she was very excited to be invited to the wedding. She promised to be there and bring her camera. They all laughed again. Ila had not thought about a photographer. "Ms. Virginia," Ila said, "do you know of a good photographer?"

"Why, yes, I do—my husband! We'll both come, but you'll have to negotiate his fee. I don't bother with his business. Let me get his business card."

Ila replied, "Now that my dead benefactor has paid for everything, I'm sure I can afford his price. Please bring your husband." They all laughed again, and Ila and Eugenia walked out the door.

Stephen must have heard them laughing because his head popped up. He soon had their precious cargo stored away in the trunk. Eugenia got in the front seat, and Ila jumped into the back. Stephen got into the car and said, "Where to, ladies?" In unison, they responded "Food!" They all laughed.

Paula was coming home from the gym when she saw the man that had moved into Ila's apartment coming out of the apartment complex. She hurried to park her car so that she could have a conversation with him and report back to Ila. She wanted to be able to tell her friend who the guy was and why he was living in her apartment. The man seemed to sense that Paula wanted to talk to him, so he did not go directly to his car; instead, he started walking up the street in the opposite direction at a fast pace.

Paula shook her head and decided she would have another opportunity to see him and would report back to Ila then. She was also going to have a conversation with the other tenants to see if they had any information on the guy now residing in 4832 #5. She walked slowly and hung around outside for a bit hoping that the man would come back, but she was still sweating from her exercise, and it was cold outside. There would be another time.

Maurice could not believe his bad luck. Just when he was coming out of the apartment, there she was—Ila's friend, Paula. He saw her rushing to lock up her car and retrieve her things from the backseat. His car was in the lot, but he would have to pass right by her in order to get to it, and he was pretty sure Paula must have told Ila there was someone living in her apartment. No one knew he was there. He had picked the lock some weeks ago. He had called the management company and told them that the Company had changed renters and that, for security reasons, he would be paying the rent directly in cash. He didn't want to leave a paper trail. Of course, the management company did not care who paid the rent as long as the rent was paid. They had sent someone out to change the locks, Maurice paid in advance for three months, and the management company maintenance person had given him a receipt when he was there to change the locks.

Eugenia, Ila, and Stephen stopped at the Chinese restaurant down the street from the apartment. Each of them ordered too much food. They all climbed the short flight of stairs to Ila's apartment. They decided they'd go back to the car for the dresses and shoes after they had put the Chinese food in the house. Not a good idea handling food and clothes at the same time, even if the clothes were protected by plastic!

Just as Ila put her key in the door, Stephen whispered, "Don't open the door! Both of you, stand back!" He gave Ila his take-away bag and said, "Ladies, sit down on the steps, let me go in first." He pulled his gun out of his holster, turned the key in the lock, slowly pushed the door open, and crawled in. If someone was in there, he or she would not be looking for Stephen on the floor.

Eugenia handed Ila her bag and unholstered her .38. She took the steps two at a time and ran around to the front door holding the .38 by her side. Eugenia stopped at the edge of the building and looked down the street toward the front door. She did not see anything suspicious. She slowly walked up the street to the front door.

Meanwhile, Stephen had crawled into the apartment. He crawled into the bathroom and stood up. He grabbed a hand mirror from the sink and stuck it outside the door to see if he could see any movement. He crawled slowly out of the bathroom to the bedroom, and then he saw all the clothes on the bed, freshly washed and folded. He stood up and walked slowly through the house, opening all the doors. He walked to the front door and opened it for Eugenia. He knew that, with her training, the first thing she would do would be to secure all exists. He laughed as he opened the door and saw her standing across the street in a strategic position. Stephen flashed her the peace sign, and she began to walk across the street. He left the door slightly open and walked back to the back door to get Ila.

Ila was still sitting there with three bags of Chinese food and doing what she had been trained to do, even though the cold made it even harder for her to stay in one place. Ila knew not to move. She had managed to get her gun out. She had released the safety and placed the gun on steps beside her just in case. *Do not move from the position that the squad leader left you in unless you are fighting for your life. The squad leader will come back for you.* "All clear," Stephen said.

"What spooked you?" Ila said.

"Not sure," Stephen replied. "I'd rather be safe than dead."

Ila could do nothing but agree with that. In the meantime. She pointed out that the Chinese food was getting cold and they were all starving. Ila put the safety back on her gun and put it back into her purse. She gathered up all the food bags and headed straight to the kitchen.

Once they were inside, Ila asked Stephen to go back out and get the dresses from the trunk. She heard Eugenia come through the front door and lock it.

Stephen went out the back door and stood on the top step for a minute. It was dark and cold, but he could feel something. He just could not put his finger on what it was. He took out his gun once again and held it down by his side. As he made it to the last step, he could hear a car approaching from the back alley. It was a Prince George's County police car. He walked slowly to the passenger side of his car, his gun in his hand. He placed his gun in between his belt and his stomach and slowly opened the trunk. He nodded at the police officer as he took out the dresses and the shoes. As he slowly walked up the steps and into the apartment, he hollered, "Anyone know anything about a PG County police officer being in the back of the apartment for any reason?" He walked into the bedroom and laid the dresses and shoes on the bed.

Eugenia replied, "Oh! What time is it?" She knew who it was. "I'll have to take my Chinese to go now." She grabbed her bag, secured her gun, and went out the back door yelling, "Don't forget to lock the door!"

Stephen and Ila both laughed until tears were in their eyes. Stephen had calmed down since he'd realized that someone from the Company had been in the apartment. Apparently, they had cleaned and had done Ila's laundry, but still there was something else. Stephen walked to the back door, secured it, and walked to the front door to make sure it was secure also. He walked back to the kitchen and sat patiently at the kitchen table while Ila placed the food on plates and put them into the microwave. She also made them drinks. When the food was ready, they both sat in silence eating slowly but steadily. When they both decided to breathe, they laughed. Ila fixed them each another drink, and they talked about work, about how exciting it was that Ila was getting married. When Stephen had finished his second drink, he looked at the clock. He stood up and placed his plate and glass in the sink. Ila said, "You leaving? It's a little spooky in here after all the drama earlier."

Stephen replied, "You're safe. When I leave, lock the back door. I'll check on you in the morning." Ila nodded her head. "Oh, by the way, the Company left clothes all over your bed. I left your gown and shoes on the bed also. You will have fine a place for all of those clothes before you go to bed." With that, he headed to the back door.

As he began to unbolt the door, Ila slid up behind him to give him a big hug as a thank you. He stood very still. She squeezed him tight, said, "Thank you," and let go.

He opened the door slowly, never looking back, and said, "You are more than welcome" and walked down the steps.

Stephen listened until he heard Ila bolt the door. It had gotten colder. He ran to the car and laughed as he looked at the PG County police car. But he certainly hoped Eugenia was making the guy wear condoms. He turned over the car engine and turned on the heat. He slowly drove home with his dick sticking straight up for blocks. He had taken care not to let Ila see it.

He thought back to their conversation. Her wedding wasn't so exciting to him, but he would never let her know how he felt. There were enough men in her life at the moment. One more would surely put her into a tailspin.

Ila was elated that her clothes had been washed, and the ones that had to be dry cleaned were now hanging in the closet. She hung the dresses in the closet too. She took the boots out of the bags and put them on the floor. She took the rest of the clothes to the living room and put them on the couch. Tomorrow she would transfer them back to boxes in the bedroom. Ila had to admit the box thing was getting old. She longed to be in her own apartment. She had cleaned up the kitchen and doubled-checked the doors. She walked to her bedroom, striped all her clothes off, leaving them on the floor. Finally, she crawled into bed and fell asleep hard and fast.

Once again, when she woke up, the cars were moving along the street. The sun was up, and she had to pee so bad she jumped up and ran to the bathroom almost tripping and killing herself because she forgot she'd left her clothes on the floor at the foot of the bed. Once in the bathroom, a pee turned into more. Chinese food always went right through her, but it tasted so good going down! She thought might as well take a shower after that episode. She turned on the water and walked back to the bedroom to get a clean towel and washcloth.

As she crossed the hall, she heard a knock at the back door. Ila ran back into the bedroom, looked swiftly for her purse, retrieved her .38, took the safety off, and stood just beyond the bedroom. "Who is it?"

"It's Eugenia. I came to get my dress."

Ila walked slowly back into the bedroom and grabbed a towel. She put the safety on her gun and laid it on the bed. She walked up the hallway slowly against the wall and looked out the side of the curtain. Ila undid the deadbolt and let Eugenia in. "Morning," Ila said.

"Morning! Stephen is right behind me with breakfast, so go put some clothes on."

Ila walked back to the bedroom and remembered that all the clean clothes were on the couch. She walked back to the living room while Eugenia went into the kitchen to make coffee. It took her three trips to get all the clothes. By that time, Stephen was walking through the back door with bagels, cream cheese, lox, bacon, and mixed fruit from the deli. Ila walked past him in only a towel, and she could see his eye light up. Ila smiled, walked to the back door, closed it, and engaged the deadbolt. "Hey!" Eugenia said. "The shower is still on in your bathroom!"

Ila ran to the bathroom to turn the shower off. She could hear Stephen and Eugenia talking is soft voices in the kitchen. She didn't know what those two had going, but she hoped it was a friendly relationship. Ila snuggled into her sweatpants and a T-shirt and walked back down the hall to the kitchen.

The food had been placed on plates, and the hot water was boiling for tea. Eugenia had taken orange juice and cranberry juice out of the refrigerator along with butter and sliced cheese. She must have had a great night because she was very hungry. Ila could only laugh.

They all sat together eating and talking about the wedding. Stephen was going to rent a car for Ila and Brock. He'd be their driver and was even willing to take them wherever they wanted to go by car after the reception for a mini-honeymoon before going on their official honeymoon. Ila thought that was so sweet and thoughtful. She would ask Brock to just get a suite at the Crystal City Marriott for two nights, and they could leave for the honeymoon after that.

The chatter was constant, and Eugenia was in a great mood. That was so rare. Ila thought the officer must be having a profound effect on her. Maybe she was even smitten a little. Ila smiled again. They talked about the menu for the wedding and how Ila had to talk to the caterer next week and get the invitations out to the students who wanted to come who were not going home for the holidays. The school would be closed for almost two weeks for the Christmas and New Year holidays. She could not believe that next Wednesday was there last day of school, and she would be getting married that following Saturday evening, New Year's Eve. They chatted more about where they hoped their next assignment would be and how this one had been good except it had come with all the drama—the police chief, his protégé, Hunter, and Maurice. Every assignment had its downfall, but as assignments went, they had all enjoyed the whine down at the college. Ila and Eugenia had talked several times about going to school for their master's degrees so they could teach at a college or university. Stephen said he was a lifer and would be with the Company until he retired. Ila and Eugenia laughed because they both knew he was telling the truth.

They sat in silence for a few minutes before Eugenia got up and began cleaning up. Stephen and Ila sat and chatted about the upcoming vacation time from work. Stephen reminded Ila that he was the maintenance man and that he had to work most of the holiday. Ila reminded Stephen that the wedding was at six o'clock on New Year's Eve, and he'd better be there. They both laughed.

Eugenia looked at Stephen with sad eyes. It was a quick glance, but one the Ila felt. Stephen then got up and said, "I really enjoyed breakfast, but it's time for me to go work off this breakfast."

Ila replied, "Where are you going?"

"I'm going to run the track at the university. Do you want to come to do your slow walk around the track as I pass you running?" They all laughed.

"Yes," Ila replied. "You guys didn't give me a chance to take a shower, so, yes, I want to come. Eugenia you going to join us?"

Eugenia said in her low sexy voice, "I have had my workout. I'm going to the apartment to take a nap." Everyone pitched in to finish clearing up the kitchen. Ila ran to her bedroom to put on her tennis shoes, a crewneck sweatshirt, and a hooded sweatshirt. It was cold outside. She looked for her gloves, but she felt it was not that cold. Once dressed, she went back into the kitchen. She found Eugenia and Stephen once again in deep conversation. She was going to ask Stephen … well, maybe not. It really was none of her business. The one thing about truth is that it will eventually come out. You just have to wait for it.

Ila bounced into the kitchen and said, "Ready!"

Eugenia said, "Where are my dress and boots?"

"Oh, they're in the closet," Ila said. "Stephen, you should see Eugenia in this dress. You're going to get an erection just looking at her."

Stephen said, "I get an erection every time I look at either of you." They all laughed again.

Ila went to the bedroom and got the garment bag and the shoes out of the closet. Eugenia walked up behind her. Her eyes were misty. Ila handed her the bag. Eugenia said, "I'm so happy for you and Brock. This is going to be an incredible night." Ila smiled and hugged Eugenia. Eugenia's body was tight a first, but she loosened up enough to hug Ila back.

Stephen said, "Group hug!" Eugenia said, "No! You might get a hard-on." They all laughed again.

They were all walking to the back door when Stephen said, "Let's leave by the front." Operatives hardly ever questioned their colleague's senses. The women turned around immediately and headed toward the front door while Stephen checked the back door. When he joined them, Ila walked through the front entry and turned right toward the alley. Eugenia turned left and headed down the block where she would turn around midway and head back to the apartment.

Stephen walked outside and secured the door. When he looked around, he spotted the dark-blue sedan. Maurice was in the driver's seat, just lurking. Stephen knew that Maurice wanted to tell Ila about his HIV status so that he could ruin everything for her, but Stephen was not going to let that happen. He looked at Maurice and made sure he knew he had been spotted. Then he continued to walk to the alleyway where he had parked the car behind the apartment.

There was only a back-door entrance to Eugenia's apartment because it sat up on the third floor of the brick building. She walked about a block out of the way, crossed the street, and began to walk back to the apartment just as she spotted Maurice. That man was stalking Ila, and she knew exactly why. He was not doing a very good job of being careful about his surroundings. He was so busy looking across the street at Stephen that he didn't she her walk up to him. She stood at the window of the driver's side and knocked on the glass.

Maurice jumped. She motioned for him to roll down the window. He manually rolled down the window. She already had her gun out and was holding it under the garment bag. She said to him, "Take your sick ass back to wherever you're hiding out. Trust and believe me: the next time I see you lurking out in front of this apartment, I'm going to report you. Go get some help. Have you not done enough to so many people?"

Maurice replied, "You have no idea how much I've been hurt, and Ila should know. I know you won't tell her."

"Let me just say this," warned Eugenia, "you don't want Brock to find out that you've been stalking Ila, because you'll be a headline in the newspaper, and no one will ever find out exactly what happened to you. So, get some help and move on with your life." Eugenia walked backwards from the car. She headed back down the block, crossed over the street, and came down the other side. By the time she got to the front door of Ila's apartment, Maurice was gone. She walked down the alleyway and saw that Stephen and Ila were gone. She walked up the steps and entered her apartment. She was dog tired. She double bolted the door, walked to her bedroom, hung up the bag, took off her shoes and coat. She fell across the bed and went fast to sleep.

Ila and Stephen rode in silence. She had no idea why she was taking herself to the track. She had not done it in weeks, but she didn't want to be all alone in the apartment. They parked behind the stadium. Stephen said, "Stay in the car for a minute." She watched him walk out to the stadium track and look. He must have seen appropriate security people around the building because he walked back to the car and told her to get out.

They walked together to the track. She always had to remember that Stephen was not supposed to be able to talk. She wished she knew more than rudimentary sign language. They walked in silence. When they got to the track, he checked his running shoes and took off. Ila began walking around the track. She would alternate between slow and fast. The first lap was difficult, but the second was easier, and the third was easier still.

After she did her three miles, she found a seat on the bleachers and watched Stephen as he finished running his five miles. He was in very good shape. But that Brock took the cake. He was built in places that people didn't talk about. Ila laughed to herself. She was sweating even though it was cold outside. She was going to walk back and wait in the car, but something was giving her angst. She was not sure what it was, but she decided to follow her instinct and sit still.

It took Stephen another ten minutes to finish his run. After he walked the last leg of the track to cool down, he came over and sat with Ila. He pulled out a pencil and some paper from his hooded Sweatshirt and wrote, "You ready to go?"

Ila said. "No. I don't want to be alone right now."

He wrote, "Ila, don't make me spend the day with you. You must know why."

Ila nodded and said, "Okay. Take me to the apartment." They both got up and walked slowly to the car. They rode in silence to the apartment. He saw a parking space in front of the apartment but drove past it and turned in to the back of the building. Ila got out of the car and walked slowly to the steps. She turned around when she got to the top step and waved good-bye to Stephen. She turned the key, walked into the apartment, and closed and bolted the door.

She was really going to take a shower this time. As she walked to the bedroom, the phone rang. She ran to the living room to answer. It was probably Paula. "Hello?" she said.

"Hey, Ila," Brock said.

"*Brock!*", Ila screamed. "I was just thinking about you and wondered what you were doing."

"I'm at the office finishing up this report. I'll turn it in on Monday, get released on Tuesday, and be with you by Wednesday of next week."

"*Yes!*" Ila said. "I can't wait!"

"Yes, Daddy is coming home. Get ready because it's been a long time."

"I don't have to get ready for you. Just one look and … ready!" They both laughed.

Brock said, "Okay. Love you. See you soon."

Ila said, with tears in her eyes, "Yes, see you soon." Brock disengaged the call. He was a man of few words—said what he had to say, and that was all. As a tear rolled down her face. She also laughed because, she said to herself, *What will I do in twenty years when I've run out of things to talk about and Brock really has nothing to say?* She laughed. *We'll cross that bridge when we get there.*

There was still the fact that she had not taken a shower. She walked swiftly down the hall. In her head she said, *Hurry up and take a shower before someone else—or something else—keeps you from it!*

She walked to the bathroom and turned on the shower. When it was hot, she jumped in and let the water fall on her head and slowly caress her body. She felt her pussy getting wet just thinking about Brock. She began rubbing her pussy with her fingers. She bent slightly so that she could find her clitoris. Slowing rubbed it, and then faster and harder. The water was hot, but her pussy was hotter. Within minutes her vagina swelled, and she could feel her relief coming in a huge swell. Her legs got weak, and she leaned back against the wall. Her legs started to shake, and there it was, all in her hand. It was incredible to come in the shower and think only of her man to get her there. She could not wait to take the gloves off and make love to him like she knew she could. She leaned up against the back wall of the shower for a minute just reveling in the power of a climax. Again, she had to laugh.

She picked the washcloth off the shower floor; she was not sure how it got there. Time always seemed to stand still when she was masturbating. As she began to wash her body, she thought about all the tasks at hand—send an open invitation to the students, have a conversation with the food service people at the school, decide what to do with her hair, choose the wedding song. The list went on. She finished her shower, turned off the water and the steam from the shower floating out into the hallway. She had forgotten to close the door. Ila grabbed her towel and removed the beads of water from her hair and body. She looked in the mirror and decided that she would remain natural. Her hair was completely black now; she had cut off all the blond hair. At that moment she knew how her hair looked was not the most important thing. Marrying Brock was the most important thing—becoming Mrs. Covington. Suddenly, her body became very tired. She had completely forgotten about the three miles she had walked that morning, but her body had not. She wrapped herself up in the towel and threw herself across the bed. That was it. Good night Irene. Time for a nap.

Brock hung up the phone. He placed the last piece of his report into a folder and labeled it "Final." He left his office and walked down the hall to the four-star general's office. He saluted several soldiers before he finally made it down to the General Jefferson Owens's office. He placed the folder on the general's desk and left him a note: "The assignment is complete. You know how to reach me if you have any questions. I'm going to get married in seven days, and I'll be back into the office around the 13th of January. If there is a problem with that plan, I'll need to know by Tuesday morning so that other plans can be put into place. Thank you for the opportunity to serve. BC"

When he thought about the note, he realized it sounded as if he was *telling* the general what he was going to do instead of asking permission. Brock decided to leave it that way so that the general understood that plans were already in place and changing them might be problematic. Even though he knew if the general wanted to change them, there would not be a damn thing Brock could do.

He left the office and again saluted quite a few soldiers as he went back to his office. He put the sensitive material in the safe and turned the dial three times. He moved everything from the surface of his desk into the desk draws. He looked around to see if there were any other items that might have to put away. He put a few more things into the drawers.

He looked at the phone. He hadn't heard from Morris, and he wanted to know if his was going to make it to the wedding. It was important that his best friend be there. But knowing the type of work they did, Morris could be in South Africa, Italy, Germany—anywhere by now. He decided to call him anyway to see if he was going to be able to come. Brock picked up the phone and dialed the number. Morris answered on the first ring. "Morris speaking."

"Man, you sitting on the phone?"

Morris laughed, "No, man. I was walking by the phone and it rang. You know these phones don't ring that often, and when they do, it's always someone trying to send me somewhere." They both laughed.

Brock said, "Ila wants us to wear silver tuxes, black shoes, black shirts, silver bow ties, and black cummerbunds. There was silence on the other end of the phone. Brock said, "Man, you okay? It's just for a couple of hours."

"No, man, it just dawned on me that you're getting married for real. You are a complete Company man. I never thought you would get married. No, it is wonderful. And, I'll wear purple if that's what you wanted. I've decided not to bring my wife and son because I'm supposed to go to Canada on the fifteenth of January. I'm sorry, man, but I'm going to fly in, party with you for two days, and fly back home. I hope you don't mind."

Brock replied, "No way, man. I just want you here. Oh, and go to the Men's Wearhouse there and get your measurements taken. Tell them to send those measurements to the Men's Wearhouse in DC. Then I can just pick up the tux and accessories, and you won't have to be bothered with those details. You'll just get here and get dressed and be with me as we watch the love of my life walk down the aisle." There was silence again. "Morris, man, you still there?"

"Man, I would not miss it. I'll be there Friday evening before the wedding, and I'll fly out Sunday morning. Can't wait. Make sure you have some Grey Goose waiting for me!"

"You bet," said Brock. "Have you made reservations yet? Oh, I forgot. I'll look for the 911 call on my beeper. You'll be either at the airport or on my doorstep."

Morris replied, "Man, you know me too well."

"Okay! See you in seven days. Kiss the family for me."

"Will do," said Morris. Morris stood by the phone for several minutes. He wanted to tell Brock that Ila had been the love of his life, but that was a lifetime ago. He would take that information to his grave.

Hunter was in Libya feeling terrible. He had been to the doctor several times over the past few weeks with flu-like symptoms, but the doctors could not decide what was wrong with him. Hunter believed he was allergic to sand. But the good news was that he was sick enough to be granted leave to return to the States so he could check into Walter Reed Hospital for a full physical. He would be leaving in the morning.

He had heard through the grapevine that Brock and Ila were getting married. He could not wait to see the looks on their faces when he showed up to stop that shit. When they got to the point in the ceremony where the officiant asked if anyone there believed there was a reason the couple should not get married, he was going to stand up and say, "I'm the reason they should not get married!" He laughed loud. He could not wait. Ila was his lady and his meal ticket to a better career. Nothing—no one!—was going to stop that. The medical transport would be leaving in the morning, and he would be on it.

Ila woke up. It was one o'clock in the morning. *Damn! Naked and now wide awake.* She got up and looked around the apartment. All the lights were on. She walked to the living room turned off the lights, walked to the kitchen and turned off that light, and walked down to the end of the hallway to turn off the hall light. Something told her to look out the window. Stephen was in the Cutlass asleep. It was cold outside. She was going to get the bottom of all this shit. *Why is he sleeping outside? Why were Stephen and Eugenia having whispered conversations?* There was something going on, and she was going to get to the bottom of it.

She ran into the bedroom put on her hooded sweatshirt, sweatpants, and tennis shoes. Fully dressed, she walked to the back door and turned on the outside light. She saw Stephen's eye pop open. He looked guilty for some reason. He threw his blanket into the backseat. Ila came down the steps quickly and ran to the car. She came around to the driver's side and told him to roll down the window. "What are you doing here?" she said.

"I fell asleep after that five-mile run."

"Yeah? Bullshit! Get out of this car and come into the apartment. You are *not* going to sleep out here all night."

"No, I'm going home now."

"Get the fuck out the car. We need to talk."

"Okay, but I need a shower and a drink. Can you offer a brother a shower and a drink?"

"Yes. Shower, drink, and then conversation."

Stephen rolled up the window, picked up his gun from the front seat, and got out the car. He retrieved his duffle bag from the backseat. He locked the car, and they walked to the steps together.

Eugenia had heard noise in the alley, so she got up to see what was going on. She saw Ila and Stephen walking together toward the apartment. *Shit!* she thought. *Stephen, please do not try to fuck Ila. Maybe I should get dressed and go down and join them.* She decided that Stephen had enough sense not to fuck Ila when they were waiting for their test results from Walter Reed. Eugenia hesitated for a moment and then said to herself, *Stephen is a good man; he would not do that knowing that he might be HIV positive.* She would see them both in the morning. She closed the curtain and went back to bed.

As Stephen climbed the stairs, Ila was talking. He saw the curtain separate at Eugenia's door. He knew the noise would have awakened her because, like all of them except Ila, sleeping deeply was not something they could do. Their senses were always on ten. He thought to himself, *If I had it to do all over again, I never would have had sex with Eugenia. But that was then and this is now.* They would both have to deal with the results—negative or positive—because there was not a lot known about the virus. Even if their tests were negative, they both might not be out of trouble.

He shook his head and decided not to think about it any further. He and Ila entered the apartment. Stephen walked directly to the bathroom, and Ila secured the back door and turned off the outside lights. She went into the bedroom, took off her hooded sweatshirt, and found a T-shirt. She removed her tennis shoes and put on her flip-flops. She heard the shower running. She was grateful that she had found him sleeping outside. He would have been there all night. She took a blanket off her bed and a sheet from the closet. There were no extra pillows; he would have to use the couch pillow. She was sure he would not mind. Couch, TV, drink, snacks—most men would be in heaven. That's all they need besides pussy. She laughed to herself as she tucked the sheet around the couch cushions and covered it with the blanket.

When she was finished, she went into the kitchen to fix his drink and some snacks. She made him vodka with cranberry juice, cut up some cheese and put it on a plate with some crackers. She looked around in the refrigerator and found grapes and strawberries. She really could get use to not having to do laundry or go grocery shopping any more. She laughed again. Fat chance after this assignment was over.

She took the plate and the drink to the living room and set them the coffee table. She turned on the TV and found *Gun Smoke*. He should be in heaven. As she laughed again, she looked up. There he stood in his boxers. He was carrying his bag in one hand and his gun in the other. He walked over to the couch and placed his duffle bag on the floor and his gun on the coffee table. He went to the door to make sure it was secure, and then walked back to the couch.

Ila started looking at the floor because she didn't want to look at him. She said, "Okay. You should be straight. See you in the morning. It's going to be a short night. It's already two o'clock."

He laughed and said, "That's more than enough sleep for me. For you, on the other hand, that is a different story!"

They both laughed. Ila still would not look at him. She said good night and walked quickly to bedroom. She decided to keep some clothes on just in case, so she kicked off her flips-flops and got into bed with her sweatpants and T-shirt on.

Stephen sat on the couch and thought about how Ila had looked at him—or not looked at him. He smiled. The drink was perfect, and he was hungry. He gobbled down the snack, threw back the drink, got under the covers, and watched TV for about an hour. It was three o'clock before he closed his eyes. He was a light sleeper, so he knew the minute the traffic started his eyes would open wide.

Ila vowed that, when she moved out of this apartment, she and Brock would not live on a busy street. She hated being awakened every morning by the sound of the traffic. Busy streets were the downside of Georgetown. The upside was that it was so convenient to everything. It actually would be wonderful to live there. She would be able to walk to most places she needed to go. There were several parks, and the Metro stops were convenient. She wouldn't really need a car. She and Brock would look around when they got back from their honeymoon. *Well, with the Company, you never know. They might have this place cleaned out by the time we get back, and relocated all of our items somewhere else.* She laughed. She sat up and thought she smelled bacon and coffee. Wow, Stephen must be up making breakfast.

She got up out of the bed, pulled the covers up, put on her flip-flops, and strolled down the hall to the kitchen. There he was in his boxers cooking. The TV was on some news station. Ila looked in and made a noise because she saw his gun was on the counter. He turned around and said, "Morning. How about breakfast?"

"Good morning. How about I just sit down?" They laughed. Ila walked back to the bathroom and washed her face and came back to the kitchen to eat breakfast. He had her plate ready—grapes, eggs, bacon, English muffin with grape jelly, and coffee. She sat down and waited for him. He said, "Don't wait for me. I've been eating all morning."

She said a private grace and began to eat. He eventually sat down. Ila said, "Why were you sleeping in the car, and why have you and Eugenia been having whispered conversations? What is it you don't want me to hear?"

Stephen hesitated and then said, "You have worked for the Company for many years. You know things are done on a need-to-know basis, right?"

"Yes."

Stephen said, "This you do not need to know, but you will know in time."

Ila nodded and said, "Understood." They changed the subject and talked about what food was going to be served at the wedding. He talked about how hard it was not to talk to Ila and Eugenia while they were at the university. This assignment had given him a lot of discipline.

Ila finished her breakfast, took her plate and cup to the sink, washed them, and put them in the dish drainer.

Stephen said, "I need a quick drink this morning. Shall I make one for you?"

"No. I have to deal with students this morning. If I had a drink I'm sure I'd say some inappropriate things. You don't have to talk to anyone. You just go about your day with your work orders and get the job done. As a matter of fact, you're going to be late. I know you can check in early and then come back to get me."

He replied, "That won't be necessary, I am sure there is nothing earth shattering to be done, it is almost the end of the semester."

She laughed and walked down the hall to take a quick shower. She turned on the shower before she went across the hall to the bedroom to get yet another towel. She jumped into the shower and took a quick one since she had just taken one before she went to bed. She hopped out of the shower and quickly went through her morning routine. She sprayed down the shower with shower cleaner, wrapped the towel around herself, and opened the door. There he stood. She looked at him and said, "Hey, are you not going to get dressed?"

He said, "I was just standing here waiting for you to come out of the bathroom.

Ila saw the duffle bag on the floor. She moved aside to let him enter the bathroom. "Okay. I should be ready when you come out of the bathroom," Ila said. She strolled to the bedroom and began looking for something to wear, since she had not given it a second thought before going to bed at two in the morning. It was cold outside, so she chose a red sweater and black pants, both of which were hanging in the closet after being at the cleaners. Perfect. She picked panties and bra out of the basket and laid them on the bed. She turned to get the lotion off the night stand and saw, out of the corner of her eye, that Stephen was standing there.

She had removed her towel because she thought he was in the bathroom. She completely turned around and said, "I thought you were in the shower."

"I came to ask you for a razor, and you were standing there naked. I know you don't have the perfect razor, but I just wanted to take some of this morning fuzz off my face. When I saw you naked, I froze and couldn't move."

"There are razors under the sink. I'm not sure you can use them, as they are ladies' razors, but you are more than welcome to try."

He walked slowly toward her. She was still standing there naked. "Stephen," Ila said, "please just go shave. Please don't touch me."

Stephen continued to walk toward her until he stood in front of her. His penis had grown in the few short steps he'd taken from the bedroom door. He kissed her neck and placed his hand between her legs. He could feel the heat coming from her pussy. He penetrated her pussy with his fingers and made slow-motion moves inside. Her juices flowed normally at first. He cupped her breast and sucked her nipple, slowly at first. Then he took the entire areola into his mouth, sucking slowly. He knew he could not have intercourse with her, but he was going to make love to her body without penetration.

Ila had become weak. She had stood very erect at first, but then her body had become limp. She relished the finger penetration and the sucking of her breast. She pulled away, but Stephen held her close and kissed her deeply. He slowly led her back to the bed. "Please sit down and lie back," he said. She sat on the edge of the bed and lay back because she knew what was going to happen next, and she could not wait. She inched back from the edge and bent her knees. Stephen dropped to the floor and opened her pussy with his fingers and licked inside, and then he found her clitoris. The rapid movement of his tongue was fierce. His tongue was so hard it felt like a tiny dick. She could feel him rubbing his dick in a slow motion as he licked her pussy. The faster he rubbed his dick, the faster he licked her pussy. When he was about to come, he sucked on her clitoris and held on. Ila came all over his face, and he came all over the Ila's towel, which he had place on the floor.

It was quick but sensational. He cleaned his penis, turned the towel in the opposite direction, and cleaned

Ila's pussy. She lay there in complete amazement knowing that what had just happen was like a cardinal sin, but oh how nice it was. Stephen got up, folded the towel, and put it on the bed. He looked at Ila and said, "I know this will never happen again, but I'm sure glad it did. Thank you for letting me live the fantasy I have been dreaming about since the day I met you."

All Ila could say was, "You're welcome." He walked back to the bathroom, and Ila lay there for a minute thinking, *What just happened?* He had already wiped her clean, so Ila got up and found her panties and bra. She rubbed lotion on her body, put on her earrings and bracelet, and got dressed in her sweater and pants. She was ready to go. She put her tennis shoes in her travelling bag and her gun in her purse. She took a small mirror out of her purse to check her makeup. She would have to go back into the bathroom when he was done to put jell on her hair and to get her lipstick and makeup sponge. She sat waiting patiently for Stephen to come out of the bathroom. She heard the door open, and he walked across the hall to the bedroom. "You all set?" he asked.

Ila nodded and said, "Just have to use the bathroom for a minute."

"Okay. I'll go warm up the car so it will be nice a toasty when you come out." As he headed to the back door he said, "Brock Covington is a very lucky man. If he ever fucks up …" With that he went out the door.

Ila stood in front of the mirror and said to herself, *What the fuck just happened?* She laughed, put jell in her hair, and reapplied her lipstick. She put her makeup in her purse and turned off the light. She walked to the living room and turned off the TV and the light, walked back to her bedroom, retrieved her bag and keys to the office and apartment, and headed out the door.

As she walked down the steps, she could feel Stephen watching her. There were no words exchanged between them. It had been a moment in time, never to be repeated or spoken about again. As he pulled up to the front door of the university, he handed Ila a note. She put it in her purse. "See you this evening, right?" she said.

"Nothing has changed."

Ila was running late, and it was Monday, so there were students standing around waiting for her. They had already signed in. She walked up to her office and greeted the students. She told them to give her one minute and she would be ready to see the first person on the list. She unlocked the door, turned on the lights, and walked back to her desk. After unlocking the desk, she placed her gun in the front drawer and her purse in the bottom drawer. Then she opened the safe. She placed the sign-in sheet on her desk. She would make notes on it that would help her create accurate reports later on. She walked back to the office door. Anthony DeLeo was her first student for the day.

Paula needed to find a job. She had not had to work while Drew was alive; in fact, she had not worked in five years. She had her registered nursing license, but she'd probably have to take some continuing educational classes before she could begin nursing again. She was headed to Arlington Hospital to speak to the administrator to see what was needed.

As she left the building, she ran into the police officer who lived in the basement apartment. "Patrick," she said, "who is the gentleman that moved into Ila's apartment?"

"He's with the State Department, and his name is Maurice."

Paula thanked him. She would call Ila when she got back home to let her know the gentleman's name. She saw him again, and he did not look well. He probably had the flu. Paula did not engage him in conversation the second time she saw him. He did not look like he wanted a conversation.

Paula walked to her car and wondered what it would be like to have to work every day again. She started the car and made her way to Arlington Hospital.

Brock was packing up his clothes and necessary items to take to Ila's apartment as he would be spending more time there for the next week, tidying up wedding plans. He was going to stop by the Men's Wearhouse for his tux fitting. The clerk there had told him that any alterations would take two to three days.

He finished packing his bag, locked his apartment, and walked to the Metro stop. He didn't take his car because Ila had the Cutlass. He was sure that Stephen was tired of driving her around. That would be his job for only the next couple of days. He took the Metro to the Men's Wearhouse. The bag he'd packed was heavier than he'd thought it would be and got heavier as he was walking to the store. He would probably take a cab to Ila's apartment, or maybe he would page Stephen to see if he could come pick him up.

When he got to the Men's Wearhouse, he told the sales clerk who he was and that he was there to be fitted for his tux. The store manager overhead the conversation and came right over to intervene. "Clinton," he said, "I'll handle this customer, but I'll make sure you get credit for the sale." Clinton shook Brock's hand and left. The store manager introduced himself as Peter and said he would be Brock's personal assistant for the fitting. Brock asked Peter if he had received measurements from California for from a Mr. Morris."

Before he could say Morris' last name, Peter said, "Yes we have received measurements for Mr. Morris. His suit will be ready the same day yours is ready. Possibly as early as Friday of this week."

Brock was happy everything was falling into place. Peter led Brock to the dressing room. "I have taken the liberty of pulling out several silver tuxedos to show you. Brock went into the dressing room and waited for Peter to bring the tuxedos. Peter came back quickly with a silver-gray, vested, single-breasted, two-button sharkskin suit. The jacket had two side vents, and the pants were slightly pleated in the front and satin lined to the knee. Peter also brought a black long-sleeved shirt with a silver-and-black printed bow tie. "What size shoe to do you where, Mr. Covington?" Peter asked.

Brock told Peter, "Size twelve." Peter handed Brock the assemble and went to find a pair of Johnston and Murphy black leather shoes and a silver-and-black printed handkerchief. Brock was putting his pants on when Peter came back to the dressing room with shoes, socks, and handkerchief. Peter had to call another store to find a size fourteen shoes for his best man. But they found them at the store in Montgomery County. They would be shipped there tomorrow.

Peter was glad to get this account for him and his fellow store clerk. There was a guaranteed 25 percent gratuity on the sale. He did not know who these men were, but a credit card number had already been provided to the store, all he had to do was run the number.

It took Brock a minute to put the combination together, but once he saw his reflection in the mirror, he knew he did not have to try on another tux. This was exactly what Ila wanted, and he looked damn good in it. He decided to walk out onto the show room floor to see how it felt to walk around in it. He needed a belt. "Peter," Brock said, "can you bring me a belt? Thirty-six waist."

"Certainly," Peter replied. Peter found a black leather belt with a very sophisticated buckle.

Brock loved it. "Peter, will you please make sure to provide this same leather belt for my best man?"

"Certainly," said Peter. Brock strolled around the store a few more times after putting on the belt just to make sure the pants fit properly and the suit was comfortable. The jacket was a perfect fit, but the pants had to be hemmed and cuffed. Brock had to have cuffs on his pants. He went back to the dressing after getting the attention of most of the store personnel and patrons. He looked good, and that was exactly what he wanted.

Peter followed right behind him with pins to make sure the pants were hemmed and cuffed to perfection.

While Peter was pinning, Brock asked Peter to make sure his best man's tux would also be perfect. It was important that they both looked like something off a fashion runway. It took Peter about twenty minutes to make sure everything was perfect. When he was finally finished, Peter told Brock to be very careful taking off the pants to make sure the pins did not move—or scratch him! Peter left the dressing room. Brock was very careful to not disturb the pins. He placed the rest of the ensemble back on the hangers even though he knew that the entire assemble would be repressed and ready for pickup.

Brock got dressed and left the dressing room. He saw Peter at the counter waiting on another customer. He didn't want to carry his bag all the way to Ila's apartment or to the university. He had to call Stephen. He walked up to the counter and waited patiently for Peter to finish with his customer. Brock told Peter he was through and that ensemble was just what he wanted. He asked Peter to prepare the bill for both tuxedoes along with all the accessories. "By the way," Brock said, "is there a phone I can use?"

"Why, of course," Peter said. He handed Brock the phone from behind the counter. Brock had to think a minute before he remembered the number for the university's maintenance department. The Company did not allow operatives to write down numbers. They had to memorize all the important numbers. After Brock stood there for a minute, the number popped into his head. He dialed, and Stephen answered on the first ring. "Hey, Stephen. It's Brock. Are you busy, man? If you're not, I certainly could use a ride to Ila's apartment or to the university." Stephen must have been there by himself or he would not have answered the phone. Then Brock remembered that most of the staff and students had probably already gone on vacation for the holidays. Stephen was problem a one man show at this point.

Stephen replied, "I'm in the middle of something right now, but I can come and get you in about thirty minutes. Can you wait that long?"

"Sure. I'll go have a bite to eat. You can meet me right outside Ford's Theater. I'll go grab a hotdog on the corner and wait for you there."

"Perfect."

Brock thanked Peter for using the phone. He stood there for a few minutes and finally said, "Peter, may I have the bill today? I don't want to have to mess around with it later in the week. I just want to come grab the suits and go."

Peter looked at Brock and said, "Your bill has already been paid."

"By whom?" Brock replied.

"A young lady came in and gave us a Department of Defense credit card. We ran it to make sure it was good, and it was. It has a credit limit for this purchase of $2,000, and we are well under that number."

Brock said, "May I have a receipt?"

Peter replied, "We were told to send the receipt to a post office box in Arlington, Virginia. I wouldn't worry, Mr. Covington. Your colleagues probably all got together to give you a wedding present."

Brock nodded, thanked Peter, and left the building. He turned right on 14th Street because he knew that, not far away, there was a hotdog vendor who sold the best hotdogs in town. He walked about two blocks with that heavy ass bag and finally got to the corner. He requested a *Nathan's* hotdog with mustard, relish, and ketchup. He also asked for soda. The gentleman knew who Brock was but made no motion to acknowledge that fact. The one thing about working in DC—it was very important not to acknowledge people you know maybe undercover or who may work in compromising situations. You just nodded and kept moving right along. Brock walked back to a bench and sat and watched the sites of DC along with relishing the smells and the sounds. There was nothing like DC, even in the winter. He had been sitting for what seemed like an hour before Stephen pulled up.

Stephen hung up the phone and started to sweat. He knew he had left the razor and the towel with semen on it in Ila's bedroom. The bed linen was on the couch, and he had thrown the razor into the garbage can in the bathroom. He ran over to Ila's office. She was with a student, but she asked the student to excuse them for a minute when Stephen came into the office. The student stepped out of the office. Stephen told Ila that Brock wanted him to pick him up on 14th Street and take him to her apartment. Ila said, "Okay, no problem. I can't wait to see him."

Stephen said, "There's a problem. I left the bed linen on the couch, a razor in the bathroom, and the towel on the bed full of semen. And, the dishes from this morning prove that more than one person was there eating.

Ila responded, "Yup. Here are my keys. Please go clean that mess up. I'm so glad he called you. I don't know how I could have explained that scenario."

Stephen looked at her and laughed. "There is no way you could have explained that scenario less than two weeks away from your wedding day." Stephen left Ila's office thinking he had just dodged a bullet. Not that Brock would have known it was him, but he would have known it was someone. Stephen raced to the car and went straight to Kmart to get a new set of sheets and a blanket. Of course, it took forever because he was in a hurry. He went straight to the apartment, unlocked the door, and headed to the bathroom. He took the trash bag to the kitchen and added it to the bag that was there. He found plastic bags for the bathroom wastebasket under the sink. He went to the bathroom and replaced the bag. He looked around the bathroom. Out of the corner of his eye, he saw beard hairs in the sink. He quickly washed them out. He took the gel Ila used to shave her legs and placed it back under the sink. He took another look around and left the bathroom. In the bedroom, he picked up the towel, took it to the kitchen, and put it into the trash bag. He went back to the bedroom to see if anything else looked out of place. He made the bed and looked around again just to make sure.

He left the bedroom and went to the living room. He had left his cup on the table. He picked it up along with the sheet and blanket. He took everything to the kitchen, put the bedding into the trash bag, and washed the cup and the rest of the dishes in the sink and put them all away except for one cup and one dish. Washed the bacon pan and put it away. He went back to the living room for one last look. He went back into the kitchen, got wet paper towels, took them back to the living room, and wiped down the coffee table. He took the new sheets and blanket out of the packages and put them in the closet, adding the packaging to the trash bag in the kitchen. He stood in the kitchen for a minute. It dawned on him that he had left his washcloth in the bathroom. He ran back to the bathroom and retrieved it and then added it to the rest of the trash. He took a stroll through the apartment for one last look. He had taken care of everything.

He grabbed the kitchen garbage bag and tied it up. He placed another bag into the wastebasket.

Finally, he was ready to pick up Brock. Stephen had broken out into a sweat. Brock was a silent kind of crazy. Stephen was not sure Ila really knew Brock. He and Brock went way back, and he knew that Brock could break a man's neck in less than fifteen seconds. He was deadly and smart. But Stephen could only pray for Ila and himself. If Brock ever found out what had happened, he would probably kill both of them.

Stephen walked backwards out of the apartment, turned around, and locked the back door. As he walked to the Dumpster, he thought he saw the dark-blue sedan that Maurice had been driving go down the alley. He didn't have time to investigate. He threw the garbage into the Dumpster and ran to the Cutlass. He had kept Brock waiting long enough.

Stephen wove his way through traffic, which was never good in DC no matter what time of day it was. He slowly inched down Pennsylvania Avenue to H Street and made a right on 14th Street. And there he saw Brock sitting on a bench. Brock jumped up when he saw the Cutlass. Stephen pulled up slowly, and Brock ran around to the passenger side and got in the car. Stephen knew that it was illegal to make a U-turn on 14th Street, but as soon as three cars passed him, he made a U-turn anyway and headed back to H Street.

Brock looked at Stephen and said, "Man, I'm so glad you came to get me. I packed this bag, and it didn't take long for me to understand that the bag was very heavy. I didn't want to carry it on the Metro and walk the four blocks from the subway to Ila's apartment. Getting out of shape. Been in this civilian life too long." They both laughed, and they both knew that Brock didn't want to go back overseas. Marrying Ila would keep him in the United States, or at least just at its borders. He could get Mexico or Canada, but he would not be placed far away because of his time in grade and his married status. And, if Ila got pregnant, he was guaranteed a desk position somewhere.

Stephen laughed to himself. He knew that Brock would be fucking Ila every waking moment just to make sure she got pregnant. Brock thanked Stephen for all he had done and wondered if Stephen would be able to get another vehicle because he and Ila would need the Cutlass until they left for their honeymoon.

Stephen explained to Brock that he used the car only because it was the one assigned to Ila. When he was given the assignment, her life was in danger, so he had just made sure she got from point A to point B without any trouble. Brock thanked him again. And all Stephen could think about was how he'd had Ila's clitoris in his lips the night before. They rode in silence. Stephen explained to Brock that he had a maintenance operations vehicle he could use for the remainder of the assignment with no problem.

They pulled up in the alley behind the apartment just as Eugenia was coming out of her apartment. She seemed excited to see Brock. They hugged and exchanged small talk before Eugenia took off running. She was serious about her workouts even in the cold.

Brock took the steps two at a time. He waited for Stephen to climb the steps and open the door. Brock asked, "Is there another set of keys somewhere?"

"I'm not sure. Be sure to ask Ila when she gets home." Stephen looked at the keys for a moment and tried to pretend he didn't know exactly what key he needed. He turned the key in the lock and pushed the door open. Brock walked through the door and hesitated. He placed his hand on his gun holster and looked at Stephen, who immediately got on the ground with his gun in his hand. Brock walked slowly to the bedroom and looked around. All clear. He walked to the bathroom. Stephen was still on the floor like a serpent slowly wiggling his way down the hall. Suddenly, they heard a voice.

"Brock!" Ila screamed. She came out of the kitchen. She hadn't put the dead bolt back because she knew that they should be arriving any minute. Eugenia had brought her home early after Ila saw her last student. Eugenia wanted to run the streets instead of the track, so she wanted to come home and get extra clothing because it was colder on the street than on the track. The track was enclosed by the stadium, so it was warmer.

Brock ran into the kitchen and grabbed Ila and hugged her until her breath was taken away. They were in deep conversation, so Stephen left the keys to the apartment on the bed and walked out the back door. He would bring the keys to the car to them in the morning. He was sure they were not going anywhere tonight. As Stephen bounded down the steps, he thought to himself, *Man, if you fuck up, I'll be there waiting.* He got into the Cutlass and drove off but not before he saw the dark-blue sedan sitting in the shadows. He drove up to the street made a right and came down the other alleyway. He drove very slowly. Halfway down the alley, he parked the car and got out.

Maurice was so fixated on the apartment he didn't hear or see Stephen come alongside the car on the passenger side. Stephen opened the door and slid into the car. He took Maurice's gun off the seat and pressed the muzzle of the his gun to Maurice's temple. "Maurice, man, what the fuck do you want?"

Maurice began to cry. "I want my life back."

Stephen, lowered his gun, placed Maurice's gun in his pocket, and got out of the car. He knew Maurice probably had another gun on his ankle. Stephen stood at the door and said, "You can't get your life back by trying to fuck everyone else's up. And we both know that, if Brock finds you out here, he's going to kill you. There are no second chances with Brock. He will kill you and take you to the Southeast dump and leave you there for the animals to eat. Whatever life you have left, you should be trying to live it with friends and family."

Maurice looked up at Stephen and said, "The Company is all the family I have."

Stephen slowly walked away. When he got to the university he would call Brock and let him know that Maurice was lurking around. He would tell him why later.

Maurice was sick that day. He watched while Stephen walked away. He really could have killed Stephen, and the Company would have made up a story about Maurice and why he was in the area, and that would be it. But they all had come up through the ranks together, and Stephen was a straight-up guy. Maurice's stomach felt like mice were running around inside. He opened the car door and threw up. He decided he needed to get to Walter Reed for a blood transfusion if they would give him one, and any medication he could take in this stage of his disease. He started the car and slowly drove off. Then he thought, *That bitch took my gun!* He started to laugh because he would have done the same thing. He drove to Walter Reed, entered through the emergency department, and showed his credentials and his status papers. People stood back for a moment. Someone placed a call, and within minutes, doctors and nurses wearing full quarantine clothes arrived with a gurney. One of the nurses said, "He probably has a gun. Let's find it before we take him in the back." Maurice pointed at his ankle. That was the last thing he remembered.

Ila finally said, "Honey, I can't breathe." Brock released the vice grip he had on Ila and stood and looked at her. He was really going to enjoy being married and living the rest of his life with this woman. He looked around the kitchen and wondered if she had anything to drink. Ila said, "You want a drink?"

Brock laughed. "Are you reading my mind already?" They both laughed. Brock remembered that Stephen had been there. He started to laugh and went to the door to get his bag, which he had left on the step. Stephen must have put it in the hallway before he left. Brock placed the dead bolt on, walked to the bedroom, and dropped his bag. He walked back to the kitchen. Ila had fixed him vodka and cranberry juice with a slice of lemon. He sat at the table and savored the drink. He had not really had much to drink since he left his assignment. He had worked day and night putting that report together. There hadn't been enough time to play. He looked at Ila and said, "The tuxedoes will be ready Friday, and I look really good in mine." They both laughed.

Ila said, "What about your best man? Is he going to be able to make it?"

"He'll be here, but he's leaving his family behind. He wouldn't miss our celebration."

"Great," Ila said. "Both Paula and Eugenia look fabulous in their dresses and boots. Paula's aunt took very good care of us. You'll be a proud man when you see me walk down the aisle."

"Ila, I'm already proud." Ila took and seat and watched him as he drank his drink. When he had finished, he lifted his glass for another one. Ila smiled and got up and fixed him another drink. She sat back down at the table and said, "We have to go to the school's food service tomorrow and pick out a menu for the reception."

"Oh, I thought we were going to *McDonald's*," Brock said.

Ila smacked him playfully on the arm. "No *McDonald's*, Mr. Covington," Ila replied.

Brock sipped his drink slowly. He looked at Ila and said, "I don't care about what we have to eat. I don't care who comes. I just want to be your husband and spend the rest of my life with you."

Ila started to cry for so many reasons—Hunter, the police officer, Stephen, masturbating—all the things that she should not have done but had done.

"Don't cry. Let's go make love to each other," Brock said. Brock threw his drink back and set the glass on the table. He took Ila's hand, and once again, all she wanted to do was take a shower first. But that was not going to happen. They walked to the bedroom. He started taking off her clothes as they walked down the hall. He left her blouse and bra on the floor. As they entered the bedroom, he stood still and took his pants off, leaving them on the floor. He took off his jacket, shirt, undershirt, socks, and underwear and left them on the floor. Ila did the same. She crawled into bed, and Brock slid in beside her. He turned her body around so that her butt was smack in front of his dick. He began caressing her breasts and kissing her neck. Ila was so hot.

She wanted him so bad. Then the caressing slowed down. The next think Ila heard was a snore. She laughed out loud, placed his arm around her waist, put her head in the crook of his arm, and was out like a light.

Eugenia had completed her five-mile run. She was happy for Ila. Brock was a great man. Ila was going to have a great life. Eugenia was walking at this point cooling down. She had gotten a call from headquarters and had been told that Hunter was on his way back to the States because he had caught a virus while in Libya. They were shipping him back to the States for a complete medical workup.

Eugenia stood at the corner of the building and started to throw up. She was going to Walter Reed this Thursday to take her test. How could something so vile spread so fast? Tears rolled down her cheeks. With all that she had been through—all the dangerous positions she had been in, all the dangerous places she had been—this disease had her scarred for her life. She leaned against the wall of the building letting the coldness go all through her body. Finally, she made peace with herself and said out loud, "God, if this how I'm supposed to leave this earth, it has been one hell of a ride." She walked slowly around the back of the building and climbed the stairs to her apartment. When she got up to the top step, she threw up again, this time pretty much all over herself. *Damn!* She put the key in the lock, opened the door, ran to the bathroom, and she threw up again.

Stephen drove to the university and decided to stay on campus. They had provided a room with a bathroom for him that he could use on the days that he was on call. He had to share with one other principal maintenance person, but he lived in Georgetown with his wife who was a teacher. He never stayed at the university. In fact, he didn't even have a key.

Stephen entered the room, took off his clothes, and took a shower. As he exited the shower, his stomach started to growl. He had not eaten. There was a small kitchenette in the room with a refrigerator, microwave, and sink. He went to the refrigerator, opened the carton and milk, smelled it, and looked at the date. He was in luck; it was still good. He went into the small cabinet and found small boxes of *Frosted Flakes* that the cafeteria lady always gave him at the end of the week. He poured three boxes of cereal into a Tupperware bowl he got from who knows where. He found a huge spoon—another item he'd confiscated in his travels. He poured the milk until it crested right to the top of the cereal. He put the milk carton back in the refrigerator and walked over to the bed. He put the cereal on the bed and walked over to his small black-and-white television. He could get only local channels, but for the time he spent in the room, that TV was perfect. He found a *Dark Shadows* rerun. He tried to concentrate on the show while he ate his cereal like a little kid. He loved *Frosted Flakes*. He could eat them without milk if he had to.

He knew Maurice was really sick. He'd looked worse today than he had just the other day. His own HIV test should be back on Friday. He felt cold in the pit of his stomach every time he thought about it. He would leave it up to the will of God. He finished his cereal. His stomach was full, and his eyes were heavy. He would have to get up early pick up Ila and Brock and then get back to the university to pick up the maintenance car. He laid his head on his pillow and found restful sleep, something he did not get often.

Morning came soon for everyone. Eugenia got up hoping that she could at least hold some food down. She wanted to get in a three-mile run this morning, but her body would not let her. She would try again in the evening. She walked into the bathroom and looked in the cabinet underneath the sink. Just bending over made her sick. *What the fuck is going on?* She reached into the cabinet for more soap. The piece she was using should have been thrown away yesterday. As she reached for the soap, she glanced at her tampons and started to cry. *Shit, I have not used those in a while.* Not only could she have HIV, she could be pregnant. This day must get better. She grabbed the soap, set it on the sink, turned on the shower, and then walked down the hall to get something to drink.

She took orange juice and water out of the refrigerator. She drank a large glass of orange juice, put the glass in the sink, and then poured a large glass of water into another glass and headed to the bathroom. The shower water should be hot by now. It felt as if the weather had gotten colder outside. She jumped into the shower and stayed there until the water ran cold. She and Ila had gotten used to their short hair. She didn't think she'd ever let hers grow back. Her stomach felt funny. She reached out of the shower to get the glass of water and took several gulps. Her stomach calmed down. She would have to call Walter Reed when she got to work to make an appointment to have a pregnancy test. They would probably draw more blood. She knew now that she could buy a urine pregnancy test, but she didn't trust the new technology. She wanted a blood test.

Brock was up with the sun. He looked at Ila. She was not moving. He peeled her from under him and slid out of the bed. He wondered what time Stephen usually got there to pick her up. He decided to go for a run. He took his duffle bag into the living room where he put on sweatpants, a regular sweatshirt, a hooded sweatshirt, two pairs of socks, and his Nike running shoes. He could feel in the apartment that it had gotten colder. The heat had come on frequently. Ila liked it cold, so it had to be chilly for the heat to come on. He laughed. He decided to go out the front door. That way he could run to the deli on his way back and pick up coffee, crisp bacon, bagels, cream cheese, and lox. He would run to the university which was about three miles away, turn around, and run back. By that time the deli should be open and ready for business.

He stood at the front door for a moment. He was not going to carry his gun, but he felt naked without it. He went back into the house, took off his hooded sweatshirt, put his holster on, put his gun in the holster, put his hooded sweatshirt back on, and headed for the door. Then he heard Ila call out, "Cinnamon raisin, please."

He laughed out loud. "Yes, honey. Come bolt the door since you're up." Ila walked to the front door naked. Brock looked at her, and his dick instantly got hard. He said, "Do not get dressed until I return." They both laughed. He dashed out the door and came right back before she could bolt the door. He ran back to the door and kissed her hard before he turned and ran down the street.

Brock understood loving to run the streets, smelling the gas fumes, seeing people coming and going, watching shops open for the day, greeting runners who understand that, if you don't run for a few days, your entire body starts to feel different. It had been a few days for him, so his stride was slow at first, and he picked up after he had run about a mile. He was hyped to see so many runners. He'd forgotten he was in a university town. The students were runners. When he reached the front gate of the university in a short time, he turned around and headed back to the deli.

People were really moving around now. Stores were opening. The newspaper stand was open and ready for business. Brock made a quick stop to picked up a *Washington Post*. He kept his stride until he got to the apartment. From there, he walked to the deli.

The deli was full of people already. He stood in line and waited his turn. After he ordered, he stood to the side until he heard his name called. The gentleman handed him a big bag and cups. He did not believe he'd ordered that much food, but he was hungry. He walked over to the coffee service and poured two cups of roasted coffee—lots of cream and sugar for Ila, and black coffee for him. The aromas coming from the deli filled the air. He wanted to just sit down and eat everything right there. He laughed and walked out the door.

Back at the apartment, he stopped at the alley and decided to go through the back door. He had a sense about something but was not sure what it was. He walked slowly down the side alley to the steps to the apartment. He looked about but did not see or feel anything. He walked back to the front door and knocked. Ila came to the window, peeked through the curtains, and opened the door slowly because, as he had requested, she was still naked. But she had taken a shower. Brock walked in and headed to the kitchen. Ila bolted the door and headed for the kitchen. Brock spread the food out on the table and headed for the bathroom. He turned the water on and called Ila, asking her to bring him a towel and washcloth. She strolled down the hall and got him a towel and washcloth from the bedroom and took them to the bathroom. He was already in the shower. She reached in to give him the washcloth, and he pulled her into the shower. She laughed and stood behind him as he washed his body. He turned around and began washing her. It was always a pleasure taking a shower with Brock. She knew that, when he turned around, he would be hard. As he washed her body, it was all she could do not to drop to her knees. Instead he turned her around and lifted her body and entered her from the back. He made her bend over so that he could get his full penis into her pussy. He was so big, Ila could feel his hardness against the walls of her vagina, and with every stroke her pussy got wetter and wetter. She screamed with pleasure as his dick grew bigger and began pulsating inside her. It felt like a heartbeat. He grabbed her around the waist and groaned like a hurt animal in the forest. She could feel his dick vibrating as his semen came inside of her. She felt brand new.

This was the one. This was the man she would spend the rest of her life with. He pulled out very slowly, picked up the washcloth, soaped it up, and cleaned his dick. He then rinsed it, applied additional soap, and washed up all over again. He then took the wash cloth put additional soap on it and washed Ila's body as well.

They exited the shower and used the same towel to dry off. Ila walked toward the bedroom, and Brock said, "No, lady. I need you naked." They both walked to the kitchen naked to have breakfast. Ila looked at the clock on the microwave. It was 6:45. Stephen would be there no later than 7:45. He would probably wait a little later. He was usually there at 7:30 a.m. Ila was due to work at 8:00. "Stop looking at the clock, Ila. Stephen will wait for you."

Just then the phone rang, startling them. Ila got up to answer the phone. "Hello?"

"Hi, Ila. It's Stephen. I'll be there at seven forty-five to pick you up, and I'll return later with the car for Brock."

Ila started laughing. "Yes, Stephen, that would be wonderful. Thank you very much." She hung up the phone.

Stephen looked at the phone and wondered what was so funny. He hung up the phone and cleaned the bowl out that he had last night, refilled it with Frosted Flakes and milk and sat and watched the news.

Hunter's medical transport was scheduled to land at 10:00 a.m. The flight from Libya took about fourteen hours; it was not like flying a commercial jet. He was not feeling well at all. He had an IV drip in his arm, and the nurse came to change it every five hours. Doctors had prescribed an antibiotic, which had been added to the saline drip; they had no idea what was wrong with him. He could not wait to get to Walter Reed so that specialists there could get to the bottom of his disease. These amateurs did not have the medical knowledge that the doctors had at Walter Reed. Plus, he has a date at the Covington wedding: If anyone can show just cause why this couple cannot lawfully be joined together in matrimony, let them speak now or forever hold their peace. *I'm going to hold my piece all right—right in my holster until the appropriate time.* Hunter laughed so loud the other patients turned around. "Turn the fuck around," Hunter said and laughed again.

Brock and Ila had a heart-to-heart talk about the wedding. He told her that he loved her, but he would have gone to the justice of the peace and they would be married by now. He told Ila that she need only to ask him for the money she needed. He had his tux and Morris' tux. The rests was completely up to her. Ila told him that she was a little disappointed that he did not want to have a greater part in planning the ceremony, but he pointed out that, because he had no opinions, planning should be easier for her.

Stephen arrived exactly 7:45 a.m. He was waiting in the alleyway when Ila hit the door. Brock said he was going to sit around, eat, watch TV, take a nap, eat again, and watch more TV. He said that he had spent so many late nights on the report, all he wanted to do was vegetate for the day. He told Ila that he would help her pick out the wedding song. They were being married in a Catholic chapel, so it could not be something secular. But he loved the song "I Want to Know What Love Is" by Mariah Carey. A gospel group provided backup in her recording. Maybe they could use that song. It wouldn't hurt to ask. Ila would be glad he'd come up with a contribution to the wedding. He was so proud of himself. He decided to start his day on the couch with a shot of vodka.

As Ila walked down the steps and got into the car. "Morning, Stephen." Stephen nodded. Ila didn't know what was wrong, but she decided not to find out. It was difficult enough looking at him after their brief encounter.

Stephen said, "You never mentioned the note I gave you."

"What note?"

"The one I wrote. You put it in your purse."

"In my purse? It is probably still there. Do you want me to look for it now?"

"No," Stephen said. "It can wait.

"Okay," said Ila. She made a mental note to look for the note. She honestly did not remember the note. *Damn! Now I want to find it and see what it says.* She just shook her head. Stephen didn't say another word. He drove up to Healy Hall and stopped. Ila looked at him and said, "It will have to wait until another lifetime. This one belongs to Brock."

"I know. Oh—please call Brock and ask him what time he wants the car."

Ila said, "I don't think you have to worry about Brock today. All he wants to do today is lie around, eat, drink, and nap."

She got out of the car and looked back as he drove off. She walked slowly to her office. There were only a few students waiting for her. But the list of students coming to the wedding had grown from fifty to about a hundred. She'd had no idea that so many students would still be on campus or in town. As she walked to the door, one of the students asked, "Can we come to the wedding?" Another said, "The sign-up page is full, but we could write our names on the back."

Ila laughed. "Yes, but you guys will have to be the last ones. Do you want to me to be living in the poor house after the wedding? I have to feed all of you!"

"Yeah," said the first student, and the others nodded in agreement. With that, they all went down the hall.

It was going to be a long two weeks for Ila with most of the students gone. She picked up the list, let herself into her office, turned on the lights, and walked back to her desk. Gun in drawer, purse in the drawer, list on the desk, safe open. Ready for business. She was glad she had no students; she really needed to get to her paperwork. All the reports had to be done in long hand because there were so many boxes to check. Her reports had not been computerized. Plus, everyone still wanted paper trails when it came to complaints or problems with the students. This way people could see where and when things were resolved or not resolved for the students. Ila believed in the system but thought there must be a better way to do it on the computer. She thought that, when her assignment was over, she would come back to the university and work with the admissions department to see if they could computerize this position.

She worked diligently all morning. She looked up at the clock over the door. It was already 1:00 p.m. There was a heavy knock at the door. "Come in," Ila said as she opened her top desk drawer. In walked a very tall black gentlemen dressed in white and wearing a chef's toque. "Hello," Ila said.

"Hello. I'm Chef Charles. I understand you're getting married on New Year's Eve. We're excited about being able to serve you that night. I've brought some hors d'oeuvres menus because I understand that's what you want served after the ceremony. We were thinking about a champagne fountain, but then I was told you were going to have students, so we'll have to change that to nonalcoholic champagne, sweet tea, water with lemons, coffee, and punch."

Ila was so grateful. This way she could take the menus to the apartment, and she and Brock could make their choices. It was something they could do together. Chef Charles continued, "We'll need your decision by Friday because we may have to order some items. I believe we have enough in the pantries and freezers to accommodate your event, but I won't know until I see the menu."

"Thank you so much," Ila said. "By the way, do you know a good florist?"

The chef started to laugh. "Ms. Montgomery, we have a hothouse on campus. We grow our own flowers. Just tell me what you'd like for your bouquets and what type of flower you want the men to wear, and we'll make them up and add the charge to you invoice."

She could not be happier. Less work. "Thank you so much," she said. He left the menus and a brochure full of pictures of assorted pastries. Ila did not want a wedding cake, so assorted pastries was the way to go. He must have talked to Eugenia. She was glad. This way she didn't have to explain anything. The chef had come prepared to make her happy. A lady could not ask for more.

When he left, it seemed he had taken some of the air out of the room. He was a tall good-looking man with a full presence. People would not forget him after meeting him. Ila laughed. Then she heard a strange noise, it was her stomach. It was already almost two o'clock. The cafeteria was probably closed. She looked for her keys, got her badge out of her desk, and headed for the door. She would probably have to settle for a peanut butter and jelly sandwich, but that would be okay. She and Brock would have dinner together, so eating light was probably a good thing. She walked through the door, locked it, and headed up the hall. And, yes, the cafeteria was closed. Fortunately, Chef Charles and the security guard were inside talking.

The security guard came and opened the door. "Ms. Montgomery, there's hardly anything left from lunch."

"Thank you. Maybe if I had some bread, I could put together a peanut butter and jelly sandwich. The ingredients are in the condiment area, right?" Ila said. They both laughed.

Chef Charles said, "I think we can help you out with that." He went back into the kitchen and brought out two pieces of wheat bread on a paper plate, along with a banana and a container of yogurt. Ila was very happy with the spread. She took the plate from the chef and carried it to the condiment table where she made her sandwich. She grabbed a spoon for her yogurt and went to the drink fountain for water. She thanked them both.

Ila said, "Chef, how should I pay for this? There's no one at the register."

"That gourmet meal is on the house." They all laughed. The security guard walked her to the door. He was still laughing as Ila walked down the hall.

There she was again at her door with too much in her hands, and there he was again with the key to her office. It seemed Stephen was always around when she needed him. He smiled as he opened the door and let her in. She thanked him. He pushed the door open let her walk through, and then closed it behind her, not uttering a word as he walked away. Wow, he really played the part at work. Ila sat at her desk and remembered she had not looked for the note that Stephen had given her. She turned her purse upside down and couldn't find it. She hoped that it hadn't fallen out in the apartment. She decided to not give it any more thought. As long as it didn't say something like "you were delicious last night," it should be good. Ila finished her gourmet lunch and went back to work. When she looked up again, Stephen was walking through the door, ready to take her home. She took her purse and her gun out of her desk and placed all the material she was working on in the safe. She grabbed her jacket and was ready to go.

Stephen and Ila walked out together after she turned off the lights and locked the door. They walked to the car slowly. A light snow had fallen, and of course it would take twice as long as usual to get to the apartment because the drivers in Washington DC were afraid of snow. She hopped into the back, and he hopped in the front. They were about to pull out of the parking lot when they heard someone call out "Ila!" It was Eugenia running to the car to get a ride home. Ila wasn't sure why she needed a ride home unless she had run all the way to work and hadn't driven her car. Eugenia hopped into the front seat and said quickly, "I ran to work and changed when I got here. I didn't bring my car."

Stephen nodded. Ila said, "I thought so. Hey, I have the menus for the wedding. Why don't you guys come by the apartment and have a drink and we can look at the menus together? Brock could probably care less, but this way we all can have input and make sure there are things on the menu we all like. Paula likes all kinds of food, so it won't matter to her. I have no idea how she stays so thin. She loves to eat." But truth be told, she ran every day, and that really helped her stay thin. Ila understood that type of regimen; she just wished she could stick with one.

Eugenia said she was game to look at the menus and so was Stephen. Ila hoped Brock would have clothes on when they got there. She laughed to herself again. The ten-to-fifteen-minute ride turned into thirty minutes. They could not believe it. They laughed at the drivers. Stephen finally turned down the driveway into the alley. They all piled out of the car. Stephen made sure every door was locked. They climbed the steps. Ila put the key in the lock and pushed the door open. "Brock!" she said. "We have company. Do you have clothes on?"

Brock called out from the living room, "Yup. Not naked." They all piled into the apartment. Brock had done exactly what he'd said he was going to do that day. He'd walked from one room to the other with food and one hand and a drink in the other. He had not been able to "do nothing" for some time. It was a welcome change, this relief from responsibility. Brock, at one point, had decided to go to the bedroom and take a nap. On his way, he saw small piece of paper on the floor. He bent down to pick it up and was about to toss it into the wastebasket, but instead he opened it up to make sure it was not a receipt of some sort that Ila might need. He was very surprised to read: "Unrequited loved is better than no love at all. Stephen." *Well, well*, he thought. He would have to make sure he kept his eye on Stephen. Poor fellow; he would settle for love from across the room. But that was good, because if Brock thought that there was more to this note than what it said, Stephen would have some explaining to do. He laughed. *Poor fellow.* He then tossed the note in the trash and fell across the bed to take a nap.

Ila went to the bedroom and dropped all her stuff while Eugenia and Stephen headed toward the kitchen to make drinks. Brock came to the kitchen, and they all sat around talking. Eugenia set out drinks for everyone and put a plate of cheese and crackers in the middle of the table. Ila joined them and sat the menus around the table. They were all talking at once. Ila got up to get a piece of writing paper from her bag. She walked to the bedroom and came back. All three were calling out what they wanted. Ila told the group that there would be no alcohol at the reception because of the students. Everyone understood.

After several drinks and many laughs, they had a menu on paper. Ila would take it to Chef Charles tomorrow. They all sat for about an hour after the menu had been completed. Eugenia was the first one to get up. She started to clean up her area, but Brock said, "Don't worry about that. We'll take care of it." With that, Eugenia grabbed her stuff and said her good-byes. Stephen was in tow, following her lead. Brock walked them both to the door.

As they were walking to the door, Stephen said to Brock, "We need to talk."

Brock said, "Don't worry, my brother, I love her too."

Stephen looked surprised with that answer. He wanted to tell him about Maurice. *Shit! He must have found the note. God damn it! Ila was careless.* But then he thought, *I should never have written the note anyway.* Brock turned on the outside light so they could see as they left. Brock didn't ask for the car because he was going to do the same thing tomorrow he'd done today. It felt good to relax. He needed that.

Ila had gone to the bedroom to get out of her street clothes. She planned to go back and clean up the kitchen. Brock walked by and said, "Honey, I got the kitchen." Ila was grateful. She was tired. She hung up her clothes, took her panties and bra off, and prepared to take a shower. She thought, *I'll just lie across the bed for a minute.* She'd had had two drinks and was feeling no pain. Lights out—that thought was her last thought.

Brock finished cleaning up the kitchen. He could not wait to make love to Ila. He hadn't taken the opportunity yesterday. He turned off the light in the kitchen and walked down the hall to the bedroom. It seemed mighty quiet. There she was, lying across the bed sideways, asleep. She had been living here too long by herself. He laughed to himself. He went over to her and pulled her legs up onto the bed and covered her. They would have a lifetime to make love. It was just his joy to be happy and in love finally. He walked back to the living room, turned the TV back on, and sat on the couch. Soon he was fast asleep.

Hunter's medical transport plane arrived on time. They bundled him into a military ambulance along with two other soldiers who were also being transported to Walter Reed Hospital. It seemed to take forever to get there from Dulles Airport. Hunter wondered why they couldn't land at Washington National Airport, which was so much closer. It was a bumpy ride down Route 50. Hunter finally fell to sleep, and when he woke up, they were at the emergency entrance to Walter Reed. Three wheel chairs were waiting.

The person pushing the chair to which Hunter was directed was covered in protective clothing from head to toe, including a mask. Hunter thought they were being extra cautious because he had a virus and they were unsure how it spread or how he'd got it. He understood the extra precaution. The transport person rolled Hunter to the elevator, and they went to the third floor where they turned right into a restricted area. There was a pharmacy dedicated to just that floor, and all the areas were protected by double doors. Everyone behind the double doors was dressed in full protective gear.

Hunter stated getting nervous. *What the fuck do they think I have?* The transport person pushed him down the hall and into room 309. It was a small room with no windows. Hunter saw a bathroom, a comfortable looking chair, a TV, and a bed. The transport person told Hunter that the doctor would be in momentarily. He told him to relax and have a seat in the chair.

Hunter sat down but felt very uneasy. First, he did not have his gun. Second, he was in a quarantined wing of the hospital. *What the fuck is going on?* He waited for what seemed an hour before the doctor walked into the room. "Hello, Hunter. My name is Dr. Ortega, and I'm a specialist in autoimmune disorders. While you were in Libya, the doctors found that your blood did not look quite right, but they weren't sure what they were looking out, so they sent you home so that you could get a complete workup.

"Why am I in a quarantined wing of the hospital?" Hunter asked.

Dr. Ortega replied, "Because we don't know what you have. It could be something as simple as very bad viral infection, or it could be something more complicated. There is a gown in the bathroom. After you take a shower, the phlebotomist will come in and draw five vials of blood. The cafeteria staff will bring you some dinner, and a certified nurse's assistant will come and check on your comfort. I'll be back in the morning. With that, Dr. Ortego left the room.

Dr. Ortega didn't want to get into specifics with Hunter, but he was almost sure that Hunter had HIV—not the complete virus yet, but his blood test had detected HIV antibodies. They would check for HIV antigen, a protein called p24 that's part of the virus that shows up two to four weeks after infection, as well as HIV antibodies. He was afraid he would be the one to tell

Hunter this news sometime tomorrow after all the tests were returned from the lab.

Hunter did what the doctor had suggested. He went into the bathroom to take a long hot shower. It had been a long journey, and he was very tired. He turned the shower on, and it instantly got hot. He could not wait to take off all his clothes and stand under the shower. He let all his clothes hit the floor, and then he jumped into the shower. The warmth of the water was heavenly. He had to make sure that, whatever he had, it would be cleared up in a few days. He had a wedding to attend. He stayed in the shower for a long time just letting the water drop down over his head to his feet. He heard a voice from inside the room. "Mr. Hunter, are you almost finished?" the phlebotomist called out.

"Yes," Hunter yelled. "Out in a second." Hunter finished his shower and dried off quickly. He picked up his clothes from the floor, folded them, grabbed the gown that was on the back of the door, and put it on. It was not the perfect fit, but it covered all the pertinent parts. He laughed to himself. He opened the door to the bathroom to see the phlebotomist standing there in full protective clothing. He was really beginning to worry. She had taken the food tray table from the other side of the bed, and she asked him to sit down. She asked him to make a fist and squeeze it several times. Hunter had great veins, so she would have no problem getting blood. She quickly took the vials of blood. She was an expert; it did not even hurt, and Hunter actually watched. When she completed her tasks, she told Hunter to relax. Someone would be bringing him food and ice water.

After she left the room, Hunter lay down in the bed and turned on the TV. They had even provided him with cozy socks. He had not been watching TV for five minutes before the cafeteria lady came with food. Suddenly, he was hungry. She was very pleasant. The food was on a tray and was covered with a cloche. There was water in one paper cup and ice in another cup. There was also apple juice and cranberry juice. She told Hunter to just leave everything on the tray and someone would be back to get it later. He lifted the cloche. There was steam coming from the food. It was hospital food, but he was starving, and anything would be good right now. He attacks the food as if it was steak and lobster. After devouring the food, he drank all the apple juice and cranberry juice. He pushed the tray to the side and lay down again. The cafeteria lady had closed the door completely, so he turned off the lights. That was the last thing he remembered. Hunter had no idea that Maurice was down the hall.

Ila woke up at around three in the morning. She could not believe she had fallen asleep. She had taken her clothes off, but that was as far as she'd got. Brock had shut down the house and was sleeping on the couch. She laughed; they were acting like an old married couple already. She got up, turned on the light, and walked over to the bathroom. She started the shower, as it took forever to get hot. She walked back to the bedroom to get a T-shirt to sleep in. She was really going to enjoy the shower after getting a few hours of sleep. By the time she came back, the shower was steamy. She hopped in, and it felt wonderful.

Brock heard the water running. He knew that Ila knew the water would wake him up. That was why she'd left the door open. Well, he was going to take her up on the offer. He jumped up off the couch and walked quickly down the hall. When he got to the bathroom, he dropped his shorts on the floor and entered the shower.

Ila started to laugh. She had known the shower would wake him up. They both laughed because they both understood her plan. They washed each other up and had to use the same towel to dry off because Brock, of course, had not brought a towel to the bathroom. They walked hand and hand to the bedroom. Brock's dick was hard. He wanted to wait and really make love to her, but his dick was about to burst. He pulled back the covers on the bed. Ila walked around him and rolled into the bed. She lay on her back and just looked into those huge brown eyes. She knew that she was in love.

He began to kiss her lightly then with more intensity. He cupped her breast and licked the right one and then the left one. He held her right breast in his mouth and sucked it like a baby sucks a bottle. She knew he was either going to come all over himself or enjoy the pleasure of coming inside Ila. He grabbed her butt and lifted it toward his dick. He slowly put his dick inside her, just the head at first. In and out. She could not believe how big his dick was; she really enjoyed feeling him inside her.

He started thrusting his dick into her pussy. He was about to explode, but he pulled out and gave it a rest. He kissed her again and again. He turned her sideways so that he could enter her pussy from behind and hold on to her breasts at the same time. He believed that was her favorite position. It felt so intimate. He kissed her on her neck and held her breasts tight and entered her slowly. He could hear her soft moans and could feel her heart beating faster and faster. Then, it happened—she bent over, and her pussy was dripping. Her heart was beating fast and he knew she was in full orgasm. His body stiffened up. Her pussy was dripping and she was moaning. Now he could come. He lifted her butt just slightly to make sure he got his entire dick inside her, and he let go. His body stiffened and he groaned aloud.

Ila let out a little scream. She knew he had been pleased, and she was happy about that. They were in each other arms until the morning light.

They woke up to morning traffic, sunlight, and a cold apartment. The temperature outside must have dropped drastically overnight. Ila got up and peeled Brock off her. She walked quietly down the hall to turn the heat up. She knew he was awake. There was no way she could get out of the bed without him knowing it. She walked to the kitchen and turned on the light. She was going to make a quick breakfast for them. She retrieved eggs, bread, and turkey sausage from the refrigerator. She put the kettle on for tea because they really both preferred tea over coffee. She heard him cross the floor to the bathroom and start the shower. Ila broke the eggs, put the sausage in a pan, and put three slices of bread into the toaster. There was cranberry juice, of course, and mango juice in the refrigerator. Since she didn't have to do the shopping, she never complained about what was purchased. She retrieved glasses from the cabinet and poured them both glasses of mango juice.

Brock came from the shower with his boxers on and brought the towel so that Ila could sit in the kitchen chair and have breakfast. She was still naked. The sausage was ready, and she put the eggs in the pan and scrambled them until they were soft. The toast popped up, and she got butter and grape jam from the refrigerator. Everything was ready. She made green tea for both of them.

She was hungry after that night of making love, and Brock was always hungry. They talked very little while eating, enjoying the fact that they were together. Ila got up to cleaned up the kitchen, but Brock said that he would take care of it because his little lady had to go to work. All he had to do was sit and watch television. Ila threw a huge wad of paper towels at him and left the kitchen.

She went straight to the bathroom. Stephen would be there within twenty minutes. She quickly took a shower and ran back across the hall to get dressed—sweater, pants, leather jacket, gloves, and possibly a hat today. She put on her panties and bra, found her makeup bag, and ran back across to the bathroom to put her makeup on.

Brock had cleaned up the kitchen and was headed to the couch to spend yet another day watching TV and enjoying the time he had away from his desk and duties. Ila heard a knock at the back door and knew it was Stephen coming to get her. She ran to the living room and kissed Brock good-bye. Of course, he was sitting there with his gun in his hand preparing to walk to the back door. Ila told him it was Stephen coming to get her and not to worry. But of course, he walked slowly to the back door and looked out the window and saw the car. Ila grabbed her purse, made sure her gun was there, grabbed her bag that held her tennis shoes and other necessities, and walked to the back door. Brock stood at the door until she got into the car.

"Morning," Ila said.

Stephen said, "Morning to you. You look like you've just been tossed." They both laughed. It was a cold day, but the sun was shining. Ila hoped desperately that the weather would hold for her wedding. It did not matter if it was cold; she just didn't want it to snow. DC came to a standstill when it snowed. It of course didn't take long to get to the university. Stephen asked, "Does Brock want the car?"

Ila responded, "When I left, he was watching TV, so I'll say no." They both laughed again. Ila got out of the car and walked to her office.

The university was silent; most of the students had already gone home. The faculty was there just finishing up grades, revamping schedules, and preparing for the next semester, which would begin in January. Ila had not had a chance to get to know any of the faculty really as she was isolated in Healy Hall, and most of the faculty didn't have the time to deal with student concerns. They were glad Ila had the position so they could send the students to her. As she walked to her office, she could see two students waiting. This would be an easy day. She could continue to write up the cases and turn them in by the end of the week so that next week could be devoted to putting the finishing touches on the wedding. She opened her office, did her ritual, and went back to the door to invite the first student in.

The day went by fast. Ila had a two o'clock appointment in the cafeteria with Chef Charles to go over the menu. She looked at the clock at 1:45 p.m. She had not eaten lunch, so it was going to be yogurt and peanut butter sandwich again today since the cafeteria was essentially closed. It would close for the holiday at noon on Friday. Ila wondered what the students did when the cafeteria closed. She would have to ask one of the students who stayed during the holiday how they survived while the cafeteria was closed.

When she walked in to the cafeteria, Chef Charles and the security guard were there talking. They were both laughing hard as she walked over to the table. Chef Charles said, "We took the liberty of making you lunch— yogurt, peanut butter and jelly, and hot tea." They all laughed, and Ila thanked them. The security guard got up and walked to the front of the cafeteria.

Ila had brought the menus, and she laughed because there were so many items circled. Chef Charles looked at the circles and said, "Ila, now you are having only about a hundred people, maybe, and most of those are students. I don't want you to waste money and food on people whose favorite foods are French fries and burgers." Ila laughed.

Chef Charles said, "Why don't you consider a burger bar—turkey and beef—and a spread with all the fixings. We could include fruit salad, mixed cheeses, a baked potato bar with all the fixings, sweet tea, water, soda, and non-alcoholic champagne. You and your friends can go to a fancy restaurant after the wedding or go somewhere nice for breakfast the next day. We'll put everything in the hallway by the cafeteria so that we can replenish the fixings bar and anything else you would like. And, we'll make special cupcakes in different flavors as your dessert. I understand you don't want a wedding cake, so I think that would work, right?"

Ila nodded her head. She was not crazy about the menu, but she knew he was right. Why spend money on baby quiche, salmon, beef brisket, and other treats? The students would not eat that sort of food. She would make reservations for the bridal party at a nice restaurant. If the ceremony was at six, they could be at the restaurant by ten. And, on New Year 's Eve, everything would be staying open late. Chef Charles said, "I am really good friends with the head chef at the Portofino Restaurant in Arlington. I'd be happy to request a small room in the back that sits about fifteen people. He can provide you with your own private server. How does that sound?"

Ila almost reached across the table and kissed him. She could not have chosen a better place. She said, "Thank you so much. That would be wonderful and perfect. Let me know if I need to put down a deposit on dinner, or whatever is necessary."

Chef Charles said, "What is necessary is for you to pay for the reception tomorrow so that I can order the food. With the university essentially shut down I'll have to order almost everything."

"How much do you think it will be?"

"I can do it all for two thousand—food, servers, setup, and cleanup. Does that fit your budget?"

Ila again wanted to reach over and kiss him. She replied, "Yes! Let me go get my checkbook." They laughed.

Chef Charles said, "Enjoy your gourmet lunch. We can sit and chat for a minute about the time line of the wedding so that we are sure the food is hot and ready by the end of the ceremony. I'll walk you to your office and get the check when we're finished here." They sat and chatted, and he wrote down some notes.

After the chef left, she still had a lot of notes to write up so she decided not to let her mind wander. She focused on finishing up her tasks so that next week, she would have nothing to do but plan the wedding.

Stephen was on his way to Walter Reed Hospital to get his results. He was nervous. He didn't know what he would do if the results were positive. He didn't feel sick, but there was not a lot of research yet on the disease. It had been called the gay man's disease for so long. He had no idea he would ever be thinking about something as disastrous as HIV. There was no cure, and the medicine currently used to treat the disease made patients sick. It was like chemo therapy—you're damned if you take it and damned if you don't take it.

He drove into the emergency room parking lot because the hematology department was right by the emergency room. As he parked his car, he saw Maurice exiting the hospital and heading toward his dark-blue sedan. He looked better. Stephen wondered if he had had a treatment while he was at the hospital. Stephen waited for Maurice to pull off before getting out of the car. He walked through emergency to the hematology department, signed in, and waited for the nurse to call him back.

Stephen had gotten word last night that Hunter was back in the country and was here at Walter Reed Hospital. He could not believe how this thing had gotten totally out of control, and because each of them could not be responsible enough to wear condoms, they had all put their lives in danger. He sat for what seemed like hours but was really only twenty-five minutes. This was a short period of time considering it looked like some people had been there for some time.

The nurse opened the door and called Stephen's name. She escorted him to room number three and told him to have a seat; the doctor would be right in. He sat and waited again. Did these people not know how anxious he was? It wasn't long before the doctor came in, but again it seemed like a lifetime. The doctor sat in a chair with the folder. He had a look of distain on his face. Stephen wanted to cry. "Hi, Stephen. I'm Doctor Ortega. It seems you have dodged a bullet this time. Your blood work shows no indication of HIV antibodies, but we need you to come back and take another blood test in thirty days, just to make sure. In the meantime, do not have sexual relations without a condom. We have prepared a package of condoms along with lubrication for you to take with you. Please have your partner get tested also, as you both are in real danger if you believe you have been exposed. Do you have any questions?" Stephen just shook his head. "Okay, then. Here is my card. Contact me if you think of anything after you leave." With that, Dr. Ortega left the room.

As Dr. Ortega left the room, he looked at Stephen's chart again and realized that there were two other men from the Company at Walter Reed. They probably all ran in the same circles. He just shook his head. He was on his way to the quarantine area to give another patient some not-so-good news. It was going to be a long day.

Stephen jumped up out of the chair. He wanted to run back to the university to tell Eugenia that he had not tested positive. But he knew from during research that it was easier for women to contract the virus than men because women were receivers and men were givers. He just shook his head, and a tear ran down his cheek. He had indeed dodged a bullet.

He picked up the bag of condoms and put them in his pocket. Then he headed for his car. In the parking lot, he saw Eugenia's car drive up and park at the back of the building. Eugenia knew the Cutlass, but when she got out of her car, she seemed busy looking at her beeper and did not see Stephen. He remembered that this was the day she was going to take her HIV tests. The results may not be back before the wedding. He thought she would rather not know one way or the other before the wedding anyway. That way she could enjoy the festivities without knowledge. What she would be glad to hear was that *he* did not have AIDS. He would let her know this evening.

Maurice walked slowly from the hospital to his car. He was feeling much better after a complete blood transfusion, but he'd been warned that that the transfusion was not a fix for the virus. He was also given a medication called azidothymidine (AZT). It was not a new medication. It was originally introduced as a cancer drug, but clinical trials showed that it could reduce the amount of human immunodeficiency virus (HIV) in the body. He really wanted to get back to Ila's apartment and just go to bed. He had not been able to sleep in the hospital. The doctor said he didn't have to return for several weeks unless he had an adverse reaction to the AZT. Maurice was going to rest up for a couple of days and then try again to reach Ila.

Dr. Ortega walked into Hunter's room. They had given Hunter a saline IV with some antibiotics. Dr. Ortega would be prescribing the new AZT drug to hold down the antibodies, so hopefully Hunter would not get the full HIV for some time if at all. The drug was so new. There were other drugs in the trial stages, but they had not been released by the Food and Drug Administration yet.

Hunter had just finished breakfast and was watching the news. He sat straight up as the doctor entered the room. "Morning, Doc," he said.

"Good morning, Hunter," the doctor replied. "I want to tell you about what we have found in your blood work. It seems you have the HIV antibodies in your blood, and that is what is giving you the flu-like symptoms."

Hunter marinated on those words for a minute and said, "Give that to me again."

Dr. Ortega repeated his statement. Hunter was silent. The doctor went on to say, "We are going to do some additional blood work, just as a double check. We don't want to be wrong about this situation. Then, if that blood work comes back with the same result, we'll consider a diet regimen, vitamins, and AZT, which is a new drug that has shown to slow down the progression of the disease. Do you have any questions, Mr. Hunter?"

Hunter shook his head. Doctor Ortega told Hunter, that the phlebotomist would be back to take additional blood and that the nurses and certified nursing assistants would be coming and going most of the day to make sure he was comfortable. "Are you sure you don't have any questions?" Dr. Ortega said again. Hunter shook his head. "Okay, then. I'll be back to see you in the morning. In the meantime, if you experience any pain, please don't hesitate to push the call button for the nurse." Hunter nodded.

Dr. Ortega left the room. As he was walking down the hall, he thought to himself, *That went too well. Something is brewing.* He could not alert the Company of Hunter's status. He would have to try to find a way to let them know something might be going on between Eugenia, Hunter, Stephen, and Maurice.

Hunter was fuming. He was going to kill Maurice. He knew Maurice had had sex with other men, but he didn't know that he had it enough to catch HIV. Maurice had had sex only with men, but Hunter had had sex with men and women, including Ila. This was not going to stop his plan. He and Ila would just have to have sex with condoms from now on. This new drug would probably stop the progression of the disease, so he could move forward with his plans, one and two: Stop the wedding! Kill Maurice!

Ila was done for the day. She had finished almost all her paperwork. There were only a few cases left. Tomorrow she would speak to the non-denominational Pastor who was going to marry them and get the rules for using the chapel. She was getting so excited. Brock would pick up the tuxedoes possibly on Friday. Brock would not get his hair cut until Thursday of next week, so that it would look fresh, but not too fresh. He was very particular about his hair. She wondered if Morris had an afro, which would be all right. Most of the men were wearing afros but the Company was strict about hair, so Brock's was always short, and his beard, when he had one, was always well manicured. He would be wearing a beard for the wedding. He was growing it now, and it was looking fabulous. She loved hair on a man's face.

She looked at the clock and wondered why she had not heard from Eugenia or Stephen all day. *They both must have had full schedules*. She really didn't want to walk back to the apartment; it was so cold. But she had her tennis shoes in her bag, so if she had to get some exercise, she would. Ila laughed because she really hated to exercise. She would rather starve herself than sweat. She laughed again. She slowly started closing up her office hoping that Stephen would show up.

Stephen drove from the hospital to Ila's apartment. He had to let Brock know that Hunter and Maurice were in town. As he drove through the maze of traffic, he heard his stomach growl. He had not eaten. He decided to stop at the Chinese restaurant not far from the apartment and pick up Chinese for him and Brock. As he entered the street, he could see that parking would be problematic, so he decided to park the car behind the apartment. He'd ask Brock if he wanted to walk to the restaurant for lunch.

After Stephen parked the car, he looked around carefully before getting out, just to make sure neither Maurice nor Hunter was lurking around. Comfortable that there was no one around, he got out of the car, but not before placing his gun in his holster under his jacket. He climbed the stairs two at a time and knocked on the back door.

Brock heard the knock and instantly got his gun. He was dressed, so he decided to exit through the front door and walk around to the back door. He picked up the keys, holstered his gun, put on his jacket, and went out the front door. He walked quickly to the driveway and walked slowly to the alley. He stopped at the edge of the building when he saw the Cutlass. He called out, "Stephen? Man, what's up?"

When Stephen saw Brock at the edge of the building, he bounded down the steps two at a time and walked up to Brock. "Man, I thought we would get some lunch. Then we could drive to the university. You can keep the car, and I'll get a maintenance vehicle for the weekend.

Brock said, "Cool. But, you know, I wasn't expecting anyone, so I went into full mode. Why didn't you beep me?"

Stephen said, "Man, I have had a lot on my mind. When this assignment is over, I don't know where they're going to send me. This has been a great assignment. Not too much stress. I was hoping that you could talk to the general for me to see if I could be assigned somewhere in the United States at least."

Brock nodded and said, "That's not a problem. I'll take care of it when I get back from our honeymoon."

Stephen said, "Great. By the time you get back, Eugenia and I both will be ready for new assignments.

Brock replied, "You know I probably can't do anything for Eugenia because she plays both sides of the fence. Her situation is very complicated."

Stephen replied, "I know. Eugenia will take care of herself, I have no doubt." They both laughed and walked quickly to the Chinese restaurant.

The placed was crowded. Brock said to Stephen, "Do you mind if we take this back to the apartment?" Stephen didn't respond. Then Brock remembered. He stood in front of Stephen and ask the same question. Stephen nodded his head yes. Both men were very hungry and ordered too much food, but Brock knew Ila would be hungry when she got home, so his would not go to waste. Their orders were soon ready.

Brock and Stephen shared small talk until they got to the apartment and turned down the driveway. Never come and go the same way—too funny, it was something they did automatically. The both climbed the steps. Brock already had his keys out to open the door. They entered and turned on all the lights and did a quick sweep, just in case. All was clear. They placed all the food on the table and got out plates, but they started eating out of the cartons before the food even hit the plate. They both laughed.

Brock fixed himself a vodka and cranberry juice, and he poured Stephen a cold glass of water. After a bit more small talk, Stephen said, "Man, I needed to tell you that Hunter and Maurice are in town. Maurice, we believe, is living in Ila's old apartment without permission from the

Company. Hunter is now at Walter Reed Hospital with some kind of virus. They shipped him home, and he got here yesterday or the day before. My intel was not really clear. But I'm sure he is here in the hospital.

Brock did not say a word. He just nodded his head. Stephen seemed surprised by his reaction. Then Brock said, "Thank you for the intel. Please know that what you have told me is on a need-to-know basis, and Ila does not need to know."

Stephen replied, "Ila already knows about Maurice, but she doesn't know about Hunter." Brock nodded, and Stephen said, "Is there anything I can do to help with this situation?"

Brock shook his head and said, "This sounds like a job for Eugenia." They both laughed. "But seriously, Stephen, thanks for telling me. I'll take care of it." They finished their late lunch, cleaned up the mess in the kitchen, and proceeded out the front door. Stephen gave the keys to the car to Brock, and he headed north walking to the university. He just wanted to clear his head. Brock headed south down the street to the driveway to the alley, got into the Cutlass, and proceeded up the back alleyway toward the university to pick up Ila.

Ila looked at the clock. *Shit! I'm going to have to walk. Stephen must be tied up.* She went from slow mode to fast mode as she really didn't want to walk in the dark with crazy Maurice still hanging around somewhere. She placed everything in the safe, put her gun in her purse, changed her shoes, and was ready to walk out of her office when the door slowly opened. She froze. Stephen usually knocked, and most of the students had gone home for the day. She backed up a little, and Brock shouted, "Honey, it's me!"

Ila laughed ran to the door. That man did not know he was about to be shot. They both laughed because they both knew how quickly something could get out of hand in the business they were in. He walked up to her and kissed her hard. "Hey," he said, "I stopped and got Chinese food, so you can come home, take off your shoes, and relax."

Ila was truly grateful for that. She replied, "I believe you have a date, Mr. Covington." As they were walking to the car, they saw Eugenia going into the building. They looked at each other as they both wondered why Eugenia was going into the building and not away from the building. As they slipped into the car, Ila told herself that she'd ask Eugenia why she had to work so late.

Brock thought to himself, *I needed to talk to Eugenia so I can make sure she can keep those punks from interrupting our wedding day.*

Eugenia had been at Walter Reed early getting her HIV test done. After five vials of blood and ten to fifteen pieces of paper to fill out, she was done. She decided to blow the day, go shopping, and have lunch at a nice restaurant. Then she would go back to work. The night before she had gotten intel that Hunter was at Walter Reed Hospital because he'd got sick in Libya, and no one knew what it was, so they'd transferred him to Walter Reed hospital by transport.

She was going to kill both those motherfuckers for ruining her life. She had been feeling weak lately. Her daily three-mile run was even hard for her. If those bitches had given her HIV ... well, she was not going to wait for the test results. She was going to devise a way to kill both of them right before the wedding and then get reassigned.

Before she left the hospital, she had given the receptionist $200 to tell her where Hunter's room was and an additional $200 to take a note to him. The young lady was more than happy to get the extra money. She took the note from Eugenia and promised that she would deliver it to Hunter that day. Eugenia asked the receptionist to put the note into a sealed envelope, which she did in front of Eugenia. "Remember," Eugenia told the young lady, "it is very important that he gets the note." The young lady nodded her head.

When Eugenia was done with her appointment and her other business, she headed to her car. It was a nice cold, crisp day, and she felt like some shopping therapy. She would go to the Crystal City to shop, and while she was there, she would book a room for next Wednesday through the following Monday. She had to stop and get cash from the bank because she wanted to pay in cash and use one of her aliases.

She drove to Federal Credit Union and withdrew $3,000. Then she drove to the Marriott and booked a room from Wednesday to Monday. She used her alias identification and told the hotel agent that her boyfriend would be coming to town and to make a note in the system to give him a key, but that he had to show his ID. His name was Hunter. The agent explained to Eugenia that hotel policy did not allow for that type of transaction but that she would be there most of the day on Wednesday. She asked Eugenia, "Do you know what time Hunter will be here?"

Eugenia replied, "Yes. He should be here on Wednesday of next week two in the afternoon." The agent said that she would be on duty that day and would take care of it. Eugenia gave her $1,000 for the room and an additional $200 tip for her service. Eugenia said, "Please make sure the suite is at the end of the hall by the steps. Hunter has a thing about elevators."

The agent replied, "No problem." Eugenia made sure she looked at her name tag—Tina.

Now she had to find out where Maurice was hanging out. That shouldn't be hard. She'd make a few calls from a pay phone to get the information. She took the elevator to the basement, which gave her entrance to the Metro, which would be her plan for escape. She looked around to make sure she knew how she was going to leave the hotel.

Satisfied with her escape route, she decided that she would take the Metro to the hotel that day and leave her car at the university. She'd be wearing a large blonde afro wig, a mini skirt, a black top, leather jacket, and thigh-high boots. She went back to the elevator and took it to the parking garage where she'd left her car. She drove back to DC with the intention of spending some money at Dillard's, but she decided to grab a bite to eat and head back to the university instead. She did not want to be missing in action all day even though she didn't have a set schedule now with the students essentially gone from the university.

She had had a full day. She stopped in one of her favorite restaurants and had fresh salmon, asparagus, new potatoes, and a glass of wine. She sat at a table by the window watching the people and traffic go by as she went over her plan to make sure there were no holes. Her mind drifted to when she was the only woman in training for the Company. There had been so many changes since then. Woman were now allowed to apply for any positions. She'd had to work her way up, threaten to sue, and scrap to get her position as an agent. It had been worth all the work and heartache. Her only regret ... she had no children, and it looked as if children were not in her future. This was no life for a child anyway. She would have to leave the child with its father or with her parents, which was not an idea she liked to think about. Her father was a colonel in the army, and he'd always run their entire household as if they lived in barracks. Her mother used to pack her father's bag quickly when he announced that he had to go on assignment. Eugenia and her brother would dance in their bedrooms knowing that their father might be gone for several months. Her brother was a lifer in the air force, and he also was not married and had no children. They would meet in faraway places when their jobs allowed and have dinner and spend a few days together. The last time she'd seen him, they were in Germany in the city of Stuttgart. What a wonderful time they'd had, drinking terrible beer and eating terrible food, but having a blast catching up on the many aspects of their careers. She looked at her watch. *Damn!* She needed to get back to the university. If nothing else, she should try to return her calls before it got too late.

Stephen did not know why he hadn't ridden back to the university with Brock. He just wanted to walk and clear his head. He really hoped Brock could help him stay in the United States, but just like Brock and Hunter, agents who were not married and had no children, nine times out of ten were sent overseas. Those two to three miles to the university felt like ten miles. It had gotten very cold, and frankly he was dressed for diving, not walking. He picked up the pace to try to get there quicker. If he'd had running shoes on, he would run, but he was wearing work boots, and they were too heavy for running. He could see the university up ahead. It looked like Oz. He couldn't wait to get to his room, turn up the heat, eat Frosted Flakes with no milk and call it a day.

As he entered the drive way to Healy Hall, he saw Eugenia's car. *What is she doing at the university this time of night?* He wondered how her appointment had gone. He would check in with her tomorrow, but then, as he walked past her office, he decided to stick his head in. He knocked on the door. There was no immediate response. He knew she was getting her gun and preparing for him to enter the office. There were no windows in any of the office doors; the building had been built so long ago. He turned the handle and wondered, why the door was not locked. He entered, closed the door, and yelled, "It's me, Stephen!"

She said, from behind a partition, "Please lock the door." Stephen turned around and locked the door. He walked down past the partition and found her. She looked gorgeous. She was a very attractive woman in a butch kind of way. He laughed to himself. He sat down. She was in full work mode.

"Why are you sitting here at night with the door open?" Stephen said.

Eugenia replied, "Well, I thought it would be better if someone entered the room instead of me going to the door opening it to find out that it might be trouble. This way trouble can enter the room and I can be prepared."

Stephen laughed, "Yup—just what I thought." They both laughed. "So, I got some intel that you should be aware of." Eugenia nodded her head, and he continued, "Hunter is at Walter Reed Hospital with a virus, and Maurice is probably hanging out at Ila's old apartment without permission from the Company."

Eugenia nodded and said, "How did Maurice manage to get into Ila's apartment?"

"He probably picked the lock. Remember, he's a lock specialist. He can hear a tumbler on a safe better than any of us, so he could break into it without much trouble. Do you not remember his specialty during training?"

Eugenia said, "Do you know how many years ago that was? Of course, I don't remember." They both laughed.

But Stephen remembered that Eugenia had a photographic memory and consequently did not forget a person, place, or thing. "How long are you planning on staying here tonight?" Stephen said.

"I just came to check my messages," Eugenia replied.

"Well, I do have good news," said Stephen. "I didn't test positive for HIV."

Eugenia jumped up in the air, which was way out of character. "I'm so happy for you," she said. "That is a reason to celebrate. We'll have drinks at my apartment this weekend!"

Stephen nodded and thought to himself, *But there will be no sex with you until you get your results.* And, really, they should not have sex with each other anyway; sex just made things difficult. "Drinks it is," said Stephen. "Now wrap this stuff up so I can walk you to your car."

Eugenia began putting things away, but then she started to cry. Heavy tears streaked her face. Stephen could not believe it. In all the years he had known Eugenia, he'd never seen her even whimper let alone a cry. She sat down in the chair and cried hard. Stephen was motionless. Then he ran to the door unlocked it and ran out down the hall to the men's room to get tissues. He was in shock. When he ran back to her office, she was still in full crying mode. He handed her the tissue. Eugenia looked at it and had to laugh. "Toilet tissue, Stephen?" He just nodded and let her have a good cry. Stephen had a seat by the door until she was done. "I don't want to die," Eugenia said. Stephen just nodded again. There were really no words.

She finally stood up and finished cleaning up her desk and locking things away. She picked up her coat, purse, and keys and was ready to go. Stephen held the door for her and turned off the light. She locked the door, and they headed to the parking lot. There was nothing left to say on the HIV subject, so Stephen said, "Saturday or Sunday and what time?"

"We'll do it on Saturday and invite Ila and Brock and pretend we are doing a small celebration for them. It will be fun. So, Saturday at four? I'll let Ila know."

He nodded and said, "Perfect." He took her keys and unlocked her car for her. Then he opened the door, and she got in.

"See you tomorrow," she said. Stephen nodded and smiled, and she drove off. He walked swiftly to his room.

It had gotten extremely cold outside. Once inside, he bolted the door and pushed a chair under the doorknob. He turned on the shower and waited for it to get hot. He peeled off his work clothes and placed them in a basket. As he stood under the hot water, he got emotional himself. He was so relieved that his life had been spared.

Hunter was looking at television contemplating how he was going to get a release from the hospital. He knew they wanted to keep him, but he was ready to go find Maurice's ass and kill him and then get to the wedding and stop that shit before it was too late. He heard the door open, and in walked a beautiful young nurse. She said, "Hunter, someone left an envelope for you at the nurse's station. Any other time we would be more cautious, but it came from the receptionist."

Hunter thanked the pretty lady, and she left. He opened the envelope. It was a note from Eugenia: "Hey, heard you were back in the States and in the hospital. If they let you out by Wednesday meet me at the Marriott Hotel in Chrystal City so we can party one last time before we get reassigned. I'll be there a 2:00 p.m. Just check in at the hotel desk. I'll be waiting for you."

She must not be getting any dick on this assignment. Hunter and Eugenia did have really good chemistry, not like he had with Ila. But he was not going to turn down a good piece of ass. He would be sure to be out of there by Wednesday and take some condoms with him. He guessed the intel she got did not have all the details. He was glad about that. It was going to be a long five days, but if they let him out early, he would just go home to his apartment and rest. He had not heard from the Company, so he assumed he was on TDY until further notice.

Eugenia drove home slowly. It took all she could not to ride to Arlington and kill Maurice tonight. But she wanted to stick to the plan. She drove into the long alleyway and turned into the area behind the apartment. Ila and Brock were home. She knew they were really enjoying themselves. She was aware she had a brief jealous streak. She shook it off. This was the life she had chosen so long ago. She sat in the car looking at her surroundings before she opened the door. Her gun was holstered. She laughed imagining a life without a gun holstered. She shook her head. Not something she wanted to do. She got out of the car and walked quickly up the steps. She had her keys out knowing how quickly someone could bound up the steps and catch her off guard, especially at night. She entered her apartment, bolted the door, walked through the apartment, and turned on all the lights. She did not have the privilege of having food and cleaning service like Ila, who was being treated as if she was in the witness protection program until after things had settled with the Chief Chambers. And Brock must have given his final report to the general or he would still be at the Pentagon. After finding the apartment all clear, she started turning off lights and walked to the bedroom. She sat on the bed and removed all her clothes. She was tired this evening. She got up and walked to the bathroom and turned on the shower. She wondered if Ila had the same problem, having to wait five minutes for the water to get hot. She walked to the kitchen and poured herself a tall glass of wine.

She just wanted to come up with a plan to get Maurice to the hotel room. She could leave him a note. Better yet, she was going to go to Ila's apartment and tell him that the Company knew where he was and to stay there until they could figure out what his next step would be. He was really considered AWOL, but when they found him, he was ordered to stand down and wait for the Company to advise him. That was a plan. He was not the only one who could pick a lock. Eugenia was pretty good at it herself. She walked back down the hall and jumped into the shower. She let hot water caress her body. She picked up soap and covered her body with suds. She never liked using washcloths. She wasn't sure when she stopped, but it had been years. She lathered up and rinsed off. She was not one to linger in the shower, but tonight it felt like a full-body massage. The water began to run tepid; she turned off the shower and reached for her towel. She hated to drip water onto the rug in the bathroom. She always dried off in the shower. She wrapped the towel around her after drying off, stepped onto the rug, and then reached for her glass of wine. Eugenia walked to her bedroom with nothing but sleep on her mind. She put the glass on the night stand, unwrapped the towel, and slipped into bed. She sat up hoping that she could devise a plan before she went to sleep. But alas, the plan just did not come together before she fell into a hard sleep. Her sleep was fretful because she knew there was not much time to put a plan together.

Brock heard Eugenia come up the wooden steps. He had a keen sense of hearing. It was one of the reasons he'd been recruited. That, and he was a sharpshooter. When he was younger, he and his cousin would go out into the woods of North Carolina and shoot squirrels, rabbits, and cans—anything that was not against the law. Both boys became sharpshooters, and both went into the Marines for four years. Brock went on to college and then went to the police academy, graduating as an officer. He was promoted to detective and was then recruited into the Company.

Ila had fallen asleep on the couch while he watched *The Rifleman*. He had gotten up to get something to eat, and that was when he'd heard Eugenia come home. He thought about knocking on her door to talk, but it was late; he would find an opportunity to speak to her tomorrow.

Eugenia caught her breath and sat straight up: Rohypnol, weed, Captain Morgan, Jack Daniels, and Clorox. She would need some help. She would talk to Stephen later that day to see if she could recruit him to help her get rid of the two people who could have ruined his life forever and probably had ruined hers. She did not think it would be a hard sell. She calmly went back to sleep knowing how it would go down. She just had to get them to the hotel together.

Ila woke up on the couch and wondered why Brock had not awakened her to go to bed. She got up, turned off the TV and the light, and walked back to the bedroom. Brock was sitting up in the bed. A sliver of moonlight was coming through the window.

He watched her as she entered the room and thought to himself, *If that mother fucker thinks he is going to stop my wedding and keep me from marrying Ila, he has another thought coming.*

Ila looked at Brock hard and said, "Why didn't you wake me up?" Brock did not answer. She hated it when he gave her the silent treatment. She removed her clothes and put them in the laundry basket, and then she walked to the bathroom to take a shower. She turned on the shower and grabbed her washcloth. When she turned to the sink to wash her face, she looked at the mirror, and there it was—Brock's promise. Her eyes welled up in tears. Could he be everything she had ever wanted and more? Could she really have this life of happiness, knowing that she was protected and safe, resting her head in the crook of his arm? Is that what her life would be like from this day forward? She laughed as she thought of the wedding vows. She quickly got into the shower and thought to herself, *What am I going to wear to work tomorrow?* She didn't want to have to think in the morning. Her royal blue sweater and denim jeans—it was Friday—and tennis shoes. She would just be finishing up paperwork, and there were probably not going to be any students there, so it should be a quiet day. Brock was going to go pick up the tuxedos, and then he would come back early to pick her up and that would be it. The rest of the time would be spent on wedding plans until next Saturday when she would become Mrs. Brock Covington.

After quickly washed all pertinent places, she got out of the shower, dried off, wrapped the towel around her, and walked to the bedroom. Brock was no longer sitting up. She laid the towel on the edge of the bed and got into the bed very quietly, inching over until she could hear his quiet breathing. It was like listening to waves in the ocean. It was great to sleep next to him like this.

Brock felt Ila get into bed and waited for her to inch closer. He grabbed her around the waist and pulled her into him. He kissed the back of her neck and began licking her down the middle of her back to her butt. He licked the crack of her ass and went down and came up under her so that he could eat the sweet nectar of her pussy. Ila was very still. He knew she was enjoying every moment. She was trying not to move too much as he enjoyed making love to her as she lay perfectly still. He opened the lips of her pussy until he could feel her clitoris, and he latched on to it and licked it with darting pulses until Ila could not hold on to her stiff body. She began to moan, and at that moment he sucked her clit as if he was sucking a straw, and Ila came in his face. He began to laugh loud and hard. He reached back and grabbed the towel Ila had placed on the bed. He wiped his face and then wiped her pussy. After throwing the towel back to the edge of the bed, he came from up under Ila, rolled over into a fetal position, and fell asleep.

Ila lay there thinking, *What just happened? How could that have been so good so fast?* Those were her last thoughts.

The morning came as usual, with the noise of traffic and people moving around—not as much as usual because the university was essentially closed, but the holiday visitors had started to arrive in the city before Christmas to see the lighting of the Christmas tree and other festivities that were held on the Mall. Christmas had fallen on a Sunday this year so the university was closed only on Friday and Monday, and essential personnel or anyone who wanted to report to work did. Any students who needed to work in the labs or see Ila or students on athletic teams were all still at the university, but this would be the last day for everyone except security until the second week in January.

Ila nudged Brock as he had managed to practically lay his entire body over hers. Sometimes she had a hard time breathing, but somehow, she usually got some sleep. He woke up instantly, looking and reaching. She rubbed his stomach and could feel his pulse calm down. He looked at Ila and said, "Do you really have to go to work?"

Ila replied, "It's the last day. When we return from our honeymoon, and hopefully are assigned to White House detail or Atlanta or Miami, we'll have many days and nights together."

Brock just laughed and said, "We'll probably be sent to Utah." They both laughed. Utah was a possibility because they'd both been involved with such an important case locally. But Ila did not care. Wherever he was assigned, she would go without hesitation. She rolled out of bed and walked to the kitchen to put the kettle on and make a light breakfast of bacon, toast, and eggs. She could hear Brock's heavy steps coming toward the kitchen. As he stood in the doorway, his presence took the air out of the room. He looked at her and then looked down at his penis. Ila immediately turned off the kettle and ran back to the bedroom. Thirty minutes later they had to start the process of getting dressed all over again.

Eugenia was up early. It was cold outside but not cold enough to keep her from running. She had not been running because she had been sick to her stomach most mornings. The one thing she had not considered until last night was that she might be pregnant. She'd had sex with the police officer twice two months ago without condoms because she'd run out, and he never brought any because she always had them. But of course, both times they used the pull-out method. Maybe she did not have HIV. Maybe she was pregnant. She thought the health department would give her a free pregnancy test, but she decided to go to the free clinic after the wedding in the Southeast and get a test there.

It was about 6:30 a.m. The sun was peeking through the sky. She put her work outfit in a garment bag, put her other tennis shoes in the bottom of the bag, and put her underwear in a plastic bag in the bottom of the garment bag. She would be able to keep on her sports bra on because the outfit was very casual, and it was her last day at work until after the New Year—maybe. They all might be reassigned after the New Year. Ila's students would miss her; she had really built a rapport with them.

Eugenia grabbed her gun and holster and put it on, making sure the safety was on. She put on a red sweatshirt, a red hooded sweatshirt, and red sweat pants, gloves, and a hat. She was ready to go to the track. It was easier and safer than running in the streets. There was also security. Everything in hand, she headed for the door.

Opening the door, she looked around and saw the blue sedan lurking at the end of the parking lot toward the back alley. Maurice was either losing his skills or he wanted her to see him. She believed it was the later, so she acknowledged seeing him. She walked down the steps and went to her car. She opened the back door and laid her clothing bag on the backseat. She got into the front seat, turned the engine over, and waited about three minutes before pulling out of the parking space. She wanted to make sure there was nobody else lurking around. She rounded the driveway and headed to O Street, waited a minute in the driveway, and then pulled out onto O Street headed toward the university. She drove slowly thinking that Maurice would follow her, but she didn't see him behind her.

Maurice waited patiently in the car. It was cold. He had used up a quarter tank of gas waiting for Eugenia to make a move. He knew she was a runner, and he figured that, on this Friday, she would make a way to get in some exercise. He had pulled into the back of the driveway at around 6:00 a.m. He turned the car off and on repeatedly for forty-five minutes before Eugenia made an appearance. He knew she would spot him. He was not really trying to hide. He still really wanted to talk to Ila. He was going to have another conversation with Eugenia to see if she could make the meeting happen for him.

After Eugenia got into the car, Maurice turned his car around, went out the back way, and entered O Street by turning right and then left onto the street. He saw Eugenia pass. He let two or three cars go by and then pulled out. She was dressed for running, so he would go straight to the track. He was glad he'd brought his credentials; otherwise, there was no way he could get to the track.

Eugenia looked at every cross street on her way to O Street. He had to have turned around and come out the back way. Three blocks down, there he was, sitting at O and 34th Streets on the left. She kept driving. When she reached the university, she drove to the back of Healy Hall where she normally parked her car. Then she decided to get closer to the track. She kept driving until she got to the gate of the stadium. The gate was closed, but a security guard was standing by to open the gate. She slowly drove up to the gate and showed her credentials to a guard inside the guard station. He opened the gate, and she drove through slowly. She still had to walk about a half of mile to get to the track, but it was better than parking in her space at Healy Hall. She drove to an end spot and looked around again, thinking that Maurice would show up any minute.

She got out of the car and did some stretching. The sun was completely up, and the cold chill was leaving the air. She locked the door and began to jog to the steps of the stadium. Much to her surprise, Maurice was already there. He had used the back entrance and had come through the tunnel. He was sitting on the first row of the bleachers as Eugenia came down the steps. At the bottom, Eugenia stopped. "Good morning. And to what do I owe this pleasure?"

Maurice said, "Stop playing games. You know I want to talk to Ila, and you are the only one who can make that happen."

Eugenia said, "You know, Brock is with her twenty-four seven. How do you think I can make it happen?"

Maurice looked at her and said, "I either talk to Ila or I talk to Brock—one or the other. I want him to know that he is about to marry someone who might just have HIV."

Eugenia said, "I have to get my workout in. Why don't you go sit in the tunnel out of the cold, and we'll talk when I'm through. I'm going to run three miles. Should take me around forty minutes.

Maurice said "I'll wait right here. The sun is coming out. It should get warmer by the minute."

Eugenia left him sitting there. She walked the track for about ten minutes, and then started to run. She loved to run. It emptied her mind and her body. For forty minutes she would just zone in on the exercise and clear her head. She had started to sweat, and suddenly, her stomach churned. It felt like an influx of acid from her stomach came into her throat. She stopped and walked over to the grass and threw up water and very little food. She began to sweat more. She stood in the grassy area for a minute and decided that walking was going to be her best bet today. Her exercise would take about sixty minutes instead of forty. Maurice would just have to wait. As she rounded the track near where Maurice was sitting, she stopped to tell him that she had pulled a muscle and would have to walk and run in combination.

He said, "What happened over there? Were you throwing up?"

Eugenia said "Yes. You should never run on an empty stomach." She continued her walk. The air was starting to warm up, but she thought it would be a good idea to stay dressed warm.

Maurice sat in the cold for the entire time wanting to just say "Fuck it!" He would ambush Ila when she came to work and make her talk to him. The only problem with that plan was Brock. He had to laugh; Brock was just not a motherfucker you messed with. He was strong, smart, and a sharp shooter. He laughed again and decided that, if he was going to die, it would not be because Brock put a bullet through his head from a hundred yards away. He waited until Eugenia rounded her last lap and she sat down beside him. He waited for her to catch her breath. "So how are you going to make it happen?" he said.

Eugenia replied, "Did I tell you that Hunter and I are going to party one last time at the Marriott on Wednesday in Crystal City? Oh, that's right you didn't know he was back in town. Well he is, and we're going to party before the wedding because we all will probably be reassigned after the wedding."

Maurice said, "What about my condition?"

Eugenia said, "You'll have to use a condom … maybe two." They both laughed.

Maurice's dick got hard just thinking about having sex with Hunter again. He didn't care that he had to wear a condom. "What time on Wednesday are you meeting at the Marriott?" Maurice said.

"Two in the afternoon," said Eugenia. "After we have our party, then we'll find time to talk to Ila. Let her enjoy her time with Brock before you break the news to her that she might have HIV. She promised him that they would meet with her on Thursday. I'll invite her to lunch, and you can meet us there. It would be better to tell her in a public place, since she's days away from her wedding. I know Ila and Brock are having unprotected sex. But you do understand that, if all of us test HIV positive, you are a dead man, right? You understand that?"

Maurice nodded. "Yes, either way I'm dead."

"Okay then," Eugenia said, "let's party protected on Wednesday and then let the chips fall where they may. You must know that, whatever happens, we've have had a wonderful ride. We've all come from different backgrounds, but our lives have been the kind that people have in the movies!" They both laughed. "So, let's party one last time, and then we'll tell Ila. She'll have time to call the wedding off, and she can get tested. Once the test results come back, we'll cross that bridge when we have too."

Maurice shook his head. "Yes, you're right. What should I bring to the party?"

Eugenia replied, "What else? Captain Morgan and Jack Daniels. I'll bring the chasers, and I'll ask Hunter to bring some food.

"Do you know where Hunter is hanging out?" Maurice said.

"Yes, but I'm not going to tell you. Do you want him to know where you are, or do you want to surprise him and watch his big black dick get so hard you'll be able to play jump rope with it?"

Maurice could not wait. He looked at Eugenia and said, "Thank you for not hating me. This is not how I thought my life would end. Have you gotten tested yet?"

"Yes. I went to Walter Reed, and I'm waiting for the results so, in the meantime we'll use condoms and party. I wish we could get some coke. You know they won't test us again until we are reassigned. I guess we'll have to settle for weed. Can you get weed?"

Maurice said, "Certainly. That won't be a problem."

"Great! This is going to be a great party. Thank you, and I promise we'll meet with Ila on Thursday. Let her enjoy some festivities before we drop the hammer on her."

Eugenia started walking up the steps, and Maurice called out, "Please don't let Brock shoot me in the head if Ila comes back positive."

Eugenia said, "I promise. My gut tells me that Ila doesn't have it, but we won't know until she is tested. Okay, Maurice, see you on Wednesday. I can't wait. You remember when we walked out of the room after our last party? We walked over Ila like she was a homeless person on a grate." They both laughed.

"See you on Wednesday," Maurice said.

Eugenia climbed the steps and walked to her car. She couldn't wait to take a shower in the university faculty lounge. Even when it was cold, Eugenia sweated a lot. And, she also could not wait to eat something—anything.

Maurice walked slowly down the tunnel to the back entrance toward his car. He would stop at the package store and pick up the Captain Morgan and Jack Daniels today. He had been given condoms at the hospital, so that was all he would need for the party. As he drove to the package store, he decided to have breakfast at the Waffle House. There was no place like the Waffle House for breakfast, and he surely would not run into anyone he knew.

Eugenia drove to the faculty lounge. She walked to the back of the building where the showers were located, dragging all her stuff with her and thinking that she would have to get Stephen involved with the plan. There was no one in the locker room. Most of the professors had left the campus for the holidays. She checked all the doors and made sure they were locked from the inside. She took off her clothes and walked to the showers. The difference between these showers and the one in the apartment was that, here, the water got hot instantly. She stood under the shower and realized that she hadn't brought anything to wash up with, so she took some liquid jell soap from the wall dispenser and made that work. As the water rolled down her back, she remembered that one of her Company classmates worked at the *Eckerd* Pharmacy in Arlington. She would run over there after lunch today and ask her classmate if she could get some liquid Rohypnol. She was sure Iris would give it to her. After all, Eugenia had cut the throat of the man who had Iris trapped in a bathroom in New York's Grand Central Station years ago. If it were not for Eugenia, who at the time had been disguised as a homeless person, Iris would not be alive today. Eugenia had never thought she would need to call in a favor, but now was the time.

She dried off and got dressed. She unlocked the door. She hadn't heard anyone knock, so it was safe to surmise that no one had tried to use the facility. As she entered the hallway, she remembered that the cafeteria was probably not open. Or maybe there was limited service today. She was starving in a way that was most unusual for her. As she thought back over the month, she realized she had not had a period, but that was not unusual for her because sometimes too much running would throw her cycle off. As she turned down the second hallway, she saw Ila and Stephen walking into the building holding bags that looked as if they might hold food. She so hoped it was food and coffee because she was going to mooch some if it was.

Ila got out of bed for the second time that morning and hurried around getting dressed. Brock was still in bed contemplating world affairs. Ila laughed and ran back into the bedroom, picked up a pillow, and hit Brock across the belly. "Get up! You've already made me late for work, and you have to go pick up the tuxedoes for you and Morris."

Brock groaned said, "Come back to bed. It's your last day! No one will miss you!"

Ila replied, "You might be right, but if there is one student there who needs help today, I want to be there for him or her." Brock groaned again and rose up out the bed.

Ila came back from the bathroom and looked at him. It was cold outside, and he had dressed in sweat pants and a sweatshirt. His leather jacket was on the bed. He'd already put on his socks and tennis shoes. She guessed it was not his intention to take a shower or brush his teeth or comb his hair. Brock said, "Stop looking at me! I'm going to at least brush my teeth and comb my hair." They both laughed. It was too late to fix breakfast, so they would stop at the deli down the street and get breakfast for Eugenia and Stephen. Ila knew that the cafeteria would probably either be closed or have a limited menu.

They finally rolled out, got into the car, and headed to the deli. Of course, it was packed. It was Friday, and a lot of people were on vacation. Brock couldn't find a place to park the Cutlass, so Ila hopped out to get breakfast. There was plenty of counter help on hand, so the line moved fast. She had ordered six bagels, lox, cream cheese, fruit bowls, and coffee, all of which required two large bags and a carrier for the coffee. She had asked the server to put Brock's breakfast in a separate bag so that he could eat either at the apartment or on his way to the tuxedo shop.

She knew that Brock was circling the block. He was just pulling up outside the deli when she came out with the food. Ila gave the coffee carrier to Brock to hold as she climbed into the car with the two bags. Of course, people were blowing their horns behind them, but, that was life in DC. They both laughed because they loved the city. To make matter worse, Brock made a U-turn, and the horns went wild. The laughed ever louder.

Once they arrived at Healy Hall, Ila gave Brock his coffee. She put the drink carrier on the dashboard, got out of the car with her purse and bag of food, reached back in for the carrier, and closed the door with her butt. She did not have all the baggage she normally carried because she knew Brock would be back to get her in the early afternoon. He honked the horn and drove off. They were both laughing.

She carefully walked up the steps and thought, *Okay, how am I going to open these doors?* Usually there were tons of people around opening and closing the door. She looked around, and from out of nowhere there was Stephen. He was like Underdog—Speed of lightning, roar of thunder, fighting all who rob or plunder! Underdog! Ila laughed to herself until tears came to her eyes.

Stephen opened the door and looked at her. He wondered why she had tears in her eyes. He was hoping this was not going to another crying episode; he could not handle that this cold morning. As they were walking down the hall, they could see Eugenia walking toward them. Ila yelled, "Breakfast!" and Eugenia started walking faster. Stephen opened Ila's office door and turned on the light. There was a small conference table to the left of the entrance. Ila set all the food on the table along with the coffee. She went to her desk area, took off her coat, put her purse in the bottom drawer and her gun in the top drawer, and unlocked the safe. She could hear Stephen going through the bags.

Eugenia walked through the door, put all her belongings on the floor, and sat at the table. By the time Ila got back to the conference table, the conversation had stopped and the eating frenzy had begun.

There was a knock on the door. Ila got up, and Stephen put his hand on his gun. Eugenia rolled her eyes. Her gun was on the floor by the door, and Ila had left hers in her desk drawer. Ila opened the door, standing behind it so that she could reach Eugenia's gun if necessary. The young student Anthony DeLeo walked in. Eugenia said, "Hi, Anthony. Why are you still on campus?" He told them that his father was supposed to be there early that morning to pick up him, but he had not arrived yet. He'd seen Ms. Montgomery with bags and was hoping that it was food. They all laughed, and Ila fixed him a bagel with lots of cream cheese. He devoured it in no time and thanked them. He said that he needed to go back out to the quad. Hopefully his father would be there in a few minutes to pick him up. He got up and left the office.

Ila looked at Stephen and Eugenia as she walked over and locked the door. "Do you know anything about that student?" she asked them. "He showed up on campus right at the end of the first semester. I really never gave him a thought, but it seems odd that he's still on campus."

Stephen said, "I'll look into his background and get back to you. But, really does it matter? None of us will be here next semester. He'll be another undercover's problem." The all laughed and continued eating.

Eugenia said, "Hey, why don't you and Brock come up to my apartment on Saturday? We can have a little celebration in honor of your wedding. You know—a few drinks and some food. We could play a game of cards or team Scrabble or go down to the Waterside Mall and listen to some jazz." They all looked at each other and laughed, "Maybe not." That was where all the craziness with the police chief had started.

Then they looked at each other and said, "The Fox Trap!"

Stephen got really quiet. Ila said, "What's wrong?"

He replied, "You know, if we leave the apartment I can't talk and I can't drink, because then I forget I can't talk."

They all busted out laughing. Ila said, "Okay—we'll stay in, get drunk, and play board games. That's what Brock would want to do anyway. After one hour at the Fox Trap he'd be ready to come home." They all laughed again.

Eugenia said, "Okay. Four o'clock on Saturday. I'll have to pick up food from somewhere and you guys bring alcohol and mixers. They all laughed again while they cleaned up their mess. It was amazing how much mess bagels, cream cheese, and lox could make. When they were finished, Eugenia picked up her bags and left to go to her office. Stephen left right behind her. It was Ila's intention to finish all her cases today including Anthony DeLeo's. That had been a very strange visit. She was sure that Stephen was going to run him through the system just to see who exactly he and his father were. Ila decided to lock the door and finish her work. She was sure Brock would be arriving shortly after two o'clock to pick her up.

Brock decided to park in the parking lot on campus to drink his coffee and eat his bagel, lox, and cream cheese. He would call Morris from the apartment when he got back to make sure his arrangements had been made. The weather had been so bad all over the United States, but Morris would have a straight flight into Washington DC International, so there was a slim chance that he would get stuck, unless they needed to make an emergency landing somewhere. He could not wait to spend time with his friend again. They'd had a great time in North Carolina, but that was a sad occasion. This was a joyous occasion, and they would probably go to Blues Alley after the wedding and have dinner, listen to some jazz, and have a good time. Brock would stop by Blues Alley that day to make reservations for nine o'clock. He was not sure who the twelve would be, but he knew Ila, and inviting twelve people to dinner would be easy.

He finished his breakfast, started the car up, and eased out of the parking lot. He saw a young man come out of Healy Hall and jump into the passenger side of a black Riviera. An older gentleman was behind the wheel.

Brock drove slowly past the car and made a mental note of the license plate. He went through the gate and made his way down O Street. It was good not to be stuck in the Pentagon writing up reports. It was easy to get stuck in that mindset and forget that life was really going on. He drove to the Men's Wearhouse and was excited about trying on his tux. He thought about overnighting Morris his tux but decided that he did not want anything to happen during shipping. He was sure the tux would fit him. The measurements had been sent along with shoe and shirt size. Everything should be fine. He decided he would call Morris from the Men's Wearhouse. As he entered the store, Peter, the store manager, walked right over to him. "Mr. Covington, you are going to be so pleased with your ensemble. As a matter of fact, we have it on display for others to use in their weddings!"

Brock walked over to the display and just nodded. It looked very *GQ*. He could not wait to try it on. Peter went to the back of the store and came back with two large garment bags. Everything was contained in the bags. Peter took one bag to the changing room and took the other one to the front desk. The sign on the room said "changing room" instead of "dressing room." Brock laughed. He had not noticed that before.

In the changing room, he began the process of putting on everything, including the socks. It took about fifteen minutes. Brock stood in the mirror and got misty eyed. He had thought this day would never happen for him. He had decided he was going to be a Company man— no distractions, no commitments, no ties. But then he'd met Ila. He'd never known that a woman could change his mind about anything. But she was easy, gentle, and dangerous all wrapped up in one. What more could a man ask for? He laughed out loud.

He could hear someone walking toward the dressing room, which was dangerous for the other person. As the person walked into the room, Brock reached for his gun. Peter said, "Mr. Covington, is everything all right? Do you need anything?"

Brock laughed again, "No, Peter. Everything is perfect. I'll be right out." Brock took his time putting everything back together. This outfit was everything Ila wanted, and she deserved it. He would call Morris from the front desk at the Men's Wearhouse, as he was not sure of the security of the phone at the apartment. Something told him to call from the store. He walked out to the front desk. Peter was taking care of another customer. Brock laid the clothing bag across the counter and sat in a chair just next to the counter. He kept an eye on the door. One day he would not always be looking for exists, making sure that he could always see the front door. He wouldn't always scan everyone in the room into memory just in case. He sat patiently while Peter finished with his customer. Peter turned to Brock when the customer walked away.

"Peter, is it possible for me to make a long-distance call on your phone?" Brock said.

"Of course," Peter replied.

"Is it also possible that you might be able to walk away for about five minutes while I carry on the conversation?"

Peter replied, "Of course." He lifted the phone off the desk, handed the receiver to Brock, and walked away.

Brock had Morris' number etched in his brain. He dialed, and Morris picked up on the second ring. "Morris here."

"Hey, man, it's Brock. I was just wondering what time you're going to get here on Friday."

"Man, change of plans," said Morris. "I have to take the five o'clock on Saturday morning and turn around and take the red-eye back at midnight. My new plans include a trip overseas. We'll talk more when I get there. I can't wait, man. I'm so excited for you!"

Brock replied, "Okay, man. I have your suit. And I'll make a reservation at the Georgetown Inn today. That way we'll have a nice place to change clothes. It's close to the university. I'll also see if Stephen can pick you up and take you back to the airport."

Morris said, "Stephen? Man, who is Stephen? Never mind, you can send whomever you like. I just want to be there for you."

Brock laughed. "He'll be the man waiting for you with a sign in his hand. Since you're taking Company transport, there should be no delays. He'll pick you up at the airport at eleven thirty at the central gate."

Morris said, "You bet. See you then."

Morris hung up the phone and decided that he would not tell Brock that he knew his bride and that flying in and out would be the best thing. There would be no time for discussion, and he was sure that Ila would maintain a certain decorum and not let Brock know. He also didn't want Brock to know he had paid for the tuxedoes—just a present to his friend. They had been through so much together over the years and were like brothers, but Morris had never told Brock about Ila.

Brock stood at the desk for a moment trying to get Peter's attention. He had asked him to leave the area but not leave the building. Brock started to laugh. He looked up and saw Peter coming into the building from outside. He wondered for a second why the man had left the building. Once Peter got closer, Brock could smell why he had left the building—Peter was a smoker. Peter walked quickly to the counter. "Yes, Mr. Covington. Everything was perfect for you? I worked with the tailor on the alterations myself."

Brock replied, "Perfect. Are you sure I don't owe you anything for the tuxedoes?"

"No, Mr. Covington, your bill is paid in full."

Brock said, "Okay. Thanks so much." He picked up the garment bags and walked out of the store. Back at the Cutlass, he opened the trunk so that he could lay the bags flat. He was surprised to see that his trunk was a mini arsenal—full of guns. He laughed out loud. Did Stephen think that the revolution would start tomorrow? He closed the trunk quickly. He had errands to run, and he needed to get cash from the bank for the room at the Georgetown Inn, and he needed to leave a deposit at Blues Alley for dinner.

Eugenia decided not to go to her office; rather, she headed to the drugstore in Arlington to get the liquid Rohypnol. And she'd stop at a package store for a bottle each of Captain Morgan and Jack Daniels. She would have four bottles in the room; her plan was to put Rohypnol in her bottles and Maurice's would not. She eased her way to her car feeling good about the plan. As she turned the corner to the parking lot, Stephen was standing near the back gate, pretending that he was fixing something. He was very good at looking busy and really just doing surveillance. She laughed. It seemed to have gotten colder in just a few hours. She put on her coat. She got into the car and drove up to the back gate, got out of the car and walked around to talk to Stephen. She said, "Please get in the car. There is something I would like to talk to you about."

Stephen nodded, turned and picked up his tools, and walked toward the car. Eugenia walked back to the car and waited for Stephen. He put the tool box on the floor of the backseat of the, car and he jumped into the front. They pulled out the back gate slowly. She turned onto O Street so that she could cross the 14th Street Bridge to head toward Arlington. For about fifteen minutes, Eugenia did not say a word. Stephen waited patiently. "Stephen, I need your help in killing Maurice and Hunter," Eugenia said. Stephen said nothing. Eugenia continued. "A couple of years ago, Maurice, Hunter, and I all use to party together. The last time was at the end of our last assignments. At the time, Ila was seeing Hunter. He was narcissistic—anything he wanted was great, anything she wanted was problematic. At the end of the assignment, Maurice, Hunter, and I had a threesome in the safe house apartment. Ila had left, but she'd left something behind, or she'd decided to bring back the car for him or something. Anyway, she walked in on us. Hunter was in me, and Maurice was in Hunter. It was the most erotic experience I'd ever had. We had no intention of letting her know, but she came back, heard the music, opened the door, and collapsed to the floor. We immediately got dressed and ended our sexual encounter. I got dressed the fastest because it really hurt me to see the look on her face. But I had to pretend it didn't matter to me one way or the other. I even smiled at her when I opened the door. Long story short, I walked out of the bedroom, stepped over her, and left the apartment. I believe everyone else did the same. But somehow Brock and Hunter had an encounter. I was gone by then so I'm not sure what exactly happened, because no one, to my knowledge, has talked about that day to this day. And over the years, we have gotten together from time to time. But never did Maurice say he had HIV, or even hint that he might possibly have HIV. To my knowledge, Hunter's only experience with another man was with Maurice. He somehow justified his relationship with him so that it didn't mean he was gay. Not sure how you wrap your mind around that, but there are a lot of guys who keep their sexuality on the down low now, so he felt justified I think."

Stephen did not say a word. They had reached the drugstore. Eugenia parked the car and asked Stephen if he was coming in. He looked at her and got out the car. They walked into the drugstore and walked back to the pharmacy. Eugenia could see her friend, Iris, in her white coat and name tag. As they approached the counter, an assistant walked up to help them. Eugenia told the assistant that she was here to see the pharmacist. The young lady went to Iris and told her that someone was there to see her. Iris walked up slowly and placed her hand close to her heart where the name tag was. The name on the tag was Margaret Bowen. "Hello there. How can I help you?" Iris said. Eugenia thought she was out of the Company business, but her name tag said Margaret Bowen.

Eugenia responded, "My friend here is hearing impaired and sometimes has difficulty reading lips." She turned to Stephen and said, "Do you want me write down the medication you need?" Stephen nodded his head. Eugenia turned back around and ask the pharmacist for a pen and pencil. The pharmacist took a pad and pencil from under the counter. Eugenia wrote "Liquid Rohypnol by Tuesday of next week."

Iris said to Eugenia, "We don't have that here, but you may be able to get it from another store. Where is the closest drugstore to your home?"

Eugenia said, "He lives in Georgetown."

Iris picked up the pad and wrote, "Meet me in the Giant Food parking lot in five minutes." She ripped the piece of paper off the pad and said to Eugenia, "Please try this pharmacy. They may have the medication you need."

Eugenia thanked her and looked at Stephen while Iris took the pad and placed in it in her pocket. Eugenia and Stephen turned and headed to the front door. They got into the car and headed across the street to the Giant Food store. They parked to the far right of the lot, which was virtually empty, so that when Iris arrived they could flash their light to get her attention. They waited, and right on cue, they saw Iris at the traffic light across the street headed to the parking lot. She parked and got out of the car quickly, obviously waiting to see flashing lights or something that would indicate where Eugenia and her friend were.

When Eugenia flashed her lights, Iris came from the far end of the parking lot walked up to the car. Eugenia rolled down the window. Iris had taken her pharmacy coat off and had put on heavy winter leather jacket and a hat. She looked like a different person. Eugenia guessed that was the point. Iris handed Eugenia the bag and said, "Read the directions carefully." She walked away from the car and went into the Giant Food store. Eugenia waited to see if there was anyone following her. She had already retrieved her gun, and Stephen was always packing. They sat for about ten minutes and saw no unusual movement. Eugenia started the engine and drove off.

She did not have to drive far to find a liquor store. She got out, bought the Captain Morgan and Jack Daniels, and got back into the car. Stephen still had not said a word. She decided to take Route 50 back into the city. Stephen finally spoke: "So, once they have been given Rohypnol and have passed out, then what?"

"That's where you come in, Stephen. I need you to come into the room to help me move them into the bathtub. In two days, the bodies will start to decompose, which means they will start to smell. I need you to bring five bottles of Clorox. We'll put it in the bathtub along with some water. It will keep the smell down and will help to quickly decompose the bodies.

"Okay," he said, "but Rohypnol will not kill them."

Eugenia said, "We'll slit their wrists—like in *The Godfather*—and they'll bleed to death. I'll give them enough to keep them out for hours. It will look like a lover's suicide pact. The cuts will have to be perfectly precise—if we cut the arteries wide enough, they'll bleed sufficiently to cause a heart attack within about one to two minutes. So you have to bring Clorox, a fresh box cutter, gloves, and we will also use the Clorox to get rid of our finger prints. But knowing the Company, once word gets out who they are, the room will be quarantined and labeled a crime scene, and we'll never hear about it again. Letters will be sent to their families stating they were killed in the line of duty overseas and their bodies were recovered, but they were cremated before they were transported home."

Stephen was very quiet. Eugenia went on, "If we don't do this, I know they will come to the wedding and start shit. I know that is what Hunter wants to do. And Maurice just wants to tell Ila about his HIV status. Hunter does not want Ila to marry Brock. Both these parasites need to leave this earth."

Stephen was silent again. They listened to the music of the traffic and the tires on the road. Eugenia was pulling into the parking lot of the university. She looked at Stephen with tears in her eyes. "I need your help." She parked in the back lot. They both sat silent for a few minutes.

Finally, Stephen said, "When are we going to do the deed?"

Eugenia could breathe again. "Wednesday at two in the afternoon. We're supposed to meet at the Marriott Hotel in Crystal City. It will take me about two hours to get the party started and over with. Unfortunately, you'll have to climb the stairs with all of that Clorox. I'll make sure the room is by the stairwell. I've paid cash for the room, and I'll leave looking like a different person. The only problem is that the agent who works there has seen me as Eugenia. I'll come back dressed differently and looking different, but I'll use the same ID—not mine of course. But she is the least of my worries. Once I get the keys, I'll go up and prepare the room. I'll leave a key at the front desk for Hunter, and I'll send the room number to Maurice on his beeper. For some reason, if the plan does not go as expected, I'll nine-one-one your beeper, and that will mean you should stand down until you hear from me again. So, if you arrive at four o'clock, the party should be over, and they should be knocked out. I'll also send the room number to your beeper. Once in the room, I'll order room service so that there will be food there to distract them while I fix their drinks. But Hunter is slick. He'll want me to drink a drink out of the bottle that they are drinking out of. So, I can do shots and put the Rohypnol in beer. I don't drink beer, so they won't be surprised if I don't have any. I'll have the St. Pauli Girl in the refrigerator with the mixture already made up. Beer is bitter, and anyway they won't notice it after three or four shots. Once they've drunk the St. Pauli Girl, I'll get the party started by taking off my clothes and lying on the bed. Maurice will come in the door with his dick hard, so it won't be all that difficult to get it started." They both laughed a nervous laugh.

Stephen put his hand on the door handle and said, "What should I bring tomorrow?"

"Bring some St. Pauli Girl!" Eugenia said. They laughed.

Stephen said, "Okay. I'll see you tomorrow at four and then on Wednesday at four. This is going to change our lives. You do understand that, right?"

Eugenia nodded. "They could have changed your life forever, and I'll know next Friday if they have changed my life forever."

Stephen said, "Remember, the university is officially closed down today, so you'll have to have all of your passes, key cards, and so forth to get on campus if you come back on Monday."

Eugenia said, "I'm officially on vacation as of right now." They both laughed again, and Stephen got out the car. He had forgotten how cold it was, and started running to his room. The campus was virtually empty. He got to his room and turned the heat up before taking off his coat. Then it dawned on him how hungry he was. Well, it was going to be Frosted Flakes and milk again. He laughed, hung his coat up, and went to the kitchen to get his Tupperware bowl for his Frosted Flakes and milk.

Eugenia pulled out of the parking lot and felt the fatigue of the day come down on her, plus her stomach was giving her hell for not putting food into it since breakfast. As she drove slowly to the apartment, she noticed that the small pizza place was still open. She did a U-turn and found a parking space not far from the restaurant. It was getting late. She took her gun out of her purse and holstered it. She placed her purse in the glove compartment and took just twenty dollars out of her wallet. She locked the glove compartment and waited for traffic to die down before trying to get out of the car. Once she was out and, on the sidewalk, her stomach rumbled as if someone had given her Pepto-Bismol. She leaned over the front of the car and heaved. There was not much to come up because she had not eaten since breakfast. She looked around to see if anyone had seen that disgusting site. She began to laugh. There was no doubt in her mind now that she was pregnant. She just hoped she also did not have HIV. *Shit … that would be more than I could handle.* She went back around the car and got into the driver's side. She turned the engine over and made another left turn into oncoming traffic. She decided to go home, have some tea, toast, and cheese and call it a night.

Ila was finishing up the paperwork for her last three cases when there was a knock at the door. She got her gun out of the top drawer, took her heels off, and walked silently to the door. She stood to the right side of the door and asked, "Who it is please?"

"It's Chef Charles."

She slowly opened the door, and there he stood—a massive man. She smiled and said, "Hi there. How are you today?"

Chef Charles responded, "I'm fine. Pastor Raleigh is right behind me. We just have some final arrangements to go over, and we must talk about payments.

"Oh, no problem," Ila said. "Please come in." She slid the gun into her pants pocket. Chef Charles and Pastor Raleigh sat down. Ila walked back to her desk and dropped the gun into the top desk drawer. She walked back to the front of the office and sat down.

Pastor Raleigh spoke first, "Since this will not be a traditional wedding, are you going to write your wedding vows?"

Ila thought a minute and said, "If it is possible, we would like to do the traditional wedding vows. This moment has been a long time coming for both of us, and we want to make sure the covenant is binding. I think the traditional wedding vows pretty much sum it up."

Pastor Raleigh looked relieved. "Great!" he said. "And the music?"

"Well," Ila replied, "since it is not a traditional wedding, I was thinking about something more contemporary. But then I thought, if you could possibly get an organist and someone to sing "Ave Maria," that would be beautiful."

He looked relieved again and said, "Thank you. That will work out fabulously."

She looked at Chef Charles, and he said, "Do you have any changes to the menu?"

"No, the menu you decided on is great. We all sat around talking about selections, but we never really came up with a good menu. I'm going to leave that in your hands. Do you need additional money for the flowers? I've decided on a large bouquet of carnations—white for me, and white with a few red ones for my maid of honor."

"Easy to do," said Chef Charles, "and no, you will not need any additional funds. We received a credit card from your Company along with a note authorizing us to use the card for all costs relating to your wedding. And if additional funding was needed, additional funding would be placed on the card. They also returned your check. We were told to contact them only if there was not enough money on the credit card."

Ila sat with her mouth open. Who at the Company would pay for her wedding? She finally said, "I want to thank whoever it is, or at least contact them and invite them to the wedding."

Chef Charles shrugged his shoulders and said, "I don't know what to tell you, but if it were me, I would just thank God and keep it moving. It is really a blessing." The Pastor agreed by nodding his head.

Ila sat for a minute and said finally, "Well, now that I have been blessed beyond measure, is there anything else we have to talk cover?"

Chef Charles said, "No. All done." He and the non-denominational Pastor rose, and Chef Charles said, "See you on your wedding day!"

Pastor Raleigh said, "Are you getting dressed in the chapel dressing room?"

"Yes, and there will be two others. I'm not sure what the guys are going to do yet," Ila said.

"Okay," said Pastor Raleigh. "If they decide to get dressed here, just let us know by Friday of next week so that we can have the other dressing room prepared and ready for occupancy. What time will your wedding party be arriving to get dressed?"

Ila replied, "We'll all be here by six. We have to get married when the clock hand is going up, so I'll be walking down the aisle at six thirty."

"That is an old tradition, Ila. It's not necessary to do that anymore," he replied.

Ila said, "According to my grandmother, who is unable to be here, it is the only tradition. My parents and grandmother are not able to travel, so that is one wish I can give her in her absence."

They both laughed. Pastor Raleigh said, "We understand." With that they both left the office.

Ila locked the door behind them. It was getting late, and she had just a one more case to complete. She walked back to her desk. It took about an hour to finish the case. She beeped Brock: 18, 5, 1, 4, 25 ("ready").

Brock looked at his beeper. Ila was ready. He had just completed booking the room at the Georgetown Inn and was on his way make reservations at the Blues Alley for dinner after the wedding. He had to remember to tell Ila what that plan was. He beeped her back 15, 11 ("OK").

Ila got his response and started to clean up her office. She suddenly remembered that she might never come back to that office, so she began writing notes for whoever would have her job after the first of the year. She was sure they would all be reassigned by then. She got a little misty eyed because she had really enjoyed working with the students. Maybe in another life she would be able to help people as her life's mission. She shook her head. For now, this was her life, and it was the only one she was going to get. Marrying Brock and having his children was the only thing she wanted to focus on from now on. She smiled.

Eugenia woke up feeling as if a she was pregnant, but not sure because she had not been pregnant since she was in her twenties. Then she had become pregnant by a guy named … she was not ever sure now, but she knew back then that she would not be marrying him. They had spoken briefly about him being the father of the child. He had said that he wanted children. Eugenia was not hearing that, however. She was in college and was not going to spend her twenties being a mommy. She remembered he was very sad that she would not consider having his baby. Damn why could she not remember his name? She had to laugh out loud. She was supposed to have a photographic memory.

She went into the bathroom, looked in the bottom of the cabinet, and found a full box of tampons. It hadn't even been opened. Well, that was really a sign. So much had been going on she had not even noticed not having a period. She decided not to change anything until she was sure. Next Friday she would get her HIV results, and then she would take a pregnancy test. But then she decided to get a pregnancy test from the drugstore while she was out shopping for the party that afternoon.

Eugenia picked up her washcloth from the shower and began to wash up. She would take a shower when she returned. It was Saturday morning, and people would be moving around early. She wanted to get out and back before noon. When she doubled over in pain, she remembered that she had not eaten. Whomever was growing inside of her was not going to let her go any further without eating. She laughed and walked swiftly to the kitchen before she called "ralph" again.

She plugged in the toaster and slid an English muffin into the slots. She got some cheese from the refrigerator and began cutting it up on a plate. Next, she pulled out the grape jam. The child growing inside her had a different kind of appetite. She never would have thought to eat an English muffin, cheese and jam. She laughed out loud again. The very sad part about it all was that, if she had HIV, there was no way she would bring a child into the world that could be infected with HIV. That would not be something she could do to a child. The English muffin popped up. She spread so much jam on it the muffin was heavy. She placed it on the plate with the cheese and walked to the refrigerator and got water from the pitcher. Whoever this baby was, it wanted to eat healthy. She sat at the table and enjoyed the delicacy. The apartment phone rang, scaring her because it never rang. She ran down the hall as the telephone was in the living room. "Yes?" she said.

Stephen said, "Come get me. I'll go to the store with you and get what we need for both parties."

Eugenia said, "Okay. Give me thirty minutes. She hung up the phone, walked back to the kitchen, cleaned up quickly, went back to the bedroom, grabbed a pair of jeans and a cowl-neck sweater and panties. She had to wear dirty socks because she could not find clean ones. She would buy more while she was out today. Triflin... she laughed again. At least this baby situation made her laugh. She did not remember laughing so much.

She hurried and got dressed, put her holster on, grabbed her leather coat, gloves, and a small purse that contained her credit card. She checked her IDs to make sure they matched the credit card she was using for the party. What a life. She looked for her keys and found them on the kitchen table. She walked through the apartment and turned off everything. As she headed for the door, her Spidey sense caused a sensation on her neck. She looked out the door and did not see anything—no sedan no police car. Just the Cutlass parked at the bottom of the steps. She opened the door and turned to lock the door. Just then she heard a car drive up. She turned quickly to see someone just turning around in the driveway. At first, she did not recognize the car or the people inside, but then her brain went into its instant recall. She realized the passenger was Ila's student, Anthony DeLeo. She bounded down the steps and ran to her car. She wanted to follow them if she could, but by the time she got to the end of the alley, the car was gone. She took a left toward the school and wondered if Stephen had had time to do a background check on that young man. She pulled into the back gate to the university. All the front gates were closed, and visitors had to have credentials to get into the parking lot. She sat for a few minutes. Stephen was usually prompt. She soon saw him running across the parking lot. She wondered how it was to not be able to talk all day. But she believed that most people did not bother him. His superiors at the university left written orders in his mailbox in the maintenance room. He would write back to let them know when tasks were completed. She manually unlocked the door, and he hopped into the passenger side. He nodded at her, and they pulled off.

She had decided to go to Giant Food in Hyattsville, Maryland, to buy the things they needed. If it all came down, investigators would have to do a lot of research to find where they had bought their products. She also decided to stop at an ATM and get cash instead of using the credit card. She drove up to an ATM at a Regions Bank and got cash, then headed to the Giant. Once there, they got five bottles of Clorox, rubber gloves, long-burning candles, cheese, crackers, chicken fingers, wine, grapes, baby quiche, potato salad, and meatballs. The food could all be heated in the oven or in a pot. They both laughed as they shopped because neither wanted to cook anything. Once they paid for their purchases, they packed all the items in the car and headed back to Georgetown. It was getting late. Eugenia asked Stephen if he was going back to the university. He said, "No, I'm in it for the long haul today. You can drop me and the items for the other party off after our celebratory reception for me, Ila, and Brock."

Ila was ready to go. Where was Brock? She had written all her notes, cleaned up the office for the next person, left the combination in the top drawer, locked it, and taped the keys under the chair. She would let administration know after the first of the year where everything was. Then her beeper went off: 8, 5, 18, 5 ("here"). She scrambled to get everything and remembered that the key to the door was taped under the chair. She retrieved the keys, got the key to the front door off, and taped the keys once again to the bottom of the chair. She looked around because she knew this was the last time she would be seeing this office. It had been great being in this environment for almost seven months. But as the Company told operatives all the time, don't get attached to people, places, or things you cannot leave behind. When you do, it is time to do something different with your life. Hands full, she walked to the door, opened it, and turned and locked it for the last time.

She had to walk down a very long hallway to the back gate. Brock did not have credentials to get in through the gate, so she had to walk to the back gate and beyond to get to the car. He was a very patient man when he wanted to be. It was Friday, and there was no need for them to get up early on Saturday. They could just lie around until the little reception at Eugenia's.

She smiled when she saw him sitting in the car. He got out and opened the door for her, which was something she never got tired of. He grabbed all her things and placed them onto the backseat. He hopped into the driver's seat, turned up the radio to WHUR, and started driving. She wondered where they were going as he was headed to southwest DC. As they turned down G Street, it dawned on her that he was going to the Channel Inn, where it all had started. Ila decided now was the time to ask no questions. They drove up found a parking space. He turned off the car and said, "Let's go have dinner." Ila nodded and waited for him to come an open the door.

They walked into the restaurant at the Channel Inn. Brock had made a reservation for them, asking specifically for a window table so they could watch the boats go by and enjoy the water on a winter day. There were candles on the table, and a gold dinner plate in the middle of the table. As soon as they sat down, a server arrived to take their orders. Brock was very talkative. He told Ila he had picked up the tuxes and found an arsenal in the trunk that Stephen kept. He also told her that he wanted a Mariah Carey song sung at the wedding. Ila had to burst his bubble on that one and told him that the song had to be "Ave Maria." He shook his head and said, "The song could be 'Super Freak' by Rick James—as long as we're there together and getting married, I don't care what song they play!" They both laughed. He also told her he had made reservations at Blues Alley for after the wedding and that he and Morris were going to the Georgetown Inn on the wedding day to get dressed. She would have to make sure she told the chef to cancel the reservations at Portofino, and the Pastor that an additional dressing room was not needed. Brock was so excited about getting married! Ila had never seen this side of him. They chatted all through dinner. She also told him that Eugenia was going to give them a small reception at her apartment on Saturday at four o'clock. After about an hour and a half, they both sat back full and ready to go home. The server brought coffee and raspberry sherbet. They drank the coffee and shared the sherbet. Brock looked at Ila with an intensity that she had never seen before. It was scary at first, and then it softened. He reached into his pocket and placed a Cartier jewelry box on the gold plate. Ila looked into his eyes, and she knew this man had gotten her a ring that would make her heart stop. She slowly opened the box, and there they were—matching gold wedding bands, each with four yellow diamonds. Then he said: "I promise to take care of you. I promise to complete your happiness. I promise to be your partner, friend, and lover. I promise to protect you. I promise to give you unconditional love. I promise to be a dedicated husband and father to our children. Lastly, I promise to keep your heart from hurt, harm, and danger. Will you please marry me?"

Ila said, "Yes." He lifted her ring out of the box and placed it on her finger. He knew that she would have to take it off, but he wanted to see it on her finger. Ila began to cry. He handed her his napkin and said, "Tears are unacceptable because my heart is filled with joy, and that is all I require from you is to be happy." She cried harder. By this time the restaurant had filled up, and people were looking at them. Several who had figured out what was going on began to clap. What a wonderful night.

Ila wiped her face and blew her nose, as of course her nose had started to run when she started to cry. She was glad there were no cameras around. She removed the ring from her finger and placed it back into the box. Brock put the box back into his pocket, and they walked out of the restaurant hand in hand. People were still clapping.

The drive back to Georgetown was very quiet; there was nothing left to say. When they returned to the apartment, they emptied the car of all of Ila's stuff. They had to make two trips to get everything. Once inside, they took a shower together, and Ila sucked his dick until it hit the back of her throat and he came all in her mouth and all over her. She cleaned him up, and then cleaned herself, and they both fell into a deep sleep.

Broke heard Eugenia leave, but he thought he heard another car in the alley. He decided to get up and look out the back window. He peeled Ila off him and walked naked to the back door. He saw Eugenia get into her BMW, but he did not see anyone else. It was cold in the apartment. They had forgotten to turn the heat up when they came home—too busy making love. He laughed to himself. He decided there was no reason to move around so early. He got back into bed. Ila had woken up, but as soon as he got back into bed, she wrapped her legs around him and fell back into a deep sleep.

Maurice had been out buying the alcohol for the party. He had started feeling not so good while driving back to the apartment. He decided to stop by the Chinese restaurant and pick up some lo mein and vegetable egg rolls. As he was leaving the restaurant, he saw the lady who lived next to him. She spoke to him as they went through the doors.

Paula looked at Maurice and said to herself, *That guy looks sick.* She walked to the counter and then decided to turn around and introduce herself, but by that time, he was gone.

Maurice drove slowly to the apartment. He needed his medication, which he'd forgotten to take that morning. He got to the apartment and bounded up the stairs, Chinese food in hand. He opened the door, placed the dead bolt on from the inside, took the food to the kitchen, and ran to the bedroom to get his medication. He should have understood that this medication was his lifeline, but he was not used to taking medication. If he wanted to live, however, he would have to get used to the new regimen. He walked back to the kitchen and took the multiple pills. Then he sat down in the living room for a while to see if the medication would kick in. It was about thirty minutes before he began to feel better. He went back into the kitchen, put his food on a paper plate, and ate it standing up. When he was finished, he went to the bedroom, took off his clothes, and went to bed. He slept through the night and woke up the next day feeling worse. He took his medication again at around six in the morning. And again, in about thirty minutes, he felt better.

He had decided that it was best to leave the house only to eat. He wanted to save his strength for the party on Wednesday. Every time he thought about it, his dick got hard. He went into the kitchen and got the plastic bag the Chinese food had come in. Back in the bedroom, he poured baby oil all over the plastic bag. Then he lay across the bed, took his dick in his hand, and rubbed it with the plastic bag, slowly at first, and then faster and faster. And, as he dreamed of sticking it in Hunter's mouth, his dick exploded, semen squirting all over the bed and all over the bag. He got up, threw the plastic bag into the wastebasket, went to the bathroom, washed up, and then went back to bed. He was in the house for the long haul. Wednesday was "D day." Just the thought of the three of them together made him horny all over again.

Dr. Ortega had Hunter's results, and they were the same. He knocked and went into Hunter's room. It was early, and he had many patients to see this day. He still had not figured out how to get in touch with State Department officials but had decided that the hospital's files would be confiscated anyway in a few days. He spoke loudly so that Hunter would wake up. "Hunter! Hunter! it's Dr. Ortega. Please wake up."

Hunter heard the doctor's voice but woke up forgetting where he was. He rolled over and looked at the doctor. He pushed the appropriate buttons to raise his bed so that he could look at the doctor in the eye. "Morning, Mr. Hunter. Your labs have come back, and your condition has not changed. What we did not discuss yesterday is if you have a partner who needs to be notified of your condition."

Hunter said, "That person has already been notified."

"Okay then. But we really need to know his or her name," Dr. Ortega said.

"Really, doctor, do you believe I'm going to tell you who I've been fucking? I'll make sure they all know, and I'll make sure they get medical attention."

"Well, Hunter, I hope that you will take the high road and make sure that your partners are aware of your condition. In any event, we must notify the CDC and the Heath Department of your condition. You will probably be hearing from them. In the meantime, we are requesting that you come back to the hospital every thirty days to be tested so that we can keep control of your condition. We'll put you on a new drug, AZT, put you on a strong vitamin regimen, and give you a diet plan. All of those things should slow down the progression of the disease."

"When do you think I can leave the hospital?" Hunter said.

"We would like to keep an eye on you until Monday just to make sure you are stable enough to leave."

Hunter replied, "Monday would be great. There are things I need to get done at my apartment since I've been away for a while. Thanks, doctor. When will we start with the new AZT drug?

Dr. Ortega said, "We will give you small doses every day just to make sure you don't have a reaction. By Monday, you should be on a full dose of AZT and vitamins, so you'll be able to leave the hospital." Hunter thanked him. Dr. Ortega said, "They may come and take additional blood, so don't be surprised. They should be here with breakfast soon. Just relax. With a strict diet, exercise, vitamins, and AZT you will be able to live a semi-normal life.

"Doctor, I appreciate the pep talk, but my life was ruined when you gave me the HIV diagnoses. All I can do now is live my life knowing that dying could come sooner than I expected."

Dr. Ortega replied, "Since we are all going to die, and no one knows his or her appointed time, I suggest that now you live your best life and hope for the best. I'll check in with you daily. If you have any questions, please do not hesitate to ask the nurse or request to see me if there are questions, she cannot answer. Most of the people on this wing are HIV positive, so the nurses are knowledgeable as they can be with this new disease. I know it is disconcerting that we are all in full protective gear, but since we are still not completely sure how the virus is transmitted, we must take full precaution." Hunter nodded his head. Dr. Ortega turned and left the room. Hunter was steaming. He was going to get Maurice in the right position and put a bullet right up his ass. He would use his .22—small but quick. He could put three bullets up his ass in seconds. Maurice would die quickly.

Eugenia and Stephen were having fun preparing the food for the little reception. It also did not hurt that they were drinking Absolut shots. At exactly four o'clock, Ila and Brock knocked on the door. Brock instantly knew that Eugenia and Stephen were not feeling any pain. He said "Okay, Ila, we've got some catching up to do." They all laughed.

Ila and Brock told them all about the ceremony. They were getting married at six thirty on the following Saturday. Eugenia, Paula, and Ila would get dressed at the university, and Brock and Morris would be at the Georgetown Inn, keeping the tradition that the groom not see the bride before the ceremony. Eugenia almost spit her food out when she heard that Morris was the best man. This was going to be one hell of a wedding. There was no way she was not going to this wedding strapped. She would have to place a .22 on her ankle or between her breasts or something, because there was going to be some shit. She got up and poured herself another shot.

They played Jenga, and spades. They ate almost all the food, and before they knew it, everyone was drunk, and it was midnight. Brock got up and said, "I'm sure glad we don't have to drive." He literally had to pick Ila up; she was really drunk. They thanked their hosts and made their way down the steps and up the short flight of steps into the apartment. Ila dragged herself to the bedroom, took off all her clothes, laid them at the bottom of the bed, and got under the covers. Brock went through the apartment, locked everything down, and joined Ila in bed as he too had had too much to drink.

Stephen and Eugenia were drunk also. They did not take the time to clean up. Eugenia went to her room and took off her clothes. Stephen got a blanket out of the living room closet, took off his clothes, and got onto the couch. He immediately got back up, checked the apartment, locked it down, and turned off the lights. Eugenia was out cold. He went back to the living room, covered up on the couch, and was gone for the night. He was grateful that he did not have to eat Frosted Flakes that evening. He made a mental note that Brock was left handed and fell asleep.

Brock woke up several times during the night, as he felt something about Stephen, something that he had not seen or felt before. Or was it something about Stephen, Eugenia, and Ila? He woke up and thought about that dynamic, and then he thought about Eugenia's reaction to the name Morris. Did she know Morris? How did they know each other? Each time he woke up, he immediately went back to sleep because his head was spinning. Ila had not moved since she got into bed. He laughed to himself; she was such a lightweight when it came to drinking.

Sunday morning was a time for slow moving for everyone. Eugenia and Stephen laid around like cats, one going to the kitchen to eat leftovers, one going to the bathroom to take a shower. Then they switched. They ate and talked until it was early afternoon. After they both sobered up, they went over the plan for Wednesday's party again. Eugenia would arrive at 1:00 p.m., get the keys, and go to the room. Eugenia would send the room number to Stephen's beeper. Hunter would arrive early just to check things out, so he might be in the lobby as early as 1:00 p.m. Eugenia would park in the underground parking. Hunter was too cheap to do that; he would park outside in general parking. Eugenia would get a luggage cart and load it up with the liquor, beer, Clorox, gloves, and other supplies. She would make sure that everything was bagged just in case someone nosey got on the elevator. Stephen would arrive at about 5:30 p.m. Both men should be out cold on the bed by that time. Stephen said "I don't have a car. Brock has the Cutlass, and the last thing I need to do is bring a Georgetown University work truck into the garage. That would not be a smart idea. I'll drive with you and help you get all those items to the room. You get two room keys and leave one for Hunter at the front desk. Just make sure the agent you have working for you doesn't answer any of Hunter's questions. You know he'll probably try to drill her. Once you're set in the room, I'll go get a massage and take a swim. By that time it should be close to five thirty. I'll have a drink at the bar and wait for your nine-one-one. When Hunter arrives, he'll probably sit in the lobby for a while, go to the men's room, and then to the bar just to check everything out before going upstairs. That's standard operating procedure. Depending on how busy the hotel is, he won't take the first elevator, and depending on what floor the room's on, he'll probably take the stairs. And he will be strapped, probably with more than one gun. We cannot under estimate him."

Eugenia was thinking while Stephen was talking. *Hunter had better not underestimate me.*

Stephen continued, "Don't fill the tub up too high. Once we get the bodies in the water, the level will rise, and we'll still have to pour Clorox on them and maybe a bit more water. By the time hotel staff find them on

Monday, their skin will be peeled off, and their bodies will be waterlogged. But as soon as the officers find their credentials, they'll shut down the room and make it a secure area." Stephen sat for a moment to see if they had covered everything.

Eugenia was good with the plan. She looked at Stephen and, suddenly, she got horny. Knowing she did not have her test results back, she was grateful that she had not been sick all day, but she had been eating like a sumo wrestler. She had consumed most of the leftovers. Eugenia was going to have to slow down because her dress for Ila's wedding fit like a glove a month ago. She laughed, she might have to wear a coat over the dress.

Stephen jumped up and said, "Let's go see *Mad Max*."

Eugenia was all for that. "I'll call Ila and Brock to see if they want to go," she said. She walked to the living room. For some reason she could not remember the number. This baby was playing tricks on her body and her brain. She walked back to the bedroom. Stephen had decided to lie across the bed. She didn't want to look at him, but she couldn't help it. He was a very handsome man. His eyes popped open when she came into the room. She looked at his pants and could tell his dick was hard. She got onto the bed, climbed in between his legs, and unzipped his pants. She looked him in the eye and reached in. Out it popped. She took it into her hands and slowly rubbed it up and down. She reached over into her nightstand drawer and pulled out lube. She poured some into her hands and rubbed it up and down his penis. She was unable to get to his balls in this position. She reached up and unbuckled his belt. Then she unbuttoned his pants and shimmied his pants and boxers to his knees. Now she could get to his balls. Stephen was moaning with the thought of her biting and sucking his balls. By the time she got between his legs he was in full orgasmic mode. She sucked and licked his balls, placing one in her mouth and licking it with flickers. He was very turned on. His dick was so hard she could see the veins popping. She knew he was ready. She licked his balls and placed his entire dick into her mouth until she could feel it in the back of her throat. It felt as if it almost touched her tonsils. Then she bit his dick, and he came in her mouth like hot volcanic lava. She was not a swallower. She looked around for something to spit in. The wastebasket was across the room. She reached down and got the towel she'd left on the bed and wiped the semen from her mouth. Stephen was laughing. "Such a waste of good semen!" Eugenia took the other end of the towel and let Stephen wipe his stomach off, as some of his cum had escaped from Eugenia's mouth. She left the bedroom and went into the bathroom to rinse out her mouth.

Stephen lay there amazed at how well she could suck cock. Depleted, Stephen got up, took off his clothes, and got into the bed. He knew he could not have sex with her, but he really wanted to. Eugenia returned from the bathroom and found Stephen curled up in a fetal position. She decided to do the same thing. She took off her clothes and laid them at the foot of the bed and crawled in. She moved close to Stephen. It was nice to feel a man's body in her bed. Her police officer friend rarely stayed the night, and when he did, he was gone early the next morning. It felt good to back up against a hard body.

Stephen felt her warm body next to his. His dick instantly got hard again, but the thought of catching HIV made his dick go limp again. He turned around and moved her closer to him. The least he could do was get her off with his fingers. He had skillful hands. He slowly turned her over and placed his two middle fingers deep into her pussy. Then he felt around for her clitoris. Once he found it, he massaged it with his fingers slowly at first then faster. He could feel her legs starting to shake. He reached down and placed her entire nipple into his mouth and flick licked it while he rubbed her clitoris hard and with speed. Eugenia's mouth fell open, so Stephen took the opportunity to kiss her softly at first then passionately, forcing his tongue firmly down her throat. He could feel her start to quiver and then the moan, soft but complete. She kissed him hard. He pulled his fingers out of her wet pussy. He wanted to put his fingers in his mouth so he could taste her. But again, not knowing, he reached for the towel and wiped his fingers off. He leaned back and grabbed her around the waist, pulled her close, and they fell asleep. The movie would have to wait until next week. Actually, he had to go to work on Monday and act as if he was working. The maintenance operations staff had to work until Tuesday, and then their holiday began. Waking up was not a problem. As soon as he saw the light come in the room, he would get up and walk to the university. Hopefully he would not wake up Eugenia.

Brock and Ila lay around most of the morning and then decided to go to the Waffle House in Maryland for breakfast. They put on sweats, coat, hats, tennis shoes, guns of course, and beepers. They were about to walk out the door, when the apartment phone rang. Ila looked at Brock. There were only a few people who had that number. She ran to the living room and picked up the phone. "Hello?" Ila said.

"Hi," said Paula. "I wanted to talk to you about the man." And, then the phone went dead. Ila said "Hello? Hello?" But Paula was gone. She waited a few minutes to see if she would call her back, but she never did. Ila thought to herself, *I'll call her back after we return from breakfast*. She walked to the door where Brock was waiting. He stood at the top of the steps and turned around and made Ila go back into the apartment. He locked the back door, and they went out the front door. As they closed the door, Ila heard the phone ringing. She knew it was Paula. She would call her back when they returned.

Paula looked at the phone and could not believe they had gotten disconnected. She had seen some AT&T phone workers outside earlier, but they hadn't mentioned anything being wrong with the line. She waited a few more minutes and tried again. But there was no answer. She wanted to talk to Ila about the man in her apartment, but she figured Ila probably already knew about him. Paula was not going to worry about it any longer. But she did need to know what time she needed to arrive at the university. She would try Ila back later that day or on Monday morning.

Maurice was sitting in the apartment feeling sorry for himself and wondering, if he had to do it all again, would he do it differently. The only thing he came up with was that he would never have reached out to Hunter. That was one person he should have let pass. But Maurice was aggressive and persistent. He had wanted Hunter the first time he saw him at training camp. Hunter was not going to come to him easily, but Maurice could feel the tension between them as they ate breakfast, or did drills, or took long runs together. One morning, Maurice had come out of his room at the training center prepared to run. He'd seen Hunter at the other end of the hall preparing to do the same thing. He didn't know why they both were hell bent on running when they didn't have to for training purposes. Maurice yelled out to Hunter to see if he wanted to run with him. Hunter nodded. Maurice sprinted down the hall knowing he would have the opportunity to be next to this man. They began their five-mile run, which was a route that they had run at least two other times that week. Staying in shape while at training camp was so hard because they were fed so well. Every night they were served lots of carbs, meats, and vegetables. Then, of course, happy hour was every night from seven to nine.

They ran at a slow clip for about a mile and a half. Then they picked up the pace. At mile three, they slowed down again, turned around, and headed back to the barracks. At mile marker four, Hunter said he had to go to the bathroom, and took a left off the path. Maurice followed. He did not want to miss seeing that big black juicy dick.

Hunter felt him running behind him. He thought he would go on and they would meet up later at dinner. Once

Hunter felt he was far enough off the path, he stopped at a tree to pee. Maurice stood right beside him and peed too. Hunter stood for a minute to let Maurice get a good look at his dick. He kind of knew Maurice wanted to suck his dick, but he also knew that Maurice was on the down low and did not want anyone to know. But Hunter could feel it. Maurice got through peeing and put his dick back in his pants. Hunter turned to Maurice so that he could get a good look, and Maurice fell to his knees. Hunter's dick was hard, and he could not believe the sensation he felt when Maurice put his big mouth all over his dick and swallowed it whole until it hit the back of his throat. His mouth was hot, and his tongue was full. Maurice licked his dick with professional precision. Hunter grabbed him by the back of the head to keep his dick down his throat. He was going to make sure this fagot got it all, because it would be the last time. Then Maurice did something to the head of his penis—he opened the hole with his tongue and licked it wide. Hunter exploded in his mouth. Maurice licked all his semen and swallowed it like it was soup. He stood up, removed his shirt, turned it inside out, wiped his mouth and Hunter's dick, and put his shirt back on. Hunter had had his dick sucked by what he thought were the best, but this sensation was very different. He was afraid that he would want to feel that sensation again and again. Hunter put his dick back in his pants. He looked at Maurice, and they both started jogging back toward the path. That was the beginning.

Dr. Ortega entered Hunter's room early Monday morning. Hunter was still asleep. The doctor turned on the light, and Hunter instantly woke up, and for a minute he forgot again where he was. "Hunter," Dr. Ortega said, "good morning."

Hunter grunted, "Morning."

"We have done all the tests, and you have not had any reaction to the AZT. Your blood pressure is good, and your blood work seems to be stable. We are going to release you today. You will have a sixty-day supply of AZT, but we really want you to come to the hospital every week or every two weeks to get blood work done. We want to make sure you are stabilized. And, we'll send you home with a case of Ensure nutrition drink, which is packed with minerals. It will help you maintain your weight. Hunter just shook his head. "Do you have any questions?" Dr. Ortega said. Again, Hunter just shook his head. "Well, I have written your discharge papers. You should be discharged later this afternoon. Do you have anyone to drive you home?"

Hunter replied, "No, doctor. I'll take a cab."

Dr. Ortega said, "Okay, Hunter. We'll see you in a couple of weeks. My number is on the discharge paperwork, and there is a twenty-four-hour hotline number to call if you become ill." Again, Hunter just nodded his head. Dr. Ortega said "They will be here with breakfast soon. I want you to eat and eat well. If you find you are losing your appetite, please call the office, and we'll give you something to jumpstart your appetite." Again, Hunter nodded. With that Dr. Ortega left the room.

Hunter lay back down and fell back to sleep. A cafeteria worker brought breakfast about an hour after he fell asleep. He rose to eat and found that he was hungry. He ate his entire breakfast. All he wanted to do was leave Walter Reed at this point. He finished his breakfast and went back to sleep. When he woke up again, another cafeteria worker was bringing in lunch. He wondered what was in the IV. Whatever it was, it was great sleepy medicine. He would ask the nurse to ask the doctor for some medication to help him sleep. He knew that, once he got home to his apartment, he would not be able to sleep. There was too much going on in his head.

When the cafeteria worker entered the room, she cleared off the dishes for breakfast, and was surprised it was still there. Hunter hit the call button. He was ready to go. He thanked the lady for lunch, and she left the room. He began eating again. He was going to make sure to keep his strength up. The nurse arrived, and she asked Hunter if there was something wrong. Hunter replied, "When will I be discharged? I'm ready to go home."

She replied, "Discharge begins at two in the afternoon. We'll put you at the top of the list if we can. It will be shortly after two. We'll do the best we can, to get you on your way." Hunter thanked the nurse and asked her if they could unhook the IV so that he could take a shower. The nurse replied, "A nurse and an aide will be here to assist you to the bathroom and to unhook you from your IVs." Hunter thanked her again and began to eat his lunch. He turned on the television to distract himself. After he finished his lunch, he became agitated because no one had come yet. Just when he was about to push the button again, in walked a nurse and an aide to assist him.

The nurse removed the IV from his arm, and the aide assisted him to the bathroom. Hunter could walk on his own, but the aide was a beautiful Hispanic lady with enormous breasts, so he thought he would take the opportunity to rub up against her. He was such a dog. But the good thing about it was that he knew it. He took a long hot shower. They had hung his clothes up in the bathroom. He got dressed and looked for his shoes. He opened the bathroom door, and the aide was still there. He asked her where his shoes were. She told him they were under the bed. He got his shoes and socks from under the bed and walked over to the chair to put them on. He remembered he did not have his wallet. He knew that protocol was that hospital officials would lock his wallet and ID in a safe because he was working undercover.

The discharge nurse walked in, and the aide left. The nurse made Hunter sign for his wallet. She gave him his supply of medication, which already included sleeping pills he could take if needed, and a case of Ensure. She said, "Please put the case of Ensure on your lap when you sit in your wheel chair. The transport person will help you put it into the cab. Do you have someone at home that can help you?"

Hunter replied, "I'll ask the cab driver to help me if I need it." The nurse nodded. He did not want to say anything that would keep him at the hospital one more minute. Just then the transport guy rolled in with a wheel chair. He had already called the cab, but had not given the driver Hunter's address. Hunter told the transport guy that he would take care of it. Hunter got into the chair and placed the Ensure on his lap. He signed the remaining papers, made sure he had his medicine, and off they went. It was not a long journey to the exit because the wing was at the end of the hospital. The cab was waiting. The transport guy put the wheel chair in the locked position and loaded the Ensure into the cab. Hunter thanked the transport guy and gave him five dollars from his wallet. He got into the cab, gave the cab driver the address, and they pulled off. He could not wait to get home.

Ila and Brock were just enjoying each other. They had no real plans; they were just spending the time getting to know each other, talking about the future. They talked about moving to Georgetown permanently no matter where they were assigned. Maybe they would buy a three-level brown stone. They could rent out the bottom floor as an income apartment and keep the upstairs for their residence anytime they were in DC. They would get a management company to oversee the property if they were assigned out of the area. The subject of children came up. Brock wanted at least two children. Ila did not mention that she had gotten pregnant by Hunter and had had a miscarriage. She hoped she was still able to have children. She had been using a diaphragm, and it seemed to have been working. Her only problem was that she kept forgetting it was in, and sometimes when she pulled it out, it was disgusting. One day she was going to remove the diaphragm, and when she grabbed the container, she found the thing still in the container. She'd have to do better.

Ila finally talked to Paula. Ila explained that they were going to get dressed at the university. Paula had gotten a job at the community college in the nursing department. She was so excited. Now that she had a job, she could move out of the apartment and start a new life without Drew, which was going to be extremely hard. She started to cry when she was on the phone with Ila. Ila just listened and finally said "There will be no crying at my wedding! Understood? You are such a water faucet." They both laughed.

Paula agreed—no crying. She told Ila she would see her at five o'clock on Saturday. Paula never mentioned Maurice. Her information about him completely slipped her mind because she was so excited about her job and the wedding. They would talk after the wedding. For now she would just focus on good and happy thoughts.

Brock had talked to Morris again. Morris was still flying in on Saturday morning and would meet Brock at the Georgetown Inn around noon. Everything was falling into place.

Stephen woke up at sunrise. He rolled out of bed slowly hoping not to wake up Eugenia, but of course that was impossible. She was already awake. He greeted her: "Good morning!"

She did not do same. "Do you want breakfast?" she said.

He replied, "Don't get up. I'll walk to the deli and pick up something. Then I'll walk to the university."

She said, "No way! It's too cold to do all that walking. I'll throw on something and drive you to the deli and then to the university." He did not fight her because it *was* cold outside. He would take a shower at work after he finished whatever was on the workorder list. He knew there was painting to be done, but there were other crews for that. He would take on as little as possible to do.

He went to the bathroom and washed up, and then came back to the bedroom and put on his clothes. They had decided that he would walk to the deli and she would pick him up from the deli and drive him to the university. Eugenia was already up and was wearing sweats and tennis shoes. She was waiting for him in the living room. She had her coat, holster, gloves, and keys in hand. When Stephen came into the living room dressed ready to go, she got up, put her holster on, put her coat on, put her gloves in her coat pocket, and picked up her small purse. When she was ready to walk at the door, she said, "Stephen, are you coming back tonight?"

Stephen shook his head. "I won't be back until Wednesday at twelve thirty. That should give us plenty of time to get to the Marriott and get set up before the two-o'clock appointment time."

Eugenia said, "Let's make it noon just in case something goes estray."

"Okay. I'll be ready for pick up at noon." The both headed for the door. They could feel the chill of the outside world immediately when the door opened. Stephen placed his hood on his head and his hands in his pocket ran down the steps and started walking fast to the deli. Eugenia laughed to herself; they we both hoping for warm-weather assignments.

She turned and locked the door and walked down the steps and headed to her car. Brock came running down the other set of steps ready for his daily jog. He ran past her and said, "Got rid of your company yet?" And he started to laugh. Eugenia did not respond. She just smiled to herself and said it was very difficult working and living around other agents because the Spidey sense was always on. He had probably heard two sets of footsteps come down stairs. The apartment was only partially carpeted. But what normal person would be that observant? Then she laughed to herself. They were not normal people. If they were, they would not be working for the Company.

She got into the car and let it warm up. By that time Stephen should be coming out of the deli. She drove slowly up the driveway, made a left not a right, went down a block, and made a left, but into the back alleyway just to make sure no one was lurking. Seeing no other cars, she drove up the driveway again and make a right to go toward the deli. Stephen was standing outside. Since school was out, the deli was crowded but not standing room only as it normally was. He got into the car with coffee and bagels for both of them. He said, "Did you see Brock?"

She laughed. "Yes. He asked me if my company had left yet." They both laughed. Eugenia made a U-turn and headed toward the university. She drove around to the back gate. Stephen showed his credentials, and they moved through the gate. He gave Eugenia her coffee and bagel, and he got out of the car. "See you on Wednesday," Eugenia said. He nodded and jogged to his room.

Eugenia sat and ate her bagel, drank some of her coffee, and headed back to the apartment. When she pulled into the driveway, she beeped Ila from the car 15, 21, 20, 19, 9, 4, 5 (outside). Ila came to the window, and Eugenia got out the car and headed up the steps. Ila opened the door and started laughing. "Your company finally left." They both laughed.

"Yes. I took him to the university a few minutes ago. I saw Brock jogging."

Ila said, "Yes, he said his ass was feeling like Jello since he had been sitting on it for a week! You want some tea?"

Eugenia said, "No. I just had coffee. Are you getting excited about the wedding? In five days you will be Mrs. Ila Covington. How does that sound to you? And, where are you going on your honeymoon? Has he told you yet?

Ila replied, "I'm so excited about it all—the wedding, getting married at the university, letting the students see us get married, and finally meeting Brock's roommate, Morris. Do you know him?"

Eugenia replied, "No, I don't know Morris. What's his last name?"

Ila looked puzzled. "That's funny. Brock never says his last name. He might not know it. Like, do you remember Hunter's last name?" They both laughed. Of course, Eugenia did not forget anything, but she played it off. They sat and talked small talk. They both decided to wear their hair naturally with just a little gel, and that would be the end of it. A little makeup, and they would be ready to go. Ila said, "Do you know that almost our entire wedding has been paid for by the Company? I didn't think they did that. But all the vendors got credit cards and were told to use them for the charges. Have you ever heard of the Company doing such a thing?"

Eugenia said, "No. But you and Brock were pivotal in breaking the case, and Brock has so many friends it could be anybody. I hope when I get married someone else pays for it!" They both laughed again, and they heard Brock coming in the back door. He had a bag of bagels, lox, cream cheese, peanut butter, humus, peta bread, and small chunks of different kinds of cheese.

Brock dropped everything on the kitchen table and headed for the shower. Eugenia could not believe she was hungry again, and could not wait to be asked to breakfast one more time. Ila got up, put the kettle on, and poured everyone a glass of cranberry juice with a shot of Absolut. Let the celebration begin!

Eugenia did not want to drink the Absolut after getting so drunk the other night. And, if she was pregnant, it was not good for the baby. But she decided to keep that to herself. Her last drink would be on Wednesday, just in case.

Brock came out of the shower and ran to the bedroom to put on a pair of shorts and get his flip-flops. He felt so much better after running. He did not want to get out of shape just in case there was a prime assignment in DC he might be assigned to. White House duty was everyone's dream. But he would take an assignment anywhere in DC, Virginia or Maryland. He walked to the kitchen where the ladies were enjoying the food. He smelled alcohol. They were starting the party early. He was glad.

His drink was waiting for him at the table, and he enjoyed just having a conversation about nothing important.

Eugenia said, "Why don't we all go see *Mad Max*? Stephen and I were going to go yesterday but we couldn't get over all the alcohol we had consumed on Saturday night."

Ila said, "Yes, let's catch the early show." Brock nodded.

Eugenia said, "We'll have to go find Stephen. He'll be on campus somewhere or in his room. We'll pick him up and all go together."

When they had finished cleaning up the kitchen, Ila threw on sweats and tennis shoes. She grabbed her leather coat, put her .38 into her bag, checked to make sure she had lip gloss, and she was ready to go. Brock put on jeans, a sweatshirt, holster, gun and tennis shoes. He grabbed his leather coat and was ready to go.

Eugenia said, "Brock, do you mind driving?"

"Not at all." He went out the back door, and Eugenia and Ila went out the front door. Brock met them at the top of the driveway. In the car, Brock made a left out of the driveway and was driving down O Street when they saw Stephen. He blew the horn, and then forgot that Stephen could not react to the sound of the horn. Brock pulled over, and Eugenia jumped out of the car. Of course, Stephen had seen them, but he could not react. Eugenia ran up on him and tapped him on the shoulder. He turned around, and Eugenia said, "We're going to the movies. Do you want to come?" He nodded, and they both ran back to the car and got into the backseat. Eugenia said, "Where were you going?"

He said, "Back to your apartment. There was nothing going on at the university, and by the time I got there all the work orders had been taken. I'm glad you saw me; you guys would have been gone, and I would have had to walk all the way back in the cold! They all laughed as Brock headed to the movies.

Hunter arrived home. He paid the cab driver, picked up the Ensure, and headed to his apartment. It was good to see his home and his car. He was supposed to have several more months on this detail, so getting home early was great. The circumstances were fucked up, but being home was great. His keys were in a fake plant that sat outside his door. He really did not have much in his apartment since he was not there much—there were just the bare bones, nothing personal but clothes. Anything of value was in a safe deposit box in Maryland. He had emptied the refrigerator before he left. He placed the Ensure on the floor, picked up the phone, and called the local Chinese restaurant. He ordered lots of food—enough for two or three days. He could walk to pick it up. He did not want to go to the grocery story, so walking to the Chinese restaurant was the next best thing. They told him his food would be ready in fifteen minutes. It would take him that long to walk there, so he turned right around, turned the squealer on again, and went out the door. He was not feeling his old energetic self, but he pressed on because he did not want his diagnosis to affect his everyday living. He would continue to work out, eat healthy, and wear condoms. He had no idea how he was going to tell Ila that they could not have children together. He would have that conversation with her after he made sure that her marriage to Brock never took place. He knew it would change some things, but for the most part, they still could be married and get White House details. That was all he'd ever wanted. He knew he liked having sex with men, but he'd had only two male partners, Maurice and one other guy he'd met while on assignment in Canada. Other than that, all his sexual escapades had been with women. And he needed to tell Ila because she could be infected also. This entire conversation was going to be hard to have, but by next Monday, he would have stopped the wedding and killed Maurice. Then the conversation could take place. Stopping the wedding would be easy. Killing Maurice would be harder, but not impossible. It was chilly outside, so he picked up the pace to get the restaurant.

Tuesday sort of came and went. Stephen went back to Eugenia's apartment after the movies and spent yet another day climaxing her with his fingers and letting her suck his dick. It seemed like such an unfair tradeoff, but Eugenia did not seem to mine. He was worried that she seemed tired, and he thought he heard her throw up in the bathroom. But all that could be nerves about the test coming back on Friday, or she could be pregnant. Either way he was nervous about her health.

On Tuesday evening, they talked about the plan again. He had not bothered to go to work on Tuesday. It was the end of the semester; he would return on Monday. But, since the case was essentially closed, he would probably be reassigned next week and the university would be told by the Company that he was not coming back.

Brock and Ila got up late on Tuesday and decided to spend the day at the apartment doing close to nothing. It was going to be a busy week. Ila did suggest to Brock that he go with her to see the chapel. He asked Ila if she wanted to run to the university, see the chapel, and run back. Ila looked at him and said, "We can *walk* to the university and *walk* back, but I don't believe I could run."

Brock laughed. "Okay then. Walk it is." The put on their clothes, went out the back door, walked up the driveway, made a left, and walked briskly to the university. They had to go through the back gate. Ila was glad she'd remembered to bring her credentials. As they walked through the back gate, they ran into Chef Charles, whom Brock had not met. Chef Charles turned around and walked into the building with them.

The chapel was near the parking lot side of the building, so it was not far to walk. As they entered the chapel, the sun was beaming in on the pews, and it seemed to light up the cross Behind the altar. Brock was amazed at the beauty of the stained-glass windows and the glistening wooden pews and alter. It seemed someone had come and put a spit shine on everything. He was silent for some time. Finally, Chef Charles said, "Is there something wrong? Does the chapel not meet your expectations?"

Brock replied, "No! It is beyond what I ever dreamed of, and I'm awe struck by the beauty. I cannot wait to get married in this place. I hope our photographer takes lots of photos. I will want to remember this day forever. Brock was a little misty eyed as he turned and shook the chef's hand. Ila almost broke down and cried. She had not seen this side of Brock for some time. Brock said, "Ila mentioned to me that someone paid for the entire wedding. Are you at liberty to tell me who that was?"

Chef Charles replied, "I wish I could tell you. A credit card showed up with instructions, which included a phone number that was not supposed to be disclosed to anyone. Now I'm sure you understand taking instruction seriously, so you can understand that that is what we are doing."

Brock nodded and said, "Understood. There is nothing else for us to do but accept—and say 'I do.'" They all laughed as they walked out of the chapel together and headed to the parking lot and to their respective cars.

Once in the car Brock, did not turn the engine over right away. He turned and looked at Ila and said, "I promise." Ila began to cry softly. She was so happy. It had been a long journey to happiness. There had been a lot of loss, hurt, pain, and growth, and she was grateful for a second chance at love.

They went back to the apartment and made love all day. It had begun to rain, and the sound of the rain falling on the wooden steps and metal rails was like sleep music. They made love, ate, went to sleep, made love, ate, and went to sleep. Exhausted, they both fell asleep for the night at around eight in the evening.

The plan was to get up early on Wednesday and get gifts for Paula, Eugenia, and Morris and something for Stephen who had been her protector through this entire process. They also needed cash for the priest. Brock wanted to get his hair cut so that it would not look really fresh on the day of the wedding. It would grow in some, and all he'd have to do would be tighten up his beard. Ila could line the back of his head on Friday night.

Eugenia and Stephen woke up early. It was Wednesday. Everything was in the car. Now it was just a matter of going through with the plan. They both were silent. There was nothing left to say. They tried to eat breakfast, but all either of them could get down was toast and coffee. They took showers and prepared themselves mentally for the carnage that was about to happen.

Eugenia was going through all the ways things could go south. She had tried her best to consider every possibility. She grabbed a plastic bag from the kitchen and put a bottle opener and extra glasses in it. She put ice in a small cooler as there would probably no ice available in the suite. She hoped it wouldn't melt before they got there. But it was cold outside, and the cooler was insulated.

Stephen was sitting in the living room ready to go. He had a .44 Magnum in his holster, a .22 on his ankle, and his beeper on his belt. All the rest of his fire power was in the trunk of the Cutlass.

Eugenia had her .22 and a Glock. She also had a box cutter, which she would put in the utensil drawer when she arrived just in case she needed to get to it. Eugenia put on her fishnet pantyhose, her patent leather thigh-high boots, a sheer black blouse with no bra, a short denim skirt with a belt. She added her blonde wig, hoop earrings, and red lipstick. She clipped her beeper onto her belt. She was ready to go. Everything else was in the car.

She walked to the living room looked at Stephen. "You ready?"

"Stay ready." They both left by the back door. Stephen grabbed the cooler and the bag because Eugenia was going to have a hard time navigating the steps in those boots. He laughed to himself. Once in the car, they looked at each other. Stephen said, "Now or never."

Eugenia replied, "Now." She was about to drive off when she remembered that she would need her boom box so that music could be playing while they were partying. She wanted to play music by the Funkadelic as well as by James Brown. She put the car back in gear and asked Stephen to go back to her apartment and get the boom box and her two tapes. James Brown was already in the box, but the Funkadelic tape was on the nightstand.

Stephen bounded the steps two at a time, unlocked the door, ran into the apartment, and got the boom box and tapes. He ran back to the door, locked it, and bounced down the steps to the car. It was 12:15 p.m.

Hunter was walking around his apartment killing time. He was like a cat on a hot tin roof. He had decided that he would kill Maurice at the hotel, but he had not figured out what he was going to do with Eugenia. Knowing her, she would be all about killing him. He was not sure she knew about his diagnosis, but she was pretty intelligent. He was sure she knew by now, and that she was at risk also.

He had taken a long hot shower and dressed in jeans, boots, and a white sweater. Then he'd exchanged the white sweater for a red one just in case the opportunity came for him to kill the motherfucker. He thought maybe he would wait until Eugenia was all partied out. He and Maurice would stay at the hotel, and he would kill Maurice during the night—probably suffocate him with a pillow. He could handcuff him to the bedpost, acting as if they were going to have rough sex games, and then he could hold a pillow over his head.

Hunter went back into the bedroom, got his handcuffs, and put them in his jacket pocket. He also got condoms out of the bag that contained all the medication from the hospital. He was glad they had thought of condoms—and they were Magnums, which was good because regular condoms pinched his dick. He had his .22 on his ankle and a Glock in his holster. He was ready to go. It was 1:00 p.m. He wanted to get there early and look around—check out where the exits were located, where the stairs were, how far away he should park from the front door. He would not park in the underground parking lot because it would be harder to leave from there, and there was also an attendant. He wanted to speak to as few people as possible. He decided to drive to the Metro and take public transport to the Marriott. Better still. He grabbed his keys, his beeper and walked out the door. His dick was getting hard just thinking about fucking Maurice and Eugenia and killing Maurice, or maybe both of them. He laughed out loud. That would be a perfect ending to a story that need not be told.

Maurice had gotten out of the shower at 12:30. He was putting on cologne so that he would smell extra good for Hunter. He put on his jeans with no underwear so that he could pull his dick out faster. He wore a heavy sweatshirt with a black cashmere scarf, boots, and his leather jacket. He holstered his Glock. He was not looking for trouble, but he never left the house without his gun. He had taken his AZT and his vitamins and was feeling pretty good today. That was probably because he had rested. That was one of the thing Dr. Ortega had said was crucial—to get enough rest.

After he talked to Ila, he would report back in and tell his general the circumstances and ask to be sent to a far-off location to sit and do paperwork searches on agents. He was not going to be any good in the field. He knew that there were certain laws that were being developed to make sure that HIV patients were given equal medical treatment. But he had no idea how long that was for. He would know after his conversation with the four-star. He decided not to drive but to take the Metro. That would be much easier than navigating traffic on a Wednesday afternoon. It was 1:00 p.m.—time to head out the door. He clipped his beeper to his belt and was out the door.

Eugenia and Stephen arrived at the hotel at approximately 12:45. They parked in the garage as close to the elevator as they could get. Stephen jumped out to get a luggage cart, which was sitting by the elevator. He jogged back to the car. Eugenia popped the trunk. Stephen pulled out all the bags and loaded them onto the cart. Eugenia got the boom box and the tapes and the bag and the cooler and added them to the stuff on the cart. Once everything was on the cart, Stephen grabbed Eugenia, hugged her hard, and walked away. She locked the car, made sure everything was out of the trunk, and headed for the elevator. When she got to the elevator, her stomach cramped up. It felt like someone was pulling her kidneys out through her belly button. She left the luggage cart and walked behind the elevator and threw up. She could feel the acid in her stomach come up through her throat. She stood there a moment just to make sure she was done. *Damn it! Now is not the time!* She didn't have anything to wipe her mouth with. She used the back of her hand and did the best she could. She took several deep breaths. She actually felt better. All she could do was to laugh to herself.

There were people walking toward the elevator. She pulled herself together and grabbed the luggage cart. She waited for the people to get on the elevator. When the next car came, she got on and took it to the first level for check-in. She got off the elevator and walked to the counter. The lady she had made arrangements with was not there. *Damn it.* The gentleman asked her if he could help her, and she said no she needed to speak to Tina. "Oh," he said, "she went to lunch and should be back any moment."

Eugenia said, "I'll wait." She moved to the side so that others could check in. Time was moving on. She looked at her beeper. It was 1:00 p.m. She was starting to feel anxious. She looked around and saw Tina coming off the elevator. Tina saw Eugenia, but Eugenia was not sure the agent recognized her because she looked so different.

Tina went into the side door and came out to the counter. "Hello, miss, I can help you down here?" she said. Eugenia left the luggage cart and walked over to Tina. She told Tina that all she needed was the room number. "And Mr. Hunter will probably not come to get his key because I'm going to send the room number to him on his beeper," she added.

Tina said, "No problem. I'll keep it here just case he comes. I'm on duty until six tonight. If he doesn't come before that time, I'll put the key in the locked drawer." Eugenia thanked her and handed her another hundred-dollar bill. Tina handed Eugenia the key to room 394.

Eugenia quickly grabbed the cart and went to the elevator. Hunter would be there any minute. As she pushed the button, her heart was beating fast. After she got the cart onto the elevator, it seemed to take an hour to get to the third floor. She grabbed the cart and wheeled it into the corridor, looking at the sign on the wall to see which way she had to go. Left. She started down the hall and quickly realized that the room was at the end of the hall by the stairs. Perfect. She finally got to the end of the hall, struggling in her high-heeled boots. She had no idea how women walked in heels every day.

She unlocked the door and was pleasantly surprised at the size of the room. It was one great room with a living room area and a full kitchen, and a bedroom area off to the side, but there was no door to separate it from the rest of the large room. She walked to the bathroom and found a large shower, a large jet tub, and two sinks. There were two closets in the main room and, the open area was furnished with a red leather couch and two leather chairs. The kitchen area contained a small round wooden kitchen table with two chairs.

Eugenia went into action. After pulling the cart into the kitchen, she pulled the ice out of the cooler and put most of it into the ice area of the freezer; the rest she dumped into the ice bucket and set that on the little table. She put the bottles of St. Pauli Girl in the freezer. She would take them out in ten minutes. She put the alcohol on the little table next to the ice bucket. She took three shot glasses from the cabinet, rinsed them, and placed them on the table. She put the soda in the refrigerator, but she wanted the men to drink straight shots. Maurice was bringing drinks too, so there should be enough. She'd forgotten to ask Hunter to bring food, so she got on the house phone and ordered chicken fingers, French fries, a cheese plate, crackers, and cookies—any kind. The food service clerk told her it would be there in half an hour. It was 1:30 p.m.

Eugenia left the rubber gloves in the bag. She put the boom box on the night stand in the bedroom, loaded the Funkadelic tape, and set the machine to play. She left the James Brown tape on the table just in case they had to change the tape. She walked back to the kitchen and put the bottle opener and her box cutter in the drawer. She put her .22 in the other utility drawer. She would ask everyone to put their guns on the counter in the kitchen. She had thrown two blunts into her purse along with some matches. The police officer had given them to her, and she'd saved them. She put these items on the kitchen table next to the Captain Morgan.

She pulled the beer out of the refrigerator and opened three of them. She poured a little beer out of two of the bottles. She got the Rohypnol out of her bag. Carefully, she poured the drug into the two partially emptied bottles, half in each. She poured beer from the other bottle back into the two doctored bottles. She put the caps back on the two bottles and placed them back into the refrigerator. She poured some of the third beer into the glass so it would appear that she had been drinking before they came.

She put everything back in the bag and tied the top of the bag in a knot. She hung the bag over a hook in the back of the closet and hung her leather jacket securely over the bag.

She took her beeper off and beeped Hunter, Maurice, and Stephen "394." Stephen would be waiting for the 911, but he needed to know the room number. She left her gun empty holster to indicate that she had surrendered her gun as she would ask the others to do.

It was 1:50 p.m. Eugenia walked into the bathroom and ran the bath water so it would be really hot. They would all take a bath, and then she would let out only half the water.

Hunter walked briskly from the Metro. Fortunately, it was only one block away from the hotel. He entered the hotel at approximately 1:40 pm. He sat in the lobby for about five minutes just looking at the lay of the land. At 1:45 he got up walked to the men's bathroom. Before he took a leak, he looked around and opened all the stalls to make sure they were not occupied. He left the bathroom and went into the bar. He sat there for another five minutes. He had been there for only a few minutes before his beeper went off. It said 394. He thought he was supposed get the key from the desk. Plans must have changed. He walked up to the bar and ordered a shot of Captain Morgan. He took the shot quickly and left the bartender a ten-dollar bill. As he was walking out of the bar, he saw Maurice heading toward the elevator. He had a bag in his hand and was walking slowly. Hunter looked down at his dick, and it slowly rose. *Damn this is going to be a great afternoon!*

Maurice got on the elevator. Hunter decided to take the stairs since the room was only on the third floor. He took the steps two at a time. He reached the door of 394 just as Maurice got there.

Maurice looked up and saw Hunter, and his dick got hard. They looked at each other. Hunter looked down at Maurice's pants, grabbed his dick, and kissed him on the lips. Maurice's knees went limp. He had so been waiting to feel Hunter's touch. They both laughed and knocked on the door.

Eugenia answered the door completely naked except for her thigh-high fishnets and her boots. They all started to laugh. The men walked over to the kitchen table, took off their coats, and hung them on the chairs. Both wore holstered guns. Eugenia said, "Okay, fellas. Guns on the kitchen counter." They took off their holsters and placed them on the counter. Eugenia said, "All guns." They all laughed. When the men indicated they had no more guns, Eugenia said, "Okay. If that's all, take off your pants. They both took off their pants and laid them across the couch. Hunter was hard. Eugenia's pussy got instantly wet. *Oh, my God! He has a pretty dick.* The men walked back to the table. There was a knock at the door, and all three agents looked at their guns. Then she remembered her room service order. She walked to the door and said, "Who is it?"

"Room service."

"Oh, okay. Leave it and charge it to the room, and give yourself a ten-dollar tip. I'm naked.

He replied, "Okay. You can leave the cart and dishes in the hall when you're done. We'll pick it up later."

Eugenia said, "Thank you." She waited a few minutes and opened the door in a squatting position, looking down the hall. When she saw nothing, she stood up and pulled the cart into the room. She locked the door. It was 2:15 p.m.

She pulled the cart into the living room. She dragged the desk chair into the kitchen and joined the guys at the table. Hunter lit the blunt and poured shots. He looked at the beer and said, "Oh, you started without us!"

Eugenia said, "Yeah. I tried but that shit is nasty. I brought more for you guys, but I thought we would have a few shots first, smoke the weed, and then get nasty." They all laughed. Eugenia walked over to the boom box and hit play. They all laughed again because the last time they were together, they were playing Funkadelic tunes. She walked back to the table shaking her ass. She sat down, and they all took shots and toked the blunt. They sat and talked about old times—how they use to get high all the time and nobody cared. Now they had to take blood and pee tests after every holiday when they were covert. They were glad they didn't have to be tested again until they took a new assignment.

Eugenia poured the guys another shot. They both took it down fast. She poured one more. They sipped on that one until blunt was gone. Eugenia stated playing with her pussy at the table, and she could see Hunter's dick getting hard. Maurice did not start getting hard until he saw Hunter. Eugenia laughed to herself. Hunter finished the beer on the table and asked Eugenia if she had another beer. She got up and took a beer from the refrigerator, put it on the counter, and pretended to open it with the opener she pulled out of the utensil drawer. As she did this, she was talking loud so they would not hear that there was no pop when the bottle cap came off. The beer was nice and cold. The men sat and finished the other joint and finished the beer.

Eugenia walked over to the bed, took off her boots and stocking, and lay there with her legs wide open fingering her pussy. Hunter could not resist. As he walked toward her from the kitchen, he was talking off his clothes, and Maurice was right behind him. Hunter turned around got his condoms out of his coat pocket. Eugenia jumped up to get a small squeeze tube of Vaseline from her purse. They all started laughing. She gave the Vaseline to Maurice, and Hunter gave Maurice a condom. Hunter stood in front of Eugenia and asked her to put the condom on. She put the condom on and got back onto the bed sideways. She pushed up to the end of the bed, and Hunter lay down and wiggled up to her pussy. He started eating her, slowly at first.

Maurice's dick was solid hard. He put the condom on and lifted Hunter's ass so he could lick his asshole and suck on his balls. Hunter was getting so excited that he forgot about licking Eugenia's pussy. Maurice slowly placed the Vaseline inside Hunter's asshole and placed his two fingers in to make sure it was nice and moist. Eugenia decided to just play with herself. The music was loud, and Hunter was moaning like a horse in heat. Maurice pulled him back toward the edge of the bed and slowly entered him from behind. He started slowly, just putting the head of his dick in, moving in and out.

Hunter's dick was rock hard. Eugenia got up on her knees and started kissing Hunter's mouth and then sucking on his chest. He could not believe how much he had missed both of these individuals. Killing Maurice would be hard, but he would make sure he fucked him one more time before he killed him. Eugenia took Hunter's condom off and spread Vaseline all over his dick. She was rubbing his dick slowly and kissing him all at the same time. At this point, Maurice had his entire dick in Hunter's ass and was pounding him like a jack hammer. Between Eugenia kissing him and rubbing his dick and Hunter pounding his ass, Hunter was really enjoying himself. It was a combination of sensations he had not felt in a long time. Maurice slowed down because he was about to come. He started kissing Hunter's ass passionately. He could feel his dick swelling up. Eugenia could feel Hunter swelling up and then he exploded all over the bed. At almost the same moment, Maurice came and screamed out loud.

She was glad the music was on. Hunter fell to the bed. He said, "Damn did I drink that much?" He started to laugh." He went out. Maurice pulled his dick out of Hunter and looked at Eugenia and said, "You bitch! You drugged us!" And he fell on top of Hunter.

Eugenia jumped out of the bed and beeped 911 to Stephen's beeper.

He was standing in the stairwell because he knew it should not take more than an hour for the Rohypnol to work, and it was already 3:20 p.m. He ran to the room and knocked on the door.

Eugenia came to the door quickly. She had no idea how long the men would be out. She ran to the bathroom and let most of the water out of the tub. She had stashed the Clorox under the sink in the bathroom. Stephen went to the bed and dragged Maurice to the bathroom. He was dead weight. Eugenia waited for him so that she could help put him in the tub. She took his legs, and Stephen took his torso. Stephen went back to get Hunter, who was heavier. Stephen had broken out into a sweat. Hunter twitched, and Stephen reached for his gun. Hunter's eyes opened for a second and closed again.

Stephen had to move slower with Hunter. Eugenia stayed in the bathroom, and when Stephen reached the bathroom, she took Hunter's legs and Stephen took his torso. They laid Hunter on top of Maurice.

Stephen looked up and finally noticed that Eugenia was naked. His dick got hard. *Damn it!* Eugenia moved quickly. She went to cabinet and got the Clorox. She uncapped the first bottle and poured it over their bodies. Stephen stood there while Eugenia poured another bottle of Clorox on the bodies. Eugenia went back to the cabinet and got another two bottles. She poured both of them over the men. Hunter twitched again, and Stephen took his gun out of his holster. He pulled a silencer out of his pocket, put it into his gun, and shot both in the head.

Eugenia stood there for a minute, thinking, *That was not in the plan but that certainly ends the situation.* She stoppered the sink and filled it with a mixture of Clorox and water. She ran to the closet, got the gloves, went back to the bathroom, and got a washcloth. When she'd wet it with the bleach solution, she wiped down the bathroom. Then she began wiping down everything they had touched.

Stephen left the bathroom, went to the food cart, put food on a plate, and took it to the table. She stood in the bedroom area and looked at Stephen as he casually snacked. This man was a cold-blooded killer. This was a side of him that she had never seen. And, it turned her on tremendously. She laughed to herself and slowed down. There could be no mistakes. She left the condom on the bed and wiped the Vaseline off. She went to the kitchen and sat with Stephen. She nibbled on some food, and they each had a shot of Captain Morgan and laughed.

After eating her fill, she went back to work. She had taken off her gloves, so she put them back on and went back to the bathroom to let the water out of the sink and rinse the washcloth again. She came out and wiped the sink, the chairs, and the refrigerator door handle. She got her .22, the bottle opener, and the box cutter out of the utensil drawer. She put the beer into the garbage can. She was going to take the garbage with her. She took off her wig and put it in the garbage can. She went to the closet and put her clothes back on. She put the bag that contained the Rohypnol and the liquor into the garbage bag. She put the glasses into the garbage bag. She went back to the bathroom and got the Clorox bottles and put them into the garbage bag along with the washcloth.

She took her jacket out of the closet. She made sure her prints would not be on the closet door. She stood in the middle of the room and scanned it for anything she may have missed. She put the opened bottles of liquor into a garbage bag. She opened the other bottles and poured some down the sink. She wiped them down. She got two glasses from the cabinet. She had to re-wipe the bottles because she had to pour some of the Captain Morgan into the glasses.

Stephen was still sitting at the table while she was running around like a chicken with her head cut off. He started to laugh. "Eugenia, the minute the police come in and see this scene and look at the guys' credentials, they're going to put a crime scene tape across this room for days. By the time they find the bodies, they'll be mush. Don't forget to put the do-not-disturb sign on the door. Now, let's get out of here!"

She looked at this man and smiled. He was cool, calm, and collected. She gave him a garbage bag. He said, "Take the washcloth out and remember to wipe off the door knobs and the luggage rack. I'll take the Metro to the Air and Space Museum. Please pick me up there."

She took the washcloth out of the bag and handed the bag back to him. With that, he walked out the door. She quickly wiped down the luggage rack. She turned off all but one light, using the washcloth so she wouldn't leave prints. She'd forgotten that her gun and holster were on the counter. She retrieved them, took off her coat, put her holster back on, and put her jacket back on. She wiped the sink again and walked to the door. She wiped off the knob, opened the door, and placed the do-not-disturb sign on the doorknob, using the washcloth. She walked quickly to the opposite end of the hall and walked down the stairs. When she got to the first level, she took the elevator to the garage.

She sat in her car for a few minutes before she put the keys into the ignition and drove off. She gave the parking attendant cash for the parking fee, pulled out of the parking lot, and headed to the Air and Space Museum.

Brock laughed because Stephen had spent yet another night upstairs. They both worked hard. He and Ila were going to the store to get gifts for the bridal party. Ila wanted stainless-steel bracelets for the ladies, and Brock wanted a stainless-steel flask for Morris. The engravings would say "Thank you, Ila and Brock." Simple but nice.

He'd heard Eugenia and Stephen bumping around early that morning. Just now he'd also heard them going up and down the stairs. What were they doing? He decided to peek out the window. He saw Eugenia sitting in the car wearing a blond wig. He started to laugh. He wondered what in the world she was doing in a blond wig.

He walked back to the kitchen and joined Ila. She was making brunch because they had gotten up so late—not breakfast, and not lunch, but brunch. They sat and talked about where they would go shopping. They would start at the mall. There had to be a place there where they could have engraving done while they waited.

They slowly got moving. It was chilly outside, so they layered up and followed the familiar ritual with guns, beepers, and keys before they were out the door. As they drove to the mall in Chevy Chase, Maryland, they listened to WHUR. They had talked so much in the last two days there was not much more to say until after the wedding. It took them about an hour to get to the mall because of traffic. It was good just being out and about with no particular place to go. They had to park way in the back of the mall. Did no one work in Maryland? They walked to the mall entrance and looked at the diagram of where all the stores where. They decided their best bet for getting something done today was at a jewelry store. That would mean that Brock would have to come up with something other than a flask for Morris.

They walked into Jared's and found stainless steel bracelets for men and women. There was a place on the chain-link bracelets for a name, and each would have a tag that said "Ila and Brock" and the date. The sales lady said she could have them in three hours. Brock nodded and gave her his credit card. He looked at Ila and said, "I guess we can spend some money on this wedding." They both laughed. The lady returned the credit card, and Ila thanked her for her assistance.

They walked out of the store and decided that the only thing to do was to go tennis shoe shopping. They both loved tennis shoes of all colors, and they both loved Nikes. They walked to the Nike discount store and got lost in tennis shoes for almost two hours. Ila was looking for a pair of silver tennis shoes that she could wear once the wedding was over because she knew those leather boots would get heavy after a while, even though they were beautiful. She thought that the shoes would be a nice idea for Paula and Eugenia too. They all wore size nine. Finally, there in the corner in the back she found silver shiny Nike tennis shoes for women—and there were three in size nine. She grabbed up the boxes and headed toward the men's side of the store.

Brock had four pairs of shoes lined up: orange, dark-blue, black, and white. Ila laughed. They looked like soldiers all lined up. Brock said, "Okay, before you say anything, I have a reason for needing all of these shoes."

Ila just laughed and said, "You don't need a reason. If you want them, get them. Once we have children you'll have to wear tennis shoes that flap." The both laughed. The sales agent came over, and Brock said that he wanted all the shoes. That sales agent was a lucky young man that day because he was paid a salary, but he also received commission, and each pair of shoes cost $150. The shoes Ila had picked out were on sale for $49.99. She was about to pay for them herself when Brock took the boxes and paid for them. Ila knew not to complain; it would be futile. She was grateful to have someone who could take care of things if she came up short.

They walked out of the store with three very large bags. It was about 3:30, and they wanted to try to get back across town before rush hour. As they walked toward the jewelry store, Brock's Spidey sense was on full alert. He walked to the corner of the four-way walkway and stopped and looked around. He leaned against the wall outside one of the stores. From there he could see all four corners. Ila followed suit and did not say a word. They stood against the wall for about ten minutes. Brock was silent. They looked like tourists, looking around and watching everything and everybody. He finally said, "Let's go." He walked quickly to the jewelry store. Their purchase was ready. They picked it up, left the mall quickly, and walked purposefully to the car.

In the car Ila said, "Brock, are you all right?"

He replied, "Sometimes when I'm in confined areas and I don't know exactly where the exists are, I get anxious. I'm good now. Let's get back to Georgetown and get some ice cream." They drove in silence. Brock did not tell Ila that he only got that feeling when some shit was about to jump off. He did not want to scare her before the wedding. They drove swiftly through the traffic, and then Brock took back roads. Once in Georgetown they went to a local ice cream shop for a treat. She got rocky road; he got butter pecan. Delicious.

Eugenia pulled slowly in front of the Air and Space Museum but did not see Stephen. She drove a little further and spotted him sitting on a bench. She stopped the car in the middle of the street, and he jumped up and got in. Drivers in DC were not very polite when people slowed down like that. They both laughed as horns started to honk.

Eugenia was very hungry, and she wanted a greasy fish sandwich and fries from the corner store in Southeast Washington. When she turned the car around and headed in that direction, Stephen did not say a word. He knew they were headed to Southeast, and he was glad he had his gun. It had become dangerous over there with the introduction of crack cocaine. The entire city was on full alert. This drug was taking out families, young people, and old people. It was said that after one hit, a person would forever be looking for that same high again and again. But each time, more of the drug was needed to get there.

They took Pennsylvania Avenue to Alabama Avenue. The joint sat on the corner of Alabama and Wheeler

Road. Eugenia's mouth started to water. She could taste those greasy fries and the fish sandwich already. She had to find a parking space. There was always a long line at this place. Eugenia parked about a block away. Stephen looked at her as if to say, "Are you crazy?"

She just laughed and said, "Get out the car. You're strapped for war!" They both laughed. The line moved fast, but they still had to wait after they ordered. Eugenia ordered for them—large fries and fish sandwiches loaded with American cheese. They moved down to the other side of the window and waited for their order.

Stephen never said a word in public. He could turn that persona off and on; he was good at it. It was about fifteen minutes before the order was ready, but she knew it would be well worth it. They stood and watched the many people who were addicted to one thing or another. They all seemed to know each other. Eugenia and Stephen were not sure the people knew each other like family or if they knew each other through drug addiction. They walked back to the car and decided not to eat in the car, but to keep moving. Eugenia drove to Hains Point where they sat and ate their food. It was a beautiful chilly evening. They talked about the wedding and how they had both always thought they would never get married. They sat and watched the sunset.

Ila and Brock did not want to do too much before the wedding; they just kind of hung around on Thursday and Friday. He took a run; she went for a walk. They made dinner on Thursday night and went out on Friday night.

As the day got closer, they were both asking the ultimate questions—Is this something we should do? Is this the right person? Will Hunter show up and act like an ass? (Brock had been told by intelligence that Hunter had been MIA since being released from Walter Reed Hospital.)

But when Saturday came, all those questions went out the window. Brock woke up early, kissed Ila deeply, and made love to her softly and sweetly. When he came, he whispered in her ear, "This one has my son's name on it." She laughed, but for real because she did not have her diaphragm in so she hoped that was not the sure shot. They stayed in bed until eight, and then they both jumped up.

Brock had scattered all his Nike shoe bags around the room. Ila had left the silver tennis shoes in the car. She would get them and pass them out after the wedding. She had brought the girls' bracelets into the apartment but had left Morris's bracelet in the car so Brock would not forget it. He had left the tuxedoes in the truck. He was going to have them steam pressed at the Georgetown Inn. He wanted Ila to edge the back of his hairline quickly. He got up, went into the bathroom, and plugged in the clippers. Ila had gone to the kitchen to make coffee, not tea; it was going to be a very long day. He came and grabbed her and held her hand to the bathroom. He was so tall, that he did not need a chair; he just got on his knees and turned around. Ila quickly tightened up his hairline in the back. He had such beautiful hair. It was curly with speckles of gray, and his beard was trimmed just right.

She could feel her very soul being consumed by this man, a feeling that she loved and hated all at the same time. She was really good at cutting and managing hair even though she never wanted to do her own. She finished and set the clippers on the counter, put peroxide on a cotton ball, and rubbed it on the back of his neck. He flinched a bit because it burned. Ila laughed inside. She was finished, and now he would work on his beard.

He stood up and started complaining about why he couldn't get dressed at the apartment—they were two grown people. Now he had to take all his stuff to the Georgetown Inn to get dressed. Ila opened the cabinet, handed him his leather toiletry bag, walked out, and closed the door. She went to the kitchen to finish making coffee. She pulled turkey bacon out of the refrigerator, put ten pieces on a cookie sheet, turned on the oven, and put the pan in the oven. She pulled out bread, peanut butter, jelly, and butter. She really did not want eggs, so she peeled two apples and two oranges and put them on two plates. She put the bread in the toaster and waited for the bacon to be done before pushing down the lever for the toast. She could hear Brock in the shower trying to sing "Super Freak." She was glad he had other skills. She laughed out loud.

Brock came out of the shower in his flip-flops with a towel wrapped around his waist. He walked to the kitchen and sat down. Ila pushed the toast down and checked on the bacon. It was nice and crispy. She took it out of the oven and placed it on top of a burner. She took each piece off and laid it on a paper towel to get the grease off. The toast popped up, the coffee was done, and they were ready to eat.

They sat and talked about going to dinner at Blues Alley after the wedding. They were excited because Phyllis Hyman was being featured there Saturday night. They had to keep track of the time because it was ticking away. It was almost 9:30. Brock's roommate would be at the hotel by 11:30. He jumped up, kissed Ila, and walked quickly down the hall. As she cleaned up the kitchen, all she could think about was that this time tomorrow she would be Mrs. Covington.

Brock packed quickly. He'd had excellent training at that job. He had to laugh to himself. He picked up his leather toiletry bag, put the rings in his pocket, put on his holster, and put his gun in the holster. Finally, he put on his leather jacket and beeper. Checklist complete. Everything else was in the car along with Stephen's arsenal of guns. He walked to the kitchen, kissed Ila softly, and said, "The next time I see you, you will be my wife. She started to cry. He walked down the hall and said, "Come get the door." She walked behind him slowly. "Hurry up!" he said. She smiled and walked faster. He opened the door and went down the steps fast.

Brock had forgotten to talk to Stephen about picking up Morris, so he had to get to the airport quickly. Fortunately, his friend was coming into National Airport, which was not that far away. He went down O Street and jumped on the Freeway to the Parkway and made it there in about twenty minutes, even with traffic on a Saturday morning. Brock went to the back gate, showed his credentials, and was allowed to park very near the hanger where the transport would be coming in. He walked to the hanger and saw some people that he knew but could not acknowledge. They all knew he would not have gotten that far without credentials. He walked over to the waiting area. He was so happy that it was chilly but not butt-choking cold. It was a perfect DC day. He sat and drank more coffee. He did not make small talk with anyone. There were some old-ass magazines in the seating area, so he took the time to look through a couple. All of sudden, people started moving around. That meant the transport was coming in. Brock was excited to see his friend.

The transport was big and loud. It took a while for it to land. Transports never really parked for long. The crew was all over it as soon as it was secure. The steps came down, and Brock was amazed at how many people had been on the plane. And, there he was. Brock got up and started walking fast to meet Morris halfway. When Morris saw Brock, he started to smile. They hugged each other and walked to the car talking fast, neither really listening to the other but certainly glad they were in each other's company.

In the car Morris said, "Man, they got you driving a Cutlass?" The both laughed out loud. The ride to the hotel was filled with conversation. Morris finally asked him, "Man, are you really sure about this woman?"

Brock replied, "She is the first woman I have ever made a promise to."

Morris replied, "Works for me." They both laughed.

The Georgetown Inn was a stately place. It was filled with so much pomp and circumstance. Brock was going to have the car valet parked, but then he remembered the arsenal that was in the trunk. It would be very hard to explain to the bell hop and the valet driver. Brock drove into the garage and parked the car. There were luggage carts at the elevator, so Morris ran over and got one. They didn't have a lot of stuff, but it would be awkward walking to check-in carrying what they did have. Brock popped the trunk and took the black tuxedo bags out of the trunk. Morris looked in the trunk and looked at Brock. Brock said, "Don't ask." They both laughed again. "Remember the man I was going to have pick you up? Those are his guns."

Morris said, "I'm sure you had second thoughts about having him pick me up." They laughed yet again.

The elevator was very large—one of the differences between a three-star and a five-star hotel. They went up to the main lobby to check in. The area was busy with people bustling around. Brock had rented the penthouse suite. He and Ila could stay there after the wedding dinner. Brock got checked in, and they went to the elevator with the luggage cart in tow. When they got off the elevator on the fifth floor, it looked as if there were only ten rooms on the entire floor. Their room number was 594. The walked down a long hallway and stopped midway at their room. Brock put the key into the lock and opened the door. The suite was enormous, with a great view of the city. There were two large bedrooms and two large bathrooms, each with a large jet tub and walk-in shower with large shower head. A large bottle of Absolut sat on the bar in the common area, and the refrigerator was stocked with cranberry juice and ice. There was a note on the desk requesting that they call the front desk so that food could be sent up. Morris called the extension. He was hungry.

Brock put Morris's suitcase in one room and his overnight travel bag in another. After Morris hung up the phone, Brock picked up the phone and asked for laundry. He wanted to get the tuxedoes steam pressed. The laundry attendant said she would send someone right up, and the suits would be back by 4:15, which was perfect.

Morris went over to the bar and made them both stiff drinks. When they were ready, he handed one to Brock. He raised his drink for a toast, and Brock did the same. "To the woman who stopped you in your tracks," said Morris. "May you live each moment of your life realizing that she cannot complete you, but she can certainly be a part of you." They clicked glasses and sat on the leather sofa and talked about any and everything.

Eugenia and Stephen arrived back at the apartment full and feeling like Bonnie and Clyde. She finally asked him once they were in the apartment why he had brought the silencer because the Rohypnol would have killed them considering all that she had put into their beer. And they had the box cutter to slit their wrists as a backup plan.

Stephen said, "I have learned in the many years I have been in this business not to think *that* someone is dead but to *know* that someone is dead. We *know* they are dead."

Eugenia shook her head and said. "Yup, we know they are dead." And they both laughed. Eugenia made drinks. There was no further discussion about Maurice and Hunter; instead, they focused on the wedding and how Eugenia had to go to Walter Reed on Friday to get her tests. After they finished their drinks, they both wanted to take a shower and burn the clothes they were wearing, but Stephen did not have a change of clothes with him, so he would have to put the same clothes back on in the morning. They took a shower together, staying under the water until it ran cold. It was as if they were trying to wash away the memory of Maurice and Hunter lying on top of each other with bullets in their heads.

For a brief moment after they got out of the shower, Eugenia was frightened, and she was not sure why. She shook it off and made them each another drink. They sat in the living room drinking their drinks and watching some nonsense on TV. At about midnight, they got up and secured the doors, turned off the lights, and headed to the bedroom. They were exhausted. They pulled back the covers on opposite sides of the bed, got in, and fell fast asleep.

Morning came quickly. It was Thursday. Eugenia got up and walked around wondering what she was going to do that day. She decided that, pregnant or not, HIV or not, she needed to run. She put on her jogging outfit along with gloves, running shoes, scarf, holster, and oversized sweatshirt. She was about to head out the door when Stephen said, "Are you going to the university track? Because if you are, you can drop me off at my room. I need to take these clothes to the nearest garbage dump."

Eugenia understood that feeling. She had already put her clothes in a garbage bag and was going to take it to the university and put it in a large construction site Dumpster. The university was always building new buildings or adding on to existing buildings, so there was always some construction going on. Eugenia said, "You know, that's a great idea. Yes, I'll run the track, but first I'll put my clothes in a construction Dumpster."

He said, "That is a great idea I'll do the same. It will only take me a few minutes to get dressed. Wait for me?" Eugenia walked to the living room and put on the news. There was never any good news, so she changed the channel to more morning show nonsense. She finally just turned it off. Her stomach was feeling particularly good today. She was hungry, but she decided to eat after she ran. She did decide to get up and get a glass of water. As she walked toward the kitchen, she stopped as Stephen was leaving the bathroom with no underwear on. That man was certainly hung for pleasure. She decided not to look too hard because she would get horny again.

She made a sharp left into the kitchen to get a glass of water. When she came back from the kitchen, he was dressed. She was really glad. They headed toward the back door.

Stephen stopped at the top step and looked around. Something did not feel right. He could not put his hands or eyes on it at the moment. He hesitated for a bit longer and then started going down the stairs.

Eugenia came outside and turned to lock the door. She did not sense anything, but Stephen was a different animal. She looked around and headed down the steps. She unlocked the car, got in, and reached over to unlock Stephen's door. Her next car would have automatic locks. It was standard on BMWs now. Stephen got in the car. It was scary how, once he was out in public, he became this different person. She was about to put the car in reverse when a police car came through the back alley and put on its lights. Eugenia put the car back in park and got out of the car. She recognized the Prince George's seal on the side of the cruiser. Stephen did not move. She walked toward the lights and started to laugh. Officer Waters rolled down his window. "Hey there," he said. "I'm off the night shift. When will you be available to see me?"

Eugenia said, "I have a full weekend. Ila is getting married on Saturday, but I'll be free on Sunday or Monday."

Officer Waters said, "I'll see you on Monday morning—early— and I'll bring breakfast."

Eugenia turned and walked back to the car. Officer Waters turned the patrol car around and headed back to the back alley. Back in the car, Eugenia could feel the air evaporate. Stephen was heated. She decided not to say anything. The less said the better. They rode to the university in silence. They went through the back gate, showed their credentials, and Eugenia parked by the gate. That way she would be closer to the track. Before Stephen got out the car he said, "I'll see you on Saturday at around five thirty at the chapel. She nodded, and he got out the car.

She was very disappointed that he did not seem to care about the results of her HIV test. She picked up her glass of water, got out of the car, and headed for the track. She had to walk down the steps because she had not parked behind the track. She should have made Stephen walk. Once she got to the track, thinking about running almost made her throw up. She decided she would have to walk her five miles today. It was chilly, so she would do it as fast as possible. She left the glass of water on the bleacher seat and started her walk.

As she walked, she reviewed the last year in her mind. It had been one hell of a ride. Now it had ended in murder and marriage—*M&M*. She laughed. She could feel someone walking behind her. She slowed down and went into the furthest track lane so that the person could pass. As she moved, she unbuttoned her jacket and placed her hand on her gun. She walked over to the grassy area and turned around to see two young ladies who looked to be college age running the track. She let them pass. She walked behind them and then started to jog a little so that she could always keep them in her sight.

It took her almost two hours to do five miles. Yes, there was something really wrong. But she was glad she'd exercised. When she got to where she'd left her glass of water, she noticed it had been moved ever so slightly. She had left it on a certain marker. She decided to leave the water there just in case. She walked slowly up the steps. She no longer saw the two young ladies. When she got up to the top of the steps, she looked around again. No sight of them.

She walked to her car, got in, and turned over the engine. She looked in the backseat. The garbage bag filled with her clothes was still there. She looked up and saw Stephen coming across the parking lot with a small luggage bag and a garment bag. She was not sure what was going on. As he got closer to the car, she unlocked the door. He opened the door, put his luggage on the floor in the backseat, picked up her bag full of clothes, and laid his garment bag on the backseat. Without seeming to give it a second thought, he walked over to a Dumpster and threw the bag into it. He walked back to the car and got into the passenger side.

Eugenia put the car in drive and drove off out the back gate. When they got to O Street, Stephen said, "You didn't think I was going to let you go to Walter Reed alone did you?" Eugenia smiled and never said a word. The went back to the apartment and spent the entire day in bed. They had not realized that killing people took all of a person's emotional energy. It had been a while since Eugenia had killed anyone who was not trying to kill her.

They both woke up early on Friday morning. Eugenia had to run; she could not sit still. She put on everything she'd worn the day before and was out the door before Stephen could get dressed and protest that she was going alone. Stephen was in the kitchen when she called out, "Come get the door. I'll be back in an hour and a half."

Stephen yelled down the hall, "Wait for me!" But by that time, Eugenia was out the door and halfway down the steps. She decided to go up the back alley toward O Street and then run to the university and back. She got through the alley to O Street and ran out of steam. She began to alternate between walking fast and running. It was a cold day, and not even the layers of clothes she had on didn't help with the All mighty Hawk. She started singing the Lou Rawls song in her head: "*I was born in a city they called the 'Windy City.' And they call it the 'Windy City' because of the 'Hawk.' All mighty Hawk, Talking about Mr. Wind kind of mean around winter time. I happen to live on a street that was a dead-end street.*"

She started to laugh because those were the only words she remembered, so she sang that verse over and over until she was back at the apartment. She ran down O Street to the driveway of the apartment and made a right. When she hit the corner of the driveway, she was completely spent and had to walk very slowly down the driveway. She wanted to be at Walter Reed before ten, so she had to get moving.

As she walked up the steps, she could see Stephen standing at the window of the back door. He was really a mother hen. He had two very strong personalities—hit man and mother hen. She laughed out loud. When she hit the next to the last step the door opened. She walked past him, and he closed the door and locked it. She walked to the bedroom, took of everything, and placed it in the laundry basket, which was overflowing. As soon as the wedding was over, she was going to do her laundry.

When she turned around, Stephen was standing there with a towel and washcloth in his hand. She walked over to him, kissed him on the lips, and walked to the bathroom. He had run a bath for her. As she lowered herself into the tub, he came in with a kettle of steaming warm water and added to the bathtub water. He went back to the kitchen, put the kettle on the counter, and came back to the bathroom. He got on his knees and asked her for the washcloth. He soaped the cloth and began washing her back, her arms, breasts, and belly. He washed all the way down her legs to her feet.

She was very tense at first, but with every stroke she relented to his touch and fell into a catatonic state for a brief moment. He finished at her feet and handed her the washcloth. Then he got up off his knees and sat on the toilet seat while he watched her finish her bath. He looked at her and said, "Could you ever commit to one person like Ila and Brock are about to do?"

Eugenia thought about that for a second and said, "Consciously understanding the situation, overtly knowing where the other person stands, making sure the lines are not crossed, making each second seems like a minute, intuitively holding back, trusting that words will not be spoken, monitoring the time because it won't last forever, entering into the situation with rules of engagement, not needing security or safety nets, troubled that you believe I don't understand who you are. Are you talking about that kind of commitment?"

Stephen got up and walked out of the bathroom. Eugenia laughed. *He has got to be crazy to believe that I'm going to step into that bullshit.* She finished washing up and got out of the tub. It was clear he had taken a shower and was ready to go. She hurried to dry off. As she went into the bedroom to get her makeup bag, the smell of bacon cooking drifted in from the kitchen. Suddenly, she was very hungry. She hurried back to the bathroom. She put on what little makeup she was going to wear, picked her hair, put Vaseline on her lips, and was ready to put her clothes on. She walked back into the bedroom, got a pair of jeans out of the closet, and put them on. She put on her navy-blue cowl-neck sweater, her boots, and her holster. She made sure her credentials were in her purse, and she put on her beeper She laid her jacket and gloves across the bed and walked to the kitchen.

Stephen had fixed bacon, boiled eggs, toast, coffee, and juice. She sat down and waited to be served. She could get use to this type of treatment. They ate and drank in silence. She got up, cleaned up the kitchen, and asked Stephen if he was ready to go.

He went into the living room, grabbed his beeper and gun, and walked toward the back door. He hollered, "Come get the door. I'll walk down the street and meet you at the deli."

Eugenia walked him to the door. He opened the door swiftly, and she closed it just as swiftly and locked it. She turned off the living room light and headed down the hall. She turned off the kitchen light, walked to the bedroom, picked up her jacket, and walked to the back door. Her Spidey sense had not kicked up in a while, but she took a moment to look around before walking down the steps. In the car, she drove up the driveway, made a right onto O Street, and picked up Stephen on the corner.

They rode to Walter Reed Hospital in complete silence. There was really nothing to say after the commitment conversation. As they pulled into the back gate of the hospital, Eugenia had to show her credentials. This gate was far away from the hematology entrance, but she felt compelled to walk all the way around instead of walking right into the hematology department.

When she reached the door, her stomach turned upside down. Eugenia ran back down the hall to the ladies' room and let loose in the sink. *Damn it!* She was glad there was no one in the bathroom. She cleaned out the sink, swirled water around in her mouth, and washed her face. She stood looking in the mirror for a moment, and it seemed her color had changed. *What the hell was going on?* She pulled herself together, walked back to the hematology department, and checked in with the receptionist. She signed in and sat in the waiting room.

There were two other people there who seemed really sick. She said a silent prayer for them and for herself. It did not take long for her name to be called. The nurse opened the door and told her to go to room five. Eugenia could feel a tear coming down her face as she walked toward the room. The nurse told her to have a seat and to wait for Dr. Ortega, who would be right with her.

Eugenia sat for about ten long minutes before there was a knock on the door. Dr. Ortega walked in. "Hello, Eugenia. Thank you for coming back at your designated time. You wouldn't believe the number of people we have to track down just so we can give them their results. I'll not prolong our discussion. This must have been the longest seven or eight days of your life. Your blood work came back inconclusive for HIV. But there were some real challenges with your blood. Your iron is extremely low, and your vitamin D is so low I'm not sure how you are still walking around. You must get more sunlight and take two thousand milligrams of vitamin D and thirty milligrams of iron daily. Here are your prescriptions. Please take them to the pharmacy down the hall, and they will fill them. And, you probably know by now that you are pregnant. Please make an appointment down the hall with OBGYN so that they can find out how far along you are. They will prescribe pre-natal vitamins. Do you have any questions?"

Eugenia was stuck on his first sentence: "Your blood work came back inconclusive for HIV." She nodded and started to cry. Dr. Ortego waited just a few minutes, and then he asked, "Did you hear everything I said? And do you have any questions?" Eugenia nodded again. "Okay.

Please make sure you get those prescriptions filled and make an appointment with the OBGYN. I believe that Dr. Susan Oliver may have openings for new patients. Ask the receptionist if you can see Dr. Oliver because you need to see someone right away. Eugenia, congratulations on your pregnancy. I want you to come back in two to three weeks so that that additional blood test can be done for your HIV status. You must have felt you were in contact with someone who had HIV, or you would not have come to take the test. But we are certainly glad you did. It is so much better to be safe than sorry. I wish you all the best, and we'll see you in two to three weeks." With that Dr. Ortega left the office.

Once the doctor had closed the door, he walked to the nurses' station and told them to give Eugenia a minute and then escort her to the pharmacy and then make sure she made an appointment with Dr. Oliver. As Dr. Ortega went to the next room to tell yet another patient that he was HIV positive, he felt a warm feeling. At least today there was one person he had not had to give a death sentence to. He'd been able to give the great news that new life was coming into the world. He still felt that he should talk to someone in the Company about how many people had been there to be tested for HIV. But a person's HIV status was private, and it was against the law for him to discuss patients' status with anyone. He decided that the number of people working for the Company who had HIV was not his fight. His fight was to try to keep patients alive and give them the best possible options. He walked up to the next door, knocked, and walked in.

Eugenia sat and cried for what seemed an hour, but she was sure it was only about ten minutes. She looked around for tissue and found some on the counter. She took short long breaths. Snot had begun to run down from her nose, and she felt a scream coming from her lower abdomen up through her throat and out of her mouth. With that there was a knock on the door. The nurse knocked and came running in. "Is everything all right?" she said. Eugenia nodded her head. "Dr. Ortega wanted one of us to walk you to the pharmacy to get your prescriptions filled and then make sure you got an appointment with Dr. Oliver," the nurse said. All Eugenia could do was nod. "If you're ready, we can go now, but if you need a few more minutes, please, by all means, just sit for a bit."

Eugenia replied, "I'm ready. Thank you very much for your help."

"That's what we're here for. Okay. If you are ready, I'll walk you through this maze and make the process a little smoother for you." They walked to the pharmacy and got the prescriptions filled right away. They then walked to Dr. Oliver's office and made an appointment for January 10, which was her earliest appointment. Eugenia thanked the nurse and began the long walk back to the car. She was sure Stephen was a nervous wreck; it had been about two hours since she left the car.

As she walked toward the car, she saw Stephen walking around the parking lot. She waited until he saw her before she got into the passenger side of the car the car. He started running toward the car when he saw her.

Stephen thought as he ran toward the car, *If she got into the passenger side, the news has got to be devastating.* He walked slowly and opened the door to the driver's side and slid in. Eugenia handed him the keys. He looked at her, and she began to weep hard. Once again, he had no idea what to do. She reached in the glove compartment, pulled out some napkins, and wiped her eyes and her nose. She said, "There were no signs of HIV in my blood system, but since I have been exposed, they want me to come back in two to three weeks. But I'm pregnant."

He turned the car over and backed out of the parking lot. They were halfway back to the apartment when Stephen said, "I always wanted to have children." They both laughed. There were many reasons why that was so funny. Stephen knew good and well Eugenia's baby was not his, but he would be more than willing to take care of the child if that was what Eugenia wanted. He had grown to love her in a way he felt he could not experience again. It was very different from what he felt for Ila. He felt lust for Ila; what he felt with Eugenia was more natural, soft, and wanted.

When they returned to the apartment, they saw that Brock and Ila were home, but they decided not to stop in. Eugenia felt like a rag doll. Between the emotion from learning she didn't have HIV and the emotion from learning she was carrying a child, she had a lot to handle. She just wanted to go bed, curl up in a fetal position, and sleep as she had not slept in the last three weeks.

Eugenia and Stephen walked up the steps, and he unlocked the back door. Eugenia headed toward the bedroom, and Stephen headed toward the living room. Eugenia took off everything, laid her gun on the nightstand, got into bed, curled up, and fell into a deep sleep.

Stephen watched nonsense TV, ate sandwiches, and drank vodka. He thought Eugenia would have to wake soon up to eat. He made her a peanut butter and jelly sandwich, put a bag of chips on the plate, and grabbed a glass of water. He took the simple meal into the bedroom. When he sat on the bed, she opened her eyes and saw the sandwich.

Eugenia's stomach knew immediately that it needed nourishment. She sat up slowly, looked at Stephen, and wondered if they really could spend a lifetime together. She started to laugh to herself. The baby had her in nesting mode already. Walking a man like Stephen down the aisle would be virtually impossible. She ate the peanut butter sandwich and chips as if they were lobster. She drank the glass of water in what seemed like a couple of gulps. She gave the plate back to Stephen and said, "Thank you so much for staying and being here today. If you don't mind, I'm going back to sleep. Ila is getting married tomorrow, and I don't want to look like a monster from 'Thriller.'" They laughed, and she curled back up and fell asleep in an instant.

Stephen took the plate and glass back to the kitchen. He tidied up and poured himself another shot of vodka. Then he locked the apartment down, went into the bedroom, took off all his clothes, and got into the bed with Eugenia. He too fell fast asleep.

Ila was so excited. Brock was gone. She had cleaned up the kitchen and she wanted Eugenia to come help her at least paint her toenails and fingernails with glitter silver nail polish she had brought. She walked to living room and dialed Eugenia's number.

The phone rang, and it was loud. Stephen jumped up and look around. He had to remember where he was. He heard the phone ring again. He ran to the living room and remembered that he was not supposed to be at the apartment. So, he decided to answer but not say anything until he knew who was on the other line. He picked up the phone, and Ila said, "Eugenia, sorry. Did I wake you? I hope not! It's my wedding day!"

Stephen replied, "She's still in the bed, but I'll have her call you in a few minutes."

Ila did not say anything for a minute, Stephen's voice was not what she had expected to hear. Then she said, "Stephen, hi! Yes, please have her call me or come to the apartment. I need help preparing for the wedding."

Stephen replied, "Okay. I'll wake her up and get her going."

Stephen hung up, and Ila was still holding the phone. She laughed out loud. She thought Stephen loved *her*. That was the quickest crush ever. Ila hung up the phone and headed for the shower. She, of course, had to wait for the water to get hot. While she waited, she called Paula, who answered on the first ring. Paula was singing into the phone, "Going to the chapel, and we're going to get married …"

Ila laughed and said, "See you at five thirty. Will that give you enough time to get dressed?"

Paula replied, "Oh, yes. I'll have my makeup and hair done before I get there. I'm so excited."

"*You* are excited," Ila said. "I've peed about five times this morning. I just can't seem to hold it I'm so excited." They both laughed again.

Paula said, "See you then." They hung up the phone together. Ila ran down the hall before the hot water got cold. It never stayed hot for long. She jumped into the shower and shaved her legs and her underarms. She didn't wash her hair because it always looked better when it was a little dirty. She was getting so excited her stomach was beginning to hurt. She turned off the water and grabbed her towel. She could hear someone banging on the back door. It was probably Eugenia. "Who is it?" Ila yelled.

"Eugenia!" Ila ran down the hallway wrapped in her towel. She forgot about being cautious and opened the door. Eugenia walked in looking like shit. Ila stood and looked at her for a moment. Eugenia finally said, "I hope you have regular coffee."

And Ila said, "I hope you're going to do something about that head before the wedding." They both laughed. Ila wrapped the towel tighter and went into the bedroom to get the nail polish and an emery board. Eugenia make coffee and ate some of the bacon that was left over from breakfast. She called down the hall, "What could you possibly need done today?"

Ila was laughing as she came down the hall. "I need a mani-pedi!"

Eugenia said, "That will take us until next week." They laughed harder.

Ila said, "If you do mine I'll do yours."

"Great, because mine look a mess too." They both knew that Paula would be groomed to the nines. Her hands and feet would be perfect, and her hair would be done in a hairstyle that did not move. They talked while they did each other's mani-pedis. When they were finished, they both felt they'd done pretty professional jobs. They both looked and felt much better than they had an hour ago. They were waving their hands to dry the polish, and they had put cotton balls in between their toes while they were being polished.

Eugenia declared that the best way to get back to her apartment without messing up her toes was not to wear shoes, but it was very cold outside. Ila ran to her bedroom and got a pair of flip-flops for her to wear. They wouldn't completely protect her feet from the cold, but at least Eugenia wouldn't have to touch anything cold with the soles of her feet, and the flip-flops would not mess up her polish. Eugenia said, "Ila, I have some good news to tell you on your wedding day."

"What?"

"I'm pregnant."

Ila stood with her mouth completely open. "Pregnant! That is incredible! Can I be the godmother? I hope it's a girl! What are we going to name her? We'll have start buying stuff right after the wedding!"

Eugenia said, "Ila, take a breath! We have about seven months to work all of that out."

Ila laughed. "Yes, I guess we do have time. Congratulations! But right after the wedding, we get started on baby stuff." They laughed.

Eugenia looked at the clock. It was almost 2:00 p.m. She said, "Ila, we'll meet you at the car at five."

Ila nodded and said, "Can't wait!" She walked Eugenia to the door and watched her step quickly down the steps in the flip-flops. She laughed and closed the door. Ila headed back to the kitchen and cleaned up. She walked to the freezer, pulled out the vodka, and took two shots. This was a day she had thought would never come. She went to the bathroom and started doing her hair and makeup, all the while thinking about the promise. A tear came down her cheek—Rodney, Phoenix, LeRoy, Stephen, Officer Waters, Hunter, Brock and all the others have names you must forget because your brain will not let you believe that you fucked that many men. She laughed out loud.

When she finished her face, she was pleasantly surprised at what a good job she could do applying makeup when she took her time. It was about 3:30 p.m. Time was clicking off. She had not really thought about what she was going to wear to the university. She wanted it to be easy to remove so she wouldn't mess up her face or hair. She decided on an A-line dress that didn't have to go over her head. For convenience, she'd wear flipflops. She put on her good underwear—the hold-it-in kind and a new bra. She took the clothing bag out of the closet and checked to make sure everything was in it. She just hoped she had not gained any weight because the dress had fit like a glove. She looked at the clock again—4:45 p.m. She went to the closet and got her leather jacket. She looked at her gun and decided she was not going to carry a gun to her wedding. She threw her makeup bag and another bag that contained her ID, credit cards, and license.

She was ready—ready to become Mrs. Ila Covington. She gathered everything, turned off all the lights, and headed for the door. She looked out the window. Eugenia and Stephen were already in the car.

Eugenia was looking for her eye shadow. She wanted to look her best for Ila. She found her curling iron. She planned to curl her hair and then put jell in it so the style would last all night. She found what she needed and went to work. She was very pleased at the result, even though it took about an hour. She was so jealous of Stephen. All he had to do was take a shower. He was now watching TV. She was sure he had a nice suit to put on, but it would take him only twenty minutes to do what he had to do.

She came out of the bathroom and walked to the living room. He looked and started to laugh. "You look fabulous! I have never seen you wear that much makeup. If I had a camera, I'd take a picture." Eugenia picked up a pillow and hit him with it. Suddenly Stephen said, "Be quiet!" There was breaking news story on TV—two men had been found in the Marriott Hotel in gangland-style killing: "The men were found after a complaint had come from other hotel guests that a horrible smell was coming from the room. The maintenance men entered the room and found the two men in the bathroom. More details will be given as they become available." Stephen looked at Eugenia and said, "Believe me, when the police look at their credentials and the appropriate authorities are called, this will go in the back pages of the *Washington Post*." They both laughed and went on to get ready for the wedding. They were both ready at around 4:30, and Stephen put all their stuff in the car. He wore a silver sharkskin suit, a black shirt, a silver tie, and Stacy Adams black-and-white shoes. He looked so handsome.

He refused to go to the wedding without his holster and gun, and he wore his .22 on his ankle. Eugenia thought that was overkill, but considering that the bodies had just been found, she understood that he could be a little paranoid. Eugenia could not leave the house without a gun either. She decided to strap her .22 to her ankle. The guns were loaded but not locked because they did not have locks. When these guns were cocked, you were ready to let go on something or someone. Eugenia did not want to mess up her pedicure even though the nail polish was dry. She put on her hold-it-in underwear and a good bra. Then she put on her blue jeans and a button-down shirt so she didn't have to take anything over her head. She put on her leather jacket with a scarf, grabbed her garment bag, and was ready to go. Stephen grabbed his leather coat, took off his suit jacket and hung it on a hanger. He would hang up his suit jacket in the car. They were ready to go. They would just sit in the car and wait for Ila. They headed toward the door, made sure the apartment was secure, and headed out. It had gotten colder because the sun had gone down, and it was getting dark. Ila was blessed; it had not snowed. It was just chilly, and there was a full moon, which would make for beautiful pictures after the wedding, if they could stand to be in the cold for a few minutes.

They walked down the stairs and put everything in the trunk. Stephen hung his coat in the backseat. Eugenia had gotten into the passenger side, which he thought was interesting. She was really nesting; now she wanted to be driven around. He laughed to himself.

It was not long before they saw Ila coming down the steps. She looked so happy. She walked to the car and motioned for Eugenia to roll the window down. She stuck her head in the car and said, "I have to make two trips." She put her first load in the car and hurried back upstairs to get her second load. She did not want to leave the silver Nike's behind. They would be such a great gift after the wedding, along with the bracelets, which she planned to give to Paula and Eugenia before they walked down the aisle. She grabbed the bags and turned right around and went back out the door. She remembered to turn on the outside light by the back door, then she locked the door and headed to the car.

Stephen and Eugenia were laughing—probably laughing at her. She put the rest of her bags into the backseat. She had so much stuff she had to go on the other side and sit behind Eugenia. They were still laughing when Ila got into the car. Ila said, "You guys laughing at me?"

They both said, "Yes!" Stephen said, "It looks like you're taking the entire apartment to the wedding." Ila had to laugh with them. It was a lot of stuff. Stephen turned over the engine and pulled out of the parking space. They were all very quiet. There was such a feeling of finality among those in the car. Stephen and Eugenia knew they would never have to worry about Hunter and Maurice again. Ila was thinking that, once they all got reassigned, it may be years before they would see each other again. It made her a little sad.

It did not take them long to get to the back gate at the university, which was a blessing because the chapel was not far from there. Ila got really excited when she saw all the activity—a food truck, employees dressed in all black, students hanging around waiting for the chapel doors to open. She hoped they would open the doors soon. It was cold out in the parking area.

Stephen parked as close to the door as he could so he could help Ila and Eugenia get all their things out of the car. When Ila got out the car, she could hear one of the students yell, "Ms. Montgomery, tell them to please open the door."

Ila yelled back, "I'll see what I can do."

They all yelled, "Thank you!"

Ila picked up her two bags, Stephen grabbed both the garment bags, and Eugenia picked up Ila's extra bag and the tennis shoes. She looked in the bag and then looked at Ila.

Ila said, "You were not supposed to see them, but since you have, I know you'll really enjoy them." They both laughed.

They walked up to the huge wooden doors. There was a security officer at the door. He said, "Hello, Ms. Montgomery. Congratulations."

Ila said, "Thank you very much. Is there any way we can let the students in from the cold?"

He said, "The chef didn't want the students to start eating the food before the ceremony began. You know how students are."

Ila said, "Yes, but it is really cold out here, and they are my invited guests. Why don't you come in and stand in the hallway where the food is going to be served and direct them to the chapel. There are bathrooms right before the chapel, so there won't be any reason for them to go any further."

He thought about that for a second and said, "Okay. You go get settled in the bridal room, and I'll start letting them in."

Ila smiled and said, "Thank you so much. It means so much to me."

With that, Stephen handed him a hundred-dollar bill and said, "Happy New Year! Thank you for working today. You could have been home with your family, but you chose to help Ms. Montgomery on her wedding day. Thanks so much." Ila and Eugenia looked at each other. Wow, what a great thing to do. Stephen was accumulating more brownie points. All Eugenia and Ila could do was laugh.

Between the three of them they only had to make one trip with all the items Ila and Eugenia had brought with them. They entered the chapel, which had been decorated in white carnations. There was a bouquet attached to every pew. And from out of nowhere the photographer appeared taking pictures. He introduced himself as "Mr. Snap." They all laughed and said it was nice to meet him. "I just want to get some before pictures if you don't' mind. Eugenia and Ila started posing, making faces and acting really crazy. Just then they heard, "Don't start without me!" And in ran Paula. Her hair was wrapped, and she was wearing tennis shoes with the toes cut out. They were laughing so hard, they didn't realize that Stephen had taken all the items into the bridal room and had disappeared.

Ila, Paula, and Eugenia posed for several more pictures and stopped when the students started filing into the chapel. Ila looked down the aisle and noticed that the first three rows on both sides were roped off with white rope. She wondered why they had done that. Then it dawned on her—those seats were saved for family of the bride and groom. She had not told anyone that neither she nor Brock had family members coming. In any event, it all looked beautiful. The lights had been dimmed except for the light on the altar. It was a sight that Ila would never forget.

The ladies turned and went into the bridal room. As they were chatting and touching up their makeup and hair, a tear slowly fell down Paula's face. She said, "Drew said to tell you that he's here, congratulations, and he loves you."

Ila looked at Paula and said, "If Drew is here, tell him to get out the room and stop looking at naked women!" They all laughed. Ila didn't want to get sentimental, but she knew that Paula could feel Drew at every step because they had been inseparable during their time together.

It was about 6:15 when the photographer knocked on the door. "Come in," Ila said. Mr. Snap said he had just taken pictures of the groom and his best man and was now ready to snap pictures of the bride and her party. The ladies were ready. He took individual pictures and then he took pictures of them together.

There was a second knock at the door. It was a young lady dressed in black who brought in their bouquets. They were stunning. The frilly petals of Ila's white carnations had been trimmed in silver, and a silver ribbon ran through the bouquet. Ila almost lost it but held it together. Paula held her hand tight. And that reminded Ila of the bracelets and tennis shoes. She pulled the bracelets out of one of the bags and called her friends over. "This is just a small token of our appreciation because you are sharing this magnificent day with us. We are very grateful," Ila said. With that, she handed them their boxes. Paula and Eugenia opened their gifts at the same time and gasped. The bracelets were beautiful. They put the bracelets on each other and thanked Ila like crazy.

Ila handed them the shoe boxes. "I just wanted you to know that I thought you guys would probably kick off these beautiful silver boots immediately after the wedding, so we got you silver tennis shoes to wear after the ceremony." Ila laughed.

The ladies were very grateful because those boots were made for looking at not walking in. They laughed and hugged each other. All the while the photographer was taking pictures.

There was another knock at the door, and the same lady in black said, "We are ready. It's six thirty."

Ila looked at Paula and Eugenia and said, "Show time!" The lady opened the door. A melodic voice starting to sing "Ava Maria" accompanied by the rich tones of the organ.

Eugenia was first to head down the aisle. She could see Brock and Morris at the altar. She also saw Stephen standing in the middle pew at the end of the row, looking handsome and smiling at her. She got misty eyed. Would this ever happen for her? Once Eugenia got to the white rope, she made a left and stood at the altar. Then the lady motioned for Paula to start her decent down the long beautiful aisle.

Ila stood in the doorway to the bridal room and was amazed at how many students had showed up. She was so excited; her heart was beating fast and her mouth had gone dry. Just then the lady in black handed her a small water glass with a straw. She smiled at Ila. Ila took several sips and was very grateful for the water. *This lady has done this a thousand times before.* Once Paula was at the rope and turning left, Ila came out of the foyer stood for a minute, her eyes glued to Brock.

Brock and Morris had to take naps because they had shared one to many shots. They did not wake up until there was a persistent knock at the door. Brock jumped up, grabbed his gun, stood alongside the door, and said. "Who is it?" The person on the other side said, "Laundry." Brock laughed to himself and opened the door slowly. Morris had jumped up and grabbed his wallet to give the young lady a tip. He took the tuxedoes from her and handed her a ten-dollar bill while Brock stayed behind the door, gun still in his hand. The young lady left and they both laughed. "Shades of old times," Morris said.

Morris took his tuxedo to one room and Brock's to another. It was 4:15 p.m.; they had to hurry. They both jumped in the shower and got dressed. The tuxedoes fit them perfectly. Brock could not believe how good they looked. They were so used to seeing each other in jeans, leather coats, and tennis shoes or boots. Brock's hair had grown in just right, and Morris was wearing a well-shaped afro. He picked it for a second and said to his reflection in the mirror, "Perfection." They laughed.

Brock had put Morris's bracelet and the rings on the table. He picked up the box that held the bracelet and said, "Man, this is just a token to let you know how happy I am that you could join us. Thanks for being my brother, friend, and confident for almost twenty years. That is rare, and I want you to know I don't take it lightly." They hugged, and Brock handed him the box.

Morris pulled out the bracelet and put it on his wrist. There was nothing left to say except, "Let's ride." They laughed.

Brock put on his holster and gun. He slipped his leather jacket on, keeping his tuxedo jacket on its hanger.

Morris, on the other hand, did not want to wear a holster. He decided to carry his .22 in his jacket pocket for now. He would put it behind his back in his belt during the ceremony so it would not look like a bulge in his jacket. Morris was a little vain. He had to laugh to himself about that.

They stood at the table and took another shot before they headed for the door. They rode down the elevator and laughed about old times. They had parked in the garage, so they got off on that floor. Morris said, "Man, you know I have to rush back to the room after dinner, get my things, and catch the redeye back to California."

Brock nodded. "Man, I wish you could stay, but for now we're going to enjoy this evening. We'll get you to the transport on time." They walked to the car and could not help but look in the car windows to look at themselves. It was clear they had it going on.

It was 6:10 p.m. It would take them ten minutes to get to the university. After hanging their coats up in the back, they both jumped into the car. The ride to the university was smooth, but Brock was surprised as he drove to the back gate at how many people were there—catering trucks, students, catering workers, security personnel. Everyone was scurrying around. Brock showed his credentials at the gate, and the security guard said, "Congratulations! You're a lucky man."

Brock said, "Thank you!" He shook his head and said to Morris, "That Ila has a way with the men. I'm going to have to put her in a tower like Rapunzel."

Morris did not say a word, but to himself, he said, "Fat chance that's going to happen." He laughed out loud.

Brock said, "What's so funny?"

Morris said, "I had a visual of that Rapunzel thing … that was funny." They both laughed.

They parked as close to the door as they could; the parking lot was pretty full. They jumped out of the car, and the security guard motioned for them to go on the other side of the building to the other entrance. Brock and Morris hurried to the other door. Inside stood a woman in black. The ceiling of the foyer was a glass dome. Brock looked up and looked at the stars. For a minute he thought he saw a shooting star. He believed that was good luck.

The lady had the flowers for their lapels in boxes. She led them to a little room behind the altar. At 6:30 p.m. they would walk out to the altar and wait for the Paula and Eugenia, and then the bride. The lady said she would be back in five minutes. That gave them time to get into their tux jackets, pin on their boutonnieres, secure their guns, check themselves in the mirror, and hug again. It seemed that the lady left and came right back. She said, "Gentleman, it is time."

Brock and Morris walked through the door and stood at the altar. Out of nowhere, a beautiful black woman dressed in all white started singing "Ave Maria." The pipe organ was loud. Everyone could feel the keys pumping the music out into the chapel. The lady in black stood in the middle of the aisle and motioned for everyone to stand up. That was the moment Brock saw Eugenia head down the aisle. She looked gorgeous—beautiful and deadly. His heart was pounding so hard he thought everyone could hear it. Then he felt the rub on his back from Morris, and his heart slowed down.

Eugenia came to the end of the aisle and made a left to the altar just as Paula made her way down the aisle looking ghetto fabulous. She was Ila's best friend. She had tears in her eyes. He could not look at her because he would also tear up. Paula stood to the left of the altar next to Eugenia.

Then, the music stopped, and the organist played a snippet of Wagner's traditional "Bridal Chorus," after which she and the vocalist switched back to "Ave Maria." It was fabulous, so well done.

Brock finally looked up and locked eyes with Ila. She was so beautiful, and he knew at that moment that he had done the right thing. He felt Morris' tension change. He looked back and Morris and smiled.

Ila was midway down the aisle when she looked at the man behind Brock. Her knees turned to Jello. *Oh, my God! It's Rodney!* She stood still for a moment. They looked at each other, and Rodney shook his head. As Ila regained her composure, Stephen jumped up to help her down the aisle. He grabbed her by the arm and said, "It would be my pleasure to give you away."

Ila looked at him and said, "Thank you so much." She locked eyes on Brock, and a tear rolled down her face. *How could this shit happen?*

Rodney noticed that Stephen's pant legs were uneven—the leg on the right was almost dragging his ankle as if he had something heavy in his right-hand pocket. Rodney was thinking, *Who is this motherfucker?* He waited until they got to the end of the aisle. Then he reached behind his back, grabbed his gun, and held it down next to his right leg. He could easily put it back behind his back after they said "I do" and everyone was looking at them.

The pastor entered from a side door and stood ready to receive the bride and groom. The singer finished the last stanza of "Ave Maria," and the pipe organ stopped. The non-denominational Pastor was obviously not prepared to ask the traditional question: "Who gives this bride away?" He had been told that Ila would walk down the aisle alone.

Brock turned to look at the Pastor, and so did Ila. Stephen still had her hand. The Pastor began: "Doubly blessed is the couple who comes to the marriage altar with the approval and blessing of family members, friends, and students. Who has the honor of presenting this woman to this man for the honor of marriage?"

All the students called out, "We do!" Stephen placed Ila's hand in Brock's hand. At the same time, Stephen took his .22 out of his pocket and shot Brock in the stomach two times. "This is for the chief, motherfucker!" he said.

Too late, someone screamed, "Gun!"

Eugenia hit the floor and pulled her gun out of her ankle holster. Paula was motionless as was the Pastor. The students began to run out of the chapel as security personnel ran down the aisle.

Rodney aimed his .22 and shot Stephen in the middle of his head. Stephen dropped to the floor.

Brock had let go of Ila's hand. He was falling to the floor. Blood was dripping off her face onto her dress. One of the security guards reached the altar. Rodney dropped his gun because the security guard did not know who the shooter was. As paramedics and police officers started running into the chapel, Ila collapsed.

Look for *Ila's Diamonds IV—The House that Jack Built*. Coming soon!

About the Author

Donna M. Gray-Banks is the Founder and Director of the F.R.E.S.H. Book Festivals, www.freshbookfestivals.com, which is one of the largest book festivals held in Volusia/Flagler Counties in the State of Florida. Gray-Banks is the author of the trilogy Ila's Diamonds I II and III and she host a weekly radio show entitled "A. F.R.E.S.H. Conversation" on Joy 106.3 F.M. in Daytona Beach, FL.

Ms. Banks was born and raised in Pittsburgh, Pennsylvania and currently resides in the State of Florida. She has one Son Gregory Taylor Banks who currently resides in Pittsburgh. She also has a huge fan club in her family Sister, Christine Hogan and Brothers Gilbert and Jackson (Gray). Her purpose in life in this season of her life is to promote Literacy as a Legacy.